WHEN IT COMES TO CRIME ...
FATHER KNOWS BEST.

"Father's Day" by Ruth Rendell
"You can never love too much" is this father's favorite motto when he becomes obsessed with the idea that his wife will leave him ... but how far will he go to keep his children?

"The Good Book" by Peter Crowther
Private eye Koko Tate takes a personal interest in finding a stolen rare Bible, but the beautiful daughter of the man who owned it turns out to be trouble ... the kind that Koko can't resist.

"Mothercloud, Fatherdust" by Tracy A. Knight
A young psychologist tries to cure a retarded man of the strange psychotic episodes he experiences on just one day every year—Father's Day—and the good doctor finds out he needs more than Freud to figure out this nightmare.

"Wrong Turn" by Norman Partridge
A movie star's son writes a tell-all exposé about his famous father and discovers a skeleton in the old man's closet he never knew about ... one that's the spitting image of his own handsome self.

"Father, Son and Holy Ghost" by Barbara Collins
Police Detective Joan Munday is sent to investigate a church being haunted by a murdered woman's spirit, but she soon suspects the human heart is behind a tragedy born of desire, guilt, and carnal sin.

MURDER FOR FATHER

MURDER
FOR
FATHER

EDITED BY
Martin H. Greenberg

A SIGNET BOOK

SIGNET
Published by the Penguin Group
Penguin Books USA Inc., 375 Hudson Street,
New York, New York 10014, U.S.A.
Penguin Books Ltd, 27 Wrights Lane,
London W8 5TZ, England
Penguin Books Australia Ltd, Ringwood,
Victoria, Australia
Penguin Books Canada Ltd, 10 Alcorn Avenue,
Toronto, Ontario, Canada M4V 3B2
Penguin Books (N.Z.) Ltd, 182–190 Wairau Road,
Auckland 10, New Zealand

Penguin Books Ltd, Registered Offices:
Harmondsworth, Middlesex, England

First published by Signet,
an imprint of Dutton Signet,
a division of Penguin Books USA Inc.

First Printing, June, 1994
10 9 8 7 6 5 4 3 2 1

 REGISTERED TRADEMARK—MARCA REGISTRADA

Printed in the United States of America

(The following page constitutes an extension of this copyright page.)

Contents

Introduction

Fathers have long played a major role in world litera-
ture. If you don't think so, ask Oedipus. Or Hamlet. Or
the James Dean character in *East of Eden.*

Recently, however, the role of father has been chal-
lenged. Long gone are the days when Father Knew Best.
Indeed, fathers today are often depicted as dopes (*The
Simpsons*), ciphers (*Family Ties*) or even monsters (the
chilling and clever, *The Stepfather*).

You'll find all kinds of fathers in this collection, nice
and nasty alike.

But that's only to be expected if our social workers
are to be believed. While they often decry the absence
of fathers in many inner-city families, they also acknowledge that it is fathers far more than mothers who abuse
their children.

Do you miss the days of Dear Old Dad?

Well, so do some of the writers in this anthology. They
pretty clearly want to turn back the clock to when
Daddy ruled supreme and life was a snug and cozy
experience.

But some of the other writers ...

Well, remember what the social workers tell us about
mein papa.

How he can be the worst sort of brute ...

Here, then, the festivities themselves: Dad seen in the
funhouse mirror ...

—The Editor

Rite of Passage

by Brian Harper

"There they are."

Randolph Covin squatted on a crumbly ledge, gazing through his binoculars at the chaparral-tufted valley. Jeremy, crouching beside his father, followed the line of his sight. He saw four brownish smudges on the landscape, wavering slightly.

He shaded his eyes from the noon sun and squinted at the ripples of August heat that undulated slowly across the sere, dusty ground.

"See them, son?" Randolph Covin asked. "See them?"

Jeremy nodded. "Yeah, Dad. I see them."

"The one closest to us—that's a fine buck—he's got your name written all over him."

Jeremy said nothing to that. The rifle in his hand, a Remington Sportsman 76 with a 4X Leupold scope, seemed more ponderous than before, heavy and hot. He wished he didn't have to hold it. Wished he wasn't here at all.

Happy birthday, he told himself miserably.

For months his dad had promised him an extra-special present for his twelfth birthday, never revealing what it would be. Jeremy had fantasized about a mint-condition origin issue of either *The Incredible Hulk* or *The Fantastic Four*—his two favorite comics—or maybe, at last, cable TV in their house, so he could watch the Sci-Fi Channel and uncut movies on HBO. A subscription to *Starlog* magazine would have been okay, too.

Best of all, a miracle: his mom was coming back. But

he knew that was crazy. His mom had run off when Jeremy was only three, going who-knew-who, not bothering even to leave a good-bye note. To him she was only a blurred memory of lullabies and bedtime stories, and a few discolored Kodachromes in a photo album.

No, she wouldn't be back, not ever. She was probably in Tahiti or Hong Kong or the Amazon rain forest by now, or someplace equally remote and fantastic.

But the first issue of *The Incredible Hulk,* the one in which Bruce Banner gets caught in the A-bomb test, would have been good enough for him.

Today—Saturday, August eighteenth, his birthday—he'd awakened at dawn, roused by his father's heavy footsteps on the basement stairs.

The basement. Maybe his dad had hidden his birthday presents down there. Yeah—in the storeroom, which was always locked, a perfect hiding place. And he was bringing them up now.

Heart thumping with excitement, Jeremy left his bedroom and crept down into the kitchen.

He found no presents. Instead, his dad was leaning over the kitchen table, inspecting his Browning bolt-action rifle. He was dressed in a beige hat, tan shirt, brown corduroy pants, and boots—what Jeremy recognized as his hunting clothes.

"Well," Randolph Covin boomed, "if it isn't the birthday boy." Then he corrected himself. "Not boy. Man. When you turn twelve, you're a boy no longer."

The words, unexpected and flattering, lifted a flush to Jeremy's cheeks. He looked away, feeling childish and vulnerable in his pj's and slippers. His gaze fell on the counter, where his own Remington rifle and boxes of .30–06 Springfield shells were neatly arranged on the Formica surface.

"Why are you getting out the guns and stuff?" he mumbled.

"Promised you a birthday surprise. This is it."

Jeremy blinked, uncomprehending. "We're going to the range?"

That was nothing special. His dad took him out to the shooting range at the local gun club nearly every weekend. Jeremy had learned to be a pretty fair shot, too; he could plug the bull's-eye most of the time, at least when he was really concentrating and not letting his thoughts wander to the latest exploits of Spider-Man.

"No, not the range," Mr. Covin said patiently. "Do you think I'd get all decked out in my camouflage duds just for a trip downtown? We're going hunting, little buddy."

"Hunting?"

"You know it. There's a first time for everything, and this is it. No more target practice. I think you're ready for the real McCoy."

"You mean, you and Sam and Mack are taking me along?"

"Nope. Sam and Mack aren't invited. It'll be just the two of us. Two men, on their own, stalking the wily black-tailed deer." He clapped Jeremy on the arm. "Pretty great, huh?"

"Oh. Sure. Yeah, Dad. Really ... really great."

"Go up and get changed now. The kind of clothes I'm wearing. Hard-soled shoes with good traction. Shirt and pants that blend with the hills. Got a hat? Yeah, I know you do—that cowboy hat I bought you in Phoenix. That'll work. Go on, now. Sooner we get going, the sooner we bag ourselves a buck."

He swatted Jeremy on the rear to get him moving. Jeremy hurried away, up the stairs, into his room, and then he was shaking, shaking all over with disappointment and anger and fear.

This was the big-time birthday present. Crawling around in the dirt and weeds, in the blistered foothills of the Sierra Nevada range, where the summer sun would have burned the bluegrass to straw and dried up every water hole. Brushing sweat off your face and flies off your neck. His father's idea of a good time—not his.

But it was worse, much worse. Because suppose they

actually tracked down a black-tailed deer. Then his dad would kill it, and Jeremy would have to watch.

Down in the basement were his father's trophies, the mounted heads of nine blacktails, their glass eyes staring, double-branched antlers gleaming in the fluorescent chill. Those heads weirded him out every time he saw them, because they'd been the heads of living creatures once, creatures his dad had killed.

He didn't want to watch an animal die. Didn't want to see it field-dressed. Didn't want to grab one of its antlers and help drag it back to the campsite. Didn't want to tie it to the trunk lid and ride home with that dead weight behind him, that load of death like a burden of guilt he couldn't shake off.

That was the procedure, of course. Though he'd never gone hunting before, he'd heard his dad describe his own forays into the oak woodlands of the foothills often enough. He knew everything there was to know about hunting the black-tailed deer—except why anybody would take pleasure in that pastime, or call it sport.

Well, he told himself nervously, it won't be too bad, I guess. When he pulls the trigger, I won't have to look. . . .

Then a shiver trembled through him in time with a bad thought, a very bad thought.

What if—Jeremy shut his eyes—what if *he* was expected to pull the trigger? What if that was why his dad had so patiently trained him on the shooting range—to prepare him for this special day, this rite of passage, this initiation into manhood?

In his World Cultures class at school, Jeremy had learned about primitive tribes that required young men to mutilate themselves or submit to torture or stalk and kill an animal in order to qualify as adults. His teacher, Ms. Stone-Belfry—who was married but insisted on using both her maiden name and her husband's surname, and who got really pissed if you called her "Mrs." instead of "Ms."—had gone on and on about how wonderfully cathartic and symbolic and archetypal and mythological such customs were.

To Jeremy they were just stupid. He thought that if he were one of those kids, and the tribal elders instructed him to punch holes in his nostrils or let some nutty witch doctor carve words on his belly or tramp off into the woods and hunt a lion with a spear, he would have just told them all to go stuff it.

But he couldn't tell his dad to stuff it. So he would have to go along and hope, hope desperately, that the deer were smart enough to keep out of sight.

The drive northeast from Bakersfield via Route 178 was mostly silent, his dad's efforts at conversation unrewarded by more than monosyllabic responses. At eight-thirty their Ford Taurus pulled into the dirt parking lot of the Foxglove Meadow Campsite, deep in the foothills, where his dad had reserved a cabin.

"Let's go, let's go," Randolph Covin kept saying, as Jeremy deliberately dawdled in the cabin's bathroom. "Best time to track and hunt blacktails is between ten A.M. and two P.M. We're losing time, son."

Then they were plodding through the parched countryside, passing over stretches of tall grass seared brown or dried yellow, all of it brittle as fallen leaves. Clumps of scrub oak and groves of yellow lupine dotted the hills like reminders of life in a world of the dead. A red-tailed hawk circled overhead, tracing long, slow loops against the sky's white dimensionless glare.

Shortly after ten o'clock his dad picked up a deer trail. Four sets of dainty hoofs had left prints in an exposed strip of crumbled, powdery shale. Farther along the trail were droppings, still fresh, crawling with fat flies that glinted in the sun like bubbles of spun glass.

"We're getting closer," Randolph Covin whispered, as though the deer were hiding a few yards away and would be alerted by the sound of a human voice. "You'll get your birthday present for sure."

I hope not, Jeremy answered voicelessly.

Then a few minutes ago they had topped a rise, this

same rise where they were perched now. His father had
taken out his binoculars and glassed the land below. And
he'd spotted the deer—a family of four: a doe, two
fawns, and a buck—feeding drowsily on blue-oak acorns,
swishing their bushy tails.

"Take a better look," Mr. Covin said, breathing hard
with controlled excitement as he handed over the
glasses. Reluctantly, Jeremy tipped the binoculars to his
eyes and focused on the nearest deer.

He was an average-looking black-tailed buck, not
large, weighing perhaps seventy pounds; his ears were
the biggest thing about him. His forked antlers were im-
pressive but not spectacular, not the four-point antlers
of some of his dad's trophies; these had only two points
on each branch.

He was beautiful, though—lean and muscular, still
wearing the reddish brown coat he would shed a few
weeks from now in early September. As he lowered his
head to the fallen acorns, then lifted his head to chew,
his antlers moved shadow to sunlight, then back into
shadow again, submerging and rising like the dorsal fin
of a leaping dolphin, gone for a moment, then flashing,
bright as fire, in the painfully strong sun.

Jeremy felt his eyes water. All morning long he'd
wanted to be somewhere else, anywhere else; now that
desire became a burning need.

He just couldn't stand being here. He wanted to be
home with his comic books and his sci-fi magazines and
his weird pal Lucas and his even weirder pal Toby, sitting around arguing about whether Jack Kirby or Jim
Steranko was better at drawing the Hulk, or maybe flip-
ping on the tube to catch the Saturday afternoon *Chiller
Thriller Theater,* which featured *It Conquered the World*
today, a pretty shitty movie, but that was okay, you
could make fun of shitty movies, put even stupider dialogue in the actors' mouths, hurl insults at the obviously
zippered-up monster suit, and have yourself a great time.

Instead, here he was in the dry blaze of the mid-
morning sun, staring at a beautiful animal, graceful as a

dancer, harmless as a leaf, vital and agile, savoring the taste of acorns, languid in the sun, loving life in its word-less way. An animal with a wife, sort of, and kids. An animal soon to be blasted to his knees, dropped with a second shot, trussed, dragged to the car, driven home, butchered, his head put on display.

Jeremy was blinking back tears, hoping his dad couldn't see, when the question came, the awful, terrify-ing question he had dreaded.

"Think you can hit him from here, son?"

Panic ballooned in his chest. He sucked in a deep breath to steady himself.

"Uh-uh, Dad. No way. He's . . . he's too far."

"Nonsense. I've seen you hit the bull's-eye from this distance."

"This is . . . different."

"Try it, son. You can do it. I know you can."

Jeremy thought about refusing, telling off his dad, the way he would have told off Ms. Stone-Belfry's cherished witch doctors. But he couldn't do that. Just couldn't.

He gave back the binoculars and stretched out flat on his belly, the rifle parallel with his body. He pumped the slide to feed a shell into the chamber, then gently nudged the barrel sideways till the buck was centered in the scope.

His dad was right. He could make this shot. All he had to do was imagine that he was aiming at a paper target on the range. Then squeeze the trigger—gently, gently—and blow the deer away.

He swallowed. Pounding violence filled his head. Tremors hurried through his insides but, astonishingly, did not reach the muscles of his shoulders and arms. His grip on the gun was firm and steady.

"Do it, son," his dad breathed.

He cast a sidelong glance at his father. For a moment he glimpsed his old man's eyes. They were wide and intense and unblinking. They were fixed not on him but on the deer. The eyes of a predator, feverish with blood lust, hungry for a kill.

Jeremy had never seen his father's eyes like that. Had never guessed that such dark passions stirred within him. The thought flashed in his mind that perhaps his mom had seen the same cruel, ravenous face Jeremy was seeing now; perhaps it had frightened her; perhaps that was why she had run off, abandoning him, escaping to some unknown hideaway.

"Do it," Randolph Covin breathed, more harshly, using the edge of his voice.

Yes, Jeremy told himself. Go on. Do it. Get it over with.

The buck bent his head to scoop up another few acorns, then shifted his weight slightly.

Slowly Jeremy's finger curled around the trigger. He drew it back, taking his time, trying not to think about the beautiful deer, trying not to picture the red hole that the bullet would make, the buck's eye-rolling convulsions as he gasped his life away.

He was exerting several pounds of pressure on the trigger now. Almost enough to fire. Almost.

His father did not speak again, but Jeremy could hear his thoughts, his angry, voiceless order: Do it. *Do it.*

Jeremy fired.

But as he did, some spasm of his arm jerked the rifle an inch to the left, misdirecting the shot, sending the bullet harmlessly into the brush several yards from the target; and the four deer, alarmed by the echoing report, leaped up in one simultaneous motion and bounded away into a thicket of laurel trees, then down some invisible ravine, lost to sight, gone.

"God *damn* it!"

Randolph Covin pounded the ground in frustration, raising a puff of beige dust.

Jeremy drew a shuddering breath and licked his lips. "Sorry, Dad. I was nervous, I guess."

"Bullshit."

"I tried to hit him—"

"Fucking *bullshit.*"

Jeremy was silent.

His father stared, his cheeks tinged red by fury, the tendons of his neck standing out like taut cords, a vein in his temple pulsing angrily.

"You missed on purpose. You didn't want to hit him. You were scared to shoot. You were *scared*."

The blood lust in his eyes had turned to wild hatred and an almost inhuman contempt.

"I'm sorry," Jeremy whispered, the words catching in his throat, forced out only with trembling effort.

"Sorry." His father tossed the apology back at him with a sneer. "Yeah, you're sorry all right. A sorry excuse for a man."

Jeremy looked away, ashamed of the sudden dampness in the corners of his eyes, afraid his father would see his tears and hate him for them.

"There's too much of your mother in you," Randolph Covin said grimly. "And too little of me. Maybe . . . maybe none of me at all."

Jeremy was young, just barely twelve, but he was old enough to understand the implication of that statement. His stomach clenched. He felt a single teardrop slide down his face and rubbed it away with a clumsy, balled fist.

"I thought you were ready to prove yourself," his father went on implacably. "Ready to grow up. I guess I was wrong. You're still a baby. Playing around with comic books and watching monster movies on TV. Like a goddamn six-year-old."

The stinging words, more painful than slaps, jerked loose a brief defensive response. "I didn't want to kill him."

"Why the hell not? That's what hunting is all about."

"I never wanted to go hunting."

"Because you were scared."

His nose felt wet and runny. He sniffled, thinking miserably that he sounded like a real crybaby now, a snot-nosed blubbering little kid.

"I was scared," he acknowledged, and then he looked up at his father, honest puzzlement overcoming shame and fear. "Killing—that *ought* to be scary, right? Scary for anyone?"

His father's voice was a monotone. "If you can't face death . . . you're not a man."

Jeremy didn't know how to answer that. He turned his head away and listened to the humming silence of the world and wished, with a sudden flare-up of fury, that he had killed the fucking deer after all, slaughtered that black-tailed bastard and hacked off his damn head for a trophy.

But it was too late now.

For the rest of the day they tried to pick up the trail. Or rather, Randolph Covin tried, while his son tagged along, saying nothing.

In mid-afternoon they paused to consume a lunch of dry rations, washed down with water from their canteens. Neither spoke. Jeremy watched a crow on a tree branch, glossy and black. The crow cawed at him, its screeching cries an echo of his father's reprimand.

He understood that if the deer could be found, his father would take care of the killing this time. There would be no second chance offered to him, not on this hunting trip, perhaps not ever.

That was just as well. Despite his humiliation, despite his fierce desire to prove himself, he still doubted he could pull the trigger and destroy such a lovely, innocent thing. Even watching his dad do it would be hard enough.

The day grew old. Shadows lengthened. The sky turned a deeper shade of blue.

From his dad's stories of past hunts, Jeremy knew that the time for tracking blacktails had passed. Even if they found the buck now, even if his dad shot and wounded him, there would not be time to track him down and finish him off before the sun sank behind the western hills. To wound the animal now would be to let him die a pointless death, huddled undiscovered in the shadowed brush, his carcass unclaimed for venison or trophy.

Still his dad would not give up. He wanted that animal dead. It was as if the buck's survival were a personal affront. He could release the boiling rage within him only by placing a bullet in the deer's beating heart.

Finally, at eight o'clock, as the last light was leaking from the sky, he slumped his shoulders and exhaled a long, disgusted sigh. "No use."

Jeremy had known it was no use three hours earlier, but he didn't say so now, of course. Didn't say anything.

"Better get back," Mr. Covin said. "Barely enough sun to see by, as it is."

"We staying in the cabin tonight?" Jeremy asked.

"Damn straight we are. And tomorrow we're going out again. To get that fucker. Or another one just like him. We're not going home without a trophy."

Jeremy shut his eyes. Another day spent tramping through the deadly heat, breathing dust, gulping down the metallic water in the canteen. Another day spent reciting silent prayers for the safety of all the living creatures his father stalked so remorselessly. Another day.

The darkness was complete by the time they returned to the cabin. It was not a true cabin, more like a motel room, sharing walls with the rooms on either side. The rustic flavor was somewhat spoiled by the beat of rap music from someone's radio.

Randolph Covin heated pork and beans over a camp stove. At nine o'clock he ordered lights-out. He and Jeremy climbed into twin beds.

" 'Night, Dad," Jeremy ventured.

Silence answered him—chilly, brooding silence.

He fell asleep wondering if his dad would ever forgive him, would ever love him again.

Awake.

The clicking of his eyelashes in the dark.

The bed, strange. The smells of the room, unfamiliar. Where was he? Not at home.

The cabin. Yes, of course. He was in the cabin in the woods. Awake in the middle of the night.

Jeremy let his vision adjust gradually to the dark. Through the window behind his bed slanted a narrow beam of moonlight. It seemed to brighten as he watched, until finally its chalky radiance filled the room.

He looked at the bed next to him.

Empty.

His father was gone. Must be taking a leak or something.

But there were no bathroom noises. No noises of any kind. He was really ... *gone.*

But where would he go? There was nothing around the campsite but wilderness. Unless ...

No.

His dad wouldn't do that—wouldn't abandon him here. Wouldn't drive off and leave him alone in the foothills, fifty miles from Bakersfield.

He was upset about the deer, sure, mad as hell, but not *that* mad.

Jeremy knew it, but he knew something else too: Years ago, his mom had run off, had left him, had never come back.

Why couldn't his dad do the same?

He fretted over these ugly fears for what seemed like a very long time. Then he stiffened, hearing the soft rattle of a key in a lock.

The door eased open.

Rigid in bed, feigning sleep, Jeremy watched a dark masculine figure slip inside. He wasn't sure who it was until the man stepped forward into the moonlight.

His father.

He let out a grateful breath of relief.

Dad must have gone out for a walk, he thought. That's all. And here I am, making up all kinds of crazy stories. God, he's right about me. I really *am* a baby.

Faint footsteps, then the closing of the bathroom door. Hiss of running water in the pipes lasted for several minutes.

Silence.

The bathroom door opened, and his dad crossed the

darkness to his own bed, took off his boots, his pants, his shirt, and crawled under the covers again.

Jeremy wondered what he'd been doing in the dark. Stargazing, maybe. Or having a smoke. He still indulged in a cigarette now and then, though everyone knew it was a vile and dangerous habit.

Snores from the other bed—a soft, gentle burring.

It was good to have his dad here with him. Good to have company in darkness. Good not to be alone.

Jeremy pressed his face to his pillow and slept.

The next day his father surprised him. "We're going home," he said when Jeremy awoke to the smell of coffee and fried eggs.

"I thought . . ." He rubbed sleep out of his eyes. "I thought you wanted to go after the deer again."

"Changed my mind."

"Really?" He could not keep relief and gratitude out of his voice.

"Really. Hey, come here, son." He put an affectionate arm around Jeremy's waist. "I kind of lost my cool yesterday, you know? Got all worked up over nothing. There's no shame in not shooting that buck. Let's just forget about it, all right?"

"Sure, Dad." Sudden happiness filled him to bursting. "Thanks. Thanks a lot."

He washed his face in the bathroom sink. Drying himself, he noticed something odd on the floor. A scatter of red-brown spots. He bent to examine them.

Dried blood.

He didn't remember seeing blood on the floor yesterday evening when he'd cleaned up after the hunt.

He almost asked his dad about them, then stopped. He remembered his interlude of wakefulness last night, his father's absence, then his return. The long minutes he'd spent running water in the sink. This sink.

Washing his hands? Washing them clean of blood?

Had he found an animal in the night? A raccoon or a rabbit or something? And . . . and killed it?

The raging blood lust, the feverish need, was gone from his eyes. Exorcised—or sated?

Though the day was already warm, Jeremy found himself shivering.

The blood stains were the first bad thing. The sack was the second.

His dad was unloading the Ford in the driveway of their house when Jeremy noticed the sack. It was stuffed into a corner of the car trunk, partially hidden by an old blanket.

"Hey, what's this?"

"Nothing." His father stopped him from reaching for it.

"Looks like a bag of stuff."

"Just some tools I brought with me. In case of car trouble."

"I thought you already kept a bunch of tools with the spare tire."

"These are extras." His dad tossed him the keys. "Go inside and open up the place, will you? Must be stuffy in there with all the windows closed. Check the mail, too."

Jeremy studied him. "Sure, Dad." He glanced at the sack again before heading up the front walk.

Didn't look like it was filled with tools. Whatever was inside was lumpy and dirty and wet. Dark brown stains spotted the wrinkled canvas.

He went around the house, unlocking windows and tugging them open. At an upstairs window he paused, gazing down at the driveway. He saw his dad remove the sack from the car, then carry it to the front door.

If the bag contained tools for the car, why would he be taking it inside? Funny.

Jeremy crept downstairs, through the living room, into the kitchen. He entered in time to see his father disappear down the basement stairs.

From below, the sound of keys jangling. The storeroom door opened, then shut a few moments later.

Footsteps marched swiftly toward the stairs.

Jeremy slipped out of the kitchen. He was waiting outside by the mailbox, looking through the bills and advertising circulars that had been delivered on Saturday, when his father emerged from the house.

Looking at the mail, yes. But not seeing it.

What he was seeing was the sack, the blood on the bathroom floor, and the fevered look on Randolph Covin's face when the deer was in Jeremy's sights.

In his mind he heard the whisper of running water in the cabin's pipes, a soft, secretive sound.

It was on the TV news that night.

As usual, Jeremy and his dad were eating off trays in front of the big Panasonic set. Not TV dinners, though. Randolph Covin was a good cook, and he'd broiled up a chicken and improved it with side dishes of mashed potatoes and steamed asparagus. Jeremy was unhappily aware that his father would have preferred to be dining on venison tonight.

One of the perpetually giddy local TV newscasters assumed a momentarily dour expression suitable for a sad or disturbing report.

"In the Sierra Nevada foothills the search continues for two missing campers. Joe and Holly Plumfeld were last seen at the Foxglove Meadow campsite on Saturday night ..."

Video of the cabins, and Jeremy's blood ran cold.

"The Plumfelds' car, a 1991 Mazda 626, was found in the parking lot of the campsite. When park rangers checked their cabin this afternoon, they found the couple's belongings inside. But there has been no sign of Joe or Holly, and relatives are becoming increasingly concerned ..."

A sound-bite of a woman identified as "Holly Plumfeld's sister," expressing her fears in a tremulous voice.

"The Sheriff's Department has released photos of the couple and is asking the public for help. If you have any information, please call ..."

Snapshot portraits of a man and woman in their mid-twenties, the hotline phone number superimposed underneath.

Then on to the weather forecast, the newscaster wearing a cheerful face once more.

Jeremy took several bites and swallows, waiting for his father to make some comment, any comment at all. None came. Finally Jeremy spoke up.

"They ... they were at the campsite."

"Looks like it."

"Last night. With us."

"So?"

"So now they're missing."

His father shrugged. "Probably went out hiking and got lost. Happens all the time."

"The police are talking like it's more serious than that."

Another shrug. "That's how they always talk. Remember that kid who got separated from his Boy Scout troop down in the San Gabriels last month? They had a hundred people out looking for him. His parents were scared out of their wits, just like I'd be if you were missing. But he turned up. In good shape, too. So will these people."

"I ... I guess."

"Don't you worry about it."

But Jeremy did worry. A lot.

In his bedroom that night he lay under the sheets, staring at the dark.

He couldn't sleep. Finally, he switched on his bedside radio, dialing the volume low, and listened to music. The station he liked was one of those golden-oldie deals; it played tunes from the seventies and early eighties, an era that seemed impossibly long ago to him, though his dad often said it felt like yesterday.

At two A.M. the hourly news update came on. The lead story shocked him upright in bed.

"... campers, earlier reported missing, were found dead in the woods less than one hundred yards from their cabin. Authorities have provided no details on the condition of the bodies, other than to say that both were seriously mutilated. The cause of death, says Detective John Springer of the Kern County Sheriff's Department, was homicide . . ."

Detective Springer started talking then, saying something, but Jeremy couldn't listen anymore, couldn't think.

After a long time he turned off the radio. He rolled over on his stomach and gripped his pillow tight.

It can't be, he told himself fiercely. Can't.

He remembered the sack, bulging with wet and soiled things.

Mutilated, the report had said. Severely mutilated.

Were there . . . pieces . . . of Joe and Holly Plumfeld in that sack?

No.

This was his dad he was thinking of. His dad, who'd raised him alone ever since his mother ran away.

His dad wasn't some kind of crazy person like Jeffrey Dahmer in Milwaukee. He didn't kill people. Animals, sure. That was different. That was normal. Sort of normal, anyway. Lots of people did it, thought it was fun, and Jeremy didn't understand them, never had, but that didn't mean they were murderers.

His own dad. A killer. A psycho. Like in the movies. No way. No *fucking* way.

He didn't believe it. Wouldn't. Someone else had murdered the Plumfelds. Someone sick and twisted. He told himself he ought to be thankful that he and his dad hadn't been the victims. Ought to be glad it was poor old Joe and Holly who'd bought it instead.

Sure. Ought to be.

But he knew he would never be able to cleanse his mind of suspicion . . . unless he looked in the storeroom.

The door to that room was always locked. Jeremy had never been allowed inside. His dad kept his guns and ammo in there, along with the tanbark solution he used for tanning hides, and the other things necessary for his taxidermy projects. Things a boy shouldn't touch.

At least that was the reason his father had given for keeping the storeroom off-limits. There might be a more sinister explanation. Maybe he kept more than guns and chemicals behind that door.

Jeremy shuddered. For a moment, thinking of the Plumfelds' bloodied bodies, his nerve failed.

Then he steadied himself. What would his hero, Bruce Banner, do in a situation like this? What would Reed Richards do?

He had to go in there, to see. And he had to do it now.

He would need the key. It was on his dad's key chain. And the chain was where it always was at night—on top of the bureau in the master bedroom, near the bed where his father slept.

Soundlessly, Jeremy slipped out of bed, and padded down the hall.

The door to the master bedroom was open. He peered in. Low snoring.

He let his eyes adjust to the gloom, then entered, taking short, cautious steps and shallow breaths.

Halfway to the bureau. The low drone of this father's snores continued.

At the bureau now. The lacquered surface felt smooth to the touch. He found the contents of his father's emptied pockets: a wadded handkerchief, coins, a roll of breath mints, a blister-pack of antacid tables, and, yes, there it was, the key chain.

Carefully, he picked it up, holding his hand steady, terrified of the jangling clamor the chain would make if it slipped out of his grasp.

Keys clutched in a tight fist, he froze, listening.

Silence.

The snoring had stopped.

No, please, don't let him be awake, don't let him catch me, oh, God, don't let him catch me . . .

A raspy cough and a rustling of sheets.

He's awake, Christ, getting out of bed—
No.

Only shifting his position, making himself comfortable. A moment later, the soothing rhythm of his snores resumed.

Jeremy was shaking uncontrollably as he crept out of the room. He gripped the keys so firmly their metal teeth chewed the skin of his palm.

Along the hall to the stairs and down one step at a time, careful, careful. Stay near the wall, away from the center of the treads: fewer creaks and squeaks that way.

Couldn't really be his dad who'd done that awful thing. But if he believed that, why was he so terrified? Why did he feel the small pops of muscle spasms in his shoulders, in his legs? Why was he certain that to be discovered stealing the keys would cost him more than angry lecture, more even than physical punishment? Why did he think he could end up like the couple in the woods?

Across the living room now and into the kitchen, the tile floor cold on the soles of his feet, he eased open the basement door and started down the stairs, keeping the lights off, feeling his way.

Halfway down, he stopped, head cocked in a listening pose. He thought he'd heard the creak of a footstep upstairs—a faint, faraway creak, perhaps on the second floor. Had his dad gotten up to use the john? If so, would he check on Jeremy, find him gone, and start looking?

He waited, listening intently for another noise from above. He heard nothing.

Just his imagination.

He went down the rest of the way. The cellar floor was uncarpeted concrete, chilly and damp, like the floor of a crypt. Bad thought to have, especially when somewhere in the dark were those stuffed and mounted heads, those glass eyes that always seemed to be staring right at you, those polished antlers like raw, fleshless bone.

He crabbed along the wood-paneled wall to the far corner, then along the intersecting wall to the store-room door.

Had his breathing always been so noisy? He'd never even noticed the sound of it before. Now each intake of breath was a shuddering gasp, a wheezing moan, the loudest racket in the world.

He fumbled with the keys on the chain, trying each in turn, until he found the one that fit. The door opened under his hand, sighing on weary hinges.

He would have to turn on a light. Until now, he hadn't wanted to; he was afraid that somehow his dad would sense a bulb flicking on anywhere in the house, the way a fairy-tale giant always sensed an intruder in his castle.

His hand searched the wall, found the switch, and flipped it up.

The sudden illumination was dazzling. Jeremy shut his eyes, blinded by the abrupt plunge from darkness into glare. Then, blinking, he looked around.

The first thing he saw was the unshaded hundred-watt bulb screwed into the ceiling. It cast a harsh glow on the narrow room and its unadorned cement walls.

An armchair and ottoman sat in one corner, near a gun rack laden with rifles and shotguns. Two other rifles, his own Remington and his dad's Browning, were propped against the wall by the doorway, carelessly left there after the trip.

Along the same wall stood a large wooden cabinet, its doors shut. Opposite the cabinet, he saw a long worktable supporting an empty porcelain basin suitable for tanning hides, homemade shelves of two-by-fours and cinder blocks lined with jars of chemical solutions, and a small portable refrigerator.

The refrigerator tugged Jeremy's gaze like a magnet. Draped over it, empty and shapeless and flat, was the sack.

Whatever had been inside must be in the fridge now.

No reason to put tools in the fridge. No reason to put anything in there that wouldn't spoil.

Meat spoiled—dead meat.

He almost turned and ran, ran out of this house, ran barefoot to the open-all-night convenience store two blocks away, where he could call the cops from the pay phone.

No. Crazy. This was his dad, his *dad*.

He drew a deep breath of courage, then knelt by the refrigerator and opened the door. Wisps of cold air blew into his face like the condensed essence of winter.

"Oh," Jeremy said simply, as if merely acknowledging an obvious fact. "Oh."

The Plumfelds were in there.

Well, not all of them—only their heads.

He stared at them, and they stared back, eyes wide and astonished, the lashes dusted with frost. A brown crust of blood caked the raw, ragged stumps of their necks.

Jeremy's throat hitched with a gagging sound.

The sudden taste of vomit at the back of his mouth roused him from shock. Panic rushed over him. He couldn't linger a second longer in this place. He had to get out, get out now, *get out*!

He jumped to his feet, staggered backward, and collided with the cabinet behind him. The twin doors unlatched and swung open.

And even though he knew he shouldn't look, knew he didn't dare look, knew it was crazy to so much as *think* about looking—even though he knew all that, he turned anyway, because he had to see.

In the cabinet . . . trophies. A dozen of them. A dozen heads—stuffed and mounted.

Glass eyes gleamed in the harsh light. Mouths, sewn shut as if pursed, shone with lip gloss and Chapstick. Hair, shampooed and neatly combed, was knotted in buns and ponytails, teased into curls, sculpted with mousse.

They were mostly women, but a few men, too. Both sexes, all races, all ages. His dad hadn't played favorites. He had killed anyone available, whenever the urge moved him. Killed all these people, and preserved their heads with his taxidermic skills.

He must have been doing it for years. But he'd kept it a secret, a secret locked in this windowless underground room. Then yesterday his blood fever had been excited by the prospect of killing the deer; and when Jeremy had failed to draw blood, Randolph Covin had found another outlet for his urges. He'd broken into one of the other cabins, killed the couple inside, then taken their heads, and hidden their bodies in the brush.

No doubt he intended to preserve their heads, as well, to add them to his collection—two fine specimens, regular four-pointers, old Joe and Holly Plumfeld.

Jeremy was dizzy. He wanted to throw up.

One particular head in the cabinet kept drawing his gaze, though he wasn't sure why. A pretty blond woman, vaguely familiar . . .

"Oh, God," he whispered as recognition hit him like a blow. "Oh, God. Oh, God. Oh, God."

Though he remembered her face only from old photographs, there could be no doubt—his mom.

She hadn't run away, after all. Hadn't abandoned him. She'd been here in the house the whole time, in the cellar with his dad's other victims.

Tears watered his eyes. He spun, needing only to escape and, once he was free of this place, to scream.

Then his heart stuttered—he jerked to a halt—he stared at a looming figure in the doorway—hairy chest, loose belly, two glazed heavy-lidded eyes.

"Dad," Jeremy croaked.

Randolph Covin nodded. "So you're on to me. I was afraid of that."

He stepped into the storeroom, naked save for a wrinkled pair of Jockey shorts. In his hand was a knife—one of the big butcher knives from the rack in the kitchen. Jeremy had seen it slice meat neatly from the bone.

"I shouldn't have done it last night," his dad whispered in a dull, dazed voice. "Knew there was a risk. But, funny thing, I couldn't help myself. It's been like that, more and more, in recent years. At first I had it under control. Only did it when I wanted to. Not now."

Jeremy licked his lips. He didn't want to ask this question, but had to. Had to. "When you ... killed mom ... were you in control?"

A smile then, blooming like a pale flower on his father's beard-stubbed face. "Oh, yes. That bitch asked for it. She was no good, no good at all." His eyes narrowed, turning colder. "I never realized how much of your mother you had in you ... till yesterday. Now I see you're not my boy at all."

"Sure I am, Dad." Jeremy took a slow, sliding step backward. His peripheral vision searched the room, found the Remington and Browning propped against the wall a yard away. Probably both guns were still loaded. "I'm your flesh and blood."

"Flesh." Randolph Covin grunted, an ugly, angry sound. "And blood." His smile widened, the nicotine-stained teeth yellow against the bloodless lines of his lips. "Well ... we'll see. We'll see."

The knife flashed. Jeremy dodged it and grabbed for the rifles. His hand closed over the Browning's barrel, and then he was stumbling backward, throwing the bolt, his father in the sights.

"Get away."

"You can't shoot me, you little bastard." Soundless laughter twisted Randolph Covin's mouth. "You couldn't even shoot a fucking *deer*."

"I said, *get away!*"

His father stepped forward, raised the knife, the honed steel coruscating prettily in the glare of the unshaded bulb, cutting an arc in the musty air.

"Goddammit, Dad, I'm warning you!"

The knife descended, the blade ripping space, plunging toward his throat, and Jeremy pulled the trigger.

The gunshot exploded, rocking the narrow room. His father lurched backward, the knife slipping from his fingers. In his bare chest a ragged crater was instantly awash in blood.

Jeremy's knees loosened. He let go of the rifle.

"Dad," he whispered, his own voice inaudible to him over the ringing of his ears.

Randolph Covin dropped to his knees, then slumped over on his side. He lay there in a tangle of limbs and a spreading puddle of blood, his eyes staring up at Jeremy in mute astonishment and perhaps something more.

His mouth worked. If any words came, Jeremy couldn't hear them.

Then he shuddered all over, a ripple of muscle spasms shaking him like a boneless thing. A thin ribbon of blood unspooled from his open mouth. One last convulsion, and abruptly life left him, his body going limp, his eyes as empty as the glass orbs in his trophies.

Jeremy stood frozen for a long moment, weak with shock. Then he staggered forward and fell on his father, hugging the lifeless body with ferocious desperation. The skin was still warm, the blood skill trickling—blood as red and hot as any that flowed in the veins of a black-tailed deer.

"I did it, Dad," he gasped between shoulder-jerking sobs. "I drew blood." He was giggling, weeping, babbling. "Faced death, just like you said."

Past tears, past trauma, he was dimly aware that boyhood had ended for him tonight. He would not be reading comic books anymore, or watching *Chiller Thriller Theater* with Lucas and Toby. He had left all that behind. Having completed his mysterious rite of passage, he was now a man.

And though he knew it was crazy, he almost believed—almost—that in their last moments together, he had made his father proud.

Retribution

by Harold Adams

It was Saturday night, near 1:30 A.M., and Corden had closed down tight. The sky was clear, the air balmy, and a steady wind moaned across the prairie. I'd have been snoozing like all the rest if Helga, our newest maid, hadn't promised to come down to the lobby from her room over the hotel kitchen and talk with me after everyone was asleep. For the benefit of those who know me too well, or who are just dirty-minded, we were going to talk about Father's Day plans for the next day. At least that's what she thought.

I'd decided to give up on her when car lights flashed through the front window, coming from the highway that passed along Main Street, and slowly moved my way.

The car pulled left and angle-parked in front. The lights went out. I got up from the rocker beside the registration counter, moved to the screen door, and looked at the green 1932 facing me, dark and still except for the faint pinging of the cooling engine.

Slowly the driver's door opened and a gaunt man in funereal clothes and a wide-brimmed fedora stepped out, stood erect, reached into the back, and pulled out a small brown suitcase. His movements were stiff and deliberate.

I pushed the screen open as he approached. He lowered his head, obscuring his face, and squeezed past me, pushing the suitcase forward, then walked to the register and put down his load.

I moved behind the counter and turned the register to face him.

"How long?" I asked as he bent low over the register, showing me only the brim of his hat and shadows. He carefully wrote down John Smithson and a St. Paul, Minnesota, address.

"How much?" he asked without glancing up. The voice was deep, almost gentle.

"Dollar a night, five for a week."

He lifted his head, let me see his face, and watched for my reaction. I didn't flinch, blink, or pretend the sight was normal. His skin was mostly scar tissue—tight, hairless, shiny, and twisted. The nose was little more than a bump with open nostrils, the mouth a lipless slash across his face. His eyes seemed lidless and had no lashes.

"I don't know how long I'll stay," he said. "Probably not a week."

"Okay. Want a morning call?"

"No."

I marked him in for Room 14, moved around to pick up his suitcase, led the way past the hall running from the north side entrance beside the stairway, and caught a glimpse of Helga heading silently back toward her room over the kitchen.

At the head of the stairs I pointed out where the toilet and shower were, and after leading him into his room, explained he had to give notice if he wanted hot water and that'd cost a quarter. He nodded, took off his hat, and looked around. I had turned on only the bedside lamp so he wasn't too hard to look at. There wasn't a sign of hair on his large, scarred skull.

"You serve breakfast?"

"Not on Sunday."

"Will there be anyplace open?"

" 'Fraid not."

"How can I get something?"

"I'll see what I can do. It won't be early. Settle for fruit, coffee, and toast?"

"Anything. If you could just have it brought up and leave it by the door, with the bill ..."

As I moved toward the hall, he called, "Are you Carl Wilcox?"

I looked back and said yes.

He thanked me, said good night, and moved to the window. I returned to the lobby, and waited a while to see if Helga would come back, but finally gave up and hit the sack.

Ma didn't like the sound of things when I described our guest at breakfast, but was too busy planning the Father's Day feed to give the single guest, however unusual, much thought. Bertha fixed him up with oatmeal in addition to an orange, a pot of coffee, and buttered toast, which I delivered.

I set the tray on the floor, tapped on the door, and after hearing movement inside, went back downstairs.

About a minute after Ma and Pa left the hotel for the Congregational Church, Helga slipped into the lobby. Being Sunday, she'd enjoyed sleeping in.

"I came down last night," she began.

"Yeah, I saw you ducking down the hall. Why didn't you hang around?"

"I heard that man and looked in from the dining-room door. How could you be so calm? He was a nightmare!"

"You saw his face?"

"Just barely—I couldn't believe—who is he—what is he?"

"A guy who got his face burned. I'd guess he comes from somewhere around here—been gone a while."

"Dear God, I nearly died. And you didn't even blink."

Her face blanched when we heard steps overhead and someone started down the stairs. Helga fled.

Smithson moved into the hallway off the lobby paralleling the staircase and found the public telephone set in a booth under the steps. I didn't hear him ring for the operator and figured he must be going through the telephone book. After a while he came into the lobby.

"Looking for anybody special?" I said.

He moved toward the table under the big wall clock,

shuffled the newspapers vaguely, then turned to stare at me with his awful eyes.

"You know Mary Jane Sills?" he asked.

"Her last name's Creighton now."

"Ah." He glanced back at the paper.

"She sings in the choir at the Congregational Church. You go over, might catch her. I hear sometimes she solos."

He opened his mouth a fraction, showing teeth that looked straight and real. It was almost like a smile. Then he walked toward the door, pulling a pair of sunglasses from his breast pocket, put them on, and went out to his car. A moment later he had driven off, heading south.

Bertha, our cook, knocked herself out putting together a special dinner for my old man, Elihu, all the while bitching that it was too early for corn on the cob, his absolute favorite fodder. She had to make do with roast beef, baked potatoes, cooked cabbage, and homemade apple pie for dessert. It was all accepted by Elihu with what Ma would call ill grace since he objected to Father's Day on principle, claiming it was dreamed up by smart merchants who figured it'd make women buy a mess of junk for gifts they'd otherwise never dream of shelling out for.

We were waiting for the apple pie when Elihu looked my way with his mean squint and asked what I thought of the guest, Smithson.

"I won't forget him soon," I said.

"There's folks in town'd like to. The reason you don't know about him is, you were bumming out west when it all happened."

I wasn't bumming all the time; for a while I was cowpoking on a ranch in Montana, but it was no use correcting him.

"What'd I miss?"

Ma said it wasn't a subject we should talk about at the table and suggested he open his presents, which he did. She gave him a sweater she'd knitted, Bertha gave him red pajamas, and I'd popped for a cigar lighter. The pajamas tickled him so he couldn't hide it, and of course that galled Ma. When Bertha served him a slab of pie that'd choke an alligator, he was even more pleased. He didn't get back to the Smithson thing until after he'd stuffed the pie down and waddled back to the lobby.

"What happened," he said, tilting his swivel chair back after lighting a La Fendrich cigar, "was these two young bucks, Jack Smithson and Laird Creighton, were courting the same gal, Mary Jane Sills all that summer. Mary was a slick little article, cuter'n a spaniel pup, and about as sensible. She got a bang out of them scrapping for her. It went on until one night in late August, the two fellas got into a bang-up fight out back of the dance hall and wore each other to such a frazzle they finally gave up, bought a bottle of moonshine from your buddy Boswell, and got good and drunk. Smithson was a farm boy who'd left his folks and got himself a job at the creamery so he'd be handy for courting, and he was living in a room near the back of the Jensons' house. The story Jack told was, he got so woozy from the moonshine, Laird helped him home and put him to bed. The next thing he knew, his face was on fire. Old Olaf, his landlord, smelled smoke and met Smithson staggering toward the bedroom door, blazing like a torch. Olaf got him out and said Smithson kept screaming Laird done it.

"Joey checked into the whole thing and got everybody's story, and what it came down to was, Laird swore he'd never gone home with Jack, but had been with Mary Jane Sills at her folks' place, smooching on the front porch till all hours. Mary Jane backed up his story, and nobody else came around to support Jack's side.

"Jack was in a Minneapolis hospital over a month and never came back to the farm. Mary Jane and Laird got married that fall."

The whole business interested me enough so I went around to see Joey Paxton, our town cop. He said Elihu had it mostly straight.

"How'd the fire start?" I asked.

"Well, it looked like he fell asleep smoking in bed.

Only that didn't check out. I mean, I could smell something like gasoline—maybe lighter fluid. The way his face was burnt was like his cigarette had exploded, you know? Jack claimed he never smoked, but there was a package of Luckies by the bed, and Mary Jane insisted he smoked, but was shy about it 'cause his folks didn't approve. Of course Creighton backed her up, and I couldn't shake either one of 'em."

"So it was all their word against his, right?"

"Uh-huh."

"Did you believe her?"

He squirmed a little. "It made no never mind what I believed, long as she stuck with her story, and there was no other witnesses. And of course Jack never came back to press charges."

"How do Mary Jane and Laird get on?" I asked.

Joey has a double handicap: he doesn't like gossip, but he can't help telling the truth. After some hemming and hawing, he admitted there'd been reports it was a little stormy. He wouldn't go into details so I could only guess he'd heard stories, but refused to listen.

Boswell, my favorite news source and the best moonshiner in South Dakota, greeted me with his usual warmth when I dropped by his shack, and after his pipe-filling and lighting-up rituals were taken care of, admitted there'd been stories about the Creightons. She'd been seen with a black eye once and with a bruised cheek another time. Creighton went to work one day with a split lip he claimed he got when he slipped getting out of his tub. He worked in his old man's implement dealers shop, which he figured eventually he'd inherit.

"Jack have any brothers or sisters?" I asked.

"Not a real one. There was this girl, Elvira. She was a cousin, some removed, that the Smithsons adopted when her folks died in a accident. She was three, maybe four years younger than Jack. Pretty close, from what I hear. She works at the library. Sweet little thing. So mousy you can go in and not even notice she's there."

"Where's she live?"

"Got a room in back at the Widow Brewer's place."

I decided to go around for a visit, but was stopped by Joey along the way as he came out of the café.

"Jack come back yet?" he asked.

"No."

"Laird's all shook up. Heard he's in town and told me he's a menace. He might attack Mary Jane or him. Where you suppose he went?"

"The last I saw, he was heading south."

He shook his head. "I don't like this. I don't like any little part of it. You see him, let me know."

"Sure."

I hadn't walked a block beyond Joey when Laird pulled up beside me in his brown Dodge.

"What's this I hear," he demanded, "about Smithson showing up at the Wilcox Hotel and asking about my wife?"

"He just asked if I knew her."

"Well, what's he doing in town? The bastard's crazy, you know. Went stark raving when he got drunk and set his own damned bed on fire and tried to blame it on me."

"Tell you what, Laird, we don't have guests fill in their life's history when they register. All we get is where they're from and how long they're gonna stay. That's it."

"Well, you must know about him, for God's sake. Doesn't he have to tell you his business?"

"Nope."

"Goddammit, man, the only reason he'd come back is to get me for taking Mary Jane away from him. You and Joey've got to run him out of town or there'll be a murder. Don't you forget it."

"I'll try to remember."

The Widow Brewer lived just three blocks north of City Hall and was sitting on her front porch when I ambled up the walk. Instead of knitting like any other proper Corden widow, she was reading a book that she lowered and closed, using her forefinger as a marker while talking with me. I tried to make out the title, but she kept it covered with her left hand.

"Elvira around?" I asked.

"Why?" she asked. Her eyes narrowed suspiciously.

"Like to talk with her."

"Forget it. She's not your type."

"Never settled on any one type, Tess. Fact is, I want to talk to her about Jack."

Her expression switched from cold disapproval to hot anger.

"Why?"

"He's taken a room at the hotel. Dad told me about what happened back when I was out west, and the story got to me. Wanted to check it out a little."

"It's a dead issue. Leave her alone."

"Jack been around?"

"That's none of your business."

"I guess you like Elvira."

She wasn't about to be soothed. She said that was none of my business either. She suggested I go visit my moonshiner friend, get drunk, go back on the bum ...

I had a feeling she was going to maybe get insulting soon, but just then this slim woman showed up inside the screen door to my left.

"I'll talk to him, Mrs. Brewer."

"You don't know what you're doing," said the old woman, her voice still harsh from her attack on me.

"Please," said Elvira.

"Very well, talk to him here. I wouldn't let a man with his reputation into my house and certainly not into your room. I'll go inside. If he get fresh, yell. I'll come a-running with the rolling pin."

A moment later Elvira and I were sitting in wooden rockers, facing the quiet street out front. She had a pretty near anonymous face except for large and tragic gray eyes. I tried to remember what color Jack's had been but they were lost in the general horror of his scarred face.

"You two kept in touch?" I asked.

She nodded.

"What brought him back to town?"

She took a deep breath, leaned back, and closed her eyes.

"I heard from Mary Jane. She came to the library two weeks ago and confessed to me she'd lied about Laird being with her when Jack was set on fire. She knew he did it, but thought it was because he loved her so he'd kill to have her, and that was so exciting it made her think she was in love with him and lied to keep him from trouble. But the marriage was awful; she was full of guilt about what happened to Jack and was going to tell the truth and see to it that Laird went to jail for the awful thing he'd done."

"You wrote Jack about that?"

She nodded.

"And he came here to check it. Has he been to see you?"

"No."

"Where is he?"

"He told me on the telephone from St. Paul that when he got here he'd go swimming at the old swimming hole, walk around the sandpit out north of town, and remember good times."

Her voice broke, and for a moment she was silent. Finally, she took a deep breath, lifted her chin, and said he didn't want her to see him the way he is now. He hadn't even let his folks see him. The parents had moved to Aquatown and never wanted to come back. He hadn't told her exactly what he intended to do about Mary Jane's call to Elvira, but she suspected he intended to let Mary Jane see what her man had done to him, which would punish her and maybe spur her on to actually expose Laird's guilt.

"I guess maybe you were in love with Jack," I said.

She looked at me, and for a moment the plainness disappeared and she was near beautiful.

"Yes, I was. I am. I don't care what happened to his face. I tell him that in every letter and during every telephone call, and he can't believe it and won't come near me. Will you tell him he's wrong to hide from me?"

"If I get the chance."

"You will. The last time we talked he asked me a lot of questions about you, and I can tell he's impressed and wants to talk with you. He'll listen to you."

Back at the hotel early in the evening, I parked in the lobby with Elihu, who sat in his swivel chair, watching dead Main Street while listening to my report on the talk with Elvira.

"Why the devil," he asked, "would Jack Smithson think you were anybody?"

That bothered me more than I appreciated because nothing whatsoever came to mind for an answer. But why would she want to soft-soap me? She seemed like the last woman in town who'd ever dream of trying to play games, even innocent ones.

A little after nine Joey wheeled his Model T up in front of the hotel and came in, bustling like a man with a mission.

"Smithson back?" he demanded.

"Not yet. What's up?"

"Mary Jane Creighton's been murdered. Head's all smashed."

"Who found her?"

"Laird. Came home from the café about half an hour ago, found her in the backyard under the lilacs. My God, what a mess. Show me Smithson's room."

We found his small bag open on the bed with shirts still neatly folded. A suit hung on one of the hangers behind the door. A pair of black shoes were side by side at the edge of the bed.

"He probably left all this to throw us off," said Joey.

I didn't believe it, but couldn't offer an argument that would even convince me. We went back to the lobby where Elihu still kept watch on Main Street. Joey asked me to let him know if the man showed up. Then he hustled off to put out a pickup order to the state police.

After some jabber about developments, Elihu shook his head sadly and went to bed.

Smithson's Chevy pulled up in front just after 10:30, and the man came inside.

"Joey's looking for you," I said.

He stopped short and looked down at me with his awful eyes. "Why?"

"You better let him tell you. I'll walk along, you don't mind."

He frowned. It couldn't make him look any more threatening, but his voice was still gentle. "Why'd I mind?"

The distance to Joey's office was only half a minute, and he stood up when we entered his office. Joey looked at the awful face without blinking, thanked Jack for coming and me for bringing him, and was so polite it was painful. Then he apologized and said he had to ask some questions, and Jack said go right ahead. It seemed funny he didn't ask what was wrong, but of course he might have guessed Laird had warned Joey of dangers and expected questions.

"Where you been all day?" asked Joey.

"I went to visit my folks."

"What time you get there?"

"Well, I took a roundabout way with stops here and there, but made it well before supper."

"When'd you leave them?"

"Maybe an hour ago."

Joey asked what time exactly; he shrugged and said he hadn't been checking his watch regular, but it had to be close to nine-thirty because his folks never stayed up later than that. "You can call them or Elvira, they can tell you."

"She was there?"

"I took her there," he said. His smile shook Joey.

"Have you talked with Mary Jane Creighton since coming to Corden?" he asked after a couple of seconds' thought.

"No."

"Why were you looking her up in the telephone book?" I asked.

"Thought some of giving her a call. Decided not to. You know she's talked with my sister?"

"Elvira told me so, yeah."

Joey wanted to know what that was about, and I told him.

The news pained Joey, and he couldn't hide it. "I'll have to talk with Elvira," he complained.

"What's happened?" Jack asked.

Joey looked more pained than ever and said I should tell him.

"Mary Jane's been murdered. Somebody got to her in the backyard."

"Ah," said Jack and looked toward Joey. "What time?"

"Don't know. Seems like after dark, but it could've been earlier. Doc won't pin it exact. Never will. So you left Aquatown around nine-thirty. Was Elvira with you?"

"Yes, I gave her a ride home."

"Anybody besides your family see you in Aquatown?"

The smile was spookier than ever. "Probably. For some reason people seem to notice me."

Joey stared at him, and I figured he was thinking there was something familiar about all this. The most obvious attacker had a solid alibi from a loving woman. Only in this case, maybe a lot more.

Joey stood up. "You mind giving me the keys to your car?"

"No. But why?"

"So you won't be likely to leave town. I got to talk with Laird and Elvira."

"Fine," said Jack. "I'm going to bed. If you want me, just knock."

Joey invited me along for his visit with Elvira, and it didn't take any fuss to get the Widow Brewer to let us see her. She was in a nightgown and robe, and didn't look as if she'd been sleeping. She faced us in the small living room and confirmed all Jack had told us.

"Tell Joey," I said, "all you told me about Mary Jane's talk with you at the library."

She went through it very deliberately, in almost exactly the words I'd heard it originally.

"What'd you think of her," I asked. "Did you believe she really meant all the business about guilt, or could she have just been trying to set up things for a divorce?"

"Oh, I believed she was sincere. She struck me as much more sensitive than I'd have expected, considering what she'd done to Jack. I mean, her lying about Laird being with her that night he did the awful thing to Jack, you know? She said at the time she just didn't have any choice. She really thought she was in love with him and couldn't bear to let him go to prison, even after the awful thing he'd done, because he convinced her he couldn't live without her and that was why he tried to kill Jack. He swore he'd kill himself if she didn't save him."

Elvira told us Mary Jane claimed her husband treated her like a whore, made her do awful things in bed, and beat her almost daily. The times her face was bruised were rare only because he was usually careful to hit where it wouldn't show.

She told us a little more than I would have believed such a shy and sheltered woman would spell out. She just about wallowed in it.

Joey and I left the house and went back to City Hall without talking.

"What'd Laird have to say when he reported Mary Jane's murder?" I asked in his office.

"He said Jack did it. He also said, if I didn't get him for it, he would. He's crazy mad."

Joey didn't want to go see him again, but I argued we had to and finally we went.

The house was empty. We talked about where he might be and found his car in the garage out back.

"What did the job on Mary Jane?" I asked.

"Doc says more'n likely a hammer. The skull's all smashed. She was hit about four, five times."

"No hammer around?"

"Nope. Not in the garage or the basement where he kept his tools."

"He had tools but no hammer?"

"He admits he had one. It's gone. He says Jack must've found it, used it and taken it away."

"So Smithson is supposed to have gone in that house, walked down to the basement, found the hammer, came back upstairs, whomped Mary Jane, and carried it off? Why the hell'd he carry it with him?"

"Well, you could hardly expect a fella who'd gone through what Jack did to act like other folks."

"There was nothing crazy about the guy I signed in and talked to this morning."

"Well, he wasn't talking to one of the people that made him what he is now."

"Now wait a minute. You heard what Elvira said. You know Laird has whopped his wife before and that if she all of a sudden took back her story about him being with her when Jack got burned, he'd be in crap soup. Who'd have a better reason for murder? Especially when he had this guy, with a face that'd spook a buzzard, to blame it on?"

He didn't try to argue with me. He said what the hell, we'd sleep on it and question everybody tomorrow.

I couldn't sleep, so back in the hotel I slipped out on the balcony overlooking Main Street and watched nothing happening beyond bug action around the streetlights. The night was warm, the moon only a sliver, and stars of the Milky Way glowed across the sky.

He must have slipped around back and come along the First Avenue side of the hotel because I didn't see him until he moved out from under the balcony toward Smithson's parked Chevy. He looked around carefully, went to the car's side, and after another nervous survey, opened the left rear door. Again, like a squirrel digging for acorns, he lifted his head for a look about, then reached inside, struggled a second with the seat, got it lifted, shoved something under it, and let the seat drop. Slowly he closed the door and turned toward the hotel.

I went over the railing and dropped on him.

My weight flattened him, sprained his right ankle, and didn't do his back a lot of good. In spite of that he fought briefly like a maniac, but when I tied him up with a combination full nelson and scissors hold around the middle, he gave up and begged off.

I took him inside, limping and moaning, then parked him on a rocker and called Joey who responded like a man sleeping off a three-day drunk but finally got my drift and said he'd be right over.

"What'd you do?" I asked Laird while waiting, "wipe off your fingerprints and hide the hammer under the seat?"

"I didn't kill her, Carl. Honest to God. She was dead when I found her, and he did it. Why'd I kill her? Sure, we had arguments and I lost my temper a couple times, but I'd never do her like that. It was that goddamn Jack did it. He's crazy."

"You're saying he did it and left the hammer there so it'd look like you were the one? Now why'd you think he'd believe anybody'd go for the idea it was you instead of Jack?"

"I told you, he's nuts. I didn't have any reason—"

"Except the fact your wife was going to renig on her story that you were with her when Jack got burned. Most folks'll think that's a fine motive."

His chin dropped so bad I thought it'd hit the floor.

"That's a lie. She'd never do a thing like that. Hell, I admit we had fights, and a couple times I belted her. Know why? Because she hit me first. She even kneed me in the nuts. Where you think I got the split lip people laughed about for a week? Every time she lost her temper, she whomped me or threw something."

It was a good act. I shook my head, but didn't get to follow up at the moment because Joey came in. He looked haggard.

I told him to go out and look under the backseat of Smithson's Chevy.

"I put it there," yelled Laird. "I did it because he left it by Mary Jane there under the lilac bush—and it was my hammer and everybody'd swallow his story I did it. I was just trying to defend myself . . ."

Joey went out to the car and came back with the hammer and a pair of gloves.

"These yours?" he asked Laird.

"No, I never saw those gloves before—"

"How about the hammer?"

Laird seemed to deflate. "It's mine. I already told you that. He must've found it. I think I left it in the kitchen the last time I used it."

After that he wouldn't answer questions. He demanded we get Doc over to find out what I'd broken and promised he'd sue me.

Joey called Doc, who showed up eventually, and it was nearly 2:30 A.M. when Laird was locked up in the cell and I went to bed.

The next day between us Joey and I confirmed Jack's story through his parents and got backup from neighbors who'd seen Jack arrive in daylight before dinner. As he said, people seemed to notice him.

The clincher was the gloves. They were too small to go on Jack's hands. They fit Laird perfectly.

Laird did his damnedest to convince everybody he'd only planted the hammer and gloves to put the blame where it really belonged, and of course nobody believed him.

Finally, he confessed.

When Jack was checking out, we had the lobby to ourselves. "You worked it so good," I said, "I'm still not able to figure all the angles."

He gave me a look as innocent as his scarred face could allow. "What's bothering you?" he asked in his most gentle tone.

"Well, did Elvira dream up that story about Mary

Jane deciding to renig on her story of what happened the night you got burned, or was it your idea?"

"It was mine."

"I kind of figured that. How'd you get him the word?"

"An anonymous telephone call."

"I guess you knew Mary Jane was a fighter—liked to hurt her men?"

"Oh yes—liked to hurt and be hurt."

"I thought for a while there you had framed Laird. Of course, in a way, you did."

"In a way. Frankly, I never believed it would work out so perfectly. I'd have been pleased if they beat hell out of each other, almost satisfied if they'd divorced. But it came out just beautifully. The business of planting the hammer and gloves in my car was too wonderful. More than I ever hoped for."

"How did it happen that after several years of hiding out, you suddenly decided to visit Elvira and your parents?"

"That was the hardest decision. But after those years of thinking about what that pair did to me, it seemed the only thing I could do was let all the family know why I had to do this whole thing. Now they understand, and it's all at rest."

He paid up, carried his suitcase out to his car, and drove toward the highway. I expected he'd swing by to pick up Elvira, but he drove straight, and the last I heard, Elvira was living in Aquatown, taking care of her aging parents.

Base Corruption

by Billie Sue Mosiman

I was the quiet, shy, reserved one. I never got into trouble; I excelled in school. I graduated from college with honors; I did all the right things. But Father loved Davey best. He always did. And now look what his selfless, one-sided love has wrought.

"The ambulance is on the way. Hold on, just keep fighting it."

Father lay on the floor of the kitchen, choking. His lips were turning as white as the tile beneath his head while I watched. I felt my gut coiling from sudden fear he'd die before the paramedics could arrive. A spasm caused me to double over.

"You didn't eat it, did you?" His voice was hardly a whisper. His own agonizing pain had drawn his knees up to his chest and made his hands tremble; his fine washed-denim blue eyes glazed over every few seconds as he grappled to stay conscious.

"No, I didn't eat it."

I drew in a quick breath and held it a beat. No, Davey hadn't cared about poisoning me. He didn't care about me or my life one way or the other. He wanted our father dead, that was his goal. Who would believe it? But Davey really meant it this time. He had brought over a casserole dish filled with lasagna, knowing Father loved it, knowing we would think Angie, Davey's wife, made it special for him. Sweet Angie, another person in Davey's life who loved him without reservation, though she hadn't spent the years with him we had to know his true nature. She couldn't have and remained with him. Or so I fervently hoped.

And in the casserole Davey had put something vile, something evil and deadly. Was it the mushrooms? Were they poisonous? Or had he just sprinkled in insecticide? Whatever it was, it was fast-acting, since Father hadn't eaten but a small portion and that was no more than half an hour ago.

Davey had told me since we were children that he'd do it. He hated the old man. Maybe he hated him almost as much as our father loved him back. It was ironic to think a son, so adored, could wish harm for so many years. I had tried to warn Father before this—the time Davey "accidentally" backed the car from the garage before Father had crossed the drive with the firewood. I told the secret then for the first time. "He means to kill you," I said. "That was no accident."

Luckily Father suffered minor contusions and abrasions. I had screamed out in time, startling Davey so that he slammed his foot on the brake pedal inches before rolling over Father's head.

"Don't you dare say that to me," Father said when he was able to lift himself from the bed in the dim, narrow bedroom he had once shared with our mother. She had died giving birth. "He didn't see me. I shouldn't have been behind the car. It was just a stupid mistake."

Davey was already gone. Late for a date, he had squealed out of the driveway, impatient to be away from the scene of what could have been his crime.

"Listen," I said. "We have to talk about Davey. I never wanted to tell you, but you have to know or something terrible's going to happen."

"You're jealous of him."

As soon as he said it, I knew it was the truth, but it was not the entire truth. "I may be, who wouldn't, the way everyone loves him and he never has to work for it, earn it or require it? No one ever paid any attention to me. Why is that? Why did you ever favor Davey? Was it because he was born first? Or because he was sickly as a kid? Or because he's just so charming when he puts his mind to it?"

Father waved all this away with his hand. "Let me get up. I should wash off my knees. I think they're scraped raw."

I stood aside and helped him stand. I followed him to the bathroom and lounged in the doorway while he sat ministering to his knees with cotton balls and alcohol. He sat on the lowered toilet lid in his floppy undershorts, his legs sticking out of them like puny birch white poles. He winced when he applied the alcohol and leaned way over to blow at the reddened skin just the way he always did for us when we'd hurt ourselves and the alcohol burned. I could smell the astringent odor and remembered those days when it was always Davey who had to be taken care of, and I rarely needed a helping hand. For I was good. I was careful. I didn't climb the trees or jump from the roof of the woodshed. I was never any bother. I tried so hard not to be.

"Father, listen to me, this one time, you must listen."

"I'm tired of your complaining about your brother, Joseph. Trying to convince me he meant to run me down with the car is like telling me the moon is made of hammered gold."

It wasn't easy the first time I told him. But I knew if I didn't, Davey was going to catch him unaware. "He told me when we were seven years old that he ought to kill you, and when he got big enough, that's exactly what he was going to do." There, I'd said it and he would have to understand now. He must.

He glanced up, the bottle of alcohol and damp cotton ball smeared with droplets of his blood held out to each side of his body. A knot was rising on his forehead that would need an ice pack. The look in his eyes now questioned me. They asked silently, *could this possibly be so?* "I wouldn't make it up, Father. Davey isn't ... he isn't ... there's something *wrong* with him. There always has been."

"Why would he want to kill me? He's my son."

As if that blood tie would stop someone as determined as my brother!

"The first time he said it was because you punished him for playing in the fireplace. You remember? The time he had stuffed the hearth full of crumpled newspapers and set it on fire so that smoke billowed out into the room? You came running, thought the house was on fire, and gave him a smack on his behind. When he was in our room, I asked why he had been playing with matches, and he was purple in the face he was so mad. That's when he said he ought to kill you."

Father bent over his knees again, dabbing at the scrapes. "That was just his anger. I'd never laid a hand on him before, that's all."

"And you never did again. Yet he told me at least once every few months what he meant to do."

Father's head snapped up. "Every few months? He said this all the time? Why didn't you tell me before? I could have tried to discover what was wrong. I might have sent him to a counselor, found a psychologist . . ."

"He scared me. He threatened to kill me, too, if I told. I believed him for a long time. I saw his face, heard his voice, I thought he meant it. No, I *knew* he meant it."

"It's all nonsense. Davey's just . . . he's always been . . . spirited. Which is more than I can say for you."

That hurt. He knew it had; he stood abruptly and put aside the alcohol, then dropped the dirtied cotton in the trash basket near the toilet. His movements were agitated, and I saw his lips working, how he wrestled with what he had just said to me, the only son who truly loved him.

"I mean, Davey's got some devil in him, no doubt about that," he continued in a rush. "He needed more attention, I had to watch out for his safety, but you, you were always like a little adult, never giving me a minute's worry, and that was a good thing, it was a great help to me, Joseph. I know you have spirit, I didn't mean it in a nasty way."

He had said this with his back to me as he drew on

his ripped trousers once again. I hung my head and swung back from the doorway, trying to find my way to the living room through blurred vision. I was almost grown then. Seventeen. My brother had just tried to cripple or kill my father with the car, and I had told the secret that frightened me most of my life, and the result of my bravery was criticism for lack of *spirit*.

Why couldn't my father love me? Would he ever love me? He couldn't even take me seriously. It was a mystery that took my heart in a fist and wrung it dry, crumpled it like old newspaper set afire on a dusty hearth.

When Davey was nineteen, he tried again. I wouldn't have known this time had I not just come out the back door that summer afternoon when the light was on the wane, shadows creeping across the ground from the leafy trees like panthers belly-crawling after small game. I saw Davey give the ladder a push. At the top of the ladder Father stood poised like a long-legged stork, arms like flapping wings spread out as they clutched air, trying to snatch the rungs before it was too late.

But it was too late.

Father plummeted to the ground from the second story where he'd just come off the roof. He'd been repairing a leak, and his hands were sticky black with shingle tar. His scream was short and cut off as soon as his body struck ground. His breath was momentarily knocked out of his lungs, and the whites of his eyes rolled back in his head. I flew across the yard to the side of the house, took hold of Davey, and hurled him to the ground with a war yell that could have been heard a mile. I went on hands and knees to where Father lay, coming around now, groaning.

A broken leg. He had not been so lucky as when Davey meant to run him down with the car, but lucky enough not to have broken his neck or back. He was in a cast for months. I did most of the work around the house while Davey spent the summer courting Angie, the girl soon to be his wife. We both were supposed to return to the university in the fall, but I was the one who left for my classes while Davey dropped out, took a penny-ante job at a computer store, and married his ladylove.

Father paid for the reception, insisting he wanted to, since nothing was ever good enough for his son. There were buckets of the most lavishly expensive champagne, catered food enough for an army, and flowers decking the hall from ceilings to doors. Davey preened more than did his lovely bride. I nursed a small glass of the champagne and watched from a corner, wondering how my brother was going to support a wife without finishing his education.

After Father's mishap that broke his leg, I often wondered if he hadn't seen Davey at the bottom of the ladder, giving it the fatal shove? I finally realized, when he never brought it up, that he must not have. If he had, wouldn't he have at least set my brother down and asked him where he had come by this penultimate evil that caused him to want to commit patricide?

But now Father knew. Lying on the floor with poison slowly working its way through his system, he had to know there was no accident this time. Davey was twenty-seven years old. He had become a computer store manager, but his salary was minuscule compared to what I made as a high school teacher, though my own salary was pitiful enough. And Davey wanted an inheritance. He knew about Mother's money. It had kept Father all these years, and the trust continued to grow since Father was a wise and thrifty manager, hoping to leave the bulk of the estate for his sons.

Maybe Davey wanted the money all along—or maybe petty revenge for some small perceived wrong that only he could render.

Father had hold of my hand, and now he squeezed it tightly. "If I get out of this alive, we'll have to do something with Davey."

I nodded my head, speechless with dread that this time he *would not* make it. It would be left to me to make my brother pay.

The siren of the ambulance wailed just outside the door. Father closed his eyes, hearing it. The pain was so bad now his color was green, and his lips that were earlier whitened were now gray as slugs lying motionless across his face. "Hold on," I whispered. "Just a little while. They're here."

They were there, and it made no difference. They whisked him away and tried in vain to keep his heart beating, his lungs breathing, until they could get him to the hospital to pump his stomach, but from the front seat of the ambulance where they made me sit, I was turned, caught in the seat belt, feeling the careening of the big white van through the streets while Father convulsed. His mouth opened, and like a fish he gulped for air, his hands stiffened and clawed at his sides, his chest expanded to the point it looked as if it might burst. I began to scream above the siren's call, above the traffic sounds, above the admonitions of the paramedics to sit back, to calm down. I couldn't stop the scream that spiraled above the roar of my heart, could not stop the words he must hear before he left me that I loved him, I loved him, I would not let him die for I loved him, and I was the only one who ever did, the only one he never believed. The only one.

When we buried Father, I watched for Davey, my gaze wandering past the gravesite to the tall monuments and tombstones and strikingly tall cypress tress, hunting for a shadow of him. The police watched, too, hoping to catch him out. But would a man who murdered his father pay his respects? It was as unlikely as a dawn that never brightens to day.

Once the estate was settled, and Davey seemed to have disappeared off the face of the earth—Angie didn't know where he'd gone, and she didn't care when the authorities told her he was wanted for murder—I knew all I had to do was wait. He'd be in touch. He wanted the money, didn't he? He'd try to force it from me in some way, through threats or real injury.

Even I was surprised at the amount of the stock holdings and cash available in our father's accounts. I expected Davey knew it all to the penny. He must have known for a very long time.

It was months before he materialized. I had almost fallen into a reverie of false hope, believing that Davey would stay in hiding for the rest of our days, that he would not dare approach me when he knew I despised him so.

It was six months after the funeral—a day so gray and dismal the watery light outside was the color of oyster shell. I sat before the fireplace, nodding off in my chair, a book of Steinbeck's journal about writing *The Grapes of Wrath* open in my lap. I still taught senior English, and I wanted to choose some of Steinbeck's entries to illustrate to my students how a great man had done his work even though he felt it was probably a mistake to think he was doing any good.

"So there you are, all alone."

My head jerked up and back at the voice. *Davey.* I dropped the book from my knees and twisted in the chair to look behind me. The sound of the crackling fire intensified in my ears. "I've been waiting for you," I said.

He looked the worse for wear. His clothes were ragged and stained, his shoes worn thin and dull. His thick brown hair had grown out to cover his ears. He needed a shave. There was a new hardness in his eyes and new lines in his face that had never been there before. Rather like my own, his face was a weary mask perched precariously on shoulders beginning to slope under the relentless assault of troublesome events.

"Then you know," he said, coming closer into the golden light of the fire, "that I expect half of the money. At least half."

I laughed with all the bitterness and sarcasm I was able to muster. "You're a fool, Davey. You should have been smothered the moment you came out of our mother's womb."

"And not you? The cowering, tail-tucking dog that you are?"

"Even a dog wouldn't murder his father."

"Our father, Joseph, was the only goddamned fool in this family."

"Because he loved you too much."

"Give me a check, and I won't bother you again. I don't care to rehash old grievances."

"I wouldn't give you the sweat off my back. I wouldn't give you a nickel if you were starving."

"I was afraid you'd be that way."

"Why did you have to kill him?"

"Why did you think that I wouldn't, little brother?"

I felt a storm cloud of fury sweep over me when he said that. I was up from the chair and had laid hold of him before he could manage to sidestep me. I had my hands around his throat, pressing for his life, but then he laughed, that horrible black laughter he reserved for when he found me ridiculous, and all I wanted to do was true murder, real and true and immediate so that he could never laugh or cry or have time to repent.

That's when I felt the cold round object pushing against my belly, and my fingers stilled against the pulse of his throat. I looked into his eyes. The man peering back at me was as emotionless as a snake poised to strike.

I relaxed my hands and brought them away from him. I stepped back slightly. I felt the spit dry in my mouth. I smelled the fire at my back, heard my brother's heavy ragged breathing. Davey was winning again; he always won out, every time.

He kept the pistol trained on my midsection. "You thought I'd come unarmed? Then you're also a fool. Now write me a check and we'll go together to the bank to get my money—*my* money."

In the next three seconds I had a decision to make. I could try for the gun and stop him once and for all, or give in to his demands and be the pushover he accused me of being, the tail-tucking dog he had known all his life.

Then a small voice spoke inside my head, the one there since I was a boy wondering late in the night why my father never loved me as he loved Davey, why he never cared for me at all, apparently, never gave to me what I so desperately needed from a father. The voice said *if you want anything in this life, you should take lessons from your brother; you should take the wheel into your hand and steer the vessel steady on and straight without a backward glance, for if you don't, there can never be hope for you as a man, no more than there was for you as a son.*

I had knocked the gun aside, and the resultant explosion deafened me, but even as my ears rang and my nostrils flared at the scent of cordite, I had my arms around Davey's body, hauling him down with me in a bear hug. We fell together, the gun still in his hand as it clattered against the wooden floor. He tried to bring that hand up and between us, but this time he would not succeed. I swore it with hot breath into his face, "You won't kill me, you won't kill me before I kill you!"

During the fight, as evenly paired as we were in stature and weight, I never knew when my arm would give out or his, when my muscles would overpower or be overpowered, not until the gun roared a second time and Davey fell still as stone. I pushed him off me, off my legs, and scrambled to my feet, trying to get as far away as possible from the blood and the death of the one person I had tried so often to save.

I sat in the gloom while waiting for the police to come. I rocked near the fire, the Steinbeck book lying exactly where it had fallen when Davey intruded. I sat watching my brother, my dead brother finally so quiet, where he lay crumpled on the floor.

When the police arrived, I let them in and stepped away from the body. "He tried to kill me. He wanted half the money our father left."

They could see a scuffle had occurred. Davey still had

the gun in his right hand, where it was bent underneath his bloody corpse.

One of the policemen turned Davey over first to check the wound and then his unmarred face. "He looks just like you!" the young officer said. "You're twins?"

"Identical," I said. "But not in the ways that count."

And now he was dead. My entire family was dead, and I would resemble no one ever again. I would not be a beloved son or brother. I would not be, ever again, so bereft of spirit that I could not find my quiet, shy, reserved way through what was left of my life.

Father, Son
and Holy Ghost

by Barbara Collins

My Sunday afternoons are sacred. Hubby is glued to his easy chair, watching football. The kids are down in the rec room, playing video games, out of my hair. And I'm cloistered in the bedroom, under the rumpled sheets, enjoying an old movie on the VCR, and eating a box of sinful chocolates I keep hidden in my underwear drawer.

But sometimes my sacred Sundays get ruined.

I'm Joan Munday, one of six detectives on the Port City Police Department, in a town with a population of about twenty-five thousand, give or take a soul.

It was 2:33 P.M., October 25, when the phone rang on the nightstand by the bed. I knew it was Captain Velez because even my own mother knows better than to bother me on a Sunday afternoon. The captain told me to call my partner, Frank Lausen, and get over to St. Mark's Church right away. He said Father O'Brien had called the station, very upset. The priest was claiming his church had been possessed by a ghost—and not the holy kind.

I hung up, then dialed Frank, and ruined *his* Sunday. I told him I'd be by to pick him up in a few minutes.

Frank lived in a split-level home in a new addition not far from our old two-story clapboard. He was twenty-eight years old—a decade younger than I—and had a wife who taught elementary school, and two small children.

He was buttoning up a wrinkled white shirt beneath

a navy jacket when he came out of his house, red tie hanging loose around his neck like a noose. His thick, sandy hair was tousled, his face unshaven.

He grunted a greeting as he got into the car. Quickly, he reached for the dial on the radio, turning it on, and tuning it in to the Bengals–Browns football game he'd been watching.

I looked in the rearview mirror, catching my own image, and cringed a little as I pulled away from the curb; with my own hastily made-up face and brown hair in need of a coif, we looked like a couple that really tied one on the night before.

Port City was beautiful in the fall. Nestled on the Mississippi River among rolling hills, the town was blessed with many trees, vibrant with color now—reds as red as blood, oranges as orange as the pumpkins sitting on porches of houses that we sped by on our way to the church. Halloween was making a big comeback here, after a slow couple of years, following some treaters getting cyanide-laced tricks. Black cats and witches clung to doors and windows, while white-sheet ghosts hung twisting by their necks from trees.

I turned my car into a cobblestone drive that led up a narrow winding road to St. Mark's Church. The huge Gothic building, pale gray granite trimmed in carved limestone, looked down ominously at us—and the rest of the city—from its hilltop perch. I thought the old Protestant church I attended was austere; this looming edifice was downright intimidating.

I parked the car in the lot and we got out.

Father O'Brien stood waiting for us at the front door of the rectory, a simple gray three-story building next door. He wasn't at all the jolly Friar Tuck-type I had naively imagined. Tall, bearlike, he was an imposing figure all in black, except for the traditional white collar. His dark hair was carefully combed, the gray at his temples hinting of middle age. While his facial features seemed benevolently boyish, a square jaw and jutting chin gave the impression he was no pushover. Outwardly the priest looked composed, but his eyes betrayed something else.

Frank and I approached. "Father O'Brien," I said, "I'm Joan Munday, and this is Frank Lausen, from the Police Department."

"Thank you for coming," he said solemnly. "And I'm sorry to take you away from your families on a Sunday afternoon."

I smiled. "I don't think they'll miss me," I admitted. I couldn't lie to a priest.

"What's this about a ghost, Father?" Frank asked.

Father O'Brien gestured toward the doorway. "We'll talk inside."

We followed Father O'Brien into the rectory, down a dark, drafty hallway lined with portraits of priests. Who they were, I couldn't say, but one of them reminded me uncomfortably of that old *Saturday Night Live* character, Father Guido Sarducci.

Father O'Brien led us into what I assumed was his office. It was cozy and comfortable—a large oak desk, a file cabinet, a picture of Pope John Paul II on the wall, and two chairs. Occupying the chairs was another priest and a woman. The priest, also dressed in black slacks and jacket, rose as we entered. He was older than Father O'Brien, tall and slender, with a handsome but world-weary face.

The woman, who remained seated, was about my age. She had short, straight brown hair, and wore little makeup on her plain but not unattractive face. Her burgundy blouse and skirt were at least ten years out of style. She looked at me with apprehension.

"This is Elizabeth Keyes," Father O'Brien said, making the introductions. "She's church organist and also helps out in the office."

Frank and I nodded at her.

"And this is Father Hanson," Father O'Brien continued. "He gives the early morning mass."

"Would you like to sit down?" Father Hanson asked. He gestured to his empty chair. "I can get another ..."

"We'll stand if you don't mind," Frank answered, almost curtly. "Now, who wants to tell us about this 'ghost'?"

Frank wasn't usually so brusque. He just wanted to get home in time for the second half.

Father O'Brien moved behind his desk. "It began about three weeks ago," he said, sitting down; the chair creaked beneath his weight. He put his elbows on the desk and pressed his hands together, prayerlike. The pope peeked over his shoulder. "October sixth, I remember because the day before was a funeral for one of our parishioners. Afterward, the family donated the flowers to the church for mass the next morning."

He paused. We waited.

"But when I went into the church that Sunday morning," he continued, "something was terribly wrong with the flowers—all of them were wilting and dying."

There was silence. Then Frank said, "That's it? Dead flowers?"

I gave Frank a wilting look; his rudeness to these men of the cloth surprised me. But then, they had interrupted *his* religion, football.

"Father O'Brien," I said. "Have you had any trouble with flowers since?"

"Oh, yes," the priest said and sighed. "We've finally resorted to using artificial ones."

"What else can you tell us?" I asked.

"There's an odor," he said. "A smell ... a *stench* really ... so unpleasant I have to open every window to get rid of it."

"Do you recognize this odor?" I asked. "Or can you describe it?"

Father O'Brien furrowed his brow. "No," he said slowly, thinking. "I can't."

"Maybe it's just a dead, decaying rat," Frank offered. "I mean, you probably have a few in an old building like this!"

Frank was in rare form today.

Father Hanson spoke. "It's not a dead, decaying rat,"

he said politely. "Many of us have encountered this odor and in different places in the church. It's like walking into a fog—that's how I would describe it."

Elizabeth Keyes, who was nodding in agreement, leaned toward Father O'Brien. "Tell them about the music," she said, conspiratorially.

"Our 'ghost' plays the organ," he said, "and quite well. Father Hanson and I can hear it at night from our rooms here in the rectory."

"The organ," I said to Elizabeth, "*can* it play by itself?"

"No," she said almost huffily. "It's a pipe organ, not a synthesizer."

"Just what kind of music does this ghost like to play?" Frank asked, smirking. " 'The Monster Mash'?"

"Hymns," Elizabeth Keyes answered tersely.

"Any *particular* hymns?" I asked.

The two priests and organist exchanged glances. Then Father O'Brien said, "It seems to favor 'Ave Maria.' "

Frank snorted. "Look, somebody's just pulling your chain. Your flock's got a disgruntled sheep, is all this is. Or a neighborhood kid playing a Halloween prank. And if that's the case, we'll catch him." Frank raised an eyebrow. "But if this *is* some ghost, some spirit of the other world . . . well, why don't you just *exorcise* it?"

Patient until now, Father O'Brien stood up, face flushed, and leaned with both hands on the desk. "Mr. Lausen," he said angrily, obviously frustrated, "this isn't some Hollywood horror show. Father Hanson's mass this morning was interrupted by screams so blood-curdling it cleared the congregation out of the church! Whatever it is *has* to *stop*!"

A strained silence fell over the room. I shifted uncomfortably from one foot to the other. I looked at Frank.

"We could stake out the church next week," I offered.

Frank sighed and nodded. Then he looked at the priests. "I've got no experience in the ghost-busting business," he said, "but I'm willing to give it a try . . . if one of you can tell me who or what I'm expected to bust."

"*I* can tell you," Elizabeth Keyes said, her voice strange, eyes haunted. "I've *seen* her."

"Her?" Frank and I said.

"Rebecca Madden."

"Now I'm confused," I admitted, looking from Father Hanson to Elizabeth to Father O'Brien. "If you know who it is why don't you ... ?"

"You don't understand," Father O'Brien said softly. "Rebecca Madden was murdered in the woods behind this church ten years ago."

It was 4:45 P.M. when I dropped Frank off at his house. We decided to alternate nights at the church; the priests could keep an eye on things during the day. I thought it was sweet of Frank to offer to take the first watch, so I could have Sunday evening with my family. Then I figured out he wanted tomorrow night off so he could watch Monday Night Football.

I drove over to the station and pulled the folder on Rebecca Madden—it was still in the active file.

The manila envelope was thick with papers and notes and newspaper clippings. It had all the earmarks of an officer obsessed with a case.

The name of Sergeant Richard Lynn was printed in ink on the outside of the envelope. I'd heard he left us for the Chicago PD a few years back, before I arrived.

I looked at the autopsy report. It said the thirty-three-year-old, female Caucasian died from strangulation. The only evidence gathered at the scene—a quarter-inch thick brown rope, four and a half feet long—was listed in the evidence locker, number JW714. The woman had not been sexually molested.

Among the clippings was Rebecca Madden's obit from the local newspaper, dated October 10, with accompanying photo.

Long tresses that looked like angel's hair encircled her head like a huge halo. Her delicate features, eyes large and demanding, were that of a porcelain doll. She was smiling, but it somehow seemed sad. A hauntingly beautiful woman ...

The obit read like a pitch for sainthood—assistant organist at St. Mark's Church, part-time Catholic elementary school teacher, charity work that would have made Mother Teresa proud. She left behind both parents, who at that time were still living in town, and a ten-year-old son. She was preceded in death by her husband.

I leafed back through the file and noticed Sergeant Lynn had kept track of the family. Rebecca's parents had moved to Naples, Florida, three years ago. The son, Chris, enrolled at the University of Iowa, in Iowa City.

If the boy was still in college, he would be a junior today.

That night I couldn't sleep. I lay in bed next to my husband, thinking about that poor woman, and that sad little boy. I got up and put on my old white robe and tiptoed in to my sleeping kids and kissed their faces. Then I went downstairs to watch TV.

Sometime around three I fell asleep for what seemed like a second when the shrill ring of the phone woke me. It was Frank.

"What time is it?" I asked groggily.

"Six forty-five," he answered, sounding the same.

"Anything happen?"

"Yes."

That woke me up. "What?"

"I hurt my back, that's what happened," he said crossly. "Here's a piece of advice ... never sleep on a goddamn church pew."

The phone clicked in my ear.

I got up and showered and dressed and got my kids off to school. Then I kissed my husband good-bye and wished him a good day at the bank.

I went out to my car.

The drive to Iowa City, which was forty-five miles north of Port City, was as refreshing as a cool drink of water. I cracked a window and let in the crisp fall air. Farm fields were brown with ripened corn, ready for harvesting, and the colorful trees, bathed in the morning sun, glistened like an artist's lovely landscape not yet fully dried.

I loved the energy of a college town and envied the students in their new coats and sweaters, faces flushed, rushing to and from class with the knowledge that their whole lives lay ahead of them.

Obtaining Chris Madden's class schedule from the dean was easy enough, but I did have some trouble finding the Arts Building where Chris was supposed to be. Locating a parking place was the hard part. After circling the packed lot a few times, I invented a spot. What were those campus rent-a-cops going to do—arrest me?

Chris was in the theater, backstage, painting a prop, brush in one hand. Other students were around, working on the sets, but I easily picked him out.

He was of average height, slender, but muscular in a blue T-shirt and black jeans. His tan tennis shoes were splotched with the green paint he was using. He had a mop of thick curly brown hair and a small mustache. The ten-year-old boy was now a twenty-year-old man.

He must have sensed me watching him from the wings because he turned and looked at me with his mother's eyes.

"Something?" he asked politely, but with an edge that said, "I'm busy."

I crossed the stage, shoes echoing off the floorboards, and told him who I was.

He set the brush down on the top of the paint can. "This is about my mother, isn't it?" he asked, but it was more like a statement than a question.

I nodded.

"Somehow I knew it," he said.

"Could we go somewhere and talk?"

He gestured toward the prop tree he was painting. "I've got to finish this," he said. "But I could meet you in the cafeteria, around noon."

"How about Bushnell's Turtle?" I suggested.

"Fine," he said.

I turned and left the stage, feeling his eyes on my back. I went outside to my car, where a fifteen-dollar parking ticket was pinned under a wiper. I guess that answered my question about what the rent-a-cops could do to me.

Bushnell's Turtle was famous for its sub sandwiches. The restaurant got its name from the man who invented the first submarine. Anyway, so the card on the table said. Established in the early 1970s, the eatery had something most other hippie-era restaurants didn't have: great food.

The place was packed right now. I grabbed a wooden booth in the back along a wall of framed photos of dogs playing cards, leaving my jacket to claim the booth before going back up to the counter to order.

At 12:13 Chris came in the front door. I waved to him as he stood in line to get his food. I had already gotten mine—carrot soup, a veggie salad with peppercorn dressing, a super sub deluxe, and chocolate cake. I had given up losing those ten pounds a long time ago.

After a few minutes Chris came back with his lunch—a bottle of "natural" soda. He slid into the booth across from me.

"I don't have much time," he said apologetically. He took a sip of the pop, then ran one finger over his mustache.

I put down my super sub deluxe and told him about the strange things that Father O'Brien had said had been happening at St. Mark's Church. I told him Elizabeth Keyes claimed to have seen his mother, in a pink floral dress, standing in the balcony of the sanctuary one night.

A peculiar look came over his face. "You don't know how relieved I am to hear this," he said softly, "because I thought *I* was going crazy."

I waited for him to explain.

He looked up at me with tortured eyes. "You see," he said, "I've seen my mother, too."

I leaned forward. "Where?"

"In my dreams," he said. "Although lately I can sort

of sense her"—he ran one hand through his hair—"I can't exactly explain it, but it's *more* than a feeling."

"Tell me about the dreams."

He leaned toward me and lowered his voice. "She's floating above me—in a white robe, not a pink floral dress. She's trying to tell me something . . . her lips are moving, but I can't tell what she's saying. Then I wake up, drenched in sweat."

I studied his face. Then I asked, "What can you tell me about Elizabeth Keyes?"

He shrugged and took another drink of his soda. "Not much," he said. "I haven't seen her for years. But I remember that she and my mother were very close . . . almost like sisters. She was always over at our house. And she was very kind to me after my mother died."

"And Father O'Brien and Father Hanson? Do you see them often?"

"Father Hanson will drop by my dorm whenever he's in town. He comes up to visit parish members who are at the University Hospital." He paused. "I haven't seen Father O'Brien in quite some time. But both Father Hanson and Father O'Brien were responsible for me getting that church scholarship to go to college here."

"I see."

Chris pushed his now empty pop bottle away. "Look," he said, his eyes searching my face, "I don't know what's going on, but I think someone at that church knows something about my mother's death."

"What makes you think that?" I asked.

He shrugged again. "Why else would she be haunting it?"

I didn't have an answer for him.

I finished my food, and we left the booth and went outside. The sky had clouded over, and the chill in the air was a promise of winter, or maybe a threat.

"I'll be in touch," I told him.

Chris took a few steps from me, then stopped and looked back over his shoulder. "Oh, one thing," he said.

"That pink floral dress Elizabeth saw my mother wearing?"

"Yes?"

"That was the dress she was buried in."

He walked away, down the street, a solitary figure among the crowd. I watched him until I couldn't see him any more.

Sitting in the dark in St. Mark's Church, I wished I was any place else. My rear end hurt from the hard wooden pew I'd been planted on for the past four hours, having positioned myself in the back row by the double doors that lead out into the vestibule. I'd brought along a flashlight, a Thermos of strong coffee, and my .38 snubnose.

It was 1:58 A.M., and I was cold and tired. Outside, the wind picked up, rattling the stained glass windows, making it even more drafty inside. The light of the moon, filtering in through the windows, cast long, distorting shadows, making everything look like a potential ghost.

It gave me the creeps to be here. I tried not to think of that woman. I was afraid if I did, she might suddenly materialize, her mouth moving silently, just as Chris had said, in a desperate attempt to tell me who her murderer was.

But wasn't that what I wanted? For our "ghost" to make an appearance? I was a cop—I didn't believe in apparitions or the supernatural or any such nonsense.

Or did I? God! This dark cavern of a church was driving me crazy!

I stood up and stretched, then walked along the outside of the pews, down toward the sanctuary. I stopped and looked up at a statue of the Madonna and Child. The sculpture was recessed into the wall in a small alcove. Moonlight fell on her face, which had the expression of both joy and sadness. It was the joy a mother feels having a child, and the sadness of knowing that that child could be taken away.

I peered closer. A tear seemed to trickle down her cheek.

My mouth fell open in a gasp, and I backed up into the side of a pew, lost my footing, and sat down hard on the seat.

Somewhere a door slammed. I jumped up and raced to the back and got my gun and flashlight. Quickly I crouched down against the wall by the double doors.

I held my breath and commanded my heart to stop thumping. Seconds seemed like minutes. Then slowly one of the doors began to open.

I rose, planting my feet, aiming the gun in one hand, the flashlight in the other.

A dark, formless figure emerged.

I said, "Hold it right there," and clicked on the light.

Father Hanson's hands flew up to his face. "It's just me!" he said, shielding his eyes from the glare. "Don't shoot!"

"Father!" I said, relieved, lowering the gun. I directed the flashlight's beam off his face. "You could've been hurt."

"I'm ... I'm sorry," Father Hanson said, "I wasn't thinking. I just came to tell you I'd turned up the heat."

"It *is* cold in here," I admitted. Wasn't that why I was shivering?

There was an awkward silence. Then Father Hanson said, "Nothing yet?"

"Nothing yet."

"And I don't suppose there *will* be after my little entrance."

I smiled. "That's okay," I said. "I think if anything was going to happen, it would have by now."

We fell silent again, and when he made no move to leave, I said, "I have some coffee; will you join me?"

"Yes, yes I will. I can't seem to sleep."

We moved to the pew where I'd left the Thermos and sat down. I poured some coffee into the lid and handed it to the priest.

"Father," I said, "I was looking at the Madonna ...
I could swear she was crying."

In the semidarkness Father Hanson smiled a little.
"Many people say that," he said. He took a sip of the
hot coffee.

"Is it real or my imagination?"

He stared at the coffee he held in both hands, warming them. "Who can say for sure?" he asked softly, then
added, "But I rather think that the sculptor intended it
to appear that way."

I nodded and took a drink from the Thermos. The
coffee tasted bitter. We sat for a while without saying
anything.

"Father," I finally said, "what happens if a Catholic
dies before she, or he, gets the last rites?"

"In the first place," Father Hanson replied, "it's not
called the 'last rites.' You've been watching too much
television." His tone was not condescending, merely informative. He went on to explain. "The Sacrament of
the Sick is intended to be given to the seriously ill while
they are able to spiritually benefit from it, not a last-
minute prayer to console relatives—or a ticket to
heaven, if that's what you're getting at ..."

"Oh."

We fell back into silence. I felt slightly embarrassed.

"Father," I said again, "if you believed in ... spirits
... how might a soul get caught in limbo? I mean, not
go to heaven ... or hell, for that matter."

He took a deep breath, and his first few words came
out a sigh, as if he were tired. "As far as the Church is
concerned, the concept of limbo has pretty much gone
out the window. It was something thought up because
St. Augustine was willing to permit unbaptized babies to
go to Hell. People didn't much like that. And so, Purgatory was kind of a compromise."

"I thought Purgatory *was* Hell."

"No. There is a difference. Purgatory is a place where
we can catch up, so to speak, on our growing, on the
preparation we didn't get a chance to do on earth."

"I see," I said. "Sort of a detention room." I paused. "But I can't imagine a person with the pristine background of Rebecca Madden being condemned to Purgatory. It's not her fault she was brutally murdered. And if the absence of the last rites—excuse me, Sacrament of the Sick—has no bearing on her entry to heaven ... well, then, I just don't get it."

He turned to look at me. "I don't know why you seem so convinced Catholic theology holds the answer to this problem." There was an edge to his voice.

"I just want to understand it," I said. "Is there something wrong with that?"

He said nothing.

I pressed on. "She went regularly to confession?"

"Sacrament of Reconciliation."

"Sacrament of Reconciliation," I repeated.

He nodded.

I thought for a while. "What if," I asked, "a Catholic took his life? That's a mortal sin, isn't it? A sin he couldn't very well ask for forgiveness for *after* it was done."

The priest nodded slowly.

"But what if he asked for forgiveness *before* ... ?"

Father Hanson turned his face toward me. "That's a very interesting question," he commented. "But one I'm not sure I can answer."

I looked toward the front of the church, where Christ hung on cross, his thorned head bowed.

"Many questions," I whispered, "but no real answers."

"I must go now," Father Hanson said abruptly.

He rose to leave, and that's when I said, "Chris has seen his mother, too."

Father Hanson's face turned white—as a ghost.

"I visited him today," I explained. Then, not wanting to give the priest anything further, I said, "Good night, Father Hanson."

He hesitated, just for a moment, then left. I heard the door close quietly behind me.

*   *   *

Sunday, 10:15 A.M. I was attending my second mass of the morning—my second mass ever, for that matter. The eight o'clock mass, given by Father Hanson, went without a hitch. Frank covered the back, while I sat down in front. We'd had an uneventful week of surveillance at the church.

Now Father O'Brien, in white vestment, stood at the pulpit while an assistant organist—a female college student—had replaced Elizabeth Keyes at the organ. Elizabeth Keyes and Father Hanson had returned to the rectory.

I found the service majestic but mysterious, comforting but confusing. We were into the liturgy, the reading of the Scriptures, when I felt the hair stand up on the back of my neck.

A foul odor wafted across me, permeating the air.

Somewhere in the bowels of the church a loud moan could be heard. Everyone in the church seemed to freeze. Father O'Brien stopped in midsentence, one hand up in a gesture, suspended in the air. As the moan built to a muffled scream, I looked back at Frank. He was already heading out the back double doors.

I jumped up and ran through the front of the sanctuary and into the sacristy, a room where the robes and other religious objects were kept. A door at the other end of the open-beamed room was open. It led out to a hallway, where stairs rose to rooms above.

An altar boy of perhaps ten, in white robe, stood plastered against the doorjamb, his brown eyes as big as the collection plate he was holding. He pointed a quavering finger down the hall.

"The ghost went that way!" he shouted. "It came from the basement!"

I ran past the boy and down the narrow hall and up the steps. As I came to the top, I drew my gun.

It was dark and cold up there. Another hallway stretched before me. The only source of light came from small open rooms that yawned off the hall.

A door slammed at the other end.

Oh, Christ! I thought, don't go up to the bell tower! Vertigo wasn't just a Hitchcok film where I was concerned.

I sprinted down the hallway and opened the door to another set of stairs, just in time to see a pink floral dress, white legs, and tennis shoes disappear at the top. The tennis shoes were splotched with green paint.

"I'm not coming up after you!" I shouted. "Chris!"

I waited in the awful silence.

Then the tennis shoes appeared, and the pale legs and pink floral dress, and Rebecca's face, ghostly white, eyes ringed in black, mouth painted red, blond hair long and wild. The apparition seemed to float down the steps.

"Up against the wall," I said, gesturing with the gun.

I patted him down. No weapon. I read him his rights.

Then I put my gun away and said, "Nice ensemble."

He relaxed and put his hands down from the wall. "Thank you," he said.

"The dead flowers?"

"Herbicide."

"And the odor?"

"Something a friend cooked up in chemistry lab."

"I suppose your mustache was of the spirit gum variety."

He nodded smugly. "After I shaved my real one off for this role, it was. What now? Are you going to book me?"

"That depends," I answered. "But first I thought we might have a chat with some people—that's what you *really* want, isn't it?"

"Yes." He raised one hand to remove the wig, like a gentleman about to remove his hat.

I reached out and stopped him. "No, don't," I said, smiling wickedly. "Leave it on."

Frank cleared out the church, sending the parishioners on their bewildered way home. Only a few of the die-hard curious were left loitering on the lawn, staring and whispering among themselves, as I led Chris, dressed as his late mother, into the rectory.

I instructed Frank that just Fathers O'Brien and Hanson and Elizabeth Keyes were invited to our little party.

In Father O'Brien's office Chris sat in a chair. To the others the sight of him must have been unnerving. Anyway, that's what I was counting on.

The two priests and the organist took their turns in expressing to Chris their indignation over his "inexcusable actions." I let them have at him a few minutes, then told them all to shut up.

"Let's hear what Chris has to say," I said.

"I want to know what really happened to my mother!" he demanded.

You could have heard a perfect-attendance pin drop.

Father O'Brien cleared his throat and began with some compassion. "Chris, we understand your feelings. Perhaps certain ... details were kept from you. After all, you were just a child—"

"Bullshit!" Chris snapped. He reached under the dress into the pocket of a pair of cut-off jeans, and pulled out a piece of folded white paper.

Carefully, he opened it. With liquid eyes, Chris passed the paper to me. "I found it the day after she died. I didn't show it to anybody ... it was all I had of her, to hold onto."

It was a letter to him from his mother. In it she wrote of her love for him. But she also wrote of another love. A forbidden one.

Frank, who had moved behind me, read it over my shoulder.

"It's a suicide note," Frank said flatly.

Chris nodded. "I didn't realize it then," he said, his masculine voice now sounding small and childlike. "After all, everyone said she was murdered. And I didn't show the letter to anyone because I was afraid that for some reason they would take it away from me."

He looked up at me earnestly. "But what I told you was true," he said. "A few weeks ago, my mother *did* appear to me in a dream. She was holding the letter. I woke up and jumped out of bed, and reread it. That's when it became clear to me."

"That she wasn't strangled," I said. "That she hanged herself."

Father O'Brien and Elizabeth Keyes looked stunned, but Father Hanson buried his face in his hands and began to weep.

"I took her down," the father sobbed, "from the sacristy where I found her. I moved her into the woods, to protect her, because I was afraid of how it would look in the eyes of the Church ..."

"You mean you were afraid your affair with my mother would be found out!" Chris accused.

Father Hanson wiped one hand across his wet face. "Yes," he admitted, "that, too." Then he said to Chris, beseeching him, "Don't you think I regret what I did? Don't you think I've asked for forgiveness a million times?"

Chris had only hatred in his eyes.

Father Hanson looked at me. "To answer your question, Officer Munday, you don't have to die to go to Purgatory. You can find it right here on earth."

"Rebecca wanted you to marry her," Frank said.

"Yes," Father Hanson replied, "and at first I thought I could, because I did love her. But in the end, I loved the Church more. As the years went by, she became more and more unhappy, because you see, we had a nine-year-old-son."

Chris rose from his chair, astonished.

Father Hanson told him, "About a year before you were born, your mother came to me for counseling. Her husband was abusive, and she wanted my help to secure an annulment, sanctioned by the Church. Instead, we became ... involved. Then her husband was killed in that drunken car accident, and she found herself pregnant and alone. Everyone just assumed the child was his—"

"Why didn't you tell me!" Chris said in anguish. "All these years ... all these years ..."

"I wanted to, believe me, but I was afraid. I looked after you the best I could."

Father O'Brien stepped out from behind his desk. "What's going to happen now?" he asked Frank and me.

"In the eyes of the law, you mean?" I said. "Well, Chris's crime is minor, a misdemeanor at worst, and I doubt any court would convict him anyway, due to the extenuating circumstances."

I looked at Father Hanson. "The statute of limitations makes your activities nonprosecutable."

I looked at Frank, and we exchanged glances: our work here was gone.

As we were leaving, I heard Father Hanson ask his son for forgiveness.

Whether he would get it or not, I didn't know, nor could I say what would happen between the priest and the Church. Rebecca had asked for forgiveness in her letter—had *she* been granted it?

Frank and I walked out into the crisp autumn day.

"That wraps it up, then," Frank said.

"Except for tracking down Sergeant Lynn in Chicago to let him know how his case came out."

"I'll leave that to you," Frank called from across the lot. "Game starts in fifteen minutes!"

I shook my head, laughed a little, and got in my car.

As I drove down the cobblestone drive, I caught a glimpse of St. Mark's in the rearview mirror, standing forlornly on the hill.

My husband and kids weren't going to be happy when I got home and pulled the plug on the video game and turned off the TV set ... but even if I got yelled at, I desperately needed us to do something together, as a family.

AUTHOR'S NOTE: I wish to acknowledge the nonfiction works of Father Andrew Greeley.

His Father's Ghost

by Max Allan Collins

The bus dropped him off at a truck stop two miles from Greenwood, and Jeff had milk and homemade cherry pie before walking the two miles to the little town. It was May, a sunny cool afternoon that couldn't make up its mind whether to be spring or summer, and the walk along the blacktop up and over rolling hills was pleasant enough.

On the last of these hills—overlooking where the undulating Grant Wood farmland flattened out to nestle the small collection of houses and buildings labeled "Greenwood" by the water tower—was the cemetery. The breeze riffled the leaves of trees that shaded the gravestones; it seemed to Jeff that someone was whispering to him, but he couldn't make out what they were saying.

Nobody rich was buried here—no fancy monuments, anyway. He stopped at the top and worked his way down. The boy—Jeff was barely twenty-one—in his faded jeans and new running shoes and Desert Storm sweatshirt, duffel bag slung over his arm, walked backward, eyes slowly scanning the names. When he reached the bottom, he began back up the hill, still scanning, and was threading his way down again when he saw the name.

Carl Henry Hastings—Beloved Husband, Loving Father. 1954–1992.

Jeff Carson studied the gravestone; put his hand on it. Ran his hand over the chiseled inscription. He thought about dropping to his knees for a prayer. But he couldn't, somehow. He'd been raised religious—or anyway, Methodist—but he didn't have much faith in any of that, anymore.

And he couldn't feel what he wanted to feel; he felt as dead as those around him, as cold inside as the marble of the tombstone.

The wind whispered to him through the trees, but he still couldn't make out what it said to him, and so just walked on into the little town, stopping at a motel just beyond the billboard announcing NEW JERSEY'S CLEANEST LITTLE CITY and a sign marking the city limits and population, six thousand.

He tapped the bell on the counter to summon a woman he could see in a room back behind there, to the right of the wall of keys, in what seemed to be living quarters, watching a soap opera, the volume so loud it was distorting. Maybe she didn't want to hear the bell.

But she heard it anyway, a heavyset woman in a floral muumuu with black beehive hair and Cleopatra eye makeup, hauling herself out of a chair as overstuffed as she was; twenty years ago she probably looked like Elizabeth Taylor. Now she looked more like John Belushi *doing* Elizabeth Taylor.

"Twenty-six dollars," she informed him, pushing the register his way. "Cash, check, or credit card?"

"Cash."

She looked at him for the first time, and her heavily mascaraed eyes froze.

"Jesus Christ," she said.

"What's wrong, lady?"

"Nuh . . . nothing."

He signed the register, and she stood there gaping at him. She hadn't returned to her soap opera when he exited, standing there frozen, an obese Lot's wife.

In his room he tossed his duffel bag on the bureau, turned on the TV to CNN just for the noise, and sat on the bed by the nightstand. He found the slim Greenwood phone book in the top drawer, next to the Gideon Bible, and he thumbed through it, looking for an address. He wrote it down on the notepad by the phone.

It was getting close enough to supper time that he couldn't go calling on people. But small-town people ate early, so by seven or maybe even six-thirty he could risk it. He'd been raised in a small town himself, back in Indiana—not this small, but small enough.

He showered, shaved, and after he'd splashed cold water on his face, he studied it in the bathroom mirror as if looking for clues: gray-blue eyes, high cheekbones, narrow nose, dimpled chin. Then he shrugged at himself and ran a hand through his long, shaggy, wheat-colored hair; that was all the more attention he ever paid to it.

Slipping back into his jeans and pulling on a light blue polo shirt, he hoped he looked presentable enough not to get chased away when he showed up on a certain doorstep. He breathed deep—half sigh, half determination.

He'd not be turned away.

Greenwood wasn't big enough to rate a McDonald's, apparently, but there was a Dairy Freez and a Mr. Quik-Burger, whatever that was. He passed up both, walking along a shady, idyllic residential street, with homes dating mostly to the 1920s or before he'd guess, and well-kept up. Finally, he came to the downtown, which seemed relatively prosperous: a corner supermarket, video store, numerous bars, and a café called Mom's.

Somebody somewhere had told him that one of the three rules of life was not eating at any restaurant called Mom's; one of the others was not playing cards with anybody named Doc. He'd forgotten the third and proved the first wrong by having the chicken-fried steak, American fries with gravy, corn, and slaw, and finding them delicious.

The only thing wrong with Mom's was that it was fairly busy—farm families, blue-collar folks—all of whom kept looking at him. It was as if he were wearing a KICK ME sign, only they weren't smirking; they had wide, hollow eyes and whispered. Husband and wives would put their heads together; mothers would place lips near a child's ear for a hushed explanation.

Jeff's dad, back in Indiana, was not much of a man's man; Dad was a drama teacher at a small college, and if it hadn't been for Uncle Fred, Jeff would never have learned to hunt and fish and shoot. But Jeff's dad's guilty pleasure (Dad's term) was John Wayne movies and other westerns. Jeff loved them, too. *The Searchers* he had seen maybe a million times—wore out the video tape.

But right now he felt like Randolph Scott or maybe Audie Murphy in one of those fifties westerns where a stranger came to town and everybody looked at him funny.

Or maybe it was just his imagination. He was sitting in the corner of the café, and to his left, up on the wall, after all, was a little chalkboard with the specials of the day.

His waitress wasn't looking at him funny; she was a blonde of perhaps fifteen, pretty and plump, about to burst the buttons of her waitress uniform. She wanted to flirt, but Jeff wasn't in the mood.

When she brought the bill, however, he asked her directions to the address he'd written on the note paper.

"That's just up the street to Main and two blocks left and one more right," she said. "I could show you ... I get off at eight."

"That's okay. How old are you?"

"Eighteen. That little pin you're wearing ... were you really in Desert Storm?"

He forgotten it was on there. "Uh, yeah."

"See any action?"

He nodded, digging some paper money out of his pocket. "Yeah, a little."

Her round pretty face beamed. "Greenwood's gonna seem awful dull, after that. My name's Tabitha, but my friends call me Tabby."

"Hi, Tabby."

"My folks just moved here, six months ago. Dad works at Chemco?"

"Mmmm," Jeff said, as if that meant something to him. He was leaving a five dollar bill and an extra buck, which covered the food and a tip.

"Jenkins!" somebody called.

It was the manager, or at least the guy in shirt and tie behind the register up front; he was about fifty with dark hair, a pot belly, and an irritated expression.

"You got orders up!" he said, scowling over at the girl.

Then he saw Jeff and his red face whitened.

"What's with him?" Tabby asked under her breath. "Looks like he saw a ghost. . . ."

The pleasantly plump waitress swished away quickly, and Jeff, face burning from all the eyes on him, got the hell out of there.

At dusk in the cool breeze, Greenwood seemed unreal, like something Hollywood dreamed up; as he walked back into the residential neighborhood—earlier he must have walked by within a block of the address he was seeking—he was thinking how perfect it seemed, when a red pickup rolled by with speakers blasting a Metallica song.

He hated that shit. Heavy metal was not his style, or drugs, either. His folks liked to joke about being "old hippies," and indeed he'd grown up used to the smell of incense and the sweet sickening aroma of pot. They weren't potheads or anything, but now and then, on a weekend night at home, they'd go in the den and put on Hendrix and Cream (music Jeff didn't care for in the least) and talk about the good old days.

Jeff loved his parents, but that Woodstock crap made him sick. He liked country western music—Garth Brooks, Travis Tritt—and found his folks' liberal politics naive. Some of his views came from Uncle Fred, no question; and maybe, like most kids, Jeff was just inclined to be contrary to his parents.

But a part of him had always felt apart from them. A stranger.

If it hadn't been for Dad liking western movies—Mom hated them and never had a kind word for "that fascist, John Wayne"—they might not have bonded at all. But when his father was a kid, *Gunsmoke* and *Have Gun Will Travel* were on TV, and that bug had bit his dad before the Beatles came along to screw up Jeff's parents' entire generation.

The streetlamp out front was burned out, but a light was on over of the door of the one-and-a-half-story 1950s era brick bungalow, with its four steps up to a stoop and its lighted doorbell. It was as if he were expected.

But he wasn't.

And he stood on the stoop the longest time before he finally had the nerve to push the bell.

The door opened all the way—not just a protective crack; this was still a small enough, safe enough town to warrant such confidence, or naivete. The cheerful-looking woman standing there in a yellow halter top and red shorts and yellow-and-red open-toed sandals was slender and redheaded with pale freckled-all-over skin; she was green-eyed, pug-nosed, with full lips—attractive but not beautiful, and probably about thirty.

"Danny," she began, obviously expecting somebody else, a bottle of Coors in a red-nailed hand, "I—"

Then her wide smile dissolved, and her eyes widened and saying "Jesus Christ!," she dropped the Coors; it exploded on the porch, and Jeff jumped back.

Breathing hard, she looked at him, ignoring the foaming beer and the broken glass between them.

"What ... what is ... who ..."

Her eyes tightened and shifted, as if she were trying to get him in focus.

"Mrs. Hastings, I'm sorry to jump drop in on you like this."

Her voice was breathless, disbelieving: "Carl?"

"My name is Jeff Carson, Mrs. Hastings. We spoke on the phone?"

"Step into the light. Mind the glass."

He did.

Her eyes widened again and her mouth was open, her full lips quivering. "It's not possible."

"I called inquiring about your husband. And you told me he had died recently."

"Six months ago. I don't understand . . ."

"Is there somewhere we could talk? You seem to be expecting somebody. . . ."

She nodded; then swallowed. "Mr. Carson . . . Jeff?"

"Please."

"There's a deck in back; I was just relaxing there. Would you mind walking around and meeting me there? I don't . . . don't want you walking through the house just yet. My son is playing Nintendo and I . . . don't want to disturb him."

That made as little sense as anything else, but Jeff merely nodded.

In back, up some steps onto the wooden sun deck, Jeff sat in a white metal patio chair by a white metal table under a colorful umbrella; dusk was darkening into evening, and the backyard stretched endlessly to a break of trees. A bug light snapped and popped, eating mosquitoes; but a few managed to nibble Jeff, just the same.

In a minute or so she appeared through a glass door. She had two beers this time; she handed him one and took a manlike gulp from the other.

"So you're the one who called," she said.

"That's right."

"I almost forgot about that. All you did was ask for Carl, and when I said he'd died, you just said 'oh,' and asked when, and I said not long ago, and you said you were very sorry and hung up. Right? Wasn't that the conversation?"

"That was the conversation."

"Are you his son?"

That surprised Jeff, but he nodded and said, "How did you know? Is there ... a resemblance?"

She had a mouthful of beer and almost spit it out. "Wait here."

She went inside the house and came back with a framed color photograph of a man in sheriff's uniform and hat—gray-blue eyes, high cheekbones, narrow nose, dimpled chin. Jeff might have been looking into a mirror of the future, showing him what he would look like in twenty-one years.

"No wonder everybody's been looking at me weird," he said. He couldn't stop staring at the picture; his hand shook.

"You never met him?"

"No. Except for this afternoon."

"This afternoon?"

"At the cemetery."

And then Jeff began to cry.

Mrs. Hastings rose and came over and put her arm around him; she patted his shoulder, as if to say, "There, there." "Listen ... what's your name?"

"Jeff."

She moved away as Jeff dried his eyes with his fingertips. "Jeff, I never knew about you. Carl never told me. We were married a long time, but he never said anything about you."

"He was the local sheriff?"

"Yes. City, not county. For twelve years. You don't know much about your dad, do you?"

"My dad ... my dad is a man named Stephen Carson."

"I don't understand."

"I was adopted." He said the obvious: "Carl Hastings was my natural father."

She was sitting again. She said, "Oh," drawing it out into a very long word. Then she pointed at him. "And the mother was Margie Holdaway!"

"That's right. How did you know?"

"Carl and Margie were an item in high school. Oh, I

was just in grade school at the time, myself, but I've heard all about it. Not from Carl ... from the gossips in this town that wanted to make sure I knew all about the Boy Most Likely and his hot affair with the Homecoming Queen. I just never knew anything had ... come of it."

"Tell me about him."

"You ... you don't know anything about him, do you, Jeff?"

"No. I always wanted to know who my real parents were. My *folks* knew ... they didn't get me from an agency. There was some connection between Dad, that is, Stephen Carson, and a lawyer who went to school with Margie Holdaway's father. Anyway, that's how the adoption was arranged. My parents told me that when I turned twenty-one, if I still wanted to know who my natural parents were, they'd tell me. And they did."

"And you came looking for your dad."

"Six months too late, it looks like. Tell me about him."

She told him Carl Hastings was an only child, a farm boy from around Greenwood who was one of the little town's favorite sons—a high-school football star (All-State), he had gone on a scholarship and a successful run of college ball that led to pro offers. But in his senior year Carl had broken his leg in the final game of the season. He had returned to Greenwood where he went to work for a car dealership.

"My *daddy's* business," Mrs. Hastings said, and she sipped her Coors. "I was ten years younger than Carl ... your daddy. I was working in the Greenwood Pontiac sales office, just out of high school, and things just sort of developed." She smiled and gazed upward and inward, then shook her head. "Carl was just about the handsomest man I ever saw. Least, till you came to my door."

"When did he become sheriff?"

She smirked a little, shook her head. "After we got married, Carl felt funny about working for his wife's daddy. Shouldn't have, but he did. When he got promoted to manager, he just . . . brooded. He was a funny sort of guy, your daddy—very moral. Lots of integrity. Too much, maybe."

"Why do you say that?"

"Oh, I don't know. It was his only fault, really . . . he could be kind of a stuffed shirt. Couldn't roll with the flow, or cut people much slack."

"Did that make him a good sheriff or a bad one?"

"He was re-elected five times, if that answers your question. He was the most dedicated lawman you can imagine."

"Is that what got him killed?"

The words hit her like a physical blow. She swallowed; her eyes began to go moist. She nodded. "I . . . I guess it was."

"I know it must be painful, ma'am. But what were the circumstances?"

Her expression froze, and then she smiled. "The way you said that . . . you said it, *phrased* it, just like Carl would have. Right down to the 'ma'am.' "

"How did my father die?"

"It *is* painful for me to talk about. If you wait a few minutes, Danny Simmons is stopping by—"

As if on cue, a man in the uniform of the local sheriff came out through the house via the glass doors. He was not Carl Hastings, of course: he was a tall, dark-haired man with angular features, wearing his sunglasses even though darkness had fallen.

"I let myself in, babe—I think Tim's gone numb from Nintendo . . . Judas Priest!"

The man in the sheriff's uniform whipped off his sunglasses to get a better look; his exclamation of surprise was at seeing Jeff.

"Danny, this is Carl's son." She had stood and was gesturing to Jeff, who slowly rose himself.

"Jesus, Annie." Simmons looked like he'd been poleaxed. "I didn't know Carl had a son, except for Tim."

"Neither did I," she said.

"He was my natural father," Jeff said, extending his hand, and the two men shook in the midst of the explanation.

"Adopted, huh? I'll bet I know who the mother was," Simmons said tactlessly, finding a metal patio chair to deposit his lanky frame in. "Margie Sterling."

"I thought her name was Holdaway," Jeff said.

"Maiden name," Mrs. Hastings explained. "Margie married Al Sterling right after college."

"Al Sterling?"

"His Honor Alfred Sterling," Simmons said, with a faint edge of nasty sarcasm. "Circuit judge. Of course, he wasn't a judge when Margie married him; he was just the golden boy who was supposed to take the legal profession by storm."

"And didn't?" Jeff asked.

Sheriff Simmons leaned forward, and Jeff could smell liquor on the man's breath, perhaps explaining the obnoxious behavior. "Fell on his ass in New York City with some major firm. Came crawling back to Greenwood to work in his daddy's law office. Now he's the biggest tight-ass judge around. You got a beer for me, babe?"

A little disgusted, a little irritated, Mrs. Hastings said, "Sure you need it, Danny?"

"I'd have go some, to match that lush Sterling." He turned to Jeff and shrugged and smiled. "Have to forgive me, kid. I had a long day."

"No problem. Did you work with my father?"

"Proud to say I did. I was his deputy for five, no, six years. Stepping into his shoes was the hardest, biggest thing I ever had to try to do."

"Mrs. Hastings suggested I ask you about how he died."

Simmons lost his confident, smirky expression; he seemed genuinely sorrowful when he said, "Sorry, kid—I thought you knew."

"No. That's why I'm here. I'm trying to find out about him."

Simmons seemed to be tasting something foul. "Punks ... goddamn gang scum."

"Gangs? In a little town like this?"

"Oh, they're not local. They come in from the big cities, looking for farmhouses to rent and set up as crack houses—quiet rural areas where they can do their drug trafficking out of and don't have big-city law enforcement to bother 'em."

"You've got that kind of thing going on here?"

Mrs. Hastings smiled proudly as she said, "Not now— Carl chased 'em out. He and Danny shot it out with a bad-ass bunch and chased 'em out of the county."

"No kidding," Jeff said. He felt a surge of pride. Had his real dad *been* John Wayne?

"That was about two weeks before it happened," Simmons said softly.

"Before what happened?"

Mrs. Hastings stood abruptly and said, "I'm getting myself another beer. Anybody else?"

"No thanks," Jeff said.

"I already asked for one and didn't get it," Simmons reminded her.

She nodded and went inside.

Simmons leaned forward, hands folded, elbows on his knees. "It wasn't pretty. Classic urban-style drive-by shooting—as he come out of the office, some nameless faceless asshole let loose of a twelve-gauge shotgun and ... sorry. Practically blew his head off."

Jeff winced. "Anybody see it?"

"Not a soul. It was three in the morning; we'd had a big accident out on the highway and he worked late. Office is downtown, and about then, it's deserted as hell. Practically tumbleweed blowin' through."

"Then how do you know it was that gang retaliating?"

Simmons shrugged. "Just the M.O., really. And we did have a report that a van of those Spic bastards was spotted rolling through town that afternoon."

"It was an Hispanic gang?"

"That's what I said."

"Nobody else had a motive?"

"You mean, to kill your dad? Kid, they would have elected that man president around here if they could. Everybody loved him."

"Not quite everybody," Jeff said.

Mrs. Hastings came back out and sat down with her Coors in hand. She still hadn't brought Simmons one.

"Sorry," she said. "I just didn't want to have to hear that again."

"I don't blame you," Jeff said. "I need to ask you something, and I don't mean for it to be embarrassing or anything."

"Go ahead," she said guardedly.

"Were my father and Margie Sterling still ... friends?"

Her expression froze; then she sighed. She looked at the bottle of beer as her thumb traced a line in the moisture there. "You'll have to ask her that."

"You think she'd be around?"

"Probably. I can give you the address."

"I'd appreciate that."

Then she smiled one-sidely, and it was kind of nasty. "Like to see the expression on her face when she gets a load of *you*. Excuse me a second—I'll go write that address down for you."

She got up and went inside again.

Simmons lounged his scarecrowlike body back in the patio chair and smiled affably. "So how long you going to be in town?"

"As long as it takes."

"To do what?"

"Find out why my father was killed."

The smile disappeared. "Look ... kid. We investigated ourselves; plus, we had state investigators in. It was a gang shooting."

"Really? What gang exactly?"

"We didn't take their pedigree when Carl and me ran 'em off that farm!"

"You must have had a warrant."

"We did. It was a John Doe. Hey, hell with you, kid. You don't know me, and you don't know our town, and you didn't even know your damn father."

"Why do you call my father's wife, 'babe'?"

"What?"

"You heard me."

Mrs. Hastings came back out with the address on a slip of paper. She handed it to Jeff.

"Good luck," she said, and then, suddenly, she touched his face. Her hand was cold and moist from the beer bottle she'd been holding, but the gesture was overwhelmingly warm. He looked deep into the moist green eyes and found only love for his late father.

"You can answer my question later," he said to the sheriff, and walked down the steps and away from the deck.

The Sterling house was as close to a mansion as Greenwood had. On the outskirts of town in a housing development of split-level homes that looked as expensive as they did similar, dominating a circular cul-de-sac, it was a much larger structure, plantationlike, white, with pillars; through a large multipaned octagonal window high above the entry, a chandelier glimmered.

He rang the bell, and an endlessly bing-bonging theme played behind the massive mahogany door; a tall narrow row of windows on either side of the door provided a glimpse of a marble-floored entryway beyond.

He half expected a butler to answer, but instead it was a woman in a sweatshirt and slacks; at first he thought she was the housekeeper, but she wasn't.

She was his mother.

She was small and attractive. She had been cute, no doubt, when his father had dated her a lifetime ago; now she was a pixie-woman with short brown hair and wide-set eyes and a thin, pretty mouth. The only sign of wealth was a massive glittering diamond on the hand she brought up to her mouth as she gasped at the sight of him.

"... Carl?" Her voice was high-pitched, breathy, like a little girl's.

"No," Jeff said.

"You're not Carl. Who ..."

Then she knew.

She didn't say so, but her eyes told him *she knew,* and she stepped back and slammed the door in his face.

He stood staring at it for a while, and was just starting to get angry, finger poised to press the bell again, and again, for an hour, for forever if he had to, when the door opened, slowly, and she looked at him. She had gray-blue eyes, too. Maybe his eyes had come from her, not his father.

Then the little woman threw herself around him. Held him. She was weeping. Pretty soon he was weeping, too. They stood outside the mansionlike home and held one another, comforting one another, until a male voice said, "What *is* this?"

They moved apart, then turned to see a man who could have been forty or fifty, but his dark eyes seemed dead already—a thin, gray-haired individual whose once-handsome features were tightened into a clenched fist of a face. He wore a cardigan sweater over a pale blue shirt with a tie. He had a pipe in one hand and a large cocktail glass in the other.

"What the hell is this about?" he demanded, but his voice was thin and whiny.

She pulled Jeff into the light. "Al, this is my son." Then she turned to Jeff and asked, "What's your name?"

Soon Jeff and Mrs. Sterling were seated on high chrome stools as the ceramic-tile island in the center of a large kitchen with endless dark-wood cabinets, appliance-loaded countertops, and stained glass windows. She had served him chocolate chip cookies and tea; the pot was still simmering on one of the burners opposite them on the ceramic island.

Judge Sterling had, almost immediately, gotten out of

their way, saying morosely, "You'll be wanting some privacy," and disappearing into a study.

"I told Al all about my youthful pregnancy," she said. "We're both Catholic, and I like to think he respects my decision to have you."

"I'm certainly glad you did," Jeff said, and smiled. This should have felt awkward, but it didn't. He felt he'd always known this pretty little woman.

"I didn't show at all," she said. "When we graduated, I was six months along, and no one even guessed. I had you late that summer, and then started college a few weeks later . . . never missed a beat."

She had a perky way about her that endeared her to him immediately.

"I hope . . . I hope you can forgive me for never getting in touch with you. That's just the way it was done in those days. I don't know how it is now, but when you gave up a baby back then, you gave him up. His new parents *were* his parents."

"I don't hold any grudge. Not at all. I had good parents. I had a fine childhood."

She touched his hand; stroked it, soothingly. "I hope so. And I want to hear all about it. I hope we can be . . . friends, at least."

"I hope so, too."

He told her about his parents' pledge to reveal his true parentage to him at his twenty-first birthday.

"My only regret . . . my only resentment toward my folks . . . is that, by making me wait, they cost me knowing . . . or even meeting . . . my real father."

She nodded, and her eyes were damp. "I know. That's a terrible thing. I know everyone's already told you, but you're a dead ringer for your dad. Poor choice of words. I'm sorry."

"That's why I'm here, actually. The main reason."

"What do you mean?"

"To find out why and how my father died."

"Who have you spoken to?"

He filled her in.

"Terrible thing," she said, "what those gang kids did."

"You believe he died that way?"

"Oh, yes. We were proud of him, locally"—she lowered her voice—"although the board of inquiry into the farmhouse shooting, which my husband oversaw, was pretty hard on Carl and Dan."

"Really?"

"They were both suspended without pay for a month. Excessive use of force. Overstepping certain bounds of legal procedure. I don't know what, exactly. I'm afraid . . . nothing."

"What?"

She leaned close. "I'm afraid Alfred may have used the situation to get back at Carl."

"Your . . . romance with my father—it was strictly a high-school affair, wasn't it?"

She scooted off the chrome stool to get the tea kettle and pour herself another cup. Her back was to him when she said, "It wasn't entirely a . . . high-school affair."

He nibbled at a chocolate chip cookie; it was sweet and good. He wondered if it was homemade, and if so, if a cook had made it, or if his mother had.

She was seated again, stirring sugar into her tea. "for a lot of years, we didn't even speak, your father and I. Both our parents had made sure we were kept apart. We went to different colleges. The pregnancy—please don't take this wrong—but it was tragedy in our lives, not the joy it should have been. The baby . . . you . . . broke us apart instead of bringing us together, like it should." She shook her head. "Times were different."

"You don't have to apologize. I don't need explanations. I just want to know the basic facts. The . . . truth."

"The truth is, your dad and I would see each other, around town—I moved back here, oh, ten years ago, when Al's New York law practice didn't work out—and when we passed at the grocery store or on the street, Carl and me, we'd smile kind of nervously, nod from a distance, never even speak, really."

"I understand. Kind of embarrassed about it."

"Right! Well, last year . . . no, it was a year and a half ago . . . Al and I were separated for a time. We have two children, both college age, boy and a girl—they're your half brother and sister, you know. You *do* have some catching up to do."

That was an understatement.

"Anyway, when the kids moved out, I moved out. It's . . . the details aren't important. Anyway, we were separated, and as fate would have it, Carl and Annie were having some problems, too. Carl and I, we ran into each other at one of the local bars one night, kind of started crying into each other's beer . . . and it just happened."

"You got romantic again."

She nodded; studied her tea, as if the leaves might tell her something about the future—or the past. "It was brief. Like I said, I'm Catholic and have certain beliefs, and Al and I decided to go to marriage counseling, and Carl and Annie got back together, and . . . that was the end of it."

"I see."

She touched his hand again; clutched it. "But it was a sweet two weeks, Jeff. It was a reminder of what could have been. Maybe, what should have been."

"I see. The trouble my father and his wife were having, did it have anything to do with his deputy?"

"That weasel Danny Simmons? How did *you* know?"

"He was over at her house tonight. Calling her 'babe.' "

She laughed humorlessly. "She and Danny did have an affair. Cheap fling is more like it. Danny *was* the problem between her and Carl. Your father . . . he was too straight an arrow to have ever run around on her—anyway, before she had run around on him."

"But they got back together?"

"They did. And just because Annie and Danny have drifted back together, don't take it wrong. I truly believe she loved your father, and that they'd found their way back to each other."

"Well, she's found her way back to Simmons, now."

"You shouldn't blame her. People make wrong choices sometimes ... particularly when they're at a low ebb, emotionally."

"Well ... I suppose she can use a man in her life, with a son to raise. Was there any sort of pension from my father being sheriff, or some kind of insurance? I mean, he was shot in the line of duty."

"I'm sure there is. But don't worry about Annie Hastings, financially. Her father's car dealership is one of the most successful businesses in the county, and she's an only child."

He slid off the stool. "Well, thank you, Mrs. Sterling. You've been very gracious."

"Must you go?"

"I think I should." He grinned at her. "The cookies were great. Did you make them?"

"I sure did." She climbed off her stool and came up and hugged him. "Any time you want some more, you just holler. We're going to get to know each other, Jeff. And Jeff?"

"Yes?"

"Would you work on something for me?"

"What's that?"

"See if you can work yourself up to calling me 'mom'—instead of Mrs. Sterling."

"Okay," he said.

She saw him to the door. Before he left, she tugged on his arm, pulling him sideways, and pecked his cheek. "You be good."

He started to say something, but then noticed her face was streaked with tears, and suddenly he couldn't talk. He nodded and walked away.

It was approaching ten o'clock now, and he walked back downtown; he wanted to see where his father worked, and around the corner from Mom's café—now closed—he found the County Sheriff's office, a one-story tan brick building. He stood staring at the sidewalk out front, heavily bathed in light from a nearby streetlamp.

He knelt, touched the cement, wondering where his father's blood had been. Heavy bushes stood to the right and left of the sidewalk and Jeff squinted at them. Then he looked up at the streetlamp and squinted again.

The sheriff's brown-and-white vehicle was still parked in front of the Hastings home. Jeff leaned against the car, waiting, hoping Simmons wouldn't be spending the night.

At a little after eleven, the tall sheriff came loping around from behind the house—apparently, they'd stayed out on the deck this whole time.

"Who is that?"

"Can't you see me?"

He chuckled, hung his thumbs in his leather gun belt. "The Hastings kid. No, I couldn't see you—streetlight's out."

"Actually, my name is Carson. The streetlight wasn't out in front of my father's office, was it?"

Simmons frowned; his angular face was a shadowy mask in the night. "What are you talking about?"

"Annie Hastings stands to come into her share of money, one of these days, doesn't she? Her father owns that car dealership and all."

"Yeah. So?"

"So I figure she wasn't in on it."

"On what?"

"Murdering my father."

Silence hung like a curtain. Crickets called; somewhere tires squealed.

"Your father was killed by street-gang trash."

"He was killed by trash, all right. But it wasn't a street gang. Out in front of the sheriff's office, my father couldn't have been cut down in a drive-by shooting; he'd have dived for the bushes, or back inside. He'd have got a shot off in his own defense, at least."

"That's just nonsense."

"I think it was somebody who knew him—somebody who called to him, who he turned to, who shot his head off. I think it was you. You wanted his job, and you wanted his wife."

"You're just talking."

"All I want to know is, was she in on it?"

Simmons didn't answer; he went around the car to the driver's side door.

Jeff followed, grabbed the man's wrist as he reached for the car-door handle. "Was his wife in on it? Tell me!"

Simmons shoved him away. "Go away. Go home! Go back to Iowa or wherever the hell."

"Indiana."

"Wherever the hell! Go home!"

"No. I'm staying right here in Greenwood. Asking questions. Poking my nose in. Looking at the files, the autopsy, the crime-scene report, talking to the state cops, putting it all together until you're inside a cell where you belong."

Simmons smiled. It seemed friendly. "This is just a misunderstanding," he said and slipped his arm around Jeff's shoulder, all chummy, when the gun was out of its holster in Jeff's midsection *now*.

"Let's take a walk," Simmons said, softly; the arm around Jeff's shoulder had slipped around his neck and turned into a near choke hold. "There's some trees behind the house. We'll—"

Jeff flipped the man and the sheriff landed hard on the pavement on his back, but dazed or not, Simmons brought the gun up, his face a thin satanic grimace, and fired, exploding the night.

The car window on the driver's side spiderwebbed as Jeff ducked out of the way, and with a swift martial-art kick he sent the gun flying out of Simmons's hand, and it fell, nearby, with a *thunk*. The sheriff was getting to his feet but another almost invisible kick put him back down again, unconscious.

The night was quiet. Crickets. An automobile somewhere. Despite the shot, no porch lights were popping on.

Jeff walked over to where the gun had landed. He picked it up, enjoying the cool steel feel of the revolver in his hand, walked back to the unconscious Simmons, cocked it, pointed it down, and studied the skinny son of a bitch who had killed his father.

"It's not what your father would have done," she said.

Jeff turned, and Annie Hastings was standing there. At first he thought she had a gun in her hand, but it was only another Coors.

He said, "Did you hear any of that?"

She nodded. "Enough."

"He killed your husband."

"I believe he did."

"You didn't know?"

"I didn't know."

"You weren't part of it?"

"No, I wasn't."

"Can I trust you?"

"You'll know as much," she said, swigging the beer, then smiling bitterly, "when I back you up in court."

He stood at the gravestone in the cemetery on the hillside. He studied the words: *Carl Henry Hastings— Beloved Husband, Loving Father. 1954–1992.* He touched the carved letters: *Father.* He said a silent prayer.

The wind whispered a response through the trees.

"What was he like?" he asked. "What was he *really* like?"

His mother smiled; her pretty pixie face made him happy.

"He was like you," she said. "He was just like you."

Father Figure

by Morris Hershman

She glanced back over her shoulder as she ran. In her hurry she didn't know that she had rushed into the middle of the dirt-crusted gray gutter, nor did she realize for as long as a moment that she had nearly walked up against a slowly moving green car, a Corvette if she wasn't mistaken.

The barrier forced her to pull back, but not before she threw another fearful glance over a shoulder. The juggernaut in front of her didn't seem nearly as frightening as the thought of that person who might be gaining on her.

Warily, she appraised the driver, discovering an older man of maybe fifty—strong hands and burly build, the sort of man who can enforce his will and could competently demolish anyone threatening some person for whom he had any feeling.

Not till after his eyes met hers did she make a point of glancing at the empty space next to him in the car. She supposed he was aware of that distress in her eyes, in her fluid posture, because he leaned over to unlock the door opposite him. As much as she wanted his help, she was startled because she wasn't used to having any man offer assistance and particularly not a man old enough to be her father.

That piece of minor mind reading diserved her grateful nod just before she hurried around to the side of his car.

She closed the door on herself with great force as the

traffic light changed to green, then made sure again and yet again that the door was locked.

"Get me away from here whatever else you do." And then, slowly, "Please."

"I'll take you home if it's not too far."

She approved of that smooth baritone voice even as she was shaking her head. Home was a mother with vivid red hair from a bottle, a woman whose time was taken up at working for some illegitimate businessman. Home was a retarded sister. Home didn't boast a father, though. There was no older man to contribute a rent check or do needed repairs or help a family member in bad trouble.

"I won't go home," she said, almost muttering. "*Nobody*'s going to find me there!"

And of course this secure salt-of-the-earth man understood perfectly. "If you're in any danger, I could drop you off in front of the nearest police station."

"Not now." She pushed her naturally bright red hair vigorously back. "What I need is a chance to think everything over and get a night's rest. Everything will look better in the morning."

The unspoken words *I hope* hung in the air.

She took his silence for an unasked question. "He threatened to kill me," she said quietly. "And meant it."

"If you've got the man's name and address, you could make an official complaint."

"I know only the first name he gave me." She didn't add that it was probably no more right than the name she had given him.

"I should never have gone there at all, I suppose," she mused while he drove smoothly around a giant-size truck. "The place has got a terrible reputation, but no other sort of dump is really interesting, you know?"

"When you're older, maybe you'll feel different."

"Well, I was at Wired, you know?" It was a disco where drugs changed hands a hundred times a minute. The papers had written it up. "This fellow in a gray-and-white suit came swaggering over during a lull in the music. He sounded as if he was making fun of me even while he called me 'beautiful', or said I was the prettiest girl in the place. I thought he was talking loud so he could be heard by others. Maybe he wanted to convince his friends that he could get any girl as easy as picking an apple."

"You could've told him to go roll his hoop."

"I did, but he had taken a skinful of cargo, and it didn't keep him from reaching out for me. I threw a glass of gin in his face—I know I'm not old enough to be served, but at Wired they pay the police and do what they want. When he got my message, half a dozen eyewitnesses laughed. He was real mean before the bouncers hurried over, and he said very quiet that he'd find me as soon as possible and he'd waste me."

"You don't think he'll sleep it off?"

"I heard his voice and saw the poison in his eyes."

The listener nodded slowly, accepting what she said, trusting her judgment. She had always thought that older men, teachers for instance, didn't believe that some youths might kill over a piece of clothing, a tone of voice, a glance.

"Maybe you got away at the right time."

She looked out the back window, satisfying herself that the enemy wasn't in sight on foot, at least.

Pointing needlessly as she turned back, she said, "The Hotel Rialto is right there."

The place had probably never been touched for custodial purposes. The exterior, along with every window air conditioner, needed cleaning. Spackling and painting would do wonders for the seedy porch. Even the ad card in a window of the hotel store, showing a mature man cuddling a striped tie while bright-eyed children watched adoringly, seemed rooted to the spot. Anybody who lived here was either short of money or felt that the shoddiness allowed more freedom than another hotel.

It was the right place for her. Hadn't she made it clear that she enjoyed being on propriety's edge, brushing against what was contemptible, what was unspeakable? *No other sort of pit is really interesting, you know?*

She opened the car door after he had made a typically skillful U-turn and pulled up. Rather than look back of her yet again, she forced herself to smile.

"Thanks. Thanks a whole bunch."

"So long, whoever you are."

"Grace, if anybody cares."

She knew in advance that he wouldn't say anything heavily flirtatious, like some lust-driven old fools. Not this one.

He was quiet, and she said, "I'll bet you've got a daughter and a wife and you live with them. Isn't that right?"

He looked surprised, and she guessed he didn't want to tell her about himself. With a flash of self-contempt, she hardly blamed him. Shoulders thrown back, she stepped out into the warm June evening. Confident because of his closeness, she didn't look from right to left this time while moving, nor did her stride quicken. With this man so near, she felt safe.

The man's watch appeared in sight as he was reaching for the wheel, and one sleeve was pulled back. Dealing with that girl, taking her out of the way, had made him twelve minutes late for his dinner appointment. A phone call would soothe ruffled feelings. There was probably at least one pay telephone inside the seedy hotel.

He saw no reason to change his mind about the Hotel Rialto when he reached the inside. Its lobby was poorly lit, and the furniture was old without having been preserved. Impossible to imagine himself drawing a relaxed breath around here! Most of the patrons must have been overnight lovers for whom the Rialto was nothing but a pit stop.

He made his call and apologized, saying he'd be on the scene in only a few more minutes. As far as he could tell, his apology was accepted.

From the corner of an eye, he noticed what was taking

place at the clerk's desk. A young man stood talking in front of it, his body moving restlessly from side to side. The bill that appeared in his hands suddenly moved to the clerk's side of the desk, where it vanished. The guy probably wanted to get a room for himself and a girl. Or himself and a needle.

The man might have looked away, but it became clear as the customer turned to the self-service elevators that his suit was gray and white. On a shoulder was a stain where cheap whiskey thrown at an angle into his face might well have dribbled down.

The elevator doors closed on him. No one would know from the broken indicator where he would stop in order to commit murder.

The man didn't hesitate about what to do. The girl may have been young enough to make some foolish mistakes, but she was a gutsy kid who didn't deserve what was coming toward her.

"I thought I recognized the young fellow you were talking to," he told the clerk, having decided to pass along as little valid information as possible, certainly not to a man so easily corrupted. "Isn't he a friend of the girl who went up just before and who I know slightly? You know who I mean, don't you?"

"Miss Neergard," the clerk said at sight of another bill that would be changing hands.

"I forgot a message and I have to call her. What room is she in?"

"Six-one-six, sir. The courtesy phones are at your left and around the corner."

He moved off determinedly, having decided that it was of no use to call upstairs, that if there was a house detective in this rat-heaven he'd be no use, and that the buttons wouldn't arrive on time even if they were called this minute. Only one guy could help, and he was inside his own skin.

He picked up speed when he rounded the corner, making for the dim-lit staircase past the so-called courtesy phones. One flight up, he took a darkened elevator to the top level. Half a minute's extra time got him there.

A nearby door was unlocked and another man's footsteps could be heard. A studio apartment was revealed. Grace Neergard was taking a deep breath to shout for assistance. The intruder reached a hard hand to her mouth and pushed her back. She was helpless now.

The man was running toward them, causing the original intruder to push Grace against the farthest wall before he could whirl around, fists raised.

Grace Neergard had seen the older man rush to her aid and realized she had been certain that he would appear. Without any reason to think so, she had been convinced that he could be depended on, a man who was solid, who assuredly had formed the habit of being father to some lucky girl or girls.

The young one had raised his fists too late. His neck was already in her fa ... the older man's bull grip.

The walnut eyes of the young man bulged in terror as the older one squeezed hard. Like Grace herself a few moments before, he couldn't shout or speak or even gasp. As if to make it clear there was no resistance, he raised his hands shakily in surrender. There was a sound of snapping, and the hands suddenly fell to his sides. He swayed as the older man pulled back, then dropped lifelessly.

"Should I call the doctor?" That must've been her voice, loud and shaky and at the same time deferential.

The man leaned over the younger one, a hand outstretched. He pulled it back, straightened, and shook his head.

"There's no pulse."

She kept control of herself, trusting the man who had already saved her, who would be sure to rearrange her life. "What ... what'll I do?"

"You've got two choices. The first is to check out of here and move someplace a visitor can't bribe or sneak his way into." He was speaking crisply, wasting no regrets over what had happened. "You can pass for nineteen if you're careful, so you could get into the Mannering at Oxford Street. They're as security conscious as you could want, but expensive."

"Oh. What's my other choice?"

"Go home and keep your head straight."

"I suppose I have to do that," she said after a moment, trying not to think about her accountant mother with the bright red hair colored from a bottle, trying not to think about her retarded sister, trying not to think. "I haven't done enough of anything so that I can't stop right away. Besides, I'm not sure somebody else will come along and help if I get in deep yogurt again."

His papery cheeks colored very briefly.

"I only hope there isn't any publicity," she added, looking down at her feet rather than at what lay on the floor, sprawled in death. "I want to avoid hurting ... anybody, you know?"

"Take it a day at a time, like someone does on recovery."

"Yes. Yes. And I swear that after what's happened, I'll be straight arrow as long as I live."

"All right, then, I'll take him out of here," the substitute father said decisively, making plans even as he spoke, she was sure. "I'll tell the clerk that he's my son and he's been doing drugs. A twenty dollar bill is enough to make sure that the creep turns his back when I'm leaving."

Quietly, in a different tone, he added, "And you're expected to keep your promises."

"I'll keep my promises to you." And looking intently at him, she said, "You can trust me, dadd ... I mean, you can trust me."

He had turned from her, but now he suddenly looked back.

"What did you call me?"

"Nothing. Nothing at all." It took strength of character to tell him even the slightest falsehood, to admit to herself that she had indulged in fantasy. "I just meant to say thank you."

She had actually mean to say that she wasn't surprised to be getting help from her father, even if he was only a substitute father, even if he was a complete stranger who was the only father she would ever know.

He looked away, bending over long enough to plan adjustments for weight and comfort in carrying the corpse, as well as his middle-aged strength.

Grace never saw or talked to him again.

He arrived an hour late at Donovan's Restaurant on Lyman Street. During the last twenty minutes he had driven to a circular pile of stones in the Jeffry J. Lyman Memorial Park. The body had been swiftly tucked away in the farthest recesses of the grounds. The dead man's clothes, some of which might retain fingerprints, were now deposited in the trunk of the car. He'd get rid of them in time, with a friend's help.

Kimberly Lucas smiled after the greetings and an affectionate kiss. She was a blue-eyed blonde who'd been living with him for eight years and knew nothing whatever about his real business.

"What kept you, a brunette or a redhead?" she teased.

"A bright redhead, actually." He told her some of what had happened, carefully laundering the details.

"But why did you take so much trouble to help a strange girl—or can I guess?"

"Nothing like that was in my mind, Kim."

"Oh, I know." She was smiling cynically. "This is Father's Day and you did her a favor so you can get a present later on from her."

"No, nothing like that at all." He'd been wondering, too, why he'd done it. Maybe because her worried looks reminded him of that older woman, another bright redhead, a woman he'd been assigned to waste early this afternoon, the woman who'd been keeping a client's business books and holding out on him to pay for extra care of a daughter who was retarded. Could it be that he felt called on to save some other woman's life to make up for what he'd had to do earlier?

"Maybe Father's Day did have something to do with it after all, Kim. Who knows? I must have seen the advertising signs all over and the TV ads, and I suppose a guy thinks about some things without knowing it consciously."

"You're going to make me cry, I just know it."

"I'll tell you this much, Kim," he said more seriously than he'd intended. "All the time I was with the kid, I couldn't help thinking that she's the kind of girl I'd have liked to have as a daughter."

The Good Book
A Koko Tate Tale

by Peter Crowther

James Axelrod Baker's study looked as if it had been put together for a *Life* magazine article or a 1967 psychedelic album sleeve. It smelled of paper, stale pipe smoke, and memories, in almost equal amounts, while, underneath, it reeked of the twin fears of death and progress.

My first thought was it should have been sealed up and opened in a thousand years so that our descendants might know what we were about. *These were the people that put a man on the moon?* They may well ask.

Three of the walls were fitted with floor-to-ceiling bookshelves, the books stacked and racked both vertically and horizontally. At the edges of the shelves, in front of the books, were items of bric-a-brac and memorabilia. It looked like a kindergarten 'lost and found' office, with Disney figurines, die-cast metal toy cars, and elastic-banded sets of bubble gum cards sharing cramped space with Halloween monster masks, baseball caps, and pieces of surreal pottery.

The window ledge boasted more of the same, and stacked against the wall below, were piles of folders and books, plus twin towers of old *Saturday Evening Post*, *Esquire*, and *Playboy* magazines *plus* numerous boxes bearing faded writing I couldn't read. Fixed to the wall above the storage radiator by the door were a series of framed comic books: *Batman and Robin, Casper the Friendly Ghost, Superman, Donald Duck,* and some I didn't recognize. I never was big on comic books. I fell in love with reality at an early age. It was weirder.

In the center of the room stood a large desk which held, among other things, a computer, a keyboard, a printer, two angle-poise lamps, a magnetized paper-clip mountain, a mess of matchbooks, three ashtrays, a Sellotape dispenser, a stapler, two pipe racks, an array of pens and pencils, four large tins jammed full with *more* pens and pencils, a couple of *National Geographic* maps, several more piles of books, and a lot of dust. It was spread so thick in places, I half expected to see a cow skull partially buried beside a dried-up waterhole.

In the middle of it all was a Fisher Price clock that had been customized so that it told the real time. As the big, yellow-arrowed hand moved over the 12, the study door opened and a tall man wearing a wide, gap-toothed smile walked into the room. It was quite an entrance, and punctual, too.

At first I thought it was Terry-Thomas, and I'd been caught up in an old British black-and-white movie.

"Mr. Tate, I'm Jim Baker," his voice boomed around the paper and mementos, seeming perfectly at home. He looked every inch the eccentric: a narrow, academic face, thin-lipped mouth, and pinched cheeks leading up to a wiry thatch of unkempt Einstein-style brown hair. And his clothes ... tweed jacket complete with leather edging and elbow patches, a frayed-collared, checkered shirt with a bootlace tie held tight with a brass Madonna—and not the one who wears her top clothes underneath her hosiery—a pair of scuffed, brown brogues, and obligatory odd socks into which he had tucked the legs of a singularly shapeless pair of bottle green denim pants. He made the neighborhood five-and-dime look like Saks Fifth Avenue.

I took hold of the hand at the end of the outstretched arm, noticing the cracked and tobacco-filled fingernails, and shook it firmly ... if a little distastefully. "Quite a collection," I told him. I didn't think for a minute that my four-minute appraisal would come as any surprise, but he did me the courtesy of raising his eyebrows briefly and nodding eternal gratitude.

"Thank you, Mr. Tate," he said politely. "Please, sit."

I sat in one of the chairs behind the desk, keeping my eyes fixed on the top of his head for signs of small beaks looking for bugs and watched as he lifted a pipe from one of the racks. He tapped it into his palm and then jammed it quickly into the corner of his mouth.

"I'll come straight to the point," he said around the stem. "I've had a most unusual burglary."

"From in here?"

He nodded again and removed a small leather tobacco pouch from his jacket pocket. He proceeded to extract long strands of what looked like brown crab grass and drop them into the bowl.

I waved my arms and gave him my best in incredulous expressions. "You mean there was *more* than this in here?"

Baker smiled as he flicked open a matchbook, struck it, and held it to the bowl, all with one hand. Maybe he used to drive a yellow cab. Maybe not. Cab drivers could also drive a car, hit innocent and inanimate objects and people without ever damaging their own vehicle, hurl abuse out of the open window, and watch what you were doing through the rear mirror at the same time. I didn't think Baker was that good. And, anyway, he spoke English and probably knew where the Empire State Building was. He puffed on the pipe and disappeared in a fog of smoke.

I waited, memorizing the route to the door in case I lost my bearings, and took out my ever-ready yellow Post-it pad and chewed pencil stub. Ever the professional.

"One item," he said at last, wafting away the smoke and then holding an index finger aloft in case I had trouble with the concept. "A Bible."

"A Bible?"

"It wasn't just *any* Bible, Mr. Tate." He reached into his inside jacket pocket and, amidst a spray of crumbs and lint-balls, pulled out some Polaroid photographs. "Here, take a look at these," he said, handing them over.

I took them and looked while Baker spoke.

"It was a St. James version, printed by George E. Eyre and William Spottiswoode of Fleet Street, England, in 1856. Black leather, tooled covers—front, back, and spine—and brass-bound at the edges and corners. As you can see, the brass is very decorative and extends to a hinged clasp that keeps the book closed when not in use." He puffed on his pipe and watched me thumb through the photographs. "Full Morocco gilt to page edges and a predominantly red marbling—excellent condition—to the inside covers, both front and back."

It was a good description of the book in the photographs. "When did the theft take place?"

"It was here on Monday."

Today was Wednesday. "When did you notice it was missing?"

"About three o'clock yesterday afternoon. I called the police; they came around a little after four."

"What did they say?"

"They suggested that I might have misplaced it." He laughed at the sheer absurdity of such a suggestion.

"And is that possible?" I asked, laughing along with him.

"All of my books are carefully recorded in my files when I buy them and then placed on an appropriate pile to await filing." He shifted his pipe to the other side of his mouth as he watched my face. "As a system, it works, Mr. Tate."

I looked to the shelves and let my eyes drift up and down, left and right, then looked around the room. "How did he get in?"

Baker shrugged. "No signs of breaking in anywhere."

"Are you alarmed?"

"I'm afraid not."

"Might be a good idea to give it some more consideration."

"My only concern now is to find the Bible."

I nodded agreeably. "So, the book went missing some-time between ... ?"

"I last saw it around ten o'clock on Monday night. I was in here doing some reorganization."

I wondered if the room realized it had been reorganized. I doubted it. "Okay, between ten on Monday night and three yesterday afternoon. Did you have any visitors yesterday?"

He shook his head.

"Monday night, after ten o'clock?"

"Nobody."

I smiled correctively. "You had *one,* Mr. Baker. Whenever it was, you had one."

"Mmmm."

"Was the Bible valuable?"

He shook his head. "Normally, this particular edition would be worth around two hundred dollars, maybe three. The only unusual feature of my copy was a small crest—a coat of arms, I suppose you'd call it—engraved on the clasp." He leaned over and fanned out the photographs. "Here," he said, pointing to one of them.

I was looking at a small design of blimps and squiggles, like preschool doodlings or vintage Andy Worhol, scratched onto the metal that spanned the closed pages. "You say 'normally'. Does the crest make it any more valuable?"

"A little."

"How little?"

"Maybe another fifty, a hundred at the most."

"What is it?"

"What is what?"

"The coat of arms."

"It's a personal mark indicating that the book is from the personal library of Charles Waring."

He had said the name with such implied significance that I felt like a hayseed for needing clarification. I mentally shifted the grass stem with my tongue, tried not to think about stalking jackrabbits through the swamps, and asked anyway.

"Charles Waring was one of *the* great bibliophiles."

"Was?"

"Yes, he's dead."

"Oh," I said, just to keep things ticking. Baker sat without moving, watching me. I felt there was something more. "Is there something more?"

"Well, not really. He died about two weeks ago ... tragic, really."

"Tragic? In what way?"

"An accident. He was working in his library when he fell and hit his head."

"And that was it? It killed him?"

Baker nodded, his face filled with the mock concerns of someone who really couldn't have cared less. "He was an old man, Mr. Tate. He hit his head on a table and"—Baker snapped his fingers—"that was that."

"Who found him?"

"His assistant, Elicia Barnes. Look," he said with a deep sigh. "I asked you here to investigate the theft of my Bible, Mr. Tate."

I nodded. "When did you buy the Bible—before his death or after?"

"After."

"Who sold it to you?"

"Well, I knew of its existence, of course, and when I heard of Waring's unfortunate accident, I waited a few days—for appearance's sake, you understand ..."

I waved away any hint of ghoulish opportunism.

"... And then I got in touch with Waring's daughter."

I shuffled my little pad and made ready my trusty pencil.

"Ella Thornley ... she's in the book under that name."

I wrote it down under the other names. Soon I'd need to start another sheet. "So she sold you the book?"

He shook his head. "No. When I phoned her, she said she had already sold all of her father's historical and theological books to a dealer. In fact, she sold the entire collection to various dealers and private collectors before her father was even buried."

"And you bought it from him?"

"Yes."

I held the pencil ready. "And *his* name?"

"Edgar Hooper. He has a store down in the Village ... one of the unnumbered streets, I don't remember which one." He coughed chestily and then swallowed. I made a mental note to skip lunch. "Hooper heard about the death almost as soon as it had happened, and not been one to observe many of the social graces, he got in immediate contact with Waring's daughter."

"How immediate?"

"Oh," Baker said, looking to the ceiling for inspiration. "The following day, I think. The call was ostensibly to offer condolences, but still managing to offer to take some of the collection off her hands. She took him up on it straightaway, and he bought the lot—all that he wanted—that afternoon."

"How do you know all this timing?"

"Hooper. He's a braggart."

"So, the daughter ... she needed the money?"

Baker smiled. "Constantly."

"Are there any other children?"

"No, just Ella. Ella Waring was a disappointment to her father, Mr. Tate. She married beneath her, and her father never forgave her. Jimmy Thornley has been involved in one money-chasing venture after another. None of them worked out. The pair of them were in constant need of money."

"How much did Hooper say he'd paid her?"

"Eleven thousand dollars."

I whistled. "Taking his markup into account, that's a lot of books."

"I would say so, yes."

"How much did you pay? For the Bible?"

"Four hundred and fifty dollars." Baker removed the pipe from his mouth and pursed his lips, moistening them. It made me feel queasy. "It was a fair price," he added, placing the pipe on the table in front of him. "A very fair price."

"What's so special about books from Waring's collection?"

"Items from the Waring collection always fetch a slightly higher price. Waring had a habit of personalizing his books with a mock coat of arms he appended to the fly leaf by means of an inked rubber stamp. As you can see from the photographs, the difference in the case of the Eyre and Spottiswoode is that the coat was actually engraved onto the clasp. But even then, the Bible is only worth around four or five hundred dollars—what I paid for it, in fact." He picked up the pipe again, jammed it back between newly wetted lips, and held his lighter over the bowl. And just when my tear ducts had sealed up again.

"Still seems like a lot to me," I said.

"That's the point," Baker said through a pungent cloud of smoke. "In terms of rare books—and certainly in terms of the books you can see in this room—the thief could have taken a handful worth several thousand dollars. Instead, he took only one. A four-hundred-dollar Bible."

I pulled out one of the photographs and shuffled the others together. "Okay if I keep this one?"

"Absolutely," he said with a grand wave of his arm, as though he were giving me something really valuable.

I put the photograph in my pocket, handed the others back to him, and stood up. "From what you say, wouldn't it be easier to just go out and buy another copy? It should be easy to replace, at least if you're prepared to do without the engraved clasp. And it would cost you less than hiring me to look for it."

"I agree, but the money is not important. There is only one Waring copy, Mr. Tate, and that is the copy that I want. And I want to know who would be prepared to steal to get it."

"And why?" I suggested.

Baker nodded. "And why."

The fat man was reading a Bible and muttering to himself. I looked over his shoulder at a block of yellow, highlighted print. "Good?" I asked quietly.

His shoulders started, and he looked around, shielding his eyes against the glare. "You startled me."

I nodded proudly. "It's these shoes," I explained. "Bought them from a guy named Cranston. Laughed a lot."

Edgar Hooper grunted and snapped the Bible closed. "Deuteronomy 14," he said, as if it meant something to me. It didn't. "I read it every day," he added.

"You figure you'll ever finish it?"

He squinted up at me and shook his head, the folds of skin hanging from his jawbone swinging like a turkey's gullet in a cyclone. "Did you want something here?"

I shifted my Juicy Fruit gum from one side of my mouth to the other, as if I meant business. "Looking for redemption." I pointed to the Bible trapped beneath his folded arms. "Maybe I'll find it in Deuteronomy."

Hooper leaned over and pushed the Bible into a shelf. "I don't think you would find anything in there to interest you, mister . . ."

"Tate," I said. "Koko Tate." I held out my card.

"Mmm, private investigator. What can I do for you, Mr. Tate?"

"I'm investigating the theft of a book from the private collection of Mr. James Baker." I pulled my pad and the photograph out and held it in front of him. "A Bible. Recognize it?"

"Yes." He said it with a slight tremor.

I sat on the edge of the table to Hooper's left before he got the chance to stand. "I understand that you sold him the book?" I returned the photograph to my pocket, watching Hooper's eyes follow it all the way.

"That's correct."

"You remember it very easily."

"Well, I . . . I only sold it to him last week."

It was hot, but not that hot. Telltale trickles of sweat coursed down the sides of Hooper's face. I held off asking another question and studied the scribbles on my yellow pad, looking up every few seconds. The trickles were getting thicker. "How did you know about Charles Waring's death?"

"Wha . . . I thought you were here to talk about Baker's burglary?"

"I am," I said. My mention of Charles Waring had startled him, but not in any defensive way. "It's just that Mr. Baker told me about Mr. Waring's death and I . . . well, I wondered how you'd managed to find out about the accident so fast."

Hooper shuffled in his straight-backed chair and smiled. "I have my contacts, Mr. Tate."

"Police?"

He frowned, but allowed a small smile. "There's no law against that, is there?"

"None that I know of." I looked back at the pad. "You specialize in this kind of book?"

Hooper closed one eye and rubbed it. "Well, yes, theological and religious works . . . and some history."

"You keep other types of books though?"

"Oh yes, I keep all types, except fiction." He spat the word out as if it were infested with maggots.

"How much is the book worth?"

He turned up his mouth and shrugged. "Four, five hundred dollars. What Baker paid me for it."

"Could it be worth any more?"

"I don't follow you?" Hooper's top lip was glistening now, and he licked at it with his tongue.

"I mean, could you have made a mistake. Could it, maybe, be some kind of special edition that made it worth even more than you charged Baker?"

He shook his head, then rubbed his eye again.

I folded my pad and slipped it into my inside pocket— with the photograph. Gave a big smile and made to move. Hooper returned the smile and moved forward in his seat. As I stood up I said, "Has anyone ever made inquiries for such a book? Either before Waring's death or after?"

The eye gave him more problems. He shook his head again and added a croaky no, just for good measure.

I thanked him and told him to give me a ring if anyone did. Or if he remembered anything that might prove helpful. I left him beamed in a smile that looked as though it might fall right off his face at any moment. I wished I could have been there when it did.

Charlie Bieglemann was eating when he answered the phone. The word he said sounded like 'Beeklemop', and I half imagined I heard the soft *plop* of a wedge of Yonah Shimmel knish or blueberry cheese bagel landing in the mouthpiece. Charlie's was a very staple diet.

"Charlie, it's Koko."

"Hey, how's it hanging, Koke?" he said around munches.

"Limp," I said. "Charlie, a favor."

"You ever call me for anything else?"

"The Charles Waring case. You handling it?"

"The Charles Waring *case*? I miss something? Where's the case, Koke? Guy falls off of his ladder, takes half of the top of his head off on the corner of his table." I heard him drinking. "That's it. The guy's history."

"You involved?"

"I got out there, sure. What's your interest?"

I told him.

"I think you're out of the grounds on this one, Koke. Old dame finds the guy—"

"Elicia Barnes?"

"She the assistant?"

"Yes. What's she like?"

"Granny Slocum in nice clothes." He did another *slu-urrrp,* and went on. "Yeah, she finds him sprawled on the floor beside the table, blood everywhere, including the corner of the table. That's it."

"Nothing missing?"

I could sense him shaking his head. "She checked. Everything had a place and everything was in it."

I tried to imagine it. Guy falls off a ladder, lands on the corner of the table. "The table, Charlie. What kind of a table?"

"What kind? How do *I* know what kind of a table? It was a table."

"You see it? When you went out there?"

"Yeah, I saw it. Blood on the corner. Sharp corner. Covered in books—"

"Covered in books? Waring or the table?"

"The table," he snapped in exasperation. "Apparently Waring used to pile books on the table, ready for filing them into the main collection."

"What did they look like? The piles of books?"

"Just piles of books. What're you getting at here?"

"Any of them fallen over?"

Charlie Bieglemann went quiet. "No," he said at last. "They were all just the way he'd piled them up." He suddenly sounded tired. "Can I finish my lunch now?"

The woman who answered the door wore a smart bottle green two-piece over a lime green ruffle-necked blouse, smart green suede shoes, and a cheek that looked as if it had stopped a Willie Mays fly ball. The bruise had closed her right eye and spread all the way around to her ear. I had to hand it to her as far as color coordination was concerned. I figured it was about a week old. A few days earlier she would have worn purple.

"Don't tell me," I said. "You fell over making an omelet."

"Who're you?"

"Tate. Koko Tate. It's short for Kokorian."

She frowned.

"It's Transylvanian. But don't worry, I only bite at night."

"What do you want?"

"Are you Ella Thornley?"

She looked at me.

"I'm a private detective, Mrs. Thornley. I wonder if I might come in and ask you a few questions."

"What about?"

"A burglary. Can we talk inside?"

"Do you have any ID?"

I pulled out a card, which she accepted without reading. She opened the door and nodded for me to go in. I went.

"How did you get it? The bruise."

"I fell over making an omelet." She smiled.

"Kitchens," I said, shaking my head. "Dangerous places."

"You do a lot of cooking?"

"Only when I'm hungry."

She sat on the back of a Parker-Knoll suite that looked as though it cost someone a year's salary, and lifted her foot onto the edge of a coffee table. Suddenly, she had a lot of legs. "You hungry now?"

"Not while I'm on duty, ma'am."

She laughed gently and threw back her hair. "What do you want, Mr. Tate?"

I smiled and pointed to her leg. "Well, for starters, I'd like it if you took your foot off the table. Those things mark easy. *You* should know that."

She removed her foot and walked across the floor to a breakfast bar that separated the room we were in from the kitchen. The two-piece fitted where it touched, and it touched a lot of places. As she walked, I lost about ten pounds. She picked up a pack of Chesterfields and shook one out. "You're here to talk about my father?" She lit the cigarette with a match and made a big deal out of shaking it dead. "Or my husband?"

"What makes you think it might be about your father?"

She smiled the kind of smile you give at the supermarket checkout when you've spotted that you've just been shortchanged. "The cheap crack about the coffee table."

"Oh, you got that."

"I got it."

"Sorry."

She laughed again. "Don't mention it." She moved back toward me and let out a genuine smile. "Look, come and sit down. Tell me what it is you want to know."

I walked to a chair you could have held a small party in and sat. Crossed my legs. "I'm trying to find a book for my client, Mrs. Thornley."

"Ella," she corrected. She plopped down on the couch up alongside of me.

I nodded. "A Bible. One of your father's books. My client bought it from a dealer name of Hooper. Now the book's gone AWOL. You know Hooper?"

"Yes, he telephoned me the day my father died. He bought a whole load of books from the collection."

"How come they were yours to sell?"

She blew out a column of smoke and frowned. "Pardon me?"

"I mean, how come you were able to sell the books so quickly? Didn't you have to wait for the will to be proven and all that stuff?"

"Oh, I see." She stubbed her cigarette out in a large bronze ashtray. "My father had made it so that the books immediately went to me. I always said I'd sell them straightaway. He knew that and said he wouldn't mind because he wouldn't be here."

"Did you . . . did you and your father get on . . . Ella?"

"Very much. We didn't always see eye-to-eye about a lot of things, Mr. Tate, but then that isn't unusual."

"One of those things your husband?"

She nodded and shifted her gaze down to her feet. "Daddy always felt that I was worth more."

"And were you?"

She looked up quickly. I couldn't tell what she was wanting to say.

"He do that?" I pointed to her cheek.

She reached up and gave it a gentle rub. "Doesn't hurt anymore," she said.

"But it did."

"It did, yes."

"Why?"

"Why did it hurt?"

"Why did he do it?"

"Because I'd sold some of the books. Because I'd sold them before I'd discussed it with him. He said that if we'd waited, we could have got a better price."

"Why *did* you sell them so quickly?"

"Because I knew he needed money."

"But won't there be a lot of money from your father's estate?"

She shook off her shoes and tucked her legs beneath her on the couch. "Yes, but that will take time. Jimmy doesn't have a lot of time ... at least not as far as this particular transaction goes."

"What—"

"I really don't want to say anything more about that, Mr. Tate. I've probably said too much already."

I lifted my hands to say that was okay. "Did anyone else ask about the books?"

"Oh, a lot of people. People who had been on at Daddy for years. I sold everything within a week. Got a good price, I think. Anyway, I didn't want things hanging around."

"Anyone ask about one particular book?"

She shrugged and then shook her head. "No, they were all dealers—there were a couple of collectors, but even they just bought whole shelves full so they could use the books in trade." She ran her fingers through her hair and grabbed at one thick strand. "My father's collection was highly sought after."

"So I understand."

We sat for a minute, her looking at me, me watching her fiddle with that strand of hair. "You sure you're not hungry?"

"Yeah," I said, "I'm hungry." I stood up. "Guess I'd better go get something to eat."

She followed me to the door and held it open for me. As I stepped out she said, "Thanks for calling, Mr. Tate."

"Thanks?"

She smiled at me. "You made me laugh. I don't laugh very much, Mr. Tate."

"Call me Koke," I said.

She nodded a soft slow nod and let the smile become embarrassed. "See you sometime."

"Yeah," I said. When the door slammed, I was half-way down the corridor, looking for a cold shower.

When the first call came in, I had just turned on the television. I'd been waiting for this movie all week—one of my favorites, and my *absolute* favorite western, *The Man Who Shot Liberty Valance.* I'd missed the beginning so I wasn't in the best of moods. But I was starting to feel better. I was halfway through a Sbarro pizza laced with double anchovies, and working my way through my second Lone Star beer. Jimmy Stewart had just picked up John Wayne's steak and slapped it on the table and everyone was pissed off: Wayne because he wanted Lee Marvin to pick it up; Marvin because he wanted Wayne to pick it up; Stewart because he thought they were both a couple of kids; me because the goddamn telephone was ringing.

"This better be good," I barked. It was a little before eleven.

"It *was* good," Charlie Bieglemann said. "Now it's gone all to hell in a handcart."

"Charlie?"

"I thought you'd like to know. I finished my lunch."

I laughed. "What else?"

"You got me thinking. I had Forensic check the table. No grain damage, no tissue, no nothing. Hardest thing it had been hit with is a napkin."

"What about the blood?"

"Smeared on."

"The thick plottens," I said.

"This isn't good, Koke. We should've checked all this stuff out a couple weeks ago."

"Hey, you're doing it now, Charlie."

He grunted. "I'll be getting back to you if I get anything more." He waited. "You do the same, huh?"

"Count on it," I told him.

"I am."

When the second call came, Lee Marvin had just worked over Edmond O'Brien and things were hotting up.

"Jesus Christ!" I snapped into the mouthpiece.

"No, it's Ella Thornley," Ella Thornley said.

It was one of those moments when you wished you could have the last thirty seconds back and then you could go dig a hole and bury them. "Just a second, you want Koko," I said, and I turned away from the mouthpiece and yelled my name as loud as I could. Then I turned back and said, "Koko Tate?"

She was laughing.

"Sorry," I said. "I'm making a habit of apologizing to you."

"I like it," she said, still laughing. "Listen, we had a call earlier tonight. I picked up the phone because I didn't think Jimmy had heard it." She paused.

Jimmy Stewart was strapping on a gun. "Yeah, I'm listening."

"It was Hooper."

"The dealer?"

"But he was ringing Jimmy. He was telling him he had something that he thought Jimmy wanted. Jimmy heard me on the extension and told me to get off the line."

"He said that?"

"He said, 'Get the fuck off the line, Ella.' "

"Sweet talker."

"You don't know the half of it."

"So you don't know what else he said ... Hooper?"

"No. But Jimmy paced around here for a while, drank a couple of Scotches and then went out."

"How long ago?"

"About a half an hour. I waited to make sure he wasn't just going to come right back in before I called you."

"He say where he was going?"

"No. Well, for a drink, he said."

"Okay, thanks."

"Does it mean anything?"

"No, but I never let a little thing like that stop me when I'm hot on the scent."

"That's one you owe me," she said. "Next time you call, bring your appetite."

When I replaced the receiver, I was opening and closing my mouth like a goldfish.

The night streets in the Village were a lot like the one Jimmy Stewart was walking down when I switched off the television—hot, oppressive, and dangerous. I pulled my Toyota onto a piece of sidewalk in front of a huge roll-up metal door bearing the words IN USE DAY AND NIGHT and got out. There was nobody around.

Hooper's Books was a single-window store along the street on the left. It looked closed and deserted, but then so did the rest of the street. Somewhere over the buildings I heard a police car, its lonesome wail joined by several car horns. I waited until the sound died away, heading uptown, and then walked along to the store.

Right away I could see things were not good. The door was partially open, stopped from closing by a solitary book whose pages had foxed and bent in a wedge beneath the door. Inside, the store looked dark and intimidating. I picked up the book and looked at the spine: *The Modernist Impulse in American Protestantism* by William R. Hutchison. One of the many that hadn't made the *New York Times* best-seller list.

I looked behind me, then pulled out my .38 police

special and checked the clip. Leaning against the side window, I pushed gently at the door and watched it drift open. Beyond was pure blackness, giving nothing away. I stepped inside and moved to the right. Moving to the left would have put the window behind me, ideal for target practice. I strained to hear anything, but there was nothing. I waited.

It must have been ten minutes later that I said, "Hooper?" as quietly as I could. There was no response. I said it louder. Nothing. This was it. I slipped the gun back in my waistband and pushed the door closed, hard. A little bell on the top jingled, but there was nobody there to hear. Walking crouched down, I moved along in front of the window to the far wall. The floor was littered with books. "Hooper? You in here?"

I stood up and backed along the wall until I felt a box suddenly jab into my back—light switches. I ran my hand down the switches and watched the spectacle unfold before me.

It looked like Berlin must've looked just before the war, when they dropped truckloads of books onto spare ground and burned the lot. Hooper's store was like that; all that was missing was a guy with gasoline and matches.

The store was divided into four corridors, or, at least, it had been once. Now it was a shambles of books and shelving scattered across the floor and partially burying the crumpled body of Edgar Hooper. At first I thought he was watching me, then I wondered why his face looked so strange. As I stepped over toward him, I saw that he was eating a book. I pulled out a handkerchief, crouched down, and wrapping the handkerchief around my hand, I prised the book free. As I pulled it out, a thick pool of blood bubbled once, up into his mouth, and spilled over his cheeks and his chin. The book was *The Literary Man's Bible* by W.L. Courtney. Who said humor was dead?

I lifted the books from him gently and carefully, the way I figure he'd have wanted me to—not for his sake but for the books'. After a while, I saw that someone had pulled down his pants and his shorts. Checking him over, trying to ignore the number of bruises and the swelling of his battered genitals, I noticed that, although he was lying flat on the floor, his body was arched in the middle. I removed a few more books and turned him over. The book lodged in his backside was *The Social Gospel in America,* edited by Robert T. Handy. I pulled it out with the covered hand, trying not to look at the mess it had made, and laid it with *The Literary Man's Bible* over by the door.

A few minutes later, Hooper's dignity restored, I climbed back into my Toyota and started the engine. Beside me on the seat was a book-size, handkerchief-wrapped package. Ahead of me Hooper's store was again in darkness.

He opened the door and glared. "Who're you?"

"Koko Tate," I said.

"Tough shit," he snapped and slammed the door in my face.

I rang the bell again. The door opened, and he took a step into the corridor. "Look, you got a problem, fella?"

I shook my head and smiled. "Uh-uhh."

He looked me up and down, hesitating at the package I held. I did the same with him. He was wearing a white shirt, open at the neck, a pair of expensive light-tweed pants, and what looked like Gucci loafers. But then anything made out of leather looks like Gucci loafers to me. I double-checked the pants for any telltale bulges that might prove troublesome later. There were none.

A gold identity bracelet hung from his wrist. I leaned forward and tilted my head on one side. "Jim-my," I read. I straightened up and said, "Hey, I used to have one of those, but now I remember who I am all the time."

Ella Thornley appeared at the door behind him. When she saw me, she said, "Oh, Mr. Tate, come in."

I brushed past her husband while he tried to think of something cute to say and went into the apartment, checking over my shoulder to see if there was anything jammed into his waistband at the back. All clear.

Her face was bruised on both sides now, her top lip puffed out and hanging over the bottom one. It looked sore. I turned around as Jimmy Thornley was closing the door. "You do this?" I asked him.

"What if I did?"

"Don't you know it's not polite to hit a lady?"

He smiled and punched his right hand into his left. If it hurt him, he didn't show it. "You want I should hit you instead?"

"I want you should try," I said.

"Jimmy," Ella Thornley said, "please. Mr. Tate was here earlier to ask about a theft."

"A theft?" His eyes brightened up. I had the feeling it was maybe one of the few crimes he genuinely knew nothing about. He let his arms drop to his sides and ruffled his hair. "Look, I'm sorry ..." He searched for my name. I let him search. "It's been a real tough night, and I had a few drinks, you know how it is," he added with a conspiratorial all-guys-together smile.

"I'm learning," I said.

He shrugged, ruffled his hair some more, and walked over to a well-stocked bar. As he reached for a bottle of Jim Beam, he said, "So, a theft, huh? How can we help?"

"You know a fella name of Hooper?"

I was impressed. His hand never faltered. "You want one of these?" he asked, eyebrows raised.

I shook my head. "He's a book dealer."

He took a sip of the whiskey and frowned. "Hooper ... Hooper. No, I don't believe I do. Should I?"

"I guess so. I just been over to see him. He's had an ... accident."

He ran a sad look at me. "That's too bad. Serious?"

"He wasn't laughing when I left him," I said, watching Thornley take another drink. "But he did say a few words."

Thornley looked up sharply and a thin trail of whiskey

ran down his chin. I nodded to it and said, "You should try a Tommy Tippee catch-all bib. They're real good. I used to use them myself . . . about thirty years ago."

"You're real funny, Tate. I'm beginning to worry these pants'll never dry."

"I try," I said, turning to shrug at Ella Thornley.

"So, what'd he say, this . . . Hooper?"

"He says he rang you to tell you a book you'd expressed an interest in had turned up after all. He'd managed to get a copy for you. Special book."

"Yeah?" He nodded to the package. "That it?"

I held up the two books in my handkerchief, and Ella Thornley gasped. The handkerchief was kind of discolored. "These?" I shook my head and rested them on my left hand, opening the handkerchief with my right. "No, these I took from Mr. Hooper to help his breathing and . . . and the general passing of air. But now that I've done that, you have a problem."

Thornley took another sip, realized the glass was almost empty, and reached for the bottle. "I've had it with you, Tate," he said. "I think you'd better go. Now!"

"No!" Ella Thornley snapped the word into the air, and both Thornley and I turned to face her. "I want to hear about my husband's problem."

"His problem is this, Mrs. Thornley. I think your husband killed Charles Waring. I think he battered his head in with an antique Bible, then he set the body up to look like he'd fallen from the ladder and hit his head on the corner of his desk."

Thornley stood, watching me impassively. I caught him glance across at his wife once, then take another sip.

I turned to face Thornley and went on. "You smeared his blood over the corner of the desk and put the book back on the shelf. You couldn't take the book with you because you were worried Waring's assistant might notice it was missing. Then she'd know his death wasn't an accident. You figured you'd go back for the book later." I turned to Ella Thornley. "He had to go back because, although he probably wiped it clean, there's always a danger it'll hold traces of blood and tissue. Particularly this book, Mrs. Thornley. It has metallic corner guards attached to the leather and ... well, things could have got trapped in there."

I put my own two books on the arm of one of the chairs, undid my jacket, and stepped to my left, away from Ella Thornley, still talking to her, but now watching Thornley. "So, he's done the murder, and he gets out of the way setting up alibis, just in case. When he gets back, you've already sold some of the books, including the murder weapon. This does not make him happy." I jabbed my finger into my cheek and gave her a quick glance.

"So he goes around to see Hooper and looks through the piles of books he bought from you. The Bible was the only one of your father's books that Hooper had sold, so that had to be what your husband was looking for. And, worst of all, Hooper recognized him." I stopped for a second. "How'm I doing?"

"Pure *Twilight Zone*," Thornley said and drained his glass.

I checked the room. One door behind me—the one I came in at—two doors over on the far wall, breakfast bar over on my right. I took a breath.

"At this stage Hooper gets greedy, figures he maybe screwed up on the Bible, and it was worth a lot more than the four-fifty he charged Baker. He knows Baker won't sell him the book back, so he decides to steal it. This he does.

"He checks and checks the book, can't find how it could be worth more than he originally estimated. He looks and he looks. Eventually, the inevitable happens and he realizes why the book is valuable to your husband. I'm sorry, Mrs. Thornley."

She shook her head, her finger jammed between her teeth to stop from crying. Maybe stop her doing other things, too.

"So, tonight, he calls your husband. Tells him he has the book and that it's for sale, at the right price. Jimmy here goes around to try persuade him to let the book go for no money at all. He batters the guy to a pulp. Jams books down his throat and up his ass until Hooper tells him where the Bible is. He leaves him for dead." I turned to Thornley and wagged my finger side to side. "Your first real mistake, asshole, and it happens more than you'd realize," I said, leaning toward the wall. "Right now, he's over at St. Vincent's, getting emergency treatment to his rectum and larynx, talking to a friend of mine who wears a badge and eats kosher pizza."

Thornley put down the glass and rubbed his hands together.

"Jimmy," Ella Thornley said. How could so much exhaustion, so much disappointment, and so much hatred get itself tangled up in one little word?

"Where's the Bible, Jimmy?" I said. "Time to make your peace with God."

Thornley moved fast.

He leaped forward, pulled the two books I'd brought around off the chair, and in one fluid movement tossed them straight at me. I was already moving toward him. I ducked and one of the books missed me completely. The other hit me right on the bridge of the nose, and I went down seeing whole galaxies. Somewhere off to one side, Ella Thornley screamed, and I rolled over fumbling for my gun. There was a crash and a sudden, overwhelming smell of whiskey. Everything went quiet for a second, and then the floor alongside me shook as Thornley came to keep me company. I opened my eyes and looked into three or four images of his face, all of them desperately trying to pull themselves together.

Thornley's face was a little below mine, his eyes closed, his hair soaked in a mixture of alcohol and blood. I turned around and looked up at Ella Thornley, standing beside the chair, swaying slightly, the jagged neck of a Jim Beam bottle in her right hand. Just a couple of seconds later, we were all on the floor.

*   *   *

First dates can be hell, but wakes can be worse.

This was a little of both.

The damage to Ella Thornley's face had healed up, and I'd taken her up on her suggestion that I unleash my appetite, but only after pacing around my apartment, glaring at the telephone for more than a week.

Jimmy Thornley had never regained consciousness, and I'd told her it was probably for the best. Saved the taxpayers a little money, at least. She'd hit him a good blow across the side of the head, fracturing his skull right on the temple—transected an artery. The clot started to compress the brain. They tried to operate, but it was hopeless; less than forty-eight hours after he'd been crowned with Jim Beam whiskey, Jimmy Thornley moved on to a new address—cause of death, subdural hematoma. He died with her at his side.

I told her to tell people it was drink that killed him in the end.

James Baker got his Bible back and immediately arranged for a specialist to remove the brass binding for cleaning. He was delighted, and his check showed it. Time to celebrate.

The Mon Hueng Seafood House is tucked away on a little side street off Canal Street. Once I'd decided on Chinese food, it had been a toss-up whether to go for Mon Hueng or Sam Wo's—Woody Allen rated Sam Wo's crabs so highly that he even shot some of *Manhattan* there, but the footage ended up on the cutting-room floor—but, in the end, I'd gone for Mon Hueng's.

We'd both started off with snails in garlic and black bean sauce—she said she would if I would, and I said I would if she would ... which made me excited and nervous, both at the same time—and then I'd had stir-fried crabs Cantonese, with minced pork, more black beans, and soft egg gravy. She said one plate of fish—"Snails ... *fish*?" I said—was enough and went instead for a deep dish of 'jeah jeah' chicken—the 'jeah jeah' is the sound it makes as it's sauteed—with mixed Chinese vegetables.

Over our impressively empty plates Ella Thornley said, "You know what day it is?"

"My lucky one?"

She smiled gently. "Father's Day."

"Oh."

"Yeah, 'oh'." She moved her finger around the rim of her glass and made a soft, far-off hum that sounded like fairies singing. "Is your father still alive?"

"Nope."

"You miss him?"

"I never really think about it . . . missing him, I mean. But, sure, yeah, I guess I miss him. You only get the one."

"I was thinking about that film, Kevin Costner . . . it was about baseball, but it wasn't, if you know what I mean."

"*Field of Dreams,*" I said. "Good movie, great book."

"It was a book?"

"*Shoeless Joe.* It was written by a guy called W. P. Kinsella."

"Lovely movie."

I nodded and mashed my napkin into an even smaller bundle.

"That was all about his father, wasn't it?"

"Yeah, about fathers and relationships and generally growing older. All those things." Her eyes avoided looking at me, but I could still see the shine of the lights reflected in their moisture. "It's right you should feel sad," I said. "Particularly so soon after and it being a special day."

"That's just it," she said, leaning toward me. "Every day should be special while they're here."

"They should, but they're not. You take them for granted. You know what they say: You don't miss your water till your well runs dry."

She didn't respond. Just sat there. Outside, a siren wailed.

"Let's have a drink to them."

"Our fathers?"

"Sure, why not?"

She shrugged. "Seems silly. Morbid."

"Needn't be. Death is only morbid to the living. To the dead, it's a way of life."

Her laugh was a long time coming, but when it arrived, it brought the tears with it.

Over coffee and bourbon we sat and talked until past one, when the waiters sat down at one of the little Formica tables over by the window and ate from bowls—containing delicacies that might have looked good to me about four hours earlier—as if they were in a race, chopsticks traveling the two or three inches from dish to mouth, and clattering in time to their incessant chatter.

We talked more about fathers and the special places they hold in your heart. We talked about their silences and their sternness, about how they guided us and helped us, and I told her many things that I hadn't told anyone else before ... things I should have remembered earlier.

Then we talked some more about our favorite movies—turned out she was a big fan of Jimmy Stewart, so I knew we were off to a good start—and how something had to be done about the Park in the summertime ... and, later, in a mixture of silence and the gentle movements that only two people who really know each other can do, we talked about the kind of jazz that cools down hot apartments.

We never mentioned books once.

The Pasture Mystery

by John Tigges

Everyone was naturally curious when the bodies were unearthed by the herd of pigs.

The pasture land had lain fallow for years, and when the owner, Sheriff Owen Thomas, died of a heart attack, his widow rented the pasture to the neighboring farmer who wanted to keep pigs in it. People drove by gawking at the scene of the men digging, looking for more and more dead people. When they felt assured that there were no more, the count stood at over fifty, fifty-three to be exact.

Harvey Whitney, candidate for the office of sheriff to fill the unexpired term of Owen Thomas, was keenly interested in the discovery, the count of bodies, and the manner in which Deputy "Tiny" Bell, the acting sheriff until after the election, would handle the case. That Tiny was Harvey's chief competition for the office lent an air of excitement to the overall atmosphere whenever the two met. Tiny didn't like Harvey and his honest law-enforcement platform. Tiny wanted the *status* to remain *quo* and not have any changes at all. That was the reason he was running for the office—or at least that was the reason he gave when asked.

Harvey's daughter, Dr. Andi Whitney, was just as interested since she wanted her father to be the next sheriff. First establishing her practice in Treavor Falls, she had some extra time on her hands and had offered to help Harvey run his campaign.

The special election was to be held the Tuesday after Father's Day, and she knew that winning would do her father a world of good. Her mother had died the previous year, and Harvey had found himself at loose ends. He had retired two months before surgery complications took his wife of thirty-six years, and he found himself lonely and without anyone to talk with, most of the time.

The first thing Andi asked him after Sheriff Thomas had died and the election and his candidacy were announced was: "Why on earth do you want to run for sheriff?"

"Oh, lots of reasons," Harvey said. "First, it's about time we got a new sheriff. Thomas was in office almost thirty years. It sure seems that if one belongs to the right political party in this county, one can be elected to a lifetime job."

"That isn't really true, is it, Dad?"

"I guess you haven't paid much attention to such matters, what with being away at school all those years. But you watch. The person who's elected to the office of anything in this county, is always reelected. Always. The mentality seems to be, 'My grandpa and my pa all voted the straight ticket, and by gosh I vote the same as them.' "

Andi shook her head. "That's difficult to believe. You mean there's no opposition?"

"Oh, sure. There might be opposition on occasion, but the powers in force don't like it, so the voters do their thing, and the results are always the same. Take a look at the county auditor. Sykes has been in office for twenty-four years. Bell, the deputy sheriff, would like a full-time permanent job like that. Matt Morrisey, the county coroner, has been in office, let's see . . . ," Harvey said, pausing while he counted years. "Of course. He and Thomas went into office at the same time. Now, you tell me if you believe the county is run so efficiently that being elected to office once means a lifetime career in that office?"

Andi stood and walked to the window. "All right. I'll go along with you that it isn't a very good way to have elected officials hold office. But what are you saying?

That Sheriff Thomas somehow is responsible for those bodies that have been found?"

Harvey shrugged. "I don't know. Owen was a tough, old bird. He ran the sheriff's office with an iron hand, and he always acted honest. But he sure as hell wouldn't kill anybody and be dumb enough to bury the body on his own land, for crying out loud."

"Let's agree on one thing, Dad," Andi said, turning to face her father. "It hasn't been proven yet that any of the cadavers met with violent ends. You'd better not say something like that and have it heard by the wrong people."

Harvey nodded slowly. "I see what you mean. I wonder how long it will take to have autopsies done on each one?"

She nodded. "Will Morrisey perform them?"

"I don't see how he could. He isn't a doctor."

"What?"

"He's an undertaker—a mortician. Until he's knocked out of office by a doctor, our county is stuck in the nineteenth century with a mortician for a county coroner. There's something in the state's statutes that says they can't unseat an incumbent for anything other than violation of the law in the performance of that office."

"So who's doing the autopsies?"

"Doctors at the State University. The highway patrol started taking them down there when they found the first body."

Andi smiled, her eyes sparkling. "The election is only five days off, and I still have some shopping to do. What do need, Dad? Anything special?"

"Need? For what?"

"For Father's Day. It's this Sunday. Is there anything you need special?"

"Yeah. Yeah, there is. I want to be sheriff. I think it would do me good to win and since the incumbent is dead, there *is* going to be a new sheriff, no matter what happens in the election."

"You say that as if there might be something crooked about the outcome."

"Naw. I don't think that for a minute. The people who run the elections are all good people. It's just the damned mentality of the voters at large that makes me sick."

"What about this deputy who's running against you? Will he be a shoo-in or can you beat him?"

"Tiny's kind of raw around the edges. He offends a lot of people with his rough ways. I guess he was a good enough deputy for Thomas, but would he make a good sheriff? I don't know."

Andi crossed the room and bent down to kiss Harvey on the cheek. "I've got to get going. What are your plans for today?"

"More campaigning and I'm stopping by the sheriff's office to see if there's anything new on the bodies. Now about my Father's Day gift. I don't care what the margin of victory is—just make it so I win."

Andi walked to the door and stopped to look back. "I'll see what I can do, Sheriff Whitney." She opened the door and was gone.

Harvey smiled. *Sheriff Whitney.* It had a nice ring to it.

"I don't care if you are runnin' for sheriff, Whitney," Tiny Bell said loudly, "you ain't gettin' access to nothin' to do with the matter of them bodies what was found." He pulled himself up to his 6 foot 4 inches height, emphasizing his girth when he did.

"I thought maybe you'd welcome a new outlook on it, Deputy," Harvey said evenly. He fought to control his temper. It was just like Bell to want to run the whole show himself. Not that he didn't have experience, but for the life of him, Harvey couldn't think of the last time there was a murder or any crime of violence of any sort in Treavor Falls or in McBride County itself.

"You can call me *Sheriff,* Whitney," Bell said. "And you may as well get used to callin' me that, too, since I'm goin' to win the election. Hells bells, I'll have this little mystery tied up and be elected hands down winner."

"You sound awfully sure of yourself, Bell."

"Why shouldn't I? I've got an inside track bein' in office already so to speak. And make that Sheriff Bell."

Harvey wondered about the man's sense of justice and fair play. If he wanted to boast to his friends, that would be all right. But to openly make statements such as he had just made, seemed at best, foolish and downright stupid.

"Tell me, *Sheriff*," Harvey said, his voice dripping sarcasm, "Who do you think put the bodies in the pasture? Sheriff Thomas?"

"You'd better not say things like that, Whitney. Sheriff Thomas was a good man. Look how long he was sheriff."

"That has nothing to do with it, Bell. Fifty-three bodies have been found on his property. It sure does raise some questions, doesn't it?"

"Questions? What'dya mean? Like what questions?"

"Like who's responsible? If the sheriff had anything to do with it? What sort of people did he associate with and hire in his sheriff's office and the like? You know, *Sheriff* Bell, questions?"

"Oh, questions. I see what you mean. Sure. Questions."

"You're sure you don't need any help from me?"

"None. Why should I give you the opportunity to solve this thing and be elected ahead o' me?"

Harvey said nothing and left the sheriff's office.

Clothilda Thomas sat on the couch, fidgeting with her handkerchief, occasionally shooting a quick, nervous look at her visitor, Harvey Whitney. She dabbed at her eyes.

"I sure don't like coming to you like this, Mrs. Thomas, but I believe that you want this thing cleared up more than anyone. After all, your husband owned the land where the bodies were found."

She nodded. "I know. But Owen couldn't have known about them. I lived with that man as his wife for almost forty-five years. He'd never have hurt the hair on a person's head, let alone do—do what was—was apparently done to those people."

"What do you think was done to them, Mrs. Thomas?"

"Why—weren't they murdered and all? Good heavens. They surely didn't die natural deaths. If they had, they'd be buried in the cemeteries around Treavor Falls. Owen always worried about such things. You know, serial killers and such."

Harvey made a mental note that apparently Owen Thomas confided a lot in his wife.

"Tell me, Mrs. Thomas, what did your husband use that pasture land for?"

She smiled wanly. "Owen always wanted to have some horses. He said to me, 'I gotta have the place to put them if I ever get the chance to get some.' "

"Did he ever get any?"

She shook her head. "Right after he died, Nick Jarding, the farmer next door to that land, came to me and asked if I could rent him the land. I thought it made sense since I'll need all the income I can get now that poor Owen is . . ."

"I see," Harvey said. "Well, thank you, Mrs. Thomas. If I want to ask you more questions, may I stop back?"

She nodded and saw him to the door.

Harvey had a couple of questions he wanted to ask Nick Jarding.

Short, rotund Nick Jarding spat tobacco juice to the ground and studied Harvey for several minutes. "So you're runnin' fer sheriff, huh?"

Harvey nodded.

"You ain't been elected yet. How come you want to ask me some questions 'bout my pig pasture?"

"I figure that if I am elected, I'll be off to a good start

to solving this case. Tell me, Mr. Jarding, did you ever ask Sheriff Thomas about renting his land?"

"You know, I like that." Jarding said and sent another stream of brown juice to the ground.

"Huh? Like what?" Harvey searched the man's face for some sort of explanation.

"Doin' work 'fore you're hired. That's the mark of a good man and a worker. I'll vote fer you."

"Did you ever ask Thomas about renting his land before he died?"

"Sure. 'Most every year."

"What was his reason for not renting? Or didn't he give you one?"

"Always said somethin' about wantin' to use it fer horses—and not smelly pigs."

"Why do you suppose your pigs found those bodies, Mr. Jarding?"

After emptying his mouth again, Jarding chomped on the tobacco plug for a moment. "Well sir, pigs has got an awful good smeller on 'em. They can smell food several feet under the ground, and since they root a lot, they dig up whatever they smell. They must've thought they found a bonanza or somethin' when they found them bodies." He chortled and spat again.

"Would they have eaten the bodies?"

"Sure. They'll eat 'most anythin'."

"Well thank you for your time, Mr. Jarding. You might mention my running for sheriff to your wife. Do you have any children old enough to vote?"

Jarding nodded. "They'll vote the way I tell 'em."

Harvey waved good-bye and left the farm. He was getting pieces of a puzzle or at least he thought he was. But what picture would be presented if he completed the puzzle, remained to be seen.

Harvey slowed his Chevy and turned into the town cemetery that bordered the city limits. He smiled to himself. He was thinking like a lawman already. He'd take a quick turn through and make sure that everything was all right and then head for the sheriff's office before going home. The forensics reports were to be available late that afternoon. Maybe Bell would relent and share the information.

Ahead, a late model car had pulled off to the side of the narrow driveway. Harvey slowed and looked to either side when he determined that the car was empty. To his left he made out the figure of Clothilda Thomas bent over the grave of her husband, arranging flowers on the hump of earth that covered the casket.

Harvey absently tipped his hat toward the woman and continued driving through the cemetery. He turned back toward the road and passed the section that had been put aside for a potter's field. The poor—indigents, hobos, and the like—who happened to die within the boundaries of McBride County were buried there with simple iron crosses marking the spot. He slowed and glanced toward the flat, level section, dotted with crosses.

When he reached the road, he turned toward town.

"That slob Bell wouldn't even let me see the first sheet of the forensics report. It was just coming in on the fax machine. Darn," Harvey said, dropping into his overstuffed chair, "the least he could've done was let me look at it."

"Not to worry," Andi said and crossed the room, handing him a large thick envelope. "Here is what I hope is the first part of your Father's Day gift."

"What's this?" Harvey took the envelope and turned it over, examining it.

"Open it and find out."

He slid the flap out and withdrew a stack of papers. He studied the top one, his face beaming. "This looks like the forensics reports."

"They are."

"Where'd you get them?"

"I called a friend of mine who works in Forensics at

the State lab. He arranged to send a set to me before he did to the sheriff's office here."

"That's great, Andi. How can I thank you?"

"By solving this case and being elected."

Harvey fell silent and poured over the first sheets. Then he looked up and said, "It's going to take an awfully long time to go through this and see if there's any sort of common thread."

"Not necessarily. Look at the last page."

Harvey slipped the last page from the bottom of the stack and quickly read the contents, his eyes steadily widening. "Why this is a complete breakdown of the fifty-three bodies. How did you ... ?"

"I asked Craig to run a computer analysis of the information. It didn't take long. I also asked him not to send a similar conclusion to the sheriff's office right away. I said Monday would be plenty of time."

Harvey chuckled and went back to the analysis. Most of the bodies had succumbed to natural causes. Some, better than half, were in the advanced stages of alcoholism, while the vast majority had died of malnutrition. A very small percentage had died of some sort of trauma, and a few had suffered multiple fractures.

Harvey looked up to find Andi sitting opposite him. "Did you read this?"

She nodded.

"What do you think?"

"It sounds pretty darned ordinary, doesn't it? No evidence of poisoning, or gunshot wounds, or knife wounds. Most were natural causes except for three or four who had died violently with broken bones and what have you."

"It says here that thirty-nine were male and fourteen female. The ages were twenty to seventy-two. That sure doesn't make it a serial killer's work, unless there's one running around loose that doesn't give a hoot as to who he does in. Most of the time, they're all one sex or one age or the same color hair or some other similarity."

"I don't think it's a serial killer either, Dad. There

haven't been any reports of people missing from around here."

"Good point. Did you see this part about the shortest period of time that one was in the ground, only two months and the longest twenty-seven years? Sure has been going on a long time, hasn't it?"

"Well, I've got a couple of calls to make at the hospital. See you in the morning. Think on that information, and we can go over it then." Andi stood to leave.

"I'm driving over to Salem first thing in the morning to put an ad in the *Salem Sentinel*. I want to stop at the rest home and visit around, selling myself. Let's have lunch together if you're not busy."

"I'll see you then." Andi kissed her father on the forehead and left.

The next morning Harvey drove through the business section of Treavor Falls. He already had coffee and doughnuts at Sally's Spoon and would first stop at the *Sentinel* office and then go to the rest home. The ad would be the last one, and he hoped it would help him carry Salem and that part of the county.

When he passed the courthouse, Harvey noticed Tiny Bell and Matt Morrisey, the coroner, coming out of the sheriff's office, which had its own entrance on the ground level. Before they passed from his view, he saw the two of them shake hands and Tiny clap a hand on the smaller man's back.

Harvey wondered what that was all about and continued driving toward the north end of town. Despite staying up until midnight going over the forensics reports, Harvey had slept well. True, he hadn't fallen asleep immediately. He had lain there, trying to put his finger on the *something* that had seemed out of place at the cemetery yesterday when he drove through.

Even in the light of day, the tantalizing *something* hovered just out of his reason's reach. What was it? What had been wrong? Mrs. Thomas? No, she was still in mourning and was simply putting flowers on her husband's grave. But that had been the only thing worth noting.

When he approached the first entrance to the cemetery, Harvey automatically slowed. He'd drive through once and then be on his way. He was backtracking on yesterday's pass through and came first to the potter's field. He hardly paid it any attention and turned to head for Thomas's grave.

Harvey braked to a halt and got out, a hundred feet to the dead sheriff's grave. He walked over and admired the gladioli Mrs. Thomas had lain on the fresh-turned earth and transplanted sod. Taking off his hat, Harvey breathed a silent prayer.

He slowly turned and took in every square inch of the area. Nothing was out of place. Nothing. Not even a blade of grass looked suspiciously bent or broken.

After he returned to the car, he drove to the next intersection and turned around. Maybe he'd notice the *something* if he drove in the same direction he had yesterday. Allowing the idle of the engine to pull the car along, Harvey surveyed the Thomas grave site once more. What was wrong?

Checking the dashboard clock, he chastised himself for taking so much time. He had to get going to Salem. Turning to drive to the highway, he looked out absently at the flat, treeless expanse of potter's field.

Then he slammed on his brakes. Of course! It wasn't what he had seen. It was what he *hadn't* seen that had bothered him. He couldn't go to Salem now. He had to take matters into his own hands. He wasn't sure if he could count on Tiny Bell to help. For all Harvey knew, the massive deputy was involved.

Harvey stood near the door that led from the sheriff's office. Andi sat on a straight-back chair while Tiny Bell's bulk almost covered the desk on which he sat. Off to Harvey's right Matt Morrisey, the coroner, Eldon Sykes, the auditor, and Frank Loangers, the county treasurer, huddled.

"Let's get on with this, Whitney," the deputy growled. "Just why the hell did you call us together—and on a Saturday mornin', yet?"

Just then the door opened and two highway patrolmen entered.

"What are they doin' here?" Bell asked, suddenly looking uneasy.

"I asked them to come, Deputy. I think we may need them before the morning's over."

"I'm the law here."

"Yeah," Harvey said. "Sure."

"What's up?" the taller of the two patrolmen asked.

Harvey explained that it had to do with the bodies that had been dug up over the last while, and although there wasn't any real foul play involved, nevertheless, the law, if not broken, had been badly bent or at least, misused.

With everyone's attention on him, Harvey walked to the center of the room. "First I want to ask Mr. Morrisey, when the last indigent person was buried by the county?"

"Well, I—I'm not really certain. A couple of months, I guess. I don't really remember."

"How long have you been in office?" Harvey fixed his attention on Morrisey.

"Well, I've been very fortunate in seeking re-election. I've held the position of county coroner for the last thirty years."

"And in that time span, how many people have you buried in potter's field?"

Morrisey's face ruddled until it was a deep red. "I don't know what you're talking about."

Harvey turned to the auditor and treasurer. "Mr. Sykes, do you know offhand how much the county pays a mortician to bury someone in potter's field?"

"Not right offhand, but I could find out in my office in a matter of minutes."

"Go ahead and find out if you would." Harvey waited until Sykes left the office. When the door closed on him,

Harvey turned to Frank Loangers. "Mr. Loangers, as county treasurer, you and your office write out the checks to the different morticians who bury the poor and indigent. Is that right?"

Loangers nodded. "I do."

"Can you tell me how many different undertakers are involved?"

Loangers frowned. "I'm not certain, mind you, and I can find out, but I think Matt is the only one."

"Would you check, please?"

Loangers left the room, and Harvey turned to Matt Morrisey again. "Just what is the procedure when, let's say, a hobo dies in the railroad yard. What happens?"

"The law calls me, I pick up the body, examine it, have an autopsy performed, then embalm it after trying to identify the cadaver. Then I bury it. Ah, that is, if it's my turn. Otherwise the funeral director whose name is on top of the list, is summoned."

"And the county I believe pays you for this. Is that right? I mean, you're a good citizen and all, but you don't donate your services as a mortician, do you?"

Morrisey coughed and stared at the floor. "The—the county pays me."

"And how much does the county pay you?"

Just then the door opened, and Eldon Sykes walked into the sheriff's office. "It's varied over the years, Mr. Whitney. When Matt first went into office, thirty years ago, the fee was $1,500 per case. That included the cost of a casket."

"And what is it now?" Harvey asked.

"Seventy-five hundred, including the casket."

Before anyone could speak, the door opened again and Loangers walked in. "Computers are wonderful things," he said. "The only mortician involved in indigent and poor cases in the last thirty years has been Matt Morrisey."

"What are you accusing me of, Whitney?" Morrisey asked loudly, taking a step back.

"I'm suggesting that, because you couldn't make

enough profit off the death of some poor person or indigent hobo, that you approached the late Sheriff Thomas and offered a split of some kind to simply bury such people on his property without the benefit of embalming or a casket. Is that about right?"

Morrisey's hands trembled, and he turned to Bell who had gotten off the desk. "You're in this as much as I am, Tiny. Tell 'em. Tell 'em how hard it is to break even when you deal with hoboes and such."

"Don't drag me into your mess, Morrisey. Owen said it was all your idea."

"Yeah, but you and Owen always helped. And for half, too."

The two patrolmen stepped forward and took the mortician into custody, reading him his rights at the same time. Deputy Bell was arrested as well, and after Sykes, Loangers, and the patrolmen congratulated Harvey for an excellent job of police work, they left. Bell and Morrisey were taken with the patrolmen, to be charged with malfeasance.

Andi stood. "I'm deeply impressed, Dad. How did you figure out what the real situation was?"

"When I was in the cemetery, I felt something was wrong. That was yesterday when I saw Mrs. Thomas at Owen's grave site. But I couldn't figure it out. I drove through again this morning before I was going to leave for Salem, then it suddenly struck me that it wasn't what I had seen, it was what I hadn't seen."

"And that was?"

"The fact that the potter's section of the cemetery was as flat as a billiard table. Sure the crosses were there, but there was no evidence of any grave having been dug in the longest while. There was a hump of earth over Thomas's site, but nothing other than some very old signs of graves at the back of potter's field that indicated anyone had ever been buried there."

"So Morrisey and the sheriff and deputy were burying them on the sheriff's land all the while Morrisey and Thomas were in office."

"I guess Bell thought he could work his way in and probably did."

"And now, *Sheriff Whitney*, you should be a shoo-in at Tuesday's election."

"With no opposition, it won't even be interesting."

"Then I can give you your Father's Day gift a day early instead of two days late. Happy Father's Day, Dad." Andi kissed her father on the cheek and pressed a small gift-wrapped box into his hand.

"What's this?"

"Open it and find out."

After tearing off the paper, Harvey lifted the lid and smiled when he saw the old, five-pointed star with the word "Sheriff" engraved on it.

Fathers, Inc.

by Robert David Chase

The noise you hear downstairs is just my mom and Sam getting ready to leave. Sam is my stepfather. They took up sailboating last summer, and now they're fanatics about it. They go every weekend.

My name is Bob. I'm fifteen. I'm the blond kid leaning out his bedroom window and waving to them down below on the flagstone patio. The sailboat is all rigged up to the trailer, and the new Mercedes sedan is all polished up and ready for a trip to the lake.

Actually, they're a little late and that's Mom's fault. She's never been exactly punctual. When my real dad was alive, that was one of the things they argued about, how she was always late. Of course, they also argued about how quickly she went through his paycheck, how her good looks seemed to attract flirtatious men at the country club, and how much my father drank. That one they argued about a lot, especially after my dad got mad at me one night and broke my ten-year-old nose with his forty-three-year-old fist. Mom got pretty hysterical, and not only threatened to divorce him, but actually got herself a lawyer. Kept her lawyer, too, till Dad started making all the usual promises about how he would go to Alcoholics Anonymous and wouldn't ever ever ever get violent with either Mom or me again. Solemn promise. So Dad moved back in, and everything went pretty well for about a month until he totaled his new red Corvette, which, as Mom had said, he couldn't afford in the first place.

"Hon?"

That's Mom now. Coming up the stairs. A little breathless.

She'll do what she always does, run past my room into the master bedroom, find the sunglasses or scarf or suntan lotion she left behind, then pop into my room and give me a quick kiss and tell me how this is the happiest time in her life.

"Be right back," she says as she scurries past my bedroom door.

In the master bedroom drawers open and close. I hear her say "darn" a couple of times and then "There it is!"

Half a minute later she comes into my room and takes my face in her hands and gives me a quick kiss on the lips.

"Did I ever tell you how happy I am?"

"Uh-huh." I grin.

She grins back. "I know you're tired of hearing it. But it's true. Sam is so wonderful to me—and he's so wonderful to you."

I nod. "I love Sam, Mom. You know I do."

"I talked to Diana Foster yesterday. She said Tommy is crazy about his stepfather, too. I'm so happy for both you kids."

"His stepfather's a great guy."

She pulls her blue silk headscarf over her blond head. "Remember Sunday is Father's Day."

I point to my closet. "I already got Sam a gift. A nice leather wallet with his initials embossed in gold."

"Oh, that's great."

"I even bought the most expensive gift-wrap they had."

She gives me another quick kiss. "Well, we're off. We'll be back early Sunday night. You be a good boy and make sure Marta gives you vegetables with your dinner." Marta's the maid.

"I will, Mom. You just have a good time."

Then she's gone, sounding like a teenager going down the stairs two at a time, then the heavy Mercedes doors are *chunking* shut, and car and sailboat are pulling out of the driveway.

Around three this afternoon I call Tommy, the kid Mom mentioned.

"How's it going?" I ask when he comes on the line.

"Greg took me hang-gliding this morning. It was really cool. Man, you couldn't ask for a better father than him."

I do that, too, call Sam my father instead of stepfather. It feels more natural.

"You think we're ever going to regret it?"

"No way," I say.

"That's the only thing that bugs me, Bob."

"What is?"

"You know, how we have to pay them a third of our income for the rest of our lives."

I sigh. Tommy goes through this sometimes. I always have to bring him back to reality.

"You remember how my old man broke my nose?"

"Yeah," he says.

"And how your old man gave your mom that venereal disease?"

"God, she was just lucky it wasn't any worse than clap."

"And how I could never have you or anybody else over because I never knew when my old man would go into one of his drunken rages and embarrass the hell out of me?"

Now he sighs. "You're right, Bob. You're absolutely right. I'm glad we did it. Greg is the perfect father for me and the perfect husband for my mom."

"Just keep that in mind."

"I will. I just start thinking about the money and . . . But no more. You're absolutely right."

I mean, at first the money sort of bugged me, too. A third of your income for the rest of your life. After I graduate from Harvard, I'll have a pretty good earning potential so The Company will make out pretty darn well on me. And on Tommy.

But it's been worth it. Ever since Whit Laidlaw in tenth grade told me about The Company a couple of years ago, my life's been great.

They did everything he said they would. Arranged to kill my father in a hit-and-run accident that was never solved. Arranged to find the perfect mate—not only good-looking and well-adjusted but also wealthy—for my mom. And arranged to give Sam a crash course in how to keep his stepson happy, starting with a new sports car and an American Express card. And what did Sam get out of it? Well, he was one of those guys who got his heart broken a lot. He was looking for an appealing, intelligent and faithful mate, which is just what he found in my mom. All I had to do was sign the lifelong contract they sent me in the mail.

"Wow," Tommy says on the other end of the phone.

"Wow what?"

"Greg, man. You know what he's doing?"

"Huh-uh. What?"

"He's shining up that new motorcycle he bought me yesterday."

"See what I mean? Aren't you glad you signed that contract?"

Tommy laughs. "I sure am, man. I sure am."

We wrap it up saying that I'll meet him at the mall Cineplex around seven tonight. There's a Stallone picture we both want to see.

After hanging up, I climb up on my bed and stretch out. A nap is always nice on a lazy summer afternoon.

Just before I close my eyes, I look at the framed photo of Sam I have on my desk.

You couldn't ask for a better father if you created him yourself.

Playground

by Daniel Ransom

Last night I had the dream again. Back in prison. In my cell. The guy in the bunk above me, cutting his throat with his homemade knife, and the hot blood starting to spatter over the side and hit me on the face, waking me up. Wanting more than ever to be out of the slam, but knowing I had six long years to go before they would parole me. Or at least that's what all the jail house lawyers were predicting.

Even the noises were in the dream. The noises of prison at night. Laughing. Crying. Snoring. Guy using the john. Couple of guys having moist sex. Clamping my hands on my ears. Trying as I tried every night to block out all the sounds. All of them. To exist in some dark soundless state like one of those sensory deprivation chambers that were so fashionable back in the eighties.

Yeah, that's what I wanted. Limbo. No smirking guards. No leering black bully who wanted my bod. No sad-sack cellmate who couldn't handle the notion that his old lady had dumped him and was marrying his brother. So he cut his throat ...

Now everything is utterly different.

April afternoon. Sunny. 80 degrees. Apple blossoms sweet on the air. Grade school playground. Red brick building. Several classes playing outdoors for recess, *thwock* of volley ball, *whap* of softball, *wunk* of tennis ball. And Pom Pom pull away. And jacks. And marbles. And young pretty teachers that the boys just can't help having crushes on.

She sees me then, all big blue eyes and pigtails and patent leather shoes and a very earnest seven years old.

She hesitates there by the open door, not more than twenty feet from where I stand on the sidewalk.

She whispers to her girl friend and then points in my direction. Her friend runs over to where one of the young pretty teachers stands . . .

I shouldn't be here. I know. If my parole officer ever heard that I was hanging around a grade school playground . . .

The little girl, the one I've come to see, Sara her name is, can hear me from where she stands so I raise my voice and say, "Hi."

"You're the man from before, aren't you?"

I smile. "From before?"

"Last week."

"Well, I guess I am."

"I told Mrs. Stevenson all about you. How you followed me home that day. She said you were a bad man."

"Well, I certainly wouldn't want to argue with Mrs. Stevenson."

"She said she'd call Officer Friendly."

"That's nice."

"He comes to our school all the time."

And then Mrs. Stevenson, who was perhaps the prettiest of them all, is there suddenly, standing next to Sara and watching me.

"I thought we had an agreement, Mr. Hamilton," she says.

"He's a bad man, isn't he, Mrs. Stevenson?" Sara says.

"Why don't you go play bean bags with Doris, honey? I'll talk to Mr. Hamilton."

"You think we should call Officer Friendly?"

"Not right now, sweetie."

Sara gives me a long, final stare, one that said I was just the sort of man Officer Friendly couldn't wait to get his hands on, and then drifts over to where Doris is pitching bean bags.

Mrs. Stevenson comes closer to me and says, "You're not keeping your word."

"I just wanted to see her one more time," I say. "She was only two months old when it happened. I just hope she doesn't suspect—"

Mrs. Stevenson says, "She's seven years old now, Mr. Hamilton. She's too young and innocent to suspect anything." Anger gleams in her brown eyes. "Now I want you to leave and never come back. Next time, I'll call the police. And I mean it."

"But I'm her father, I've got a right—"

"No, you don't, Mr. Hamilton. You have no right to see her, not after the way you beat her mother to death."

Manslaughter it had been. Because I'd been so drunk, I guess. And because my father was a prominent banker who'd been able to afford a good lawyer.

"As far as she knows, the man and woman who adopted her are her real parents. If you have any feeling for her at all, Mr. Hamilton, you'll let her go right on believing that."

"I guess with Father's Day coming up and all, I just thought—"

"Good-bye, Mr. Hamilton. Remember that next time, I call the police."

Then she's gone, back to the laughter and scent of apple blossoms and the high silver spray of the boys playing with the water fountain.

And then I take my last look at Sara, so much like her mother already, so much like the woman who that dark and terrible night so long, long ago had caused me to strike her until my knuckles were broken.

Mrs. Stevenson glances over at me one more time.

Just as I start to leave, I feel someone watching me, and when I turn I see Sara there in the hot, dusty air of the playground, staring at me as if she had finally figured it all out.

I do just what Mrs. Stevenson wanted me to do. I leave, and quickly.

Long Lonesome Roads

by Ed Gorman

1

They get wilder all the time. This morning for instance, soon as I saw her stuffing an expensive bar of bath soap into her purse, I went over and made the pinch. She was, after all, a shoplifter; and I was, after all, a security guard.

She was maybe fifty, wearing a fancy mauve-colored suede coat that probably cost more than the car I drive, and the kind of preppy button-down shirt and pleated paisley skirt that college girls have started wearing again. Pretty enough in a brittle way until you looked closer. And then there was something . . . wrong.

"I'd appreciate it if you'd take your hand off me."

She said it very loudly so that many people in the busy department store aisle turned to look at us.

I stage-whispered, "Ma'am, all I want is for you to walk to the manager's office with me. C'mon, now, let's not make a scene."

She slapped me, then, hard enough to fill my eyes momentarily with starry skies.

Even before I could see again, even before I had calmed myself enough not to return her slap, I clamped onto her wrist again, gave her a slight tug, and pulled her down the aisle.

We had a real audience now, staring, whispering, pointing. Just the sort of commotion management pays the security company I work for to avoid.

The left side of my face was still numb from where

she'd slapped me. I tugged her along harder than I probably needed to.

In the back were the elevators. When the left one dinged, and the doors rumbled open, I stood aside, let go of her wrist, and said, "After you."

"You're a jerk, you know that?"

Once again we were attracting onlookers. I gave her a slight shove aboard, got the doors closed, and punched 7. I leaned against one wall, she leaned against another.

"You stupid bastard, Dwyer."

Mention of my name brought my head up. How did she know my name? I looked at her again. Much more carefully this time. There was . . . something . . .

"Jack Dwyer."

"That's right," I said. "Jack Dwyer."

"Catholic high school."

"Yeah. So what?"

"Played forward your junior year then gave up basketball when your old man died because you had to get a part-time job."

I looked right at her. "What the hell's going on here?"

"You really think anybody could be as bad at lifting a bar of soap as I was? C'mon, Jack, gimme a break."

"You wanted me to catch you?"

"Absolutely."

"Why?"

"Just kind of get your heart started. You always were a hothead. Remember there was one older kid who always liked to tease you, really get you going? Steve Byrnes?"

Another lingering stare at her nice, pretty . . . but odd middle-class face. "Who the hell are you?"

"Stare at me a little more."

I stared at her a little more.

"Sally Byrnes," she said.

"My God."

"You remember Sally Byrnes?"

"Well, hell, yes, she was a year behind me in school."

A little more staring. "You've kind of changed. I

mean, you sort of look like her, but then you sort of don't."

"Maybe I look a little bit more like Steve than Sally."

"Well," I said, not sure how I was supposed to respond.

"That's who I am, Dwyer," she said. "Steve."

"Huh?"

"Steve, you dummy. I'm Steve. Her older brother. I had an operation." She smiled. "I wanted to pull your chain the way I used to when we played basketball. That's why I was stealing the bar of soap out there. Just to watch you get all steamed up."

But at the moment shoplifting was not the subject dominating my mind. I was slightly more interested in how and why Steve Byrnes, a good tough kid, had become a woman.

2

So twenty minutes later we're sitting in this Denny's and Doris a/k/a Steve is telling me all the stuff you have to go through to change sexes. The psychoanalysis, going two years in drag, taking hormone adjustments, and finally having what they call "reassignment surgery," which means lobbing off your poor little pee-pee. All the time she told me about this, I just kind of held on to my crotch.

"And now I'm happy."

"Well, uh, good," I said.

"Except for one thing."

"One thing."

"That's why I decided to look you up. In the book from our last reunion, it said you were a private detective."

"Well, actually I'm a security guard. I work for a private detective agency."

"But you do, you know, things?"

"Things?"

She sighed. "Do you remember much about me?"

"Some, I guess."

"After we got out of high school, I went straight into the Marines. I was still trying to prove something to myself. Anyway, then I came back to the Chicago area here and settled down and got married. My wife died of ovarian cancer about twenty years ago, so I raised our daughter alone."

"Yeah, I guess I do remember that."

"Well, I always had this problem. I mean, you've heard all the clichés. About how deep inside you really want to be a woman. Well, that's how I was. But I wasn't real sure my daughter could handle it. She was very straight arrow—cheerleader, football player boyfriend, you know."

"Yeah."

"So I decided to be merciful to both of us. I pretended to drown in a boating accident. The body was never found."

"I see."

"What I really did was fly to Denmark. Start the whole procedure." She sipped her coffee. She looked real dainty. Eerily so. God, the way I remembered Steve Byrnes, he was one of the meanest kids on the court. How could this woman be Steve Byrnes?

"She's in Chicago here," Doris said. "Husband, two kids, ten and twelve." She looked right at me. "I want her to know about me. Know I'm alive. Know what I've done. I've been in the area for a year, but I still haven't worked up nerve enough to call her."

"Call her. Tell her, yourself. Not me."

"She might freak out."

"Not if she loves you."

"That's only on Oprah, that 'not if she loves you' bullshit. My daughter probably still loves me—but as her father not her mother."

"Yeah, I guess that's probably a possibility."

"That's why I want to hire you."

"Me? For what?"

"To tell her. To go out to her place in Oak Park and

let her know the truth about her father." She smiled. "Father's Day is coming up. I mean, even though I'm no longer a man, I'm still her father if you know what I mean."

"God, Doris, I've got to be honest. I don't know what you mean. I'm trying to know what you mean, but I don't think I'll ever be able to."

"It kind of upsets you, doesn't it? That I'm a woman now and everything."

"I still want to call you Steve."

"But I'm not Steve. I never was Steve. Not really."

"It's pretty strange is all. I mean, I don't mean to hurt your feelings, Doris, but first you steal that bar of soap and then you lay all this on me and—"

"You're kind of whining, Dwyer. That's never becoming."

"I know I'm whining. It's just that—"

And then she changed, abruptly. "You think it was easy for me, you insensitive jerk?"

She might be mostly Doris, but there was some of the old Steve left in her, too. That temper of hers.

"I guess not."

"It isn't easy being a freak."

And with that, she turned and looked out the window at all the gourmets who were carrying discount coupons into Denny's front door. She was crying, and it was obvious that she didn't want to cry.

So I sat there and tried not to feel guilty, but it didn't quite work.

"Doris."

But she didn't respond.

"Doris."

Still no response.

"God, Doris, I'm sorry. I really am."

Instinctively, the way I would for a woman, I put my hand out to touch hers. Then I remembered and stopped myself. She was bringing out all my insecurities.

"Doris."

Nothing.

"Doris?"

"What?"

"I really am sorry."

She kind of snuffled, then turned back to me and said, "Think about it, Dwyer. Do you think any of us would wish this kind of life for ourselves? God, you people just don't think it through."

"I'll go see her."

"What?"

"Your daughter. I'll go see her. Tell her."

She smiled. "Oh, Dwyer, you always were a softie."

I laughed. "Is that a compliment?"

"Just be sure you tell her how much I love her."

"I will."

"And how much I want to see my grandkids again."

"I will."

"And how much I've missed her."

I nodded. "You going to give me a number where I can reach you?"

She wrote it down on a napkin, and then we walked out to the car.

"You're being a real gentleman about all this, Dwyer," she said when we reached her car. "And I appreciate it."

"Like I said, I can't do it tonight because I have to work. But tomorrow's my day off, and I'll do it then."

"Thanks, Dwyer. Thanks a lot. I really mean that."

For a moment I was scared she was going to lean over and give me a peck on the cheek. But fortunately she settled for a handshake.

3

Plotz the name was, one of those hard Slavic names that imply a nice neat yard, a sensible new car in the drive, and a reasonable amount of wages put into a savings account. Good citizens, I think they used to be called. The new name for them, given the welfare society, may be suckers.

I know you're not supposed to stereotype people that way—a lot of Slavs are slobs, I'm sure, and have not a dime in their savings accounts—but my stereotype turned out to be true.

Doris's daughter lived on a street where everybody seemed to have the same three things—noisy kids, big barking dogs, and vans to transport the kids and the dogs in. The lawns were scrupulously tended and just starting to go a deep green.

The house was a trim Cape Cod model, glaring white in the morning sun, and as I pulled in the drive, I saw a chunky but not unappealing young woman Windexing the front window inside. She wore a blue-and-white bandana on her hair and a blue work shirt and jeans too loose to be fashionable.

I pulled the car up to the two-stall garage, got out, and walked around to the front door.

She had the door open. "You're Mr. Dwyer?"

"Right."

"I'm Stephanie. C'mon in. I put some coffee on."

Up close she was much better looking, one of those very female melancholy faces that little girls always have in their First Communion pictures. She was her First Communion picture all grown up. The quick, intelligent blue eyes were especially nice.

I sat in a comfortable leather recliner while she went off to get the coffee. The furnishings, from the plum-colored divan to the discreet Chagall prints, were a little more arty than I might have expected, but not so arty that there wasn't a warmth to the room. Maybe it was all the photographs of her two tow-headed kids. The north wall was a shrine to them.

She came back with coffee, gave me mine, and seated herself primly on the edge of the couch. "So," she said. "You wanted to talk to me about my father?"

That's all I'd told on the phone earlier.

"Yes. About your father. This coffee's really good by the way."

"Oh, thanks." Pause. "Mr. Dwyer—"

"How about 'Jack?' I don't need to feel any older than I am."

A sweet little girl grin. "Tell me about it. I'm at the age where my mirror is starting to be very cruel." Pause. "He's dead."

"Your father?"

"Yes. I mean, in case you didn't know. I get calls every once in a while from guys he was in the Marines with. They don't know he died in a boating accident."

"Your father isn't dead."

There. That was the only way I knew to say it.

"What?"

"He isn't dead."

"Just who *are* you, Mr. Dwyer?"

"I went to high school with your father, played basketball with him, too. Now I work for a private investigative agency, and that's why he hired me."

"Who hired you?"

"Your father."

"My father's dead."

I sighed. "I know you're getting mad."

She shook her head. "What I'm getting, Mr. Dwyer, is suspicious. This sounds like some kind of confidence game or something."

"I can give you his phone number."

"My father's?"

"Right. You want it?"

But just then I saw her glance out the front window. I heard a car in the driveway.

"Just please sit right where you are, Mr. Dwyer," she said.

"Your husband."

She nodded.

He came tramping in the back door and called out, "I need a kiss from my beautiful bride!" and then passed through the kitchen and the dining room and walked into the living room.

"Oh, hello," he said when he saw me.

"Honey, this is Mr. Dwyer. This is Don, my husband."

He nodded.

"He's trying to make me believe that my father is still alive."

He'd been friendly enough in a tentative sort of way, but suddenly he wasn't friendly at all. Despite the gray in his hair, he looked a little boyish, tall and trim in a three-piece suit with a button-down white shirt and a sensible brown necktie. But now he wasn't friendly at all. His altar-boy face got a lot harder looking than I would have thought possible.

"My husband's a lawyer," she said.

"I used to work in the consumer fraud division in the Attorney General's office in Springfield," he said.

"This isn't a con."

"It is if you're trying to convince my wife that Stephen Byrnes is still alive."

"Well," I said, "he is and he isn't."

"Just what the hell is that supposed to mean?"

I could see him as a prosecutor—looks like a nice young college kid, but goes after you with pit-bull frenzy.

"He hired me to come out here and tell his daughter that he's alive and wants to see her."

"Why wouldn't he tell her for himself?"

The prosecutor had taken over entirely now. The wife was just a friendly witness to be called when he needed her.

"He has his reasons."

"And those reasons would be what, exactly?"

"Two years ago he had one of those operations where a man is changed into a woman."

I thought that there would be the shocked silence you hear in movie melodramas. Instead there was a harsh burst of laughter from Stephanie. "My father, changed into a woman? If you knew my father at all, you'd know he was a decorated Marine—for one thing, and a very good athlete, for another. Very good."

From my red windbreaker—on good days I still think of myself as James Dean's kid brother—I took the slip of paper with Doris's phone number on it.

"Why don't you call her?"

" 'Her.' I'm supposed to be calling my father who is now a 'her?' " She was starting to get shrill, which meant she was starting to get scared, which meant that she was starting to believe me.

"I'm sorry."

"Right," she said.

"Dwyer, why don't you get up and I'll walk you out to your car," Don said.

I stood up and walked over to the couch and handed her the slip of paper. "This is where . . . he . . . works. He should be there now. Ask for Doris."

"Oh, that's very funny, Dwyer. Ask for Doris."

She jerked the piece of paper from my hand. Her pretty eyes shone with tears. "Doris. Right. Doris."

"C'mon," he said, taking my arm like an arresting officer making a pinch, steering me toward the front door. "We'll talk outside."

The day was sweet with bird song and a gentle breeze just right for flying kites. I wanted to be a kid again, at least for an hour or two.

"You know I can check you out," Don Plotz said as we stood in his driveway.

"And you would if you were smart."

"This still sounds like a con to me."

"Yeah, like the ones you used to run up against in the Attorney General's office."

"Something funny about working in the Attorney General's office?"

"I guess it was just the way you sounded. So reverent and all."

"I don't like you, Dwyer."

"Well, I'm not exactly falling in love here myself."

We were leaning against his new tan Volvo. He looked away, was quiet for a time, then swung his head back to me.

"Is this for real, Dwyer?"

"It's for real."

"He became a woman?"

"Well, he became what he is now. Whatever that is. He thinks he's a woman, anyway, and I'll take him at his word, the poor bastard." I thought of how sad Doris had been back at the restaurant. "It couldn't have been very easy for him."

"God, this is crazy." He shook his head. "I mean, you assume that somebody's dead and then . . . And this on top of it."

He wasn't exactly making sense, but I didn't blame him. This wasn't the sort of incident you could make much sense of.

He sighed deeply. "You know, he never used to like me. Never thought I was smart enough for his daughter. I got let go from a couple of law firms when I was younger. That's the reason I went to the Attorney General's office. I wasn't having much luck here."

He shook his head—stared off at the pure blue sky, against which a hawk was just now soaring.

"He won't believe I have my own law firm now. I mean, getting that money awhile back. I'm not doing great yet, but I'm doing all right." He looked at me and smiled. "My wife wasn't kidding you."

"About what?"

"About Steve. He really was an athletic guy."

"Well, now he's an athletic woman."

"This is crazy," he said again. He'd be saying it for the next couple months at least.

"I know. But have her call him at that number, will you? Whatever else, he's still her father."

He smiled sourly. "Just in time for Father's Day, is that the idea?"

"You better ask Doris that."

We shook hands, said a few more words, and I walked down the drive to my car. In ten minutes, I was at a drive-up phone calling Doris.

"Did she start crying?"

"She thought I was working some kind of scam."

She laughed. "She was always like that, even as a little girl. Suspicious."

"Doris, this isn't going to be easy for her."

"I know."

"And when she talks to you ... well, she could be kind of mad."

"I expected a little of that. You said Don was there?"

"He seemed to be a little better able to handle it than your daughter."

"That surprises me, Dwyer. He's not very bright. He got fired from three different law firms before he was thirty."

I sighed. "Look, Doris, none of us are exactly perfect human beings. Your son-in-law may not be the brightest guy in the world, but he seems decent enough."

"Judgmental."

"Huh?"

"I've always been too judgmental. You're right, Don's a decent, hard-working guy, and I should be glad that my daughter married him."

"Good luck on everything," I said.

"I'll send you a check."

"It's a freebie."

"But—"

"Good luck," I said and hung up.

4

I drew a week at a discount store that mostly sold western-style clothes, which meant that I had to listen to country-western music all week. If there's a hell, it's waking up in a tiny little locked room with a record player and one album, *The Best of Hank Williams, Jr.* Talk about suffering.

On the third day of my gig I saw a lady friend of some ten years ago, and so, floating adrift on the cold dark waters of middle-age, we tried a night at her apartment with beer and Domino's pizza and a rental tape of Bogie and Gloria Grahame in *In A Lonely Place*, which is in some ways my own biography. Afterward we had a little quick nervous sex in her dark perfume-smelling cubbyhole of a bedroom, and afterward she cried and told me what a bastard he was, the guy she'd been living with six years, the guy who had three weeks ago walked out on her. I just held her and let her cry. Maybe next time I got my heart broken, she'd return the favor.

I got home just before dawn, but decided not to lie down because I'd never be able to wake up again in two hours. I kicked Mr. Coffee in the ass and set him to work and right after then, the phone rang.

"Mr. Dwyer?" A woman.

"Uh-huh."

"This is Stephanie Plotz."

Talk about two names that don't go together— Stephanie and Plotz.

"Right."

Then, being a detective and all, I thought: Maybe something's wrong here, her calling me at 6:04 A.M.

"My . . . father."

"Yes?"

"Somebody killed him."

"What?"

"His . . . friend . . . just called me. I wondered if you'd meet Don and me over there." She then gave me an address.

"Half hour, forty-five minutes, max."

"Thank you." Beat. "I'm sorry I was such a bitch the other day."

"No harm done."

"Somebody murdered him, Mr. Dwyer. Murdered him." Then she started crying so hard that Don had to take the receiver from her and say, "Please come over."

5

Knowing that the first wave of crime-scene folks would make talking to Stephanie impossible—they'd have a lot of questions for the deceased's daughter—I ate a large breakfast on a small budget at a place where they catered to truckers who seemed bent on solving the nation's problems, largely through the process of execution, which would be televised to every home in the country.

From there I called in to the security company, said I was taking the day off, and to have one of the subs cover me, and that I'd see them tomorrow.

The place I wanted was one of those old Victorian mansions, complete with spires and turrets, that had been turned into a boutique, in this case a business for interior decoration, Lochinvar, Inc.

The driveway that wound from the entrance gate to the front porch was filled with police cars of various kinds, crime lab vans, TV vans, and a Volvo I recognized from the Plotz driveway.

I stood inside the vestibule, thinking that this was the sort of place Arthur Conan Doyle had probably lived in, parquet floor, prim flocked wallpaper, a winding staircase, a hushed and somewhat shadowy air through the place. At least this was the impression you got in the vestibule. The rest of the house was different, brightly lighted rooms filled with carpet samples and paint swatches and dozens and dozens of color photographs showing homes and offices that Lochinvar had decorated. There were also some very chic pieces of furniture for sale. I lifted the price tag of a couch. No wonder I shopped at Kmart. The price for this baby was six thousand dollars.

The cops looked like infidels in a place like this, big and noisy and bold in a space that called for delicacy and quiet and tact.

Doris was still on the floor, a sheet carefully tugged over her. The wound had apparently been in the chest. At least that's where most of the darkening blood was.

I recognized Dave Kilmer immediately. We'd gone to the Police Academy together back in the days of marijuana and protest marches, when being a cop wasn't so popular.

Someone had sneaked into his house one night and

robbed him of his youth. His hair was gone, his eyes had pouches, his cheeks had jowls, his suit coat had the impossible task of trying to cover a wriggling baby whale.

He saw me and nodded for me to follow him out to the front porch. On the steps he took a deep breath of gray, overcast air and said, "Fags."

"Fags?"

"Inside. Fags. All three of them."

"Live and let live, I say."

He gave me the bad cop eye. "Yeah, but you haven't heard the worst of it."

"No?"

He shook his square bald head. "The dead woman, Doris?"

"Right."

"He used to be a guy."

I didn't want to spoil the fun he was having shocking me so I said, "Aw, bullshit."

"Honest and truly, Dwyer. He had one of those operations."

"How'd he die?"

"You don't care that he used to be a guy?"

"Right now, I'd rather know how he died."

Dave Kilmer shrugged. For him this was the boring part. He still wanted to talk about sex change operations. "This . . . person . . . had the habit of coming into the business here very early some mornings. This . . . person . . . was a sales rep for the company. Sort of laid out the day in advance before all the phones started ringing. And this morning, well, somebody shot this person." He looked at me and made a pained face. "You know those operations over in Denmark? They cut your whanger off. Can you imagine that?"

"Any suspects?"

He shrugged again. "Probably a burglar, the way I figure it."

"Yeah?"

"Back window smashed. They'd been having some

problems with their alarm system anyway, according to the head flit in there."

"So it looks good for burglary?"

"According to Chad, the head flit, there's more than three thousand dollars missing from the cash box in his office. That's why this . . . person was shot."

Kilmer's name was called from somewhere inside. "Better get back," he said. Then he poked me with a playful finger in the belly. "You're putting on a little weight."

Here was this forty-eight-year-old who looked like seventy telling me that I was the one falling apart.

"Well, I wish I could lose weight the way you did, Kilmer."

"Oh, yeah?" he said, obviously preparing himself to be flattered.

"Yeah, when all your hair fell out, you must've lost what, about twenty pounds?"

He gave me a grimace and vanished.

6

Forty-five minutes later, as the official people began to drift away, I found Stephanie and Don Plotz.

They were in a tiny kitchen area at the back of the house, having coffee with a slight, handsome man dressed in a tailored white shirt and tailored black slacks. With his dyed wavy black hair and elegant movements, he looked like a fifties rock star who was preparing a comeback.

"This is Chad Mally," Stephanie said. "Chad, this is Jack Dwyer."

He had a grip that made me wince with pain. He wanted to demonstrate that he was a strong guy, probably in all respects. He'd just made a believer out of me.

"Why don't you join us?" Don Plotz said, pushing forth the only unoccupied chair.

I sat down and pulled myself up to the table. Stephanie poured me hot coffee and pushed the cup over to me.

I glanced at walls that were like a minimuseum of black framed photographs, again showing various sites the firm had decorated.

Chad Mally said, "All these are jobs that Doris sold in the last year." His voice got rough. "We'll never replace her, that's for sure."

At the hint he might cry, the three of us sort of put our heads down so we wouldn't have to watch him. But he caught himself. "The police tell me that a lot of burglaries never get solved. They said the same thing is true even for some murders. Can you imagine that, murderers walking around free and clear?"

The hint of tears again. But he stopped himself. "I think I'll walk around and see what's going on." He stood up. "Nice to meet you, Mr. Dwyer."

"Same here." I was hoping he wouldn't throttle my hand again.

When he was gone, Stephanie said, "Chad and my father lived together."

"I see."

"Lovers, I mean."

I nodded.

"God, I feel so guilty," she said. "Here my father is dead, and I'm still disapproving of the way he lived."

"Honey, it's going to take a while to sort out our feelings," Don said. "That's all." He wore his lawyer white button-down shirt and his lawyer red power tie and his lawyer blue three-piece suit. But for all that, there was still a beaten air about the man. He carried it with him like a faint but sour odor.

"He's right," I said. "You had a shock, learning about your father the way you did. And then him dying on top of it."

"I just wish I'd been nicer to him when he called yesterday." She paused. "I wasn't mean or anything, but I wasn't very warm, either. He started to explain about the operation he'd had and I—" Her eyes filled with quick little-girl tears. "I told him I didn't want to know anything about it. That must have really hurt him, after all he'd been through, I mean."

Don put a long arm around her and drew her to him, and for the first time I liked the guy. He knew how to comfort somebody else, which is a rare enough quality in any of us, but especially so in someone who seemed as dull as Don.

He held her tight, and in that moment she was not only his wife but his daughter and his sister as well.

He gave a little tilt of the head that said I should leave now. I agreed. I left. Stephanie stayed tucked into her husband's shoulder. I didn't blame her a bit.

7

"You knew about his operation?"

"Of course. We slept together."

"Did anybody else know?"

"Not so far as I know."

"Was he handling it pretty well? Being a woman, I mean?"

"Let me ask you a question, Mr. Dwyer."

"All right."

"I spoke with Detective Kilmer."

"Uh-huh."

"And he said that if he had to bet, he'd bet it was a burglar who killed Doris."

"I see."

"So why did you hang around here long after the police left to ask me these questions?"

"Because I don't think a burglar killed him."

"And you, I suppose, know a lot more than the police?"

"Kilmer was just giving you an educated guess. That doesn't mean he was right." I leaned forward toward his desk. "Now let me ask you another question. You lived with Doris and presumably were involved with her, but

I don't see any signs of regret or anything like it. All I see is anger."

"A lot of people get angry when someone dies. They detest the whole notion of death."

"They get angry, but not this kind of angry. You haven't said one nice thing about Doris."

"That's enough, Mr. Dwyer. That's quite enough."

We were in his office on the second floor. The sun had come out and cast long shadows across the Queen Anne furnishings that filled the quiet, pleasant room. I sensed that Chad and I were not in danger of ever becoming good buddies.

"I resent you accusing me of his murder."

"I'm not accusing you of anything."

"Of course you are." He glanced at his watch then. He still looked like a faded rock star who'd kept himself in shape until you looked at the eyes—old eyes, booze eyes, sad eyes.

"I have an appointment I have to keep."

"If I have any more questions, you mind if I call you, Mr. Mally?"

"Yes," he said, pushing back from his desk. "Yes, I mind very much."

I made the mistake of shaking hands good-bye. He ground the bones in my fingers to fine white powder.

8

I was in the vestibule, ready to go outside again, when somebody whispered, "Just a minute."

I turned to see a young man with a formidable gold earring hanging from his right lobe and an expensive blue cashmere sweater tied around the neck of his blue shirt. His gray slacks and black loafers completed his male model ensemble. He didn't seem all that happy about being as pretty as he was.

"Step out on the porch," he said softly.

I stepped out on the porch. He followed, closing the

door behind him. "Chad is always spying. He'd kick my ass if he knew I was talking to you."

I wanted a cup of coffee. I also wanted a cigarette, even though I'd quit a couple of years ago.

"They fought all the time," the young man said.

"They?"

"Doris and Chad."

"I see. About anything in particular?"

"Oh, God, Chad really would kill me." He paused. "They were having some sort of argument about Channel 3."

"The TV station?"

"Right."

"But you don't know why?"

He shook his ash blond head. "Afraid I don't."

"You think there's any way Chad might have killed him?"

He hesitated, blue eyes furtive. "Well, he has a horrible temper, Chad does."

"Horrible enough for murder?"

"I suppose. But then I suppose we all do." He leaned closer and said, "But there's something else you should know, too—"

And just then I saw Chad in the glass of the door behind us. He jerked it open and pushed past the young man so he could shout in my face.

"If you want to pick Rick up for a date, Mr. Dwyer, I'm afraid you'll have to wait till he's done working for the day." He glared at Rick. "You get back inside, young man, and I mean right now."

Rick gave me a sickly, shamed look and went meekly inside.

"I don't want to see you again or hear from you again, Mr. Dwyer. Is that clear?"

"Clear."

"And now I want you to leave."

I looked at him a long moment, feeling sorry for him despite myself. His wasn't an easy life, nor had it probably ever been, so maybe he deserved a little more time at being an asshole than most of us did.

"Take care of yourself, Chad," I said and went down his stairs.

9

On the way over to Channel 3 I did what I always do when I'm starting a case—phoned the Credit Bureau and asked them to run checks on Chad as well as Mr. and Mrs. Don Plotz.

While the bureau knows all kinds of things about you it shouldn't—all kinds of things that are strictly illegal to know—it also is one of my main sources of information. Run a credit check on somebody and you get a real good notion of that person's life.

After that I ate a hamburger at Hardee's and watched a bunch of tots in their bright spring outfits trundle after their moms, and of course I got sentimental about my own kids and wished they were that age again, and then I drove over to Channel 3.

A year earlier a guy with a gun had managed to get into the news studio and hold one of the anchor men hostage for half an hour. The whole thing had been televised of course. Eventually somebody took the gun from the guy and led him away to an ambulance, but ever since Channel 3 resembled a fortress.

I went through three different guards before I got to the news director's office and asked him if anybody on his staff had been doing a story on Doris.

"The transsexual?"

So he did know. I nodded.

"Talk to Wendy Ayers. Down the hall with the rest of the reporters."

At this time of day most reporters were out on assignment. I recognized Wendy even from the back. She had long blond hair and the plain earnest looks of an overly sensitive folk singer. She always got the stories about starving old ladies and kittens who comfort the dying.

She looked awfully nice till you studied her eyes for a while. Benito Mussolini must have had eyes like those.

It was a room filled with small cubicles, like a sweat shop where they sell diamonds over the phone. In a couple of adjacent rooms people were editing video tape, the chittering chipmunk noises of fast forward filling the air.

I told Wendy who I was.

"I don't think you're a cop, are you, Mr. Dwyer?"

"Private cop."

"Ah." She was not impressed. "I'm not sure I should say anything to you. In light of the fact that Doris has been murdered."

"I'm trying to help his daughter."

" 'Her.' "

"Huh?"

" 'Her' daughter. Doris was a her."

"Oh. Right. Her."

"You didn't approve of Doris, I take it?"

My period had just kicked in. "Look, Wendy, I don't have any time for all this politically correct horseshit, all right? I used to play basketball with this tough kid named Steve Byrnes—then one day twenty-five years later, he shows up and he's Doris. I'm too old and too stupid to make sense of any of that. I'm not a wise man, and I don't pretend to be. But I do know Steve was a pretty sad person whatever sex he was, and I also know that his daughter would like to know who killed him and why."

"You're really pissed."

"Yes, I am." My breath came out ragged. "Now are you going to help me or not?"

She looked at me and shook her head, still not wanting to help me, but apparently figuring that by telling me a few things she'd at least get rid of me. I've always enjoyed being a nuisance.

"Doris was going to come out."

"Come out?"

"I was going to interview her on camera, and she was going to tell her story."

"I see."

"That's why she wanted to talk to her daughter—prepare her and the grandchildren."

"I see."

"We were going to show photographs of her life. Show that outwardly she'd been a nice normal midwestern boy who had this frantic desire to be a woman. Then Doris really started getting some static."

"Oh? From whom?"

"Have you met Chad?"

"Uh-huh."

"He's a real prick, Chad is. He was afraid that if Doris revealed herself as a transsexual, Chad's entire interior decoration business would be ruined. Chad said that the public is willing to tolerate gays, but that they would never tolerate or do business with a transsexual."

So Doris had been an outcast even among homosexuals.

"Doris told you this?" I asked.

"Ummm-hmmm. And I saw it for myself."

"Saw it?"

"In the parking lot right outside. Doris drove over one night to start preparing the interview, and Chad pulled in right behind her. Slapped her very hard."

"In front of you?"

"In front of me, yes, but he was so mad I don't think he was even aware I was there. Then he called her a lot of names. And threatened her."

"What kind of threat?"

"You know, 'If you keep this up, Doris, you'll regret it and I promise you.' That kind of thing."

"When was the last time you saw Doris?"

She thought a moment. "Day and a half ago. Late lunch."

"Doris say anything in particular?"

"Just that she still wanted to do the piece, but that Chad was really hassling her."

I nodded. "Thanks. This helps me a lot."

She smiled. "We're both kind of crabby today, I guess."

I smiled back. "Unfortunately, I'm kind of crabby like this most of the time."

"Yeah." She laughed. "That's what I figured."

10

I went for coffee and called the Credit Bureau. My contact had gotten busy all of a sudden and hadn't had time to use the computer yet. "Hey, at the rates I'm paying you?" She laughed. "You're such an asshole, Dwyer."

By the time I reached Chad's, all of the official vehicles had gone. There were just two cars in the lot to the west of the house. The Victorian looked cold as a banker's heart looming against the overcast sky.

I went inside where I found my pal Chad in the vestibule.

"I told you I'd call the police and I meant it," he said.

"You do that, Chad, and I'll tell them how you tried to stop Doris from telling her story to Channel 3."

"You bastard. You don't have any right to snoop around like this."

"Did you kill him?"

"You bastard. You fucking bastard."

With that, he turned around and mounted the narrow, winding staircase to the second floor and his office.

I followed, my steps making a hollow echo in the big empty house.

He went in and sat behind his desk. He leaned to the right, opened a desk drawer, and took out a small pistol. "I have every right to use this. You're trespassing."

"Chad, they'd get you for first-degree murder if you shot me now." I paused, looked at the gun and spoke in a gentler tone. "Chad, if you killed him, why not make it easy on yourself. Just say so."

He looked down at the gun in his hand. He no longer

looked angry. He just looked tired and sad. He put the gun back in the drawer. "You may find this hard to believe, but I loved Doris. I was only trying to protect her."

"From going public?"

"Most people are reluctantly starting to accept homosexuals—not like them, but at least tolerate them. But even so, we still get beaten up and discriminated against. You know that. But a transsexual—" He shook his head.

"An even rougher road, huh?"

"Much rougher. Doris would have become a ... laughingstock. Everybody would have known who she was. I'm sure she would have been besieged by obscene phone calls and the whole bit."

"So you wanted to stop her for her own sake?"

"I hear what you're saying, Mr. Dwyer. You're asking if I was solely concerned with Doris. Not solely, no. I loved Doris and I didn't want to see her hurt in any way—she'd had a much tougher life than I had, that whole frustration of wanting to be another sex—but I also had my business in mind. I've worked my ass off for twenty years to get this business where I want it. I don't want to lose it. And being in the public eye that way, well, Doris could have done the business some harm. No doubt about it."

"Were you ever physically violent with her?"

"A few times, I suppose. Nothing really serious."

"I'm not sure what that means."

"It means I shoved her a few times, and that once I slapped her, but that was the extent of it."

"Did you kill her?"

"No, Mr. Dwyer, I didn't kill her." He started the glancing-bat-his-watch routine. "I really need to get some work done."

"If you want to talk about it, you can call me," I said, pushing my business card across his desk. "If it happened when you were angry, unpremeditated—"

"You really think I killed Doris, don't you?"

"Yes, I do."

"I don't believe this." He sighed and waved a dismissive hand. "Just get the hell out of here."

I stood up. "If you want the name of a good lawyer, I'll be happy to give you one."

He didn't even want to look at me any longer. He turned his head and stared out the window at the fine Chicago afternoon.

In the vestibule the young man I'd spoken with before came up and said, "I was going to tell you something else when Chad made me go back inside."

"Oh?"

He nodded. "I come in early sometimes, too. The way Doris did, I mean. I have to schedule everybody's time, and it can be a real bitch." He paused. "Anyway, I got here early this morning. And just as I was pulling up, I saw somebody pulling away."

"Did you know who it was?"

He nodded again. "A guy in a tan Volvo."

"A guy?"

"Same guy in the framed photo Doris kept up in her office, her son-in-law. Don, I think his name is."

"And this was when?"

"Maybe six-twenty, six-twenty-five."

"You tell the cops this?"

"No."

"Why not?"

"Cops beat up a friend of mine not too long ago— raided a gay joint just to have a little fun. So I'm not real keen on cops at the moment."

"Not all cops are like that, you know."

"Probably not."

"Thanks for the information."

"Chad's an asshole, but he's not a killer."

"Thanks again."

11

On the way over to the Plotz home, I stopped at a Denny's for black coffee and apple pie, the same fuel I used to pack in my wintry days as a Chicago cop. I phoned my friend at the Credit Bureau, my friend who would never go out with me no matter how unsubtly I hinted that I'd like to go out with her, and she gave me three reports.

One of the reports told me very simply who the killer was—and even gave me the motive. God, it was something I should have been able to figure out by myself.

"This is great," I said. "Listen, why don't I take you out for a big steak and some wine tonight? We'll celebrate." That sounded like a pretty sneaky way to get her to go out, a celebration. I was a mastermind.

"You don't have to do that, Dwyer. Just send a check to my apartment the way you usually do."

"Do you think we'll ever go out, Linda? I mean really be honest with me so I can quit torturing myself."

"You're too crazy, Dwyer. You remind me too much of my first husband."

My curse. A lot of women have said that to me. How I remind them of their first husbands. The ones they divorced.

"Well, then, thanks for the help."

"Don't be mad."

"I'm not mad. Just humiliated."

"Take care of yourself, Dwyer. I worry about you. I really do."

12

The tan Volvo stood in the driveway of the Plotz home when I pulled up. From my glove compartment I took my old .38 Special, the one I'd had in my cop days.

Stephanie answered the door. She wore a man's blue button-down shirt and jeans. Her hair was tied back in a ponytail. She would have looked younger except for her eyes. She'd been crying.

"Hi."

"Hi, Stephanie. Is Don home?"

"He is but he's . . . asleep."

"I need to talk to him."

"Apparently, you don't hear very well. I said he was

asleep." She snuffled up some tears, wiping the back of her hand against her nose, little-girl style.

"Cut the crap, Stephanie. Go get him. I'll wait in the living room."

She glared at me a long moment, shook her head, then went off to get Don.

I went in and sat down in the leather recliner.

Don came out in less than a minute. Stephanie was right behind, watching him like a kid afraid her parent was going to do something crazy.

"I don't like you talking to my wife that way."

"I was rude. I'm sorry."

"I also don't have anything to say to you."

I sighed. "Don, let's make it easy for each other, all right?"

"What's that supposed to mean?"

"Go sit on the couch and I'll tell you."

"You're ordering me around in my own home?"

"Spare me the melodrama, Don. Just sit down and shut up a minute." I looked at Stephanie.

She nodded for Don to go sit down on the couch. She sat down right next to him.

"The other day when I was out here," I said, "you told me how you'd gotten some money a while back and that you went into law practice for yourself. I should have figured out where you got the money. When Steve faked his drowning, you and Stephanie got his life insurance—$300,000. I checked on it today. But even so, you haven't done very well, Don. Not very well at all. You've got two mortgages on this place, and one of your former clients is suing you for incompetence. You're in big trouble. But you'd be in even bigger trouble if the insurance company made you pay back the $300,000 because Steve turned up alive. That's why you killed him, Counselor. You couldn't afford to pay the money back. But if you'd done some checking, my friend, you would have found that only in fifty percent of cases like these do people pay the money back. The insurance companies forfeit rather than go through a long court battle. It's cheaper that way."

He sat with his head in his hands. Stephanie rubbed his neck and watched me. "Don isn't incompetent, Mr. Dwyer. He's just unlucky. Some people are, you know; unlucky, I mean. Like that cartoon character that always had a black cloud hanging over his head? That's how Don's been all his life."

She wasn't his wife now or even his girl friend. She was his mom.

She rubbed his neck some more.

I just sat there, watching them. They cared reverently for each other, and in these circumstances that was hard to watch because very soon now he would be in prison.

"You want me to phone the police?"

"No, thanks, Mr. Dwyer," she said, still working his neck muscles. She smiled sadly. "I'll turn myself in." The quick dead smile again. "You know when I called you after they found my father? I thought that would be a perfect cover. Why would the guilty person ask you to find the killer? I guess I'm not that smart."

I started to say something, but she stopped me. "When I spoke to my father the other day, I was really mortified at what he told me, especially the part about going on Channel 3. I thought of what that kind of publicity would do to our family, especially to our girls. And to be honest, I also thought of how we might have to return the insurance money. Most of it's gone. We're in terrible shape."

Don's hands fell away from his face. Tears darkened his eyes. "Don't say any more, honey."

"Let's get it over with," she said.

"But—"

"Please," she said. "Please." She leaned over and kissed him tenderly on the cheek. Then she turned her attention back to me.

"My father mentioned how he liked to go in early. I couldn't sleep. I left the house early and went over to Chad's offices. My father was there. We argued. He was going to Channel 3 no matter what I said. I got so angry that I shot him with the gun I'd brought along. I'd just wanted to scare him a little, so he'd see how much I was against his going public. But then I . . . shot him. I was in a kind of daze. I called Don. He came and got me. I was lying in the backseat, sobbing all the way home."

Which explained why Chad's assistant saw only Don in the car that morning.

"I really didn't mean to kill him."

"I don't suppose you did." I sighed and rubbed the back of my own neck. "It's one hell of a mess, I'll say that."

"I still can't believe that my own father had that kind of operation."

I stood up. "I'll give you twenty-four hours to turn yourself in. If you haven't done it by then, I'll do it for you. In twenty-four hours, maybe you can pull some things together. Prepare your kids and everything."

Don said, "I appreciate that, Dwyer."

He was holding his wife now, much as she'd been holding him, with great fond care. She was starting to cry in little bursts, like an engine working itself up to full capacity.

By the time I reached the front door, she was sobbing.

I got in my car and drove away. It was a beautiful spring afternoon with soft silken sunlight and monarch butterflies the size of fly swatters, but somehow I wasn't in the proper mood to appreciate it all. It would take a little while.

Roses Are Red,
You're Dead

by Richard Acton

The cold of February in Midwest City is different from
the damp cold of Norwich in England, where I normally
teach criminal law and evidence. Except for the static
electricity from the dry winter air, I like the weather
here and my life as a visiting professor at Midwest
University.

The University has put me in the Riverside Inn by the
students' union. I am very comfortable, but every time
I meet a fellow guest, hands are extended and blue
sparks jump. I consult Bridget Shannon, my waitress,
about the customs of this area and about most other
things as well. She has lived in Midwest City, a small,
intimate university town, all her life. She enters eagerly
into my conspiracy against the cholesterol police and
brings me fried eggs every morning in the hotel coffee
shop.

I feel rather sorry for Bridget, and I can't say why. I
suppose she is the same age as me, around forty, and
yet she seems older. She is good-looking enough, small
and redheaded, freckled, in fact very Irish. But she has
a sadness about her that sometimes she cannot hide. She
has told me that she was married to a businessman, but
they divorced after their son was born. Her son works
in a local business.

This morning I suddenly realized tomorrow was Valentine's Day, so I decided I must get a card for Jane
Schultz. Jane works in the University library, and we

have dinner together at least once a week or go to a film. When I first asked her out, I hoped for a romance, but that was not what she wanted, and so we've turned into brother and sister. She is the ideal companion—quick, funny, and kind. She is a blue-eyed blonde and seems to be related to all of the many people of German descent in Midwest City. Jane has kept me from being lonely and thoroughly deserves a valentine.

When Bridget brought my fried eggs, I asked her where I could get a valentine card. She thought carefully and then made her diagnosis. "Go to Gorman's Drug Store on West Street," she said firmly. "They have wonderful cards."

I decided to go at lunch time and set off for the law school. I always study the graffiti in the tunnel under the railway bridge on my walk. Today, in red, somebody had scrawled, "Disarm America." Somebody else had written in blue, "Guns are a constitutional right." The debate made me think of my forthcoming class. I have to read up on the American constitutional cases desperately each day before I confront my students.

When I reached the law school building, for the sake of my considerable figure I took the stairs to my fourth-floor office. I love my office. United States and northwestern law reports surround the walls, and to amuse the students, I keep my English barrister's wig and gown on the back of the door.

I decided to telephone Jane Schultz and ask her out to dinner that night. She sounded frantically busy, but accepted my invitation. She teased me about my girth, so we agreed to meet at a healthful salad bar in town. I often wonder if "health" is an American euphemism for "fear of death." Anyway, you can cheat at salad bars because the variety is so remarkable.

Then I went for coffee and donuts in the student lounge. I like the students enormously, but, goodness, they are serious. Although I beg them to call me Robert, they always call me Professor Lindsey. The faculty are the opposite. They all call me Bob, which makes me cringe.

The students talked politics and sports, and I did my best to join in. I mentioned that I wanted to buy a valentine card. The students insisted that I go to Bain's Hallmark in the downtown mall, where you inevitably meet everybody in town. They thought Bridget's shop was too far to walk. I announced the valentine was just for a friend, but I received universal glances of disbelief.

Class was a success, and afterwards I saw some students about their assignments. At lunch time I set out for the mall. I walked past a sports shoe shop, whose name always makes me laugh—the Athlete's Foot—and entered Bain's Hallmark next door. The place was thronged, and an untidy young man with long blond hair and freckles was sweeping around the customers' feet, which didn't make choosing cards any easier.

The array of cards was astonishing, and I leant over the rack, determined to find something unsoppy and funny for Jane. People in Midwest City say "excuse me" in loud voices whenever they even come near to touching each other. The crowd trying to get at the cards uttered an awful lot of "excuse me's." At last I found a card with a witty poem.

As I took the card in my hand, I heard a sort of gasp. Nearby a silver-haired man wearing a gray overcoat sank to his knees and then fell on his face. A hunting knife stuck out of his back. People screamed as the blood stained his coat.

Everybody crowded around. For some reason I looked at my watch; it was 1:05 P.M. The manager called for a doctor. More people came into the shop, and miraculously, one of them was indeed a doctor. He examined the silver-haired man and announced: "He's dead."

Lying near the body was an open card. I knew better than to touch it, but I leant over and looked at it. On the right-hand side was a motif of red roses and in big gold letters: "Wishing You a Happy Father's Day."

When the police arrived, the place was even more

crowded. The officers cordoned off the area between the two card racks where the body lay. They asked everybody in the shop to give them their names and addresses. No one had seen the murder.

When I gave my name and address, I mentioned the Father's Day card, and the policeman made a note. Then a blond young woman carrying some packages pressed up against the rope. "That's my father," she said and started to cry.

I knew her. It was Pat Beckman, a first-year student at the law school. I had even seen her earlier in the students' lounge. I went over and said, "It's Professor Lindsey." She looked at me blankly, and I put an arm around her to comfort her.

"I must go and tell my mother and my brother, Rick," she said. Then in a panicky voice, "Where is Rick?—I just saw him in the mall."

The police took a brief statement from Pat. The dead man was her father, Ed Beckman, a prominent businessman. She had been shopping and had no idea he was in the mall. They were a family of four. Her mother was bedridden after hurting her spine in an accident years ago. Pat had one brother, Richard, who was in the University business school. She and her brother both lived at home.

The police finished taking photographs and combing the area for evidence. One officer carefully grasped the Father's Day card with tweezers and placed it in a plastic casing. Soon the ambulance arrived, and two men took the body on a stretcher. I offered to walk Pat home, but a policeman said he would drive her.

Then the crowd dispersed, and I went over to the manager and paid for my valentine card. I commiserated with him on having a murder on the premises. He had an air of great dignity and didn't seem too shaken. I explained I was a professor of evidence at the law school, and he looked suitably impressed. He told me that he had ten people working under him in the shop.

I went back to my office, thinking about the murder.

Father's Day is no part of my life; I don't think it's nearly as important in England as in America. So I looked in an encyclopedia and found it takes place in June. What on earth was a Father's Day card doing on the floor of a card shop in February?

Suddenly the telephone rang. It was a colleague of Jane's to say that her cousin had died unexpectedly, and she would be an hour late for dinner.

I tried to prepare for my class the next day, but couldn't concentrate. Finally, I gave up and went to my room at the Riverside Inn. My heart was still beating wildly from the drama, so I took a hot shower, which calmed me down.

At dinner I told Jane, who was wearing black, that I was sorry about her cousin. "It's awful," she said. "He was murdered in the mall today."

I was incredulous. "Do you mean Ed Beckman was your cousin?" I asked. She looked equally astonished.

"I was there," I said, then blurted out, "buying a valentine."

Jane told me about the Beckmans. They were an old Midwest City family. Ed was a wealthy man and a pillar of the community. Everybody was very sorry for him because of his wife's accident, but Jane said, "It's his wife I feel sorry for." She explained that while his wife was warm and kind, she didn't like Ed much. Ed had been driving when his wife was injured.

"The community thinks he has been a model husband since then," Jane said. "But I know he was a hypocrite."

"Tell me about the children," I asked.

"Well, I've been to see them, and they are terribly upset. The strange thing is, they were both in the mall today. Rick was having lunch with somebody in a pizza place upstairs, and Pat was shopping."

Then I told Jane about the Father's Day card. "Wow," she said. "Why a Father's Day card?"

I returned to the subject of the young Beckmans. "Do you like the children?" I asked.

"Yes, I like Pat a lot. She's as kind as her mother,

and she's always involved in good causes. She spends every spare moment working with disabled children."

"Well, how about Rick?"

She considered. "Rick has a mean streak. When he was a teenager, he once beat up a girlfriend. His father persuaded her family not to bring charges. I can't say I really do like Rick."

"Let's be logical," I said. "If a rich man is killed, the people who benefit under his will must be the chief suspects. Presumably they are his wife and children. The wife is disabled, and from what you say, the daughter seems an unlikely suspect. That leaves the son. And then there is the Father's Day card . . ."

At last I had got a chance to get my teeth into real life evidence. "We're going to solve this murder, Jane. Can you find out about Ed Beckman's will?"

"Sure," said Jane. "I'll let you know."

At breakfast the next morning Bridget looked far away. She fetched my eggs, and I asked her what was wrong. "Nothing," she said. "I'm happy enough. It was my son's birthday yesterday."

"Well, don't look so glum," I said and went off to the mall, whistling.

At the card shop my friend, the manager, was just opening the glass doors. The familiar face of the floor sweeper appeared over the vacuum cleaner. I said to the manager above the noise, "When do you start selling Father's Day cards?"

"After Mother's Day—in May," he said.

"Do you have a stock now?" I asked.

"Oh, yes," he said. "Lots of them in the back of the store."

I walked to the law school and prepared for my class. Then Jane telephoned. "Except for some small charitable gifts, everything goes to the family," she reported. She added, "I found out something else. Rick was having lunch yesterday with a business school professor, Don Wilson."

Now we were getting somewhere. If Rick had already

left the professor when he met his sister in the mall, he could have committed the murder. I telephoned Professor Wilson and asked him for an urgent appointment after my class. He was obliging.

Class went well, and as I walked over to the business school, it was snowing lightly. I explained to Wilson that I had been present at the murder in the mall. Could he tell me about Rick Beckman that day?

At first Wilson was reluctant; he clearly couldn't see what business it was of mine. Then he made a decision. "Okay, I will tell you this. I was with Rick continually from 12:30 to 1:15. We both met his sister in the mall about one, and then we walked back here. I will tell you something else. Rick hated his father. He told me his father had had endless love affairs and made his mother miserable."

That was all I could get out of him. I thanked him and wandered down to the mall, lost in thought. Rick Beckman had any amount of motive, but apparently had an alibi for 1:05 P.M., the time of the murder. Pat Beckman had motive, but seemed an unlikely assassin. Their mother could not walk and couldn't possibly have done it. What about that Father's Day card? I was convinced it was the key.

At the card shop yet again, I asked the dignified manager if I could see his Father's Day stock. He was getting used to me and took me to the back of the shop. The top box on the stack was open. I looked in the box; the first card had a border of red roses and the printed gold words, "Wishing You a Happy Father's Day."

I asked the manager, "Is this a common card?"

"Oh, yes," he said. "Common as Happy Birthday."

"Happy Birthday." The words kept going around in my head. Could birthday be the answer somehow? Then I had an idea and walked to the county courthouse in the town square. I asked a baliff where I would find birth certificates, and he directed me to the Clerk of the District Court, Civil Division.

The office was a complete contrast to a musty, English

public records office—bright and modern with a smiling young woman in a green dress behind the counter. She was intrigued by my English accent and went out of her way to be helpful.

I asked her if she could trace the birthdays of Richard and Patricia Beckman. "What years were they born?" she asked. I didn't know, so I guessed, "Around 1970."

The young woman started taking out volumes of records. Then she came back with two of them. Rick Beckman had been born on June 3, 1968, and Pat on November 17, 1971.

My idea looked silly, and then I had a brain wave. "Can I trace somebody from their birth date?" I asked.

"Well," said the clerk, "do you know the year the person was born?"

I didn't. She said, "You'll just have to go through the volumes on your own."

I asked her to bring the records for 1965. Then I tried 1966, 1967, and went on year by year. By the time I reached the 1973 volume, I was in despair. Suddenly, I found what I was looking for among the birth records from the Good Samaritan Hospital. My heart jumped. Who says professors are just theorists? I had the answer. I knew who the murderer was.

Back I went to the Riverside Inn. Bridget had gone home, but the receptionist gave me the address of her trailer. I telephoned Jane and asked her to pick me up in her car. Soon she arrived, and we set off for the trailer park.

Bridget looked surprised to see us. I introduced Jane, and said, "Can we come in?"

"Sure," said Bridget doubtfully. We went into her tidy little living quarters.

"Bridget," I said. "I've been investigating the murder of Ed Beckman. I've just been to the courthouse, and I think I've solved it."

Bridget said, "Why are you telling me this?"

"There is a birth record for Edward Beckman Shannon on February 13, 1973. The mother's name is Bridget Shannon, and the father is Edward Beckman."

She gasped and went very pale, and the freckles stood out on her face. Freckles, I kept thinking. Forget the red hair, but freckles.

Suddenly she burst out, "I killed him. He let me down so many years ago. I'm a Catholic, I couldn't have an abortion. He promised to divorce his wife and marry me. But when our son was born, Ed didn't come through with marriage, money, or anything else. I registered the baby as legitimate and gave him his father's name. One day I swore I would get Ed, and yesterday I did. I saw him in the mall and followed him into the card shop, where he was buying a card for his wife. I stuck a knife in him and walked out."

"Did you see me there, Bridget?" I asked.

"No . . . yes . . . but you had your back to me."

"Why did you leave a Father's Day card?" She looked blank.

Bridget had confirmed my suspicion. "You didn't kill him, Bridget. But I know who did."

A look of terror came into her eyes.

We parked in the ramp near the mall. Jane seemed puzzled as she tried to keep up with me. We passed the Athlete's Foot and entered Bain's Hallmark.

Inside the shop I went up to him. "You're Bridget's son, aren't you?" I said. "You're Edward Beckman Shannon."

The freckled floor sweeper nodded.

"It was your twenty-first birthday yesterday."

He nodded again. Then he exploded, "I hated him! I hated my father! I hated him for what he did to my mother. I hated him for being rich and giving us nothing. I hated him for giving his other son and his daughter everything, while I'm a crummy janitor. When he saw me in the shop, he turned away and pretended he didn't see me. I went crazy. I had my knife with me. He was my father. It was my twenty-first birthday. There was no present for me. He could have a Father's Day card to celebrate. I used a handkerchief to get the card. Then I wound the handkerchief around the knife handle, pushed it into him, and dropped the card beside him. I'm glad he's dead!"

Then he started to cry.

The manager telephoned for the police. The dead man's son just stood crying.

When the officers arrived, I told them of the admission, and they took him away.

As Jane and I walked toward the car, she asked, "Was it the freckles?"

I said, "I thought there was something familiar about him when I first saw him. It had to be somebody who could get at the Father's Day cards. The Father's Day card had to mean something."

Then I felt in my coat pocket. I pulled out Jane's valentine card and gave it to her. She read the poem, threw back her head, and laughed.

"Happy Valentine's Day, Jane," I said.

The Dead Weight
of Copper Tears

by Wayne Allen Sallee

The man who murdered my father was released from Stateville today. My dad was a thirty-year cop with Gang Crimes South, working the projects. The man who killed him did not do it while my father was on duty, nor when he was off-duty, as so often happens on Chicago's South Side. He was killed after he retired, the memories of Charles Benbow and his string of victims floating in his bottles of Jack Daniel's, drained daily until his heart disintegrated. My father was fifty-nine.

Since Benbow's case was overturned, the witnesses from 1983 afraid to testify again or possibly even dead, he was released on his own recognizance pending a retrial.

My name is Vince Kane. I chose to be a con artist instead of a copper. If I had a beer gut—for this is what my father drank when he was first immersed in the Benbow killing spree—I would look quite a bit like him. He always used Grecian Formula on his hair. Chain-smoking L&Ms has made my thirty-five-year-old voice deeper. I have been following my father's murderer for three days.

I am going to kill him. Even though it is indeed the third Sunday in June, it is Father's Day in more ways than one.

I have followed Benbow the entire weekend. As a grifter, you can pretend to belong in any place, any situation. When my father's killer went into the Sunshine Inn on Muddy Waters Drive, I coasted through being the only white man there by telling the bartender I was writing a nightlife column for *Penthouse*. Only on the news stations do they send black people into black neighborhoods to cover a story of any kind.

While Benbow was there, fiving it to his old pals and listening to Johnnie Lee Hooker sing the blues, I popped some reds and thought about how this scene had come to be played out. My father had been a good cop before the first body floated up in the Chicago River with the spring thaw of fifteen years ago.

For five years Edward Kane, my father, who had a fourth-grade education yet worked as a decoder during the Korean War, hunted down the man who was murdering prostitutes in the Rush Street district. My father worked out of the sixteenth, on Chicago Avenue, and while it is true that Area 5 Homicide detectives handled the glory end of it, the average beat copper did most of the scut work.

He had been the one, along with Lee Mayr, who had canvassed the Gold Coast for witnesses, made the timetables, typed reports in triplicate, and all that shit. The detectives sat in cars with their binoculars and watched the skirts leave the gash bars, their smiles swiped right off any current cop show's opening credits.

The majority of the prostitutes, ranging in age from sixteen to thirty, had gravitated around Tourette Lautrec's, an industrial music bar on Elm and Gwynplain. So did Charlie Benbow. My father knew him from the 'hood, and he told me, in the days when he still could talk about his job without getting the shakes, that Charlie pronounced his name so that it sounded like Charlie Bimbo—cracking a clean, white smile. My father had dentures when he was forty. Different generations, variant ways of personal hygiene.

My father and Mayr had a good case against Benbow. For three years they kept tabs on him, but could never get him cold. Always on the periphery of the crime scene, like an arsonist marveling at his work of destruction.

Benbow was an unemployed construction worker, and his works of destruction involved women's faces—an eye here, a jawbone there. Never had the mutilations been post-mortem, according to the new Cook County M.E., Frank Bervid. Though he had done some things to the bodies before he killed them.

The bartender asked me for another drink, the band stopped for a short break, and I felt as old as my father would be today.

Benbow made eye contact with me for the first time, but I could not see a twitch of recognition due to the smoke from my cigarette. He walked over to the bartender to ask about the white cracker down here off Stony Island, and I wrote in my notebook because I knew the keep would tell him I was working for *Penthouse*. In actuality, I was writing these last few pages down. Somebody played a Billie Holiday song on the Seeberg juke box.

I wondered if Chicago's Finest had put a tail on him, but doubted it. The retrial was ordered because of a previous witness recanting her testimony, and because of one other thing—the way they entrapped Benbow.

It had been early August of 1983, and my father and Mayr had built up a good case against Benbow. Field reports taken from his neighbors on Sedgwick, bartenders and waitresses—the only sober people—along Rush Street, but nothing concrete.

Two of the dicks at Area 5 thought it best to catch Benbow in the act of mutilation. Their way of thinking was that, just as in a good action movie, there are always sacrificial lambs.

The lamb in question was a twenty-year-old bottle blond whose street name was Idaho. She had been trying to reform, had been staying at a halfway house in Streator, and working part-time at a hair salon on Main Street. The detectives drummed up some shit from her past that the quiet town of Streator, off Interstate 55 and in the middle of nowhere, really wouldn't take kindly to. All she had to do was go back to Chicago for one weekend—proposition Benhow while wearing a wire.

The dicks didn't want to settle for a rinky-dink john charge. They listened to the girl named Idaho scream and yet waited until the slick sound of a serrated knife through the baby fat in her cheeks before they burst on the scene.

Benbow had never seen the wire, but he had still gutted Idaho like a fish.

My father heard of their tactics through word of mouth. The detectives were promoted to office jobs at the new State of Illinois building downtown, and my father and Lee Mayr received Honorable Mentions. But my father started his descent into drinking. Ten years ago it had been Schnapps at work, Clorets to cover *that* in case anybody asked, and a twelve pack of Drewry's at night.

After a few months he was transferred to the Fillmore district on the West Side. I found out from Mayr at my father's funeral that it was because he wanted to blow the whistle on the Benbow case. The "official" reason was that my father had become dead weight because of his drinking and increasing weight problem.

The watch commander knew full well that the Fraternal Order of Police would file a grievance. Chicago will always be a politically run town. By transferring my father to Harrison and Kedzie, under the auspices of "departmental rearrangement due to the new airport district," they knew he might get scared enough to quit.

Or at the very least, killed—in the line of duty, of course.

The old man stuck through it, I'll give him that. The beer slowly became boilermakers, and finally the hard stuff was all he drank. My mother left him in 1986. I stayed home and cleaned up after him. The worst thing that ever happened was when he woke up still plastered and mistook the exercise bike for the commode. I spent two hours mopping up runny shit from the basement floor in the middle of July. He had the first heart attack three months later. The second one . . . he had no chance at all to make it through that one.

I held onto his star; when district asked about it, I played stupid. *You know he was a stinking drunk and you know why,* I intimated. *He probably lost the fucking shield for all I know or care.*

Oh, but I cared.

Benbow left the bar at four-thirty that Sunday morning. Father's Day. I watched him leave amid nicotine question marks, and followed soon after. As I said, I'm a con artist. Lee Mayr was able to tell me that Benbow was staying at the Cass Hotel on Wabash, a block from the river.

I drove my father's '77 Volaré as fast as I could, knowing that I would beat the Jimmy Walker cab taking my own personal murder victim home.

Driving straight up Michigan, blowing every light— after all, the car was registered to a dead man—I hit the Cass Hotel twenty minutes before sunrise. I reflected on things some more.

My father never slapped my mother or took his anger out on me. It was a matter of the drinking making him sullen and morose. He hunted monsters, confronted monsters, but they had stood their ground. What is one more dead prostitute, really? This is how City Hall thinks. The D.A.'s office has a saying for perps charged with significant lack of evidence. *Maybe they didn't do this, but they probably did something else, and it was just as bad.* Let the judge, jury, and executioner sort 'em out.

He never quit. Other cops would have—cops on TV and in novels. Some in real life. He called them "candy asses." I heard him cry only twice. Once, when he heard about the transfer to Fillmore, the other time years later. He had called in to say he had to have a few days off because his mother—my sole surviving grandparent—had died of cancer in Missouri.

The watch commander thought he was making excuses to cover up another drinking binge. This was why he had cried.

I was the one who had helped get Benbow released. I contacted Nora Chvatal, a reporter for the *Sun-Times* and gave her as much detail as I could. It took three years, but the story finally saw print. The defense attorney won a shot at a retrial based on new evidence. One of the detectives who "cracked the case" had died of colon cancer; the other had become a consultant for a software company and was head of security.

And now Charlie Benbow was on the streets for the last day of his life.

I wore a weight belt under my shirt to give the impression of added bulk. In the car I had changed into a cop's regulation shirt I had purchased from a thrift store on Kinzie the day before. I pinned my father's badge to the front left pocket, his name badge to the right, and waited on the front stoop—just out of sight.

The cab pulled up several cigarettes later. I waited in silence until Benbow paid the driver. The only other traffic on the street was newspaper and bakery trucks.

I stepped out of the shadows as Benbow reached for the door. He turned to look at me. I told him I wasn't carrying a piece, and I knew that he probably wasn't holding anything, even a shank, because of possible surveillance. I also knew that it was nearly time for shift-change, and in all likelihood, there were no cops around.

"You remember me, Bimbo?" I asked him, enjoying his wince. "Edward Kane, the cop who helped put you in the right place at the right time." God help us, both me and you, father, I thought.

"I heard about you." Benbow gave his pearly smile. "Word is you was a dead weight alkie."

"Think so?" I held my hands up in the air, making a

show of my fake belly. "Maybe I'm armed, maybe not. Want to run for it?"

He stuck his tongue under his lip, then spat. I knew he wasn't armed himself for certain when he started running south on Wabash.

Toward the river.

Where I wanted him.

I stayed behind him until we crossed the bridge, midway to Wacker Drive. Evidently I had fooled him into thinking that my father was still alive. He whirled around when he saw that I had caught up with him.

"Ain't got nothing on me," he said.

"That's right." While running the three blocks, I had pulled free the Velcro patches on the weight belt. I slapped Benbow against the side of his head with it.

He fell to his knees, and it was all I could do to keep from tearing his eyes out with my thumbnails. Behind us the sun had started to show beyond the Michigan Avenue hotels.

"Edward Kane died years ago, ass-wipe." I informed Benbow of this as I pummeled him senseless with the weight belt. "He's no longer the dead weight." He looked up at me. I could not read the emotion in his eyes, but I wanted it to be fear.

"See, Bimbo. You're the dead weight now."

I dropped the weight belt into the gutter and lifted the killer up. Three stories below the bridge there were several stone pilings, their tops inches above the gray-green river.

"You didn't just kill Idaho and the others. You killed my father, too." The thing that made me angriest was that Benbow said nothing in rebuttal—wasn't scared, didn't try to offer up dope, nothing. Like the guy in Texas who spit on the chaplain before he went to the electric chair.

Charlie Benbow said not a damn thing as I let him drop down onto the piling, his head cracking against concrete, his brains splattering in the water around his corpse.

The sun was higher now; the bits of brain tissue made ripples in the water as if there were a sudden, condensed rain shower.

The morning sun reflecting off the ripples reminded me of copper tears from a long time ago.

The Raven Takes Over

by Ron Goulart

Most histories of the movies of the 1940s mention him, the suave private detective of the silver screen who also solved murder mysteries in real life. None of it, which can be said for quite a bit of Hollywood history, is true at all, though it does make for entertaining reading.

Hix did the actual detective work, not the Raven. But, uncharacteristically, he never took any of the credit for solving those various movieland crimes. His motive initially was both crass and sentimental. He wanted to make sure he had enough money to get married on.

The business about the murdered mystery novelist Hix walked into by chance. That was at about eleven o'clock in the morning on a crisp, clear Tuesday in October of 1943.

The short, crinkly-haired screenwriter, decked out in umber-colored slacks, a lime polo shirt, and a pair of strange bloodred shoes he'd acquired on a recent jaunt down to Tijuana was strolling from the writers' building on the fifty-acre Star Spangled Studios lot toward Sound Stage 11.

Hix was whistling a soulful version of *Body and Soul* and about to turn to ogle further a titian-haired starlet who was riding along the palmtree-lined street on a very expensive bicycle.

"Oops, my heart belongs to another," he reminded himself, keeping his eyes on the white gravel pathway he was following. "Nice backside, however, and no lingerie under those slacks."

He was en route to watch the love of his life, Boots

McKay, do a tap number in the latest SS musical, *Hot Tamales Strike at Dawn.* Boots, a lovely dark-haired girl, was going to dance on the wing of a bomber while costumed as a riveter.

"Helps the war effort," Hix murmured, scratching at his frazzled hair.

As he went by Stage 13, the metal door lurched open and none other than Jack Greenway came tottering out. The thirty-three-year-old actor's natty tweed sport coat was askew, his regimental tie dangled at an odd angle, and his handsome tanned face had an underwater tinge.

The actor took a few unsteady steps, glanced back over his broad, well-tailored shoulder, and then leaned against the trunk of the nearest palm tree and started breathing through his mouth.

Hix approached him. "William Powell just phoned, Jack, and says he wants his mustache back."

Greenway brought a moderately shaky hand up to brush at his thin mustache. "Jove, Hix, I'm deuced glad to see you, old man."

"You know what I like about you?" inquired Hix as he bounced a few times on the bright green lawn. "The way you've never lost your hometown accent. Nope, just one sentence and I can tell you're a Youngstown, Ohio boy."

The actor clutched Hix's arm. "I've just had a bit of a scare."

"Don't go admitting things like that, it's bad for your publicity," cautioned Hix. "We're in the midst of lensing *The Raven Takes Over,* first in what I trust will be a lucrative series of dick pix. You are portraying that daring and debonair private investigator, the Raven hisself. Keep in mind that the Raven must never admit to—"

"Listen to me, Hix. In there ..." The dapper actor pointed at the big humpbacked building he'd just burst free of. "It's a ... well, dash it all, it's a corpse."

Hix blinked, his hair growing even more frazzled as he rocked on his heels. "Naw, that's been done too much," he said. "I used the body on the sound stage gimmick in *Dr. Crimebuster Goes to the Movies.* Worked a switch on the gag in *The Loco Kid Rides South,* wherein a circus comes to—"

"I'm alluding to a real incident, old man. Inside, on the set for *One of Queen Victoria's Nights.*"

The small writer scowled. "You haven't gone and bumped off some pea-brained starlet? You've been known to use bedroom sets for your amorous—"

"As a matter of fact, I had arranged a quiet rendezvous with a talented young lady who's a newcomer to the screen," admitted Greenway. "She hasn't appeared and ... this isn't she, old man. The dead woman is Rose Karr."

"Rose Karr?" His eyes widened.

"Afraid so."

Sighing, Hix ceased bouncing. "She was supposed to be barred from the lot," he said. "Chiefly because she's been threatening to sue all the Star Spangled moguls for plagiarism, slander, and other chicanery."

"You have to admit our new Raven character is deucedly close to her detective character, the Angel." The actor brushed at his mustache again. "And, since I portrayed the Angel in nine previous quickies, the public might assume—"

"Hey, they weren't quickies," contradicted Hix. "On this lot any fillum that takes a full nine days to get into the can is considered a major production. And simply because you happen to play two different and distinct detectives doesn't mean that—"

"The old girl had a point, Hix. When Star Spangled couldn't come to terms with her for more Angel films, you and your current writing partner cooked up the Raven," Greenway pointed out. "I mean to say, the very title of our new motion picture, *The Raven Takes Over,* seems to me quite clearly to indicate that—"

"Enough bickering, Jacko," decided the writer. "Let's get in there to view the scene of the crime."

"Actually I don't feel up to taking another—"

"Sure, you do. You're the Raven, and if we play our

cards right, we're going to reap a stewpot of publicity out of this old bimbo's demise."

"How do we do that?"

"You're going to solve her murder," Hix informed him.

The dead woman was sitting on the bedroom floor, thick legs spread wide, broad back slumped against the floral wallpaper. There were two bloody splotches on the front of her white mannish blouse.

"Not a pretty sight," muttered Greenway, who'd halted at the edge of the dim-lit Victorian bedroom set.

"Rosie wasn't all that terrific looking to begin with." Hix crouched slightly as he approached the body.

"I say, what's this?" Squatting, the actor plucked a matchbook from the floor. "A book of paper matches from the Club Avocado. Isn't that the night spot where your screenwriting partner whiles away most of his evenings?"

"Along with a multitude of other fans of watered booze." Hix knelt next to the dead writer and touched her bare arm. "She hasn't been dead that long."

"The lady was, I assure you, dead and gone when I arrived on the scene."

"Here's another nice touch." Hix pried the corpse's right hand open, extracting a sheet of blue memo paper. " 'We can settle this once and for all. Meet me on Stage 13 at 10:30 A.M. JPS.' "

"JPS? Jove, that must stand for J. Paul Stanhope, the very partner of yours we've been discussing."

"So it would seem." Folding the memo, Hix slipped it into his slacks.

"Ought you do be doing that, old boy? We shot a scene only yesterday in which Inspector Rattner chastised the Raven for tampering with the evidence at the scene of—"

"Somebody's already tampered with the scene of this knockoff." Hix straightened, frowning around.

"How so?"

He shook his head and his fuzzy hair jiggled. "Did you notice a gun anywhere?"

"Afraid not. Came in, noted the young lady in question wasn't about. Then spotted poor Rose Karr," said Greenway. "By the way, you must know that Rose and Stanhope have had several violent quarrels of late, most of them on this very lot. She claimed the unpublished yarn that served as the basis for our Raven film was an obvious steal from one of hers about the Angel."

"I know, yep. That's one of the reasons Rosie's been kept off the premises of late."

"Obviously, old man, she wasn't kept off today." He gestured at the sitting corpse.

Hix circled the body and kicked at the small black purse beside her on the imitation Persian rug. "Hum," he said, kneeling again to poke a finger at something next to the purse.

"Another clue?"

"Flakes of old newspaper." Gingerly, he opened the purse and probed inside it. "More newsprint crumbs within, but nary an old clipping."

"Perhaps Rose carried reviews of her many detective novels with her."

"Not worth killing for." He stood up. "Before Rosie struck it—moderately—rich with her mystery stuff, she was a reporter in the Midwest. Back a decade or so."

"And therefore?"

Hix shrugged. "Darned if I know." Sitting on a loveseat, he eyed the body.

"Should we not," suggested the uneasy actor, "notify the authorities?"

"Not right yet."

"Hix, having appeared in nine Angel movies, I have picked up a smattering of knowledge about the routine one's obliged to follow in—"

"I penned most of those," reminded the frazzle-haired writer. "But I want to make sure I get rid of all the stuff that was planted here to frame Stanhope."

"You suspect a frame? Why, old boy?"

"Here's the logic I'm applying to this caper." Hix bounced out of the chair and commenced pacing the bedroom set. "If J. Paul Stanhope—once great novelist who's reduced to slaving in a forlorn writer's cubicle but a few doors from mine—if he knocked off this bimbo, they'll more than likely toss him in the hoosegow. Should that happen, our Raven series may get canceled on account of bad publicity. I intend any edition now to pop the question to the gifted Boots McKay, currently featured in *Hot Tamales Strike at Dawn.* Therefore, I wish my income to continue evenly and smoothly as I once again sail out on the sea of matrimony. Writing these nitwit Raven features happens to be the easiest way I know of to earn a quick buck. Ergo, Stanhope has to be innocent."

Shaking his head, Greenway said, "You can't always tell what a drunk like Stanhope will do."

"A drunk who's my collaborator is bound to be as innocent as a leg of lamb. Further he . . . hum."

"Something else?"

Hix had suddenly dropped to all fours and was scraping at the rug with the side of his right hand. "A smattering of tobacco."

"Stanhope doesn't smoke."

"One of the few vices the lad doesn't practice." He rubbed a few grains of dark tobacco between his fingers, sniffing. "Pipe mixture, vaguely familiar."

"Anyone could've dropped that on the carpet, old chap. Days ago perhaps."

"Nope, you forget that Slepyan is directing this historical opus, and he has a cleanliness obsession." Standing, Hix funneled the tobacco into the breast pocket of his citrus-toned shirt. "Slep has them vacuum the sets and dust every nook and cranny at the end of each day's shoot. Whomsoever lost this pinch of tobacco did it this very day."

"Chap tugs gun out of pocket, spills tobacco pouch, eh?"

"Could be." Hix was squinting into the shadows beyond the set. Noticing a telephone on a taboret next to a swayback canvas chair, he went striding to it, hopping over cables and wires that snaked along the studio floor.

"Notifying the police at long last?"

"Eventually, eventually." Hix arranged himself in the assistant director's chair and dialed a number. "Pop? This is America's greatest living writer and ... No, not Edgar Rice Burroughs. It's Hix. The incomparable Hix as my many fans like to ... No, I don't sound anything like Mickey Mouse. Pop, cease this good-natured badinage, for which you're justly famed throughout the movie capital, and attend to me. You've been guarding the Star Spangled Studios gate since the break of day, have you not? Fine, so you allowed one Rose Karr onto the ... Who called and told you it was okay? Ah, I see. And that's who the dear lady asked after? Pop, how'd you like to suffer a mild attack of amnesia? What's it pay? Oh, say a sawbuck and ... Okay, we'll make if fifty bucks. You just can't remember whom Rosie inquired after nor who told you it was all right to lift the ban on her. Probably just until sundown today. No, you won't be compounding any felonies. Actually, you're aiding the course of true love, helping our boys in uniform, striking a blow against the Axis, and doing your bit for Uncle Sam. Nope, fifty is tops for the job. Okay, keep 'em flying. So long."

"Who asked to have her admitted?" inquired the actor as Hix hung up.

"Pop claims J. Paul Stanhope used the Ameche this A.M. to inform him that it was hunky-dory to once again allow Rosie to roam the highways and byways of Star Spangled. And Rosie told the old duffer she was here to keep an appointment with J. Paul Stanhope."

"The evidence against him is piling up, old man."

"Something is piling up." Hix frowned as he dialed another number, drumming the fingers of his free hand on the wooden arm of the chair. "The scent of that darn tobacco reminds me of something, but ... Ah, is this the office of Johnny Whistler, famed Hollywood columnist and scribe and ... It's me, Gladys. The nation's best-loved movie scripter and a ... Nope, not Ben Hecht. Hix, and no cracks about my voice. Is Johnny in? Well, put him on, I've got a momentous scoop for ... C'mon, kiddo, wasn't the last item I slipped you for his colyum a socko ... Sure, millions of people are interested in my doings. And the fact that I escorted a fast-rising hoofer to the glittering preem of *Hot Tamales over Tokyo* is newsworthy to the ... Hum? Sure, you can have a glittering opening in Glendale. Gladys, don't be so insular. Now, *muy pronto,* as I wrote in my latest Loco Kid epic, put on your boss. Okay, okay. But a cheap dinner and a meatless one to help the war effort. I'll call you to set the date. Hello, Johnny, how's the Boswell of Hollywood Boule ... Of course, it's worth your while to chat with me. This is big news *and* an exclusive to you. Rose Karr has been murdered here at the Star Spangled Studios and ... What? No, the identity of the mysterious slayer remains a deep dark mystery. However, and here's the hot part of the item, Jack Greenway, who is coincidentally starring in the currently lensing *The Raven Takes Over,* scripted by your humble servant and onetime Pulitzer Prize winner J. Paul Stanhope, is ... No, Johnny, I wouldn't call J. P. a washed-up rummy. Pay attention or you'll miss the good stuff. Jack Greenway has vowed to emulate the Raven in real life and solve the murder. He's moved by a deep and abiding admiration for the deceased and swears he'll track the killer and bring him or her, as the case may be, to justice. Eh? Nay, no, nope, Johnny, I wouldn't murder some innocent old broad for cheap publicity. And remember the name is spelled H-I-X. When you spell it H-I-C-K-S, the rubes get the idea I'm ... Thanks, Johnny. See you around."

"What deep and abiding admiration? I could barely stand the ..." Greenway paused and glanced at the body. "Rose and I weren't close chums, Hix, and to inform that scandalmonger that—"

"You weren't drinking in everything I said in my usual dulcet tones," Hix told him. "Think about headlines like such—Movie Sleuth Solves Real-life Murder Case. That'll provide a heck of a goose to your sagging career."

"See here, old man, my career is by no means sagging. Why, only last—"

"A fellow who gets third billing in *I Married A Zombie* isn't giving Spencer Tracy any sleepless nights."

Greenway told him, "I'd prefer not to dabble in detection at all and let the—"

"Of course, you ain't going to dabble." Hix left the canvas chair, poking at his narrow chest with a thumb. "I intend to solve this whole mess and then give you the credit. All you have to do is look suave and take the bows. Can you manage that?"

"Assuredly, but—"

"That's swell. Now we have to go call on Stanhope."

"Aren't you at least going to alert the studio police?"

"Shortly." Hix headed into the darkness around the set.

Hix paused as six blondes in sarongs came walking by. Four of them giggled, three waved, and two called out, "Hi ya, Hix."

"Pull up your halter, Mona," he advised. "Your tattoo is showing."

"Nertz to you."

"Ah, that poor kid's been heartbroken since I plighted my troth with another," observed Hix, resuming their walk to the writers' building. "She hides it behind a mask of hardboiled—"

"Suppose," put in Greenway, "this souse really did do in Rose? We're just—"

"Stanhope once won a Pulitzer," reminded Hix, frazzled hair dancing atop his head. "Therefore you can't call him a souse. Say rather that the guy has a moderate drinking problem."

"If it were moderate, the bloke wouldn't fall down so bloody often."

"He was a heck of a writer once. Even you must've read *A Farewell To Paradise* and *The Great Sunrise*."

"Can't say I have, old man. My idea of leisure reading is Pearl Buck."

They reached the faded two-story wooden building that housed the Star Spangled scriptwriters. "Clamp your fingers on your snout," advised Hix. "Otherwise the combined stench of stale cigars, spilled booze, and yesterday's romantic interludes will give you the bends."

"You chaps ought to demand little bungalows such as we actors enjoy."

Making a snorting sound, Hix went bounding up the creaky wooden stairway to the second floor. "Ah, the familiar sound of typewriters being pounded by palsied fingers, old MGM plots being pilfered, cocktails being shaken, bookies being pleaded with. Home."

He loped by his own office, the door of which had a large photo of Ken Maynard pasted to it upside down. Stanhope's office was three doors farther along.

Not knocking, Hix barged in.

"Jove, this looks deuced bad," commented Greenway from the threshold.

The pale blond Stanhope was slumped facedown at his desk. Near his right hand, atop a spread of old scripts, sat a .38 revolver.

Hix crossed the small, musty room and poked his collaborator in the ribs. "Arise and sing, J. P."

The author moaned, made some bubbling noises, and began snoring.

Hix tugged a polka-dot handkerchief out of his pocket, wrapped it around the gun, and picked the thing up. Sniffing at the barrel, he said, "Been fired off recently." He deposited the weapon in his pocket.

"Shouldn't the murder weapon be turned over to—"

"Hush," Hix said, picking up an empty glass from beside the pile of scripts and sniffing. "No telltale odors or . . . Shucks. This damn glass has been rinsed out."

"Could that not be a clue in itself?"

"Probably." Hix placed the glass on a cluttered shelf behind the desk. "Somebody slipped J. P. a mickey, then went about framing him for the abrupt demise of Rosie."

"Be difficult to prove the bloke was doped. Since the tumbler's been—"

"Faith and bejabbers, look at this." He was squatting next to the swivel chair of the slumbering writer. "More tobacco."

"We may be on to something."

After sniffing at the flecks of tobacco, Hix flickered them into the pocket of his shirt. "What exactly?"

The actor stroked his mustache with a forefinger. "Haven't the foggiest notion, old man," he said finally. "But if this were a Raven film, why, finding the same tobacco at two locations . . . it is the same, isn't it?"

"Yep."

"Then it must mean something."

"Mayhap the killer has some of this stuff in his pocket," speculated Hix. "When he took out his gat to pop Rosie, some spilled in Queen Vicky's boudoir. And when he planted the roscoe on J. P., more rained down."

Greenway brightened. "Exactly, yes."

Hix rested his backside against the side of the desk. "Okay, I am now going to attempt to sober J. P. up a mite. Then I intend to nose around some, hither and yon," he announced. "Wait a half hour or so and then thereafter call the studio cops. Tell them about Rosie, but don't mention the gun or the other stuff we've found."

The actor grew thoughtful. "I suppose newspapers all across the country would pick up the story should I actually solve this bally mystery."

"Sure, along with *Time*, *Life* and *Photoplay*."

"I never have had the cover of *Photoplay*."

"This'll cinch it," Hix assured him, taking hold of Stanhope under the armpits and tugging him clear of the chair. "Now help me lug J. P. to the shower stall at the end of the hall."

"I wouldn't want to do much riveting in those togs," Hix remarked to the very pretty brunette across the table from him in the crowded commissary.

"It's a stylized riveter's outfit," explained Boots. "And

quit being evasive, Hix. There are Burbank policemen all over the place, plus newspapermen and three gossip columnists. Besides which, you're wearing that daffy look you take on whenever you start playing detective."

"I'm not the op this time around. Jack Greenway is doing the honors whilst—"

"G'wan, Greenway couldn't find his elbow without a roadmap," said the dancer.

"You mustn't spread rumors like that, m'love. Loose lips sink ships, as well as my cunning scheme for keeping the nitwit Raven series afloat."

"One flicker doesn't make a series." She poked her fork into her cottage cheese.

"Precisely why I don't want either my star or my sozzled colleague hauled off to the Bastille," Hix said. "Oh, by the way, what say we get hitched?"

Her eyes widened, and she set her fork aside. "This, I take it, is a formal proposal?"

"What else? We've been seen together at all the posh Tinseltown bistros for nigh on to two years, your name's been linked with mine in many a column, and—"

"That's because you're still romancing that peroxided bimbo, Gladys, who works for Johnny Whistler and—"

"My heart belongs to you and you alone."

"That's what the count said to the peasant girl in *The Second Mrs. Monte Cristo*."

"When I cook up a terrific line, there's no sense in using it but once," he pointed out. "How about it?"

"Well, I might as well," said Boots, grinning at him. "But I won't give up my career."

"I hope not, since I'm counting on your salary from Star Spangled to help finance this marital venture." Hix reached over to pat her hand. "Along with what I make from the Raven epics."

"Okay, that's settled. Now fill me in on what's been going on."

Hix gave her, with interruptions to greet various actors, actresses, and writers who wandered in for lunch, a concise account of the murder of Rose Karr and his subsequent poking around.

"Is that lush awake yet?" she asked when he concluded.

"About halfway. He's holed up in Greenway's bungalow, guzzling black coffee."

"What's he got to say about all this?"

"Precious little," admitted Hix. "All that J. P. recalls is having a small slug of rye to limber up his brain prior to embarking on a rewrite of the dinner-party scene in our epic. He passed out shortly thereafter, which was about 9 A.M."

"Anybody who'd drink rye that early in the day would do anything," observed Boots. "Even murder. Did he really invite Rose Karr to meet him here this morning?"

"He says nay. I showed him the note I extracted from her clutches. J. P. opines he probably didn't pen it."

"Probably?"

"The guy has lapses of memory, but he's pretty sure he wasn't planning any rendezvous with the old broad." Hix noticed the ham on rye on his plate, picked it up, took a tentative bite, then put it down. "Actually, my pet, I'd have gotten more useful info out of one of those pickled brains in a jar they used in my screen masterpiece, *They Made Me a Monster.*"

Boots scanned his face for a few seconds. "You're even jumpier than usual," she noted. "That usually means you've found out something."

"While the local Keystone Kops were en route, I roamed around, snooping and asking judicious questions," he said. "It seems Rose had been having considerable money problems until about six months ago. Her literary fortunes didn't pick up, but her income sure did. Expert opinion seems to be that the old dear started up a lucrative blackmail business—using tidbits she'd picked up during her years here in the glamour capital plus a good deal of the stuff she'd unearthed whilst employed as a crime reporter in some benighted outpost such as Kansas City or Cleveland."

"Okay, so she was blackmailing people." Boots rested an elbow on the table. "Some of them on the lot here?"

"Yep. And this morning one of her clients came up with the money-saving notion of removing her from this sphere of existence."

"You can't be sure, though."

Hix said. "At the site of her bumping-off I found some crumbs of old newspaper. Occurred to me she was carrying around some old clippings, possibly stuff saved from her newspaper days. Those clippings are probably full of news that'll embarrass someone hereabouts. Rosie no doubt meant to sell them, but our murderer thought of a cheaper way to get hold of the stuff."

"Why'd she tell the gate she was coming to see Stanhope?"

"A cover-up. You don't drive up and announce to Pop, 'Howdy, I'm here to blackmail Boots McKay.' "

"I suppose not."

"Take my word for it," Hix said, trying another bite of his sandwich. "I used a similar situation in *Dr. Crimebuster's Gamble.*"

"Isn't that the one where the good doctor gets shot by the killer?"

"Only in the leg."

"I wouldn't want that to happen to you, Hix."

"Fear not."

Boots shook her head. "Let's say Stanhope is innocent," she said. "What about Greenway? He might be the one she was going to meet on Stage 13. When he bumped into you, he made up that story about finding her. Really, I've never been able to believe that guy is as dim-witted as he looks."

"You forget this is Hollywood, the dimwit center of the universe," reminded Hix. "I've written a dozen pics for Jack, and he isn't shamming denseness. Besides, he didn't have time to kill Rosie, dash over and plant the gun on Stanhope, and then get back to Stage 13 again. Even a fleet-footed little rascal like me can't do that."

"How about other suspects?"

Hunching, Hix nodded at a nearby table. "There are several sitting over yonder," he said in a lowered voice. "We have, for instance, Lou Gomper, who's a ringer for Wallace Beery's stand-in. He produced the Angel flickers and is doing the same for the Raven. He and Rose grew to loathe each other, and she'd been threatening to sue him."

"Too obvious," commented Boots, nose wrinkling. "You'd never cast such an obvious heavy for the killer."

"Note that he is, even as we speak, smoking a pipe."

"Nope. Try again."

"Sitting on his right hand, we find lanky Oscar Fairfield, youthful boy-wonder director. There've been rumors that he owes his present exalted position more to mob influence than talent," continued the fuzzy-haired screenwriter. "Could be Miss Karr had proof of that."

"He smokes cigarettes."

"But he rolls his own."

"Oscar directed me in *Hot Tamales on Broadway*. Seemed like a nice guy, for a director."

"Now over against the wall at a table by himself, we find Charley Bunyan, who's undertaking the part of Inspector Rattner in *The Raven Takes Over*," Hix continued. "His bio is vague as to who or where he was prior to his advent here in the movie mecca some six or so years back. He's a longshot, since he doesn't smoke at all and thus—" Hix suddenly straightened up, hair flickering atop his head.

"Are you having a fit?"

"No, nope. Where was I?" He paid attention to his sandwich for a while. "Ah, yes, I'm also curious about Carmelita Pepp, who's starring in your songfest. Supposedly the lady hails from Brazil, but her accent is as fake as a three-dollar bill. Could be she's a Nazi agent or—"

"Nobody who wears bananas and pineapples on her head is capable of murder." She frowned across at him. "Hix, what's come over you?"

"I've just been visited by a brilliant hunch," he admit-

ted, bouncing free of his chair. "I'll see you when evening is nigh, cookie. Don't strain your gams."

"Hix, don't go getting—"

"Farewell until then. And don't forget we have a date
to get hitched." Shoulders up, he dodged through the
crowded room and out into the bright afternoon.

"Ah, the grandeur of it all," remarked Hix, kicking
up dust on the Old West street.

"I say, old man," said Greenway, glancing uneasily
around at the false-front buildings, "I'm not at all certain
that I relish this upcoming encounter with—"

"All you have to do is recite the dialogue I worked
out for you." Tugging at the actor's tweedy sleeve, Hix
guided him around a bend and through a stretch of jun-
gle. "I wonder if Boots and I would be comfortable in
a tree house? The plumbing is probably—"

"Supposing this bloke isn't the killer?"

"Then you'll both have a good laugh," said the writer.
"And we'll set up a tête-à-tête with the next suspect
on my list. I don't, however, think I'm cockeyed in my
surmise, so—"

"Going to make me look deuced silly if you are
wrong. Chap'll consider me a bally idiot."

The tropical greenery ceased, and they were strolling
along a row of Manhattan tenements. Hix slowed.
"Okay, Jacko, the old dark house is around the next
corner," he said. "You go swaggering in there, speak the
speeches, and we'll nab our slayer."

Greenway rubbed at his mustache. "You'll be close
by?"

"Didn't I write the near-miss Oscar-winning script for
The Secret Love of Daniel Boone? I am an expert at
sneaking up on people, places, and things," Hix assured
the reluctant actor. "Now scoot, truck on down to your
rendezvous. Comes *mañana,* your photo'll be in all the
newsrags."

"Showing me, no doubt, decked out with flowers and

reposing in my coffin." Shrugging very slowly, Greenway continued on alone.

Hix waited until he'd turned down the lane that led to the ramshackle mansion where Star Spangled shot many of its spook movies.

Hix quietly sang a couple lines of "Me and My Shadow" in a rotten imitation of Ted Lewis as he scooted along an alley. He emerged at the rear of a Foreign Legion fort.

Easing along its imitation stone wall, he peered out and caught a glimpse of the sinister old house rising up out of a weedy field a hundred or so yards away. Greenway, not quite as jaunty and calm as usual, was climbing up the weathered front steps. He hesitated a few seconds before pushing the oaken door open and entering.

About three minutes later Charley Bunyan, still in the rumpled blue serge suit he wore to portray Inspector Rattner in their movie, came lumbering along. He scanned the surrounding area, then thumped up the stairs and shoved into the old dark house.

After sucking in air, Hix dashed from his hiding place and went scurrying over to the house. He made his way across the high grass of the lawn and moved to the side of the mansion.

Deftly—at least that's how he was describing it in his mind—he climbed up over the side porch rail. He skulked up to the nearest window, which was partially open, and peered in through the yellowed lace curtains.

"What's the big idea?" Bunyan was asking Greenway. "Why'd you invite me to some kind of secret meeting?"

"I'm afraid this bluff and ... um ... bluff and fluster simply won't do, old boy." Greenway was standing in front of the stone fireplace, elbow resting on the mantel.

"Bluff and *bluster*," corrected Hix under his breath.

"I don't get you, Jack."

"But I get you. You see, when I found poor Rose Karr, she wasn't quite dead."

"So what?"

"The dear lady, with her last breath, informed me where she had hidden the duplicate copies of the newspaper clippings you took from her," continued the dapper actor. "Most interesting reading they made, too. Outlining your former career as a criminal and making it evident that you're a wanted man under your true name."

"Hey, if I'm a fugitive criminal, I'd be pretty dumb showing my face in two dozen movies in the past three years," the hefty actor pointed out. "Anybody could spot me."

"Not after you had plastic surgery and put on considerable weight, old man."

"Don't be a sap, Jack. With a new face and body, how'd Rose Karr recognize me?"

"There are several possibilities there." Greenway's delivery was improving, and he was starting to sound almost confident. "You might have a birthmark or tattoo—someplace where the cinema audience can't see it—and poor departed Rose somehow got a peek at it by chance. Or, while you were appearing in some of her Angel films, you may've inadvertently said something that tipped her off. I imagine you both hail originally from the same part of the—"

"Have you told the cops any of this malarkey?"

"Not yet. I thought perhaps I might be able to sell you the clippings, along with the flakes of pipe tobacco I found at the scene. They prove—"

"Hell, I don't even smoke at all. Everybody knows that."

"Charley Bunyan doesn't smoke, old man, but Inspector Rattner does," said Greenway. "You were wearing that suit when you took poor Rose's life. You were carrying the gun in the same pocket where you keep your prop pipe and tobacco pouch. The tobacco will match, proving beyond a shadow of a doubt that you are the killer."

"You've got me, sure enough." From the pocket in question Bunyan pulled another gun, a snub-nosed .32

revolver. "What's going to happen now is sort of sad. You're going to write a note confessing to bumping off Rose Karr and then blow your brains out. I'll write the note, of course, since I'm an expert forger and—"

"I do hope you're not intending to shoot me with that particular gun." Greenway grinned.

"Huh?"

"Old man, really, I've been on to you for some time, and I took the precaution of replacing the bullets in that weapon with blanks while you were at lunch."

Bunyan stared down at the gun in his hand.

Greenway lunged, hitting at the other man's wrist with the side of his hand. The gun fell to the floor and Greenway slugged the thick-set actor twice on the chin.

Bunyan sighed, grunted, fell to the floor, and spread out on the threadbare rug.

Hix climbed in through the window. "Not a bad job."

"I hadn't expected the fellow to have *another* gun," Greenway said, using his display handkerchief to wipe at his forehead. "You didn't include anything about that possibility in the script you worked up to bluff him."

"An oversight."

"Still and all, I do believe, I ad-libbed fairly well, don't you?"

"You were sensational and terrific." Stooping, Hix grabbed up the revolver and handed it to him. "Stay here with this lout."

"You're going to fetch the police?"

"First the press, then the cops." Hix gave him a lazy salute and rushed out of the room.

Mothercloud, Fatherdust

by Tracy A. Knight

"I've got a case for you, Perry." Dr. Casey said it with such administrative aplomb I felt like Harry Morgan, staring at the business side of Jack Webb's head.

I wasn't sure I wanted to hear what kind of referral he had in mind. Only three months into my internship after earning my master's in counseling, I already had learned that intern therapists were regarded as the grunts of mental health care, perpetually assigned the tasks and clients that others had grown frustrated with or weary of—an instructional rite of passage designed to teach humility, perhaps.

Nonetheless. "What have you got?" I asked, straightening the tie to which my graduate school neck still had not become accustomed.

He tossed a file onto my desk. "Charles Lowary. He's about forty-five, moderately retarded."

"A current client?"

"No. Several years ago, he worked in our sheltered workshop for six months or so. Otherwise we've had no ongoing contact with him. He was a pretty good worker while he was with us. Didn't say much, not too verbal at all."

"So what do we need to do? Why does he need counseling?"

"I'm not sure," Dr. Casey said as he sat down in the chair opposite me. "That's what you need to figure out."

I opened my notebook, as if preparing to fashion a scribbled equation—a crisp mathematical solution to a human problem. Youthful idealism.

"Charles is a mysterious guy," Dr. Casey continued. "If he lived someplace other than Elderton, particularly a big city, he'd probably be dead or homeless and starving by now. But we take care of our own around here. In a small town folks like him are well-tolerated, almost adopted by the community."

So I'd heard.

"What does Charles do? Does he work?" I asked.

"Other than his sheltered workshop experience, I don't think he's ever worked. His mother died giving birth to him, and his father just kept him at home. No formal schooling."

"No special education?"

"You forget, Perry. This is rural America. There wasn't any special education when Charles went to school. You either sent your kids to school with everyone else's—or you didn't."

"Does he still live with his father?"

"John Lowary died in a house fire ten years ago. It was a miracle Charles survived. Luckily, the old man left enough inheritance and insurance money to take care of him for life. Charles lives alone. He has a conservator who takes care of his money and a housekeeper who keeps things clean and buys his groceries."

"So what's the problem?" I asked. It sounded like Charles Lowary had a pretty good life.

Pointing at the calendar on my desk, Dr. Casey said, "It all comes down to that. You see the date? Father's Day is this weekend. Ever since his dad died, Charles has had a psychotic break every Father's Day. Like clockwork, he just loses it completely, becomes totally nonfunctional. And every year we hospitalize him. It clears in a few days, and for the rest of the year Charles is his fine, passive, nondisruptive self. And every year the community points a finger straight at this mental health center—especially me, the director—and says, 'Why don't you people help poor Charles?' The whole town's waiting for it to happen again. This morning people started phoning me. Even the mayor called. They want to know what we are going to do. I told them I have a hot new intern I'm assigning the case to."

"So you want me to ... ?"

"Figure this thing out. Nobody has in ten years. We've even gone to his house on Father's Day, and he's never there. He just shows up on the town square about mid-morning, psychotic as hell." Dr. Casey paused for a moment, scratched his chin, and smiled. "I'll tell you what, Perry. You prevent Charles from having a psychotic break this year, and you win a gold intern star and a hell of a recommendation from me when you finish here. So it's simple, you see? You got into this field so you could perform miracles with people's lives, right? Now's your chance. Have at it."

Truth be told, I didn't get into this field to "perform miracles with people's lives" or to become my clients' Good Father. I only hoped to make my tiny corner of the world a little saner, a bit happier.

But a client with limited verbal ability would find counseling of negligible value. It sounded like the skills of a detective would prove more appropriate, that whatever clinical acumen I possessed offered precious little fuel for this particular trip. Unfortunately, to find a detective in rural America, one's only option is to turn on the television set.

Since Charles had attended vocational programming for six months, I figured a visit to the sheltered workshop on the edge of town was worth a try.

The workshop supervisor, Becky Patterson, met me at the door, brushing dust from the front of her work shirt, apparently the residue of an ongoing workshop project. Behind her the sounds of machinery and happy conversation filled the air. "Perry," she said, "what brings you to Becky's Wonderful World of Work Adjustment Training?"

"Charles Lowary."

She clapped her hands and smiled. "Charles. Boy, I

haven't thought about him for a long time. Was he referred to you?"

"Yeah. Dr. Casey said Charles has a psychotic episode every Father's Day. He wants me to figure it out or, better yet, to prevent it."

"God, that's right. You're the sacrificial intern counselor. It's your turn," she said, regarding me with an expression blending respect and pity. "Charles worked here during June of '75. I remember him acting really strange the week before Father's Day, even more withdrawn than usual. Then he didn't come to work for a couple of days and ended up in the psych unit in Galesburg that weekend. Have you met him yet?"

"I hope to later today if I can find him."

"While you're figuring things out, see if you can figure out what he keeps in his sack."

"Sack?"

"Yeah, everybody in town has wondered about it. That week he started acting strangely, he brought the sack with him every day. He wouldn't let anybody look into it. Very protective. He kept it squeezed between his knees all day while he did assembly work."

"Anything else you can tell me about Charles?"

"Not much. He was always a real gentleman around here. Cooperative, very polite and passive. Kept to himself. He didn't say much at all, though I imagine he has some verbal skills."

"Did he get some counseling while he was here?"

"No. You forget, he was here to learn some marketable work skills and habits, not to untangle any personal issues. I wish he would have stayed with us longer. I bet we could've placed him in a janitorial position."

"Well, maybe it's best if I just go see Charles, talk to the guy—the direct approach."

"Worth a shot. Good luck, intern," Becky said with an optimistic salute.

The next morning, after two appointments, I had a prelunch opening in my schedule. As it turned out, Dr.

Casey, and indeed the entire staff, knew exactly where I could find Charles: "within a block of the square, on Locust Street." Apparently, his movements could be as confidently predicted as a new moon.

Sure enough, as if adhering to an invisible script, Charles was walking down Locust Street toward his home when I first saw him. He was clutching a sack, the opening of which was rolled tightly shut.

When he saw me approaching, Charles made brief eye contact before looking again at the ground. He was over six feet tall. He wore faded jeans, an "Illinois—It's a State of Mind" T-shirt, and loafers the size of small dinghies. His shock of dark hair, poorly cut, stood out in multiple directions, declaring independence from his head. His loping walk simultaneously suggested profound relaxation and intense pursuit. Other than those attributes, he was close to handsome. Might have been a good-looking fellow were it not for a difficult birth or some subtle twisting or breakage of a chromosome, I imagined.

"Charles?" I called out as nonthreateningly as possible as I walked toward him.

Compliant, he stopped in his tracks and turned in my direction. He smiled, stubbled cheeks spreading, and I saw only shiny gums, no teeth. "Charles," he echoed.

I held out my hand, and he responded, shaking it with such vigor it was as if he had known me since childhood.

"I'm Perry Turner. I'm a counselor at the mental health center. How're you doing today?"

"Fine." Automatic, without tone. He put the sack beneath his arm and held it tightly.

"Say, Dr. Casey asked me to come and see you today. You remember Dr. Casey?"

He nodded. His smile remained.

Since he gave me little indication of his depth of understanding, I decided to jump right into it, figuring the worst that could happen was benign silence. "Dr. Casey's a little concerned about you. He told me that you have a tough time around Father's Day every year and you know, Father's Day is this weekend."

"Father's Day," Charles said. Echoing or demonstrating understanding, I could not discern.

Only one way to go. Forward. "How come you have such a rough time on Father's Day?"

He licked his lips, and I thought I saw a tear forming in his right eye. "Mothercloud, fatherdust, sharp sun," he said, consonants fogged by his lack of teeth.

"Pardon me?" It was difficult to be empathically reflective when I had no idea what he was saying.

Charles looked down at his watch. Though it was nearly noon, his watch read four-thirty. The second hand was still. Apparently, while Charles had not mastered the art of stem winding or watch reading, he had absorbed some related social customs. By looking at the watch, he was telling me he had someplace else to go, something better to do. Now.

He began walking away, and convinced I had at least established initial rapport, I chose not to pursue him.

"See you later, Charles," I suggested.

Funny how retarded folks rarely have nicknames. Without even asking, I was positive that Charles had never been Charlie or Chuck to anyone. Never was a retarded Gerald referred to as Jerry; Robert was never Bob. Perhaps it's our way of giving them a bit of formal honor that they otherwise would not enjoy; or perhaps it is just another form of the quiet separation between Us and Them.

Dr. Casey was eating a sandwich in his office when I returned. He waved me in. "Figure everything out?" he said, his inflection implying confidence that I had not. "Can we escape the community's wrath this year?"

"I met him," I said, shrugging. "He seems like a nice fellow. I tried to talk to him about Father's Day, opened up the topic for him. He didn't give me much information though. He said something like, 'Mothercloud, fatherdust, sun . . .' Well, nothing that made much sense. Charles doesn't seem like he has much insight."

"Insight?" Dr. Casey laughed. "This isn't New York City psychoanalysis, Perry. Don't worry about *his* insight, just develop some of your own. Father's Day is two days away." He pulled some papers from his drawer. "Now, it's not that I don't have faith in your abilities, but I've already made arrangements with Galesburg for his admission. This is the only case we've ever handled where we can take care of all the paperwork before anything's even happened."

As an intern, I saw Dr. Casey as somewhat of a transitional father figure helping me to develop from infant intern to grown-up counselor. But that didn't stop me from wanting to prove myself, to earn his pride, as does any son. I wasn't daunted.

I retreated to my office and placed a call to the sheriff's office. I already knew that Sim Blakely had been county sheriff for almost twenty years. And since he was usually called in to corral troublesome patients for transport to the psych unit, maybe he could tell me something.

Wrong. He spoke with the confidence of someone whose word was rarely questioned in town, even though his thinking had the distinction of being both overdramatic and droll, not to mention lacking in factual basis. He theorized with the carelessness of a lazy mad scientist.

"Always seemed to me that the fire was a mite suspicious," he said in Barney Fife tones. I could picture him hitching up his pants. "I wonder if the ree-tard did it, maybe to kill the old man. He's not as stupid as people think he is. He's been sitting pretty since his dad died." With the virtual absence of serious crime in the area, perhaps Blakely just needed a colorful story to tell at sheriffs' conventions and using the mysterious Charles Lowary as a protagonist was too full of potential to pass up. That would be a generous interpretation of his motives. "Yep, he probably toasted the old man for the insurance money, just set him ablaze."

I suspected that Sheriff Blakely didn't share in the community adoption of Charles Lowary.

I thanked him with proper humility and hung up.

Next I called Ted Yancy, the Elderton attorney who served as Charles's conservator. He admitted he hadn't talked to Charles in years. His secretary handled the disbursement of funds and the paying of Charles's bills. I asked him about Sheriff Blakely's suspicions, and he spent the next several minutes loudly proclaiming that it was impossible for Charles to have had anything to do with the fire: "It was an electrical fire, damn that Blakely. It's been proven. And as far as Charles goes, hell, son, you've never seen a boy more upset than Charles was that night. Before the fire was even under control, Charles ran back into the house and tried to drag his daddy out. Jesus, there wasn't hardly anything left of John." Yancy then used the rest of our conversation to tell me "in strictest professional confidence" what a dipshit Sheriff Blakely was.

A client canceled her appointment the following afternoon, Saturday, so I used the opportunity to drive by Charles's house on Hillcrest Street. It was an old white two-story frame house, nondescript, interchangeable with half the homes in Elderton save for its lack of a porch swing.

I knocked and Charles answered. He smiled that same smile, all gums and open space.

Behind him, I saw a woman putting away groceries in the kitchen.

"Hello again, Charles," I said as we renewed our handshake. He stepped back from the doorway, and I took this as an invitation to enter.

As Charles opened a cabinet and removed two coffee cups, I said to the woman, "Hi. I'm Perry Turner of the mental health center."

"I'm Ida Townsend," she said. Ida was at least seventy. Her face was round and bright, her head topped with dull silver hair. She crinkled her cheeks into a smile.

"You're the housekeeper?" I asked.

"Well, I'm a volunteer from the Retired Senior Volunteer Program."

"RSVP. Sure."

Charles removed two spoons from the drawer and rummaged in another cabinet until he extracted a jar of instant coffee.

"Ms. Townsend, we're a little concerned about Charles," I said, "what with Father's Day coming up tomorrow."

Charles hopped up and down twice, a mercurial burst of excitement. "Mothercloud, fatherdust, sharp sun," he said as he hopped.

"You just relax there, Charles," Ida said, then turned back to me. "Yep, it's about that time again. You know, I've been helping out here for over five years, and this boy still confounds the blazes out of me."

"Has he ever talked about his father or Father's Day to you?"

"Charles probably hasn't said more than twenty words to me in all this time," she said. Then, over her shoulder, "Have you, Charles?"

Charles put two teaspoons of coffee into each cup as he nodded to Ida.

"Have you asked him about it?" I said.

"Not much use in asking." She squeezed her eyes shut, shook her head, and pointed a thumb Charles's way.

Charles waved his hand under the running tap water, retracted it suddenly, and then put each cup in orderly fashion beneath the faucet. He placed the cups on the countertop and carefully stirred the coffee crystals. He walked over and handed me a cup proudly.

Ida Townsend cocked her head at him. "Charles, that ain't no way to be making coffee."

"No, that's okay," I interjected. Ida shook her head again. I drank half of the coffee down quickly. Actually it wasn't too bad, although some of the crystals had not dissolved in the tepid water. "Hey, that's a pretty good cup of coffee, Charles. Thanks a lot."

Ida folded the last of the emptied grocery sacks and put it in the trash. She wiped her hands together twice, then grabbed her purse. "I'll see you in a week, Charles," she said as she walked to the door. "Nice meeting you, Mr. Turner." And she was gone.

Charles and I stood looking at each other, holding our coffee cups as if waiting for someone to make a toast. He looked at me expectantly.

"Can we sit down, Charles?"

We did.

I leaned in his direction. "Charles, I know we just met yesterday, but you're a nice man, and I like you. I don't want you to have a bad time this Father's Day, that's all. Maybe if we talk about it, this Father's Day can be better."

He reached to his back pocket and pulled out a time-worn wallet. He worried his way through the transparent picture holders, most of them empty. Tongue sticking out with concentration, Charles removed a black-and-white photo, spiderwebbed with creases, and held it out to me.

The man in the picture looked either tiredly proud or proudly tired; neither quality was dominant. He held a small boy on his lap, one hand upon the child's head. Both he and the boy were smiling widely.

"That's your dad and you?"

He nodded. "Dad. Father. No more."

"No more," I said. "He's gone now."

"No more."

"Well, he looks like a wonderful father, Charles, and you sure look like a wonderful son. You miss him a lot, don't you?"

Charles peered past the kitchen doorway to the front room. I saw the sack lying on an otherwise empty book-shelf there.

With infinite care he replaced the picture in his wallet and returned the wallet to his pocket.

"Mothercloud, fatherdust, sharp sun," he said and looked to the front room again. Slowly, the corners of his mouth began pushing downward, until they almost reached his jawline. He began to moan.

I laid my hand atop his. He looked up for a second. His eyes filled with tears and he began to cry. He was a pathetic sight, drool running freely from his toothless mouth. As he wept, Charles choked and gasped so violently I worried he would hyperventilate.

"It's okay, Charles," I said gently. "It's okay."

I let him cry until he put his head down on the table, exhausted.

"That's good to cry, Charles. That's a way we say good-bye."

He wiped his eyes and nose with his shirtsleeve.

I saw the clock on the kitchen wall. It was four o'clock. I had an appointment waiting.

"Now look, Charles," I said, rising from my chair. "I have to go now. Thank you for letting me see you today. It was good you showed me your father's picture and that you cried. When Father's Day comes tomorrow, maybe you can take out your dad's picture and look at it and tell him how nice it was to be his son. Wish him a happy Father's Day. You don't need to hurt so bad this year. Okay?"

He looked toward the front room, the sack, then back to me.

"Thank you," he said clearly.

I returned to the office, so confident I actually had accomplished something important I didn't feel the need to check in with Dr. Casey. I saw my last two Saturday appointments and went home, feeling warm and full.

But that night, as I tried to fall asleep, the image of Charles Lowary kept intruding. I saw him cry. I heard him say, "Mothercloud, fatherdust, sharp sun." I saw the little boy sitting on his father's lap and pictured the photo coming to life, John Lowary patting his young son on the head, proud that with no mother, living in a small town with no opportunities for schooling or the companionship of peers, the boy was able to smile. Quite an accomplishment.

And I began to doubt myself. I felt less sure that I had made the quiet therapeutic magic happen. Normal intern doubt? Hard to say.

I set my alarm for five o'clock Father's Day morning.

As the summer sun rose over Elderton, I sat in my parked car a block away from Charles's house. I sipped coffee from a Styrofoam cup and took bites from the chocolate specimens I had bought at Daylight Donuts at five-thirty. I felt like a deputy on a stakeout and wondered if Sheriff Blakely had ever found need for a stakeout in this town.

As soon as the blacktopped streets of Elderton shone with the morning sunlight, Charles walked out his front door. He held the tattered sack tightly to his chest.

With determination and intensity, Charles began walking toward the town square.

I followed slowly in my car until he reached the far side of the square. Feeling vaguely silly driving five miles an hour and stopping every ten yards, I parked and began pursuing him on foot, careful to remain a half block behind him.

Several times as I continued following Charles, I considered running up to him and saying, "Charles, let's go back to my house. I'll make us some coffee, and we can talk some more." But at the time, that didn't seem proper. He was so purposeful. Obviously, he knew what he was doing. Keeping my distance seemed the respectful thing to do.

Five blocks later and Charles was nearly at the city limits, walking at the same brisk pace he had maintained since leaving his home.

The last block of Elderton residences abutted a large University of Illinois research farm, teeming as far as the eye could see with emerging soybean plants. Charles left the confines of Elderton and entered the field, carefully staying between the rows.

I began trotting because Charles picked up speed as he walked up then over a gracefully sloping hill, disappearing from my view momentarily.

Seconds later, when I reached the top of the hill, I lay on my belly so only my head would be exposed to him. But it didn't matter. Charles faced the other direction, toward the sun, and was too deeply engrossed in his activities to notice me.

He laid the sack on the ground at his feet, stood tall, and reached his hands toward the sky, palms out. "Mother!" He yelled it at the top of his lungs, and I wondered why, if this was something he did yearly, he had never been heard throughout the east end of town. Though the landscape was basically flat, his penetrating cry echoed around me.

"Mother!" he screamed, extending the word for seconds, simultaneously pointing a finger skyward, toward a lonely white summer cloud.

His voice became hushed for a second. Then a tiny hum slowly escalated into full-throated bleating and bawling. Charles whirled around and around, every so often stopping just long enough to point at the cloud and cry, "Mother!" He spun, a spastic pirouette, until he lost his balance and fell to the ground.

Like Charles's body, my mind whirled. Psychological theories—behaviorist, humanistic, psychoanalytic, Gestalt—each clicked into place briefly and then finding no fit, flew away. I couldn't explain what I was seeing, and I couldn't take my eyes off it.

Lying on the ground, Charles rocked violently side to side, bursts of dislodged soil set free to float in the warm morning air.

If I'd had my notebook, I would've been scribbling down notes as I watched his doleful dust dance. But I don't know what I would have written.

Suddenly, his rocking stopped as quickly as it had

begun. He lay on his back, panting, whimpering, pointing at the cloud that had started to skitter away in the distance.

Charles Lowary turned over and pushed himself up to a kneeling position. Gingerly, he picked up the sack and unfurled it. He reached inside and with noble reverence lifted out its contents.

The distance between us was just far enough so that it took me a few moments to focus in on what it was he held.

He reached to the sky, gripping the wrist of a blackened, gnarled hand. Then he stood.

"Father!" he shouted in a high, tinny voice. "Daddy!"

In response to his call, Charles tenderly brought down the hand, again and again, to his head—stroking his hair, massaging his face, patting his head.

He continued this for several minutes, silent except for brief punctuations of speech when he said softly, flowingly, "Good boy. You're a good boy, Charles. You're a sharp son."

Patting his head with the hand, puffs of dust released with each tap, floating in the sunlight. "Good boy."

Suddenly, his shoulders sagged and Charles Lowary stood motionless, his father's hand hanging from his grasp. He looked down to the open sack, dropped the hand in, and closed it up again.

Finally, he reached upward, only this time he shouted not to his mother or his father. He cried to the sky itself, his voice sustained in a loud, trembling keen that continued until he was out of breath.

Then he quickly snatched up the sack and with a pitiable wail, Charles Lowary began running, top speed, toward town.

Toward me.

If I hadn't reached up to tackle him, Charles would have run over me.

I finished my internship three months later and moved far away from the small town of Elderton. I visited

Charles twice during those last months. No one else made the trip to see him. I guess the community adoption had been quietly canceled.

Since relocating to a suburb of Chicago ten years ago and opening a private practice, I have served several thousand clients. By all accounts I am an ethical and effective counselor. I have a nice income and a solid client base.

But regardless of how many years flow by, no case has remained with me like Charles Lowary. The memory of him is a shard of glass that floats freely through the chambers of my heart, frequently nicking me deep inside.

Sure enough, after I had pulled him to the ground that Father's Day, he was totally incoherent, speaking without words, crying without emotion, present but not there. I sat on the hilltop for an hour, his head in my lap, saying, "Good boy, you're a sharp son." But that was probably as much for me as it was for him.

Charles was hospitalized in Galesburg in the bed reserved for him. But this time his week of respite and quick return home were not to be.

The local State's Attorney found out about the contents of Charles's sack and—probably feeling the same sense of power a road crew member feels the first day he gets to hold the Stop-Slow sign—decided that some obscure aspiration of justice required satisfaction.

To this day I cannot imagine what charges could have been brought against Charles, who had lovingly carried his father's hand, secretly cherishing it since the night he had retrieved it from the fire. No matter. No formal charges had to be filed. The State's Attorney convinced a local judge that Charles's possession of the hand evidenced a tendency toward unpredictability and violence. Charles was committed to the state institution in Weaver, known as the Asylum for the Criminally Insane prior to our current age of enlightenment. He has remained there ever since.

He deteriorated rapidly after being transferred to

Weaver, even being given to uncharacteristic periods of blind panic and aggression. And though I was only an intern at the time and no one would listen to me, I think I have always known why.

It counts for precious little that Elderton considered him their communal son. No one knew Charles: the things that made him laugh and cry, the things he wondered about, the things that scared him. No one bothered to make the simple human connection with him, the same connection we all need, the tender tether of belonging. I probably came the closest, but even my effort was pitifully lacking. The chasm between Charles and everyone else, though not acknowledged, was infinitely deep and wide, full to the brink with loneliness.

So Charles had created a unique, almost poetic ritual for himself, an oddly curative mental aberration, one in which he was able to call to his mother as she floated by in the distance, lost and untouchable; one in which he was again soothed and reassured by the hand of his father; one in which his internal world finally exploded much as it had the night of the fire.

Previously, that internal explosion had soon settled, and Charles had healed in a graceful denouement, consoled with the knowledge that Father's Day would come again. But since that summer when our lives intersected, Father's Day has not returned for him.

Now Charles Lowary has only a locked room with a window so small he cannot see his mother flutter by in the sky, and a father whose absence palls eternal.

Given the circumstances, it seems impossible to me that Charles can find his way back from his dark and lonely madness. But perhaps I am wrong. Perhaps the human spirit, like a flower in a cellar, continues to search out the light, no matter how distant or scarce.

Today I received a Father's Day card from Charles Lowary.

Parting Gift

by Larry Segriff

The salesman looked at me as though I was crazy.

"Are you crazy?" he asked. Obviously he didn't work on commission.

I sighed and shook my head. "Look, I don't see why you're having such a problem with this. All I asked was whether you had an appropriate gift for Father's Day."

"Yes." The clerk nodded. He couldn't have been out of high school for long. His dark, dirty hair kept falling into his eyes. "But you also said he died last week."

"That's right." I had to admit, I'd thought it a bit odd myself, but old Pembroke, our family lawyer, had read Dad's will to us just the other day. It was quite clear. All four of us kids would be taken care of no matter what, but the bulk of Dad's money would go to the one who, in Pembroke's estimation, provided the most appropriate gift for Father's Day.

Hey, it might be weird, but for an estate valued at more than ten million dollars, I didn't mind playing the fool.

The clerk with the greasy hair couldn't help me, nor could anyone in the dozens of other stores I visited that day. It just wasn't easy, picking a present for the man who has nothing.

The next day, Friday, we all met over at Evan's house. He was our big brother, the oldest of the four, and of us all, he probably needed Dad's money the least. His place was the closest thing to neutral ground we were going to find in this city.

Dee, the eldest of the two girls by just over a year,

was there ahead of me. It was not yet two o'clock, but she had a Scotch in her hand, and the look on her face suggested that it wasn't her first.

"Clyde, dear boy," she said, kissing the air next to my left ear, "so nice of you to come." She was a slinky woman in her early forties, with reddish hair done up in a long braid that fell halfway down her back. She had hazel eyes that tended more toward green and had been bloodshot for the last four years.

I nodded, then turned toward Evan, in his usual place behind the bar.

"Greetings, Clyde. What'll you have?" He had red hair, too, cut short and curling wildly. His eyes were more brown, with flecks of gold dancing near their centers. All of us were tall, but Evan, some three and a half years older than Dee, was starting to put on a little weight.

"Nothing, thanks."

"Oh, come now, dear brother," Dee said, slurring her words only a little. She would remain coherent for at least three hours yet, I knew. "Still mourning Father? What an act." She brushed by me and held her empty glass out to Evan for a refill.

He obliged, and I saw it was Chivas. As always, he poured with a liberal hand.

"No, Dee. Not mourning, but you know I can't drink." Alcoholism ran in our family; it was just that not all of us admitted it.

She sniffed and turned her back on me to accept her glass. Evan gave me a wry look as she turned back. I noticed that he was drinking mineral water.

I was sure Dee was about to cut loose with another shot, but the remaining member of our dwindling family put in her appearance just then. Dorothy, sometimes called D2 to her intense frustration, was also tall and also red-haired, but there her resemblance to her elders ended. She had a shorter nose, almost pug, that contrasted sharply with their proud beaks, and her eyes were blue.

Me, I was the misfit. I had Granddad's hair, jet black without a hint of curl, and if mine was starting to go gray at the temples at the ripe old age of twenty-nine, at least it wasn't receding like Evan's. My nose didn't match, either, being neither too long nor too short, and my eyes were as gray as my temples.

"Hello, Dorothy," I said, family rules requiring the latest arrival to greet the newcomer. "Evan's pouring. Would you like something?"

"Maybe a glass of wine," she said. "Thank you."

I strode over to the bar and accepted a glass of Riesling. With Dorothy there was only one kind of wine. She smiled when I took it over to her, but didn't say anything.

"Well," Evan said, checking the ice in the bucket. "We're all here. Should we get started?"

"Christ," Dee said. "This isn't going to be another god-damned meeting, is it? I thought we were just getting together for drinks." She gestured with her glass and would have spilled it if she hadn't already drank half of it off.

"No, Dee, not a meeting," Evan said, picking up his mineral water and stepping out from behind the bar. "I just thought, since it's almost Father's Day, we might want to talk about this whole thing. You know."

"Oh, please." She rolled her eyes, one of the few moves she could make no matter how many Scotches she'd had, and looked to Dorothy for support.

Our youngest sister shrugged. "I don't see any harm in talking about it," she said. I had the feeling that, had Dee not already spoken, Dorothy's opinion might have been quite different, but she hated to go along with Dee on anything.

"Tell me, brother," Evan said, looking at me. "Have you bought your gift yet?"

I gave a small smile and wished for a drink, if only to have a reason to stall for a moment. "No, Evan, I haven't. Have you?"

He smiled, too, rather secretively, and shook his head.

It was unclear whether he was saying he hadn't or was refusing to answer, as I was sure he intended.

"Dee?" He bounced the question to her.

She was taking a long drink at the time and almost choked on her mouthful of Scotch in her haste to reply. "Oh, sure," she said, her voice scathing. "You'd like that, wouldn't you? Find out what I bought and then try and do better. You know Pembroke has always liked my taste."

"Just because you—"

I cut in before Dorothy could finish. We all knew what she was going to say, and I didn't see how the accusation would help anything. Besides, it was ancient history.

"You know," I said, "that's not a bad idea, Dee."

She was glaring at Dorothy, fire in her red-rimmed eyes, but at my words she turned on me. "What? What's not a bad idea?"

"Think about it. We're all going to be taken care of, right? No matter how this thing tomorrow comes out? That wasn't spelled out, of course, but I think we can all assume it means that we'll each be given a significant amount of money; maybe not millions, but certainly enough to live on. So what is it that we're fighting over? Excess wealth. I mean, really, what do you do with ten million dollars? What did Dad do with it? Put it in a bank and hoard it. What if, instead, we all agreed to buy the same thing, maybe something as simple as just all signing a card for Dad. Pembroke would have to call it a tie, and we all split the pot. Two and a half mil, or more, for each of us, and no risk at all. What do you say?"

They all stood motionless, looking at me, and for a moment I thought I had them. Then Dee burst out laughing, with Evan and Dorothy quick to follow.

"Oh, Clyde," Dee said. "That's great. Wouldn't Daddy just love that? The four of us *cooperating.*"

Dorothy, siding with Dee for once, said, "A card? Now that's a wonderful idea. Here we are, talking about millions of dollars, and you think a card's an appropriate gift?"

Actually, I did. I'd seen a movie once long ago. I think Jimmy Stewart was in it. He played a young man who'd just received a million dollars inheritance, but with a catch. He could keep it, if he chose, or, if he dared, he could try to spend it all in thirty days. If he was successful, he'd inherit a full ten million dollars, but if he failed, he got nothing. I'd always expected Dad to do something like that, and not just because of the coincidence of figures. The only thing was, where Jimmy's patron was trying to teach the value of a dollar, Dad was just plain ornery.

Still, I'd thought the card idea suitable.

Evan looked at me, eyebrows askance and a wry grin upon his face.

Dee wasn't done yet. "A card," she repeated. "Yeah, how much is a buck and a quarter divided by four? Or, better yet, we could buy some construction paper and *make* one. That'd be cheaper."

I looked around at the three laughing faces and tried to keep my anger in check. "Well," I said, "I can see that this is a waste of time. Thank you, Evan, for trying, at least. Dee, Dorothy, good-bye."

I turned and walked out. Behind me one of my sisters called out, "Don't go away mad; just go away." And the other suggested, "Drop us a line, sometime, Clyde. Or, better yet, send us a card."

Their laughter followed me out. Why is it that the youngest never gets any respect?

On Sunday we all met at Pembroke's office at one o'clock. I suppose that was to give everyone time to get home from church, but in reality it allowed Dee to recover somewhat from the previous night's indulgences.

Pembroke had an office on Third Street, an old two-story brick building that was probably on some historical registry somewhere. Walking up the plushly carpeted stairs, I found myself wondering about old Pembroke. It was Father's Day. Did he have a family waiting for him at home?

I was the last to arrive, which was unusual, but it had taken me longer than I'd thought to wrap the oversize box I had brought along. Lugging it up those stairs was quite a feat, also; although it was light, it was pretty unwieldy.

I could see the lingering amusement on my siblings' faces as I entered the large, well-apportioned office. Dee was sitting next to Evan, and she mouthed the word "card" into his ear. They were both on the black leather couch that lined the wall to the right of the door. Opposite them, in an overstuffed chair to Pembroke's right, Dorothy looked up and grinned as well.

Pembroke sat behind his desk, a mahogany monster that could have served as a snooker table. He had an unlit pipe clenched in his teeth. There was no humor hiding in his eyes, so I assumed my brother and sisters hadn't told him about Friday's conference.

There was a large marble urn sitting on a blotter in the middle of that enormous desk. I didn't have to ask what was in it. I'd seen it after the funeral when the director brought it out and gave it to Mr. Pembroke.

"Yes," Pembroke said when I'd closed the door. There was another stuffed chair directly before him, and I seated myself there as he went on, "Welcome, Clyde. I am pleased to see that you have a gift with you as well."

Glancing around, I noticed that each of us four had brought a gaily wrapped parcel. Dee and Dorothy held theirs on their laps. Evan, like me, had his on the floor by his feet.

"The ground rules are these," Pembroke said, his deep, rich voice giving added weight to his words. "You will each unwrap your presents one at a time, in descending order of age. I will compare each with a list your father left in my keeping. The one of you that comes closest to matching what he'd asked for wins. The others will, as I said before, be taken care of."

Dee had risen as he spoke, the amusement draining

from her face. "Wait a minute—most closely matches what he'd asked for? That's not what you said before."

Pembroke looked at her. "I know. All is proceeding in accordance with your father's wishes."

That deflated her. Knowing Father, none of the rest of us had been at all surprised.

"Evan, we'll start with you. What gift did you select as being most appropriate for this Father's Day?"

Big Brother looked more than a little uncomfortable, a situation that was rare for him. He sent his gaze once around the room, as though seeking some kind of support, but it was a wasted effort. Clearing his throat, he bent down and retrieved the package by his feet.

About the size and shape of a shoe box, he'd wrapped it in silver paper with a blue bow. Undoing the paper, he revealed that it was a shoe box, but he didn't immediately lift the lid.

"Years ago, when I was young, Father used to do a lot of reading. Fantasy was his chosen genre, and as I recall, he was particularly fond of Tolkien. Actually, I'd commissioned this work nearly a year ago, before any of us even knew he was sick."

Yeah, I thought. *Back when you still thought you could worm your way into his good graces.*

With a little flourish Evan removed the lid of the box and drew out an exquisite figurine. Dee, sitting right next to him, gave out a little gasp, though I was sure she hated herself for doing it.

It was a dragon, done in loving detail, and he'd obviously spared no expense. The scales appeared to have been dipped in real gold, and the eyes were genuine ruby chips. Or so they appeared, and knowing Evan, I doubted they were fake. I'd read Tolkien myself, many times, though I might not have if I'd known Dad liked him, and I recognized the dragon immediately. It was Smaug, the Great Worm, killer and hoarder and keeper of the Great Ring. The thing was, the sculptor had, in an amazing display of his art, managed to give the piece an unmistakable resemblance to Dad. It was nothing obvious, nothing as simple as the shape of the nose or the cut of the mouth, but looking at that piece made me think of our father.

Even Pembroke let out a whistle at the sight, but he didn't say anything. Simply consulted a sheet of paper he kept concealed on his lap, nodded once, and made a notation with his Mont Blanc pen.

The murmurs subsided quickly, and then it was Dee's turn. She glanced one more time at the dragon in Evan's lap, smiled as if to say, "Nice try," and opened her gift.

This package was slightly larger than Evan's, and she'd chosen gold paper. She'd placed a white satin bow upon it and looked only at Pembroke as she opened it.

"Unlike Evan, I didn't commission this a year ago, but it's something I've been waiting to give him for a long time." From beneath the paper came an unmarked box, and from this she pulled a bronzed, limited edition Tonka dump truck. "As far as I know," she said, rising and stepping toward the desk, "Dad never played with one of these, but we all know how much he liked getting his ashes hauled." And she placed the reliquary squarely in the back of the truck and pushed it slowly across the desk.

Pembroke burst out laughing and my heart sank. She'd done it. We'd all known since the reading of the will that the final determination was up to old Pembroke, and she'd already had an edge with him. This had pretty well sealed it.

Tears of laughter streaming down his face, he motioned for Dee to take her seat and turned to Dorothy.

Our youngest sister stood up, glaring daggers at the two oldest members of our family. She held her gift, the size and shape of a jewelry box, wrapped in pink paper and a red ribbon.

"Unlike others present," she said, slowly turning her dark gaze on the still-chuckling Pembroke, "I am not here to take cheap shots at our father."

"Believe me," Evan interrupted, "there was nothing cheap about my shot."

Dorothy didn't even look over at him. "I loved my father," she went on, unmindful of the snickers coming from the couch, "and I am here to honor his memory."

She unwrapped her package and showed the contents to Pembroke. I had to half rise and peer over her shoulder to catch a glimpse myself, and at first, I couldn't tell what it was.

"Daddy is beyond presents now," she said, "and so I decided to make this a present to myself."

That was just like her.

She held up her gift, and now I could see that it was a little crystal pendant mounted on a fine gold chain. "I found a jeweler who could modify this for me in only a few days. It cost quite a bit, but it was worth it to have a locket that could hold both a picture of Daddy and a pinch of his ashes. Mr. Pembroke, I am here to ask you for a pinch, so that I may always carry a piece of my father with me wherever I go."

I heard a groan from the couch and didn't have to look over to know that Dee was rolling her eyes. "God," she muttered, "where's the Scotch when I need it?"

Pembroke didn't respond directly to Dorothy. He just held her gaze for a moment before making a mark on the paper on his lap. Then it was my turn.

"Clyde?" he rumbled. Dorothy went back to her seat without her pinch of Daddy.

I shrugged. "I guess I have to make a little speech, too. It took me a long time to come up with the gift that I thought best summed up my relationship to my father. I had hoped that, as a family, we might come up with something a bit more meaningful, but as that was not to be . . ." I shrugged again and turned to my box.

I had selected the most garish party paper I could find. It had clowns all over, bright spots of red and green and blue, all against a vivid yellow background. I'd put a purple bow on it, knowing the color would clash the most. Besides, Dad had always hated purple.

Ripping the paper off, I opened the large box and lifted it high. "I decided that the most appropriate gift

I could give to Dad for this Father's Day would be just what he's always given me." With that I tipped the box over, showing that it was empty.

Pembroke grunted and made another mark. I took my seat, not really surprised at the silence that had fallen over the room. Looking around the room at the festive paper strewn about and the frustrated faces my siblings bore, I couldn't help but think how much dear old Dad would have treasured this scene. He'd have probably thought it was worth dying just to be able to stage it.

Pembroke kept his head down, looking at whatever paper was on his lap, for several minutes. He still held his fountain pen, but I couldn't see that he was writing anything.

Eventually, he looked up, taking us all in one at a time, and I saw a familiar, wicked gleam in his eye.

"I had feared this was going to be difficult," he said. "Your father did indeed leave the judging to my discretion and, knowing all of you, I should not have been worried. I'm glad to say, none of you disappointed me."

He lifted the paper from his lap and dropped it on the desk in front of him, right next to the dump truck containing Father's ashes. "Your father never intended for any of you to inherit his estate. Oh," he hurried on before we could react, "there were provisions in the event that you truly surprised me. Believe it or not, he truly did care about all of you, in his own way. He'd hoped that, with both of your parents gone, you would finally be able to come together as a family. Had you done that, I would have been able to award the estate to all of you equally."

I felt three pairs of eyes turn in my direction, but I couldn't tear my gaze from Pembroke. I'd gloat later. Right now, I wanted to hear where the old bastard was leading.

"It is, therefore, with some satisfaction that I announce that the bulk of your father's estate, at last estimate valued at some ten point seven million dollars, will go to several different charities. Those, also, your father left to me to pick. His only words on the subject were, 'Just so long as none of them benefit those damn kids of mine.' "

"But what about us?" Evan protested.

"You said we would be taken care of," Dee added.

Pembroke smiled. "And so you shall. I said that the bulk of his estate is to go to charity." Beside me, Dorothy sighed with evident relief. "The remainder, approximately two and a half million"—out of the corner of my eye I could see both Dorothy and Evan grin—"will go to set up a trust fund to maintain your father's house. Any of you who choose to live there will be provided for. All your groceries will be paid for, including whatever liquor you may require, as will any and all taxes and utilities. Should any of you decide to marry and raise a family, there will be additional funds provided to add on to the existing structure. That is all."

There was a moment of stunned silence before someone—I think it was Dorothy—asked the obvious. "And those of us who choose not to live together?"

"Get nothing," Pembroke said.

I grinned. I couldn't help it. The old bastard had done it again: Set us all up and then knocked us all down.

The others were sitting motionless, their heads hanging slightly, defeated. I stood up and strode forward to the edge of Pembroke's desk.

"I can hear what each of them is thinking," I said to the old reprobate lawyer. " 'I'll live in that house, but not with any of them.' Well, Pembroke, I'll tell you right now, I'll accept Dad's offer, with or without my siblings."

I turned to regard them. "I'll be wanting to move in as soon as possible," I said, "but we'll need to work out the details, first. Please drop me a line with your decision as soon as possible. Or, better yet," I added, my grin growing even wider, "send me a card."

Wrong Turn

by Norman Partridge

The thing is, they really weigh on you. That's why digging up the dead is so tough.

And my father was a real backbreaker. I'm speaking figuratively, of course. I mean, I can't remember the last time I held a shovel in my hands, and I'm not a dirt-under-the-fingernails kind of guy. I've never played things that way. I've always liked to think that I used my head.

Not that I've gotten much of anywhere in thirty-five years. The trust fund my mother set up after she remarried has kept me afloat, but I think my monthly stipend equals the average take an inventive person can snag with welfare and food stamps. I'm certainly not one of those rich sons of privilege who motor around Maui with a wind-surfing rig when they're not busy hitting the slopes in Aspen or Vail.

Dad's name hasn't hurt me, though. There are still plenty of people who remember it. It's funny—people forget directors and writers and producers, but get your face up there on the screen and you'll be remembered for a long time, even if your claim to fame is portraying a long string of heavies and sad-eyed losers in poverty row quickies. I've made more than a few dollars by being the son of a movie star, even if Dad was a star in a lesser constellation.

Then again, most people remember Dad for the things he did when there weren't any cameras in sight. That's what puts the old shine in their eyes.

Tom Cassady—my old man. Me—Tom Cassady, Junior. I guess Dad wasn't the most inventive guy in the world. He actually had a dog named Rover.

But Dad did leave me the name and all the baggage that goes with it. That, and his face. Hard little eyes and pouting lips on a face that is otherwise completely boyish, even when I skip shaving for a day or two. Give Kurt Russell a bad attitude and you've got me. I don't have Dad's signature broken nose, of course—remember, I use my head. And I doubt that I'll ever acquire the puffy, dissipated look he had after he got out of prison, the look that made him a *primo* heavy in his second run at Hollywood, because I don't drink much.

But as I said, I've made some money with Dad's face. It's a handsome face, and I take care of what's under it. I pump iron, keep my tan just a shade this side of narcissistic, get my hair styled every other week and my back waxed at the same interval. You've probably seen me on TV—lathering my manly chest with Irish Spring, whipping a bottle of Sharpshooter barbecue sauce from a holster while I wear a squint that would have pleased Sergio Leone. Big hands with manicured nails dishing Happy Chow for some generic Rover. You've probably seen me, or at least significant portions of my anatomy.

But you didn't know who I was.

I didn't know either. That's why I dug Dad up. I wanted to find out.

I wrote the book. It was my idea. *Cassady: a Life on the Edge*. After I sold it, the publisher brought in a pro to rewrite it, a guy who'd ghosted books for several bulimic actresses, a gay running back, and a hamster that spent four years in the White House—in a cage, not in the Oval Office. The ghost spent a week with me, and I didn't shut up the whole time. I learned more about myself in that week than I've learned in thirty-five years of living. Even now, I think of the ghost's quiet questions, questions that had always been in my head, but had never escaped, and my tongue gets dry.

The ghost tried to interview my sister, but Jo wouldn't

have anything to do with him. Anyway, he rewrote the book. Just a few minor adjustments—*punched up* the prose, *punched up* the title. That's publishing talk. Changed the title to *Killer Cassady*.

As it turned out, I didn't write what was in that book, but it all came out of my mouth. I'll admit that. And even with everything down in black and white, it came out of my mouth over and over. I toured twenty cities in fourteen days, and my mouth was dry in every one. Then I spent a week under the lights with the syndicated television mud-slingers. And everywhere I ran in those three weeks—lips flapping, sucking air and trying not to sweat as much as I tried to smile—my dead father rode me piggyback.

The book tour climaxed on the day before Father's Day. That was the publisher's plan, as if people were really going to choose a book like mine as the ideal gift for dad. I took my last round of questions in a Chicago studio, sitting there with a guy who wore too much Jovan Musk and a gaggle of housewives who seemed fascinated and repulsed in equal parts.

Mr. Jovan Musk worked up to it, lobbing a volley of soft questions my way. And then he asked me, "Do you think your father exploited the fact that he was a convicted murderer to further his career?"

I didn't even blink. I took it just the way Dad would have in one of his movies. I answered in a solid, studied whisper, equal portions of sorrow and shame in my voice.

And then Mr. Jovan Musk hit me with the follow-up question, the one that surprised me.

I took that question Dad's way, too.

The next time I saw him, on television that afternoon as I passed through O'Hare, the talk show host was wearing a couple of Popsicle sticks on his nose. The sticks were held in place by a generous smattering of gummy white tape. He looked kind of like Lon Chaney, Junior, as the Mummy.

And then I got off a plane in Reno and it was all

over. Or it should have been. I drove to Lake Tahoe, stopping only for gas and a quick bite. I had to use folding money because my credit card had expired while I was on tour. That's the great thing about expense accounts. Live on one long enough and you lose track of your own money.

I awoke the next morning in the A-frame cabin I've owned for ten years, only to find the red light on my answering machine flashing wildly. I hit the play button and listened to the first three messages. Two local TV shows and a radio call-in show in Sacramento, all wanting me to keep on talking.

I cut the messages short. It was Father's Day, but somehow I didn't want anything to do with my father. Three weeks carrying him on my back, a year digging him up while I wrote the book. I didn't even want to look in the mirror because I didn't want to see his eyes staring back at me.

So I climbed out of bed and went downstairs.

And my father was sitting there on my couch, watching me, his hard little eyes peering over a copy of *Killer Cassady*.

His pouting lips twisted into that signature grin that always spelled trouble in his films. Wounded, hateful, proud—all at the same time.

"At least you spelled my name right," he said, rising from the couch. He straightened his jacket—very shiny sharkskin, the color of a hammerhead—and loosened his skinny black tie, and the way he moved he might as well have said *I'm ready to get down to business*.

I hadn't said a word, but my throat was dry. I didn't know what to say, but my mouth came open.

And then I realized that his voice was all wrong.

"Who are you?" I asked.

He dropped the book as if he'd suddenly discovered that he was holding a poisonous snake. He grinned. "Sorry to give you a scare. I couldn't resist it. I'm not a ghost. I'm your brother." I didn't say anything, so he kept on. "Yeah. It kind of surprises me, too, reading this book. I mean, you've done a lot of research. I don't know how you could have missed me."

I fished around for something to say. "Dad never mentioned—"

"Damn right, he didn't. Christ, would you go around rubbing your kid's nose in your dirty laundry?" He laughed high and nutty, more like Richard Widmark than Dad. "But maybe the old man told you that kind of stuff. Maybe he bragged about the little actress he knocked up in '58. Maybe you just forgot to put that in the book. If that's the deal, it's a shame, because you make the dirty stuff sing. Like that part where Dad kills your mother's boyfriend? Smashes the little Frenchman's head against the kitchen counter until the tiles crack? Man, I felt like I was there." He cracked his knuckles. "Man, I could almost *taste* it."

"I did a lot of research," I said. "Court transcripts, crime scene photos, things people hadn't taken time to examine."

"Yeah. Sure. I get that." He glanced at the book. "But *you're* in there, too. I mean, I'm a slow reader. I'm only a hundred pages or so into it. But the old man has already smacked you around a good dozen times. That part where he puts on the gloves and says he's going to teach you how to box? That was *brutal.* And Dad did throw a mean left hook. Remember the way he took out that pretty boy in *Wrong Turn*?" He stopped and looked at me kind of funny. "Amazing how you've still got that cute little nose after the beatings the old man dished out."

"Look," I said, knowing I had to change direction. "What do you want?"

He didn't answer. In the bedroom the phone rang. We listened as the answering machine picked up, heard the tinny voice of a producer leaving an eager message. The producer had been after me for weeks, following my book tour trail. He wanted to remake Dad's best-remembered movie, *Wrong Turn,* and he wanted me to star.

When the producer finished, the man who claimed to be my half brother pointed a thumb in the direction of the phone. "I guess I just want in on the action. I mean, we're family. We ought to look out for each other. Maybe you don't want to make that movie. Maybe you could put in a good word for me. You got the book out of Dad. It seems like I should be due for something."

I stood on the stairs, and my hands became fists, and I couldn't stop shaking. He was pressing my buttons, just dancing over them lightly, pressing just hard enough—the way people used to press Dad's buttons in the movies, *bip bip bip,* time after time until he finally smiled his little smile and exploded.

The way they pressed Dad's buttons in *Wrong Turn.*

"I think you'd better go," I said.

He was smirking, staring at my fists as if they were no more dangerous than feather dusters. He cracked his knuckles again. Thick ridges of scar tissue the color of spoiled meat seemed to swell before my eyes. "You'd better slow down." He rubbed his nose, which was flatter than Dad's, mocking me, and for the first time I noticed the net of bone-colored scars under his thinning eyebrows. "See, I've followed in the old man's footsteps, too. Oh, I haven't been in front of any cameras, unless you count cameras that shoot mug shots. I haven't made any dog food commercials, like you have. I've followed the other path. I've bashed heads against kitchen counters. But just like you, I haven't quite lived up to the old man's example. You haven't made a movie; I haven't cracked any tile."

I couldn't help it. His battered nose and scarred knuckles suddenly didn't matter. I started toward him, wearing Dad's smile.

And I was surprised by how quickly he moved away and opened the door. "You think about it," he said. "I don't need an answer today. You think about family."

"I don't need to think about anything."

"Oh, yeah, you do." His gaze found the book. "Because there's more to this than you and me. There's our darling sister, too." He shook his head. "Remember the things Dad used to do to bad girls in the movies? Remember how he'd get them to do the things he wanted? Remember what he did to that two-faced piece in *Wrong Turn*? And our sister . . . what you wrote about her . . . oh, man, she's one bad girl."

He had finally pushed the button that stopped me cold. The best I could do was whisper, "You leave Jo out of this."

"Now Tommy m'lad, you didn't leave Jo out of this, so why should I?" He stopped in the doorway for a moment, completely confident, not sparing me a backward glance. "Anyway, you think about what I said. You get in touch with that producer. I'll give you today to get it done, and I'll call you tomorrow. And then you'd better tell me what I want to hear, or else I'll be driving down to San Francisco. I don't like long drives, and I'll be thinking of our darling sister the whole time." He laughed. "And thanks for the free roost. This has been a relaxing three weeks." He started across the pine porch. "Your mail's on the kitchen table. There's beer in the fridge."

I just stood there. Dad pressed down on me, whispered in my ear, told me what to do.

But I didn't do anything.

My brother was gone.

There was another phone in the kitchen. I had to look up Jo's number in San Francisco. We weren't on the best of terms. Hell, that was sugar-coating it. We hadn't talked in five years, not since Jo got into trouble for smacking around her live-in lover. The incident made the papers, and the woman took her revenge in the courts. Lesbian battery case. The bastions of political correctness in S.F. seemed shocked by the very idea— like gay couples were immune to that kind of trouble.

Jo came to me then, expecting a sympathetic ear, and

all I could do was make smart remarks. "Like father, like daughter." The girlfriend hit Jo for a good bit of cash, and Jo got off with probation and counseling. The last I'd heard she was involved with one of San Francisco's gay theater companies, both acting and directing.

That was pretty much it with us. Until now. I dialed her number and was rewarded with an unfamiliar voice that informed me Jo and Gabrielle weren't at home; I could leave a message at the sound of the deafening applause.

Theater people—*trés* cute. But this wasn't something to do on tape, no matter how anxious I was. Who knew what Jo would do if I came at her out of the blue with a sixty-second warning? She'd most certainly seen *Killer Cassady*. By now, she'd probably read the chapter where I connected her propensity to violence to the old man. If that were the case, I figured that my sister would be ready to eat me for breakfast.

I told myself that Jo was tough. She was indeed like the old man. She could take care of herself.

I cradled the handset. I wanted to do something, but I didn't know just what. I looked across the room to the place my brother had stood. Just doing that scared me. I made my way to the door, cautiously, as if I expected him to jump out at me. I closed it, locked it, remembering the steel in his eyes and his scars.

Maybe he wasn't my brother. Half brother, I should say. Maybe he was just a nut. But even as the idea took hold, I knew it wasn't true. He had the look, all right. He had the genes. And I had twenty-four hours to figure out how much he knew, and what he could do with that knowledge.

I opened the fridge. The six-pack he'd left me was waiting. I popped a brew and sat down at the table. The key to the drawer I rented at the post office lay on the unfinished pine, along with a large stack of mail.

The bastard hadn't been kidding. He *had* picked up my mail. And, looking at the envelopes, I could tell that he'd opened it.

Three weeks' worth of mail. Not much for someone who lives as quietly as I do. I don't go in for magazines and catalogs, mainly because my work involves travel. With the drawer, which is fairly large, I can miss a couple of weeks and still not have to notify the P.O. and everyone who works there that I'm out of town and my place is ripe for burglary.

Go ahead, call me paranoid.

Hurriedly, I flipped through the mail. Mostly bills, junk. But there was a letter from the producer that had been forwarded by my agent, and a quick once-over told me that two things were missing from the large package—a contract and a script for the *Wrong Turn* remake.

That set me to thinking. Maybe my half brother *hadn't* known about the movie. Maybe he had come here with a simple shakedown in mind. I cursed myself for leaving the key to the post office box where someone could find it. My mistake had probably given the idiot ideas.

I sorted through the rest of the mail and found nothing else of interest, but I wasn't finished. I wanted to be thorough. I dumped the garbage can in the sink and sifted through the trash—hamburger wrappers, beer cans, crumpled cigarette packages, and, finally, another envelope.

It bore no return address. I sifted through more junk and found a torn chunk of a letter from my credit card company. I remembered my drive from the airport, the clerk at the gas station informing me that my card had expired.

The torn letter promised that "my new card was enclosed."

But the card wasn't in the garbage.

I knew where it was—in the wallet of a guy who thought that he was one step ahead of me.

So, my credit card had been stolen.

I breathed a sigh of relief. My half brother *was* that stupid. He had fallen victim to the old man's genes, all right. Punch your way out of problems. Snatch the easy opportunity. Don't think ahead.

That was the propensity that always got Dad into trouble. He'd snatch the fast answer because he couldn't think ahead, and then he'd end up sinking deeper into trouble. It happened to him in *Wrong Turn.* In that movie he kept the dead guy's wallet because he was afraid of a murder rap. And then the shrewish hitchhiker entered the picture and tried to force him into assuming the guy's identity so they could make a fast buck. Dad couldn't think at all after she came into it. Just like that night in the kitchen when he caught my mother with that French dandy who specialized in playing the smartass kind of guy Dad loathed. He couldn't think at all, seeing that guy with his wife. He could only *react.*

That's what my half brother was doing. He was reacting, running the *Wrong Turn* playbook, but he wasn't thinking.

I was thinking, and fast. I called the credit card company's 800 number and asked for a rundown of my latest charges. Several local restaurants turned up—Soule Domaine at Crystal Bay, Bobby's Uptown Café at Incline—better joints than I figured my *doppelgänger* for.

He was staying at the Cal-Neva Lodge on the north shore, the place Sinatra had owned before he made the mistake of inviting Sam Giancana to be his guest. It was a nice place, a tourist place. That didn't seem to fit my half brother, either.

He'd had a room at the Lodge for two weeks.

I hung up the phone. I had more questions.

And the answers were just eight miles away.

I stood in the lobby of the Cal-Neva, staring at the stuffed bobcat on the big granite fireplace, wondering if the big cat's last memory was sticking his nose somewhere that it didn't belong.

I wandered over to the main desk. An old man was trying to weasel a couple of comp rooms out of the desk clerk. The old man's young squeeze was busily tapping her toe. The trouble threw me off. I didn't want to deal with a surly clerk.

"Mr. Cassady?" A young woman stepped behind the desk. "Tom Cassady?"

"Yes." I smiled, playing it simple.

"I just want to say . . ." She blushed. "I think it was great what you did to that ass on television. I've been waiting for something like that to happen since the first time I saw him."

I kept the smile. "I just thought it was the right thing to do."

She nodded. "Well, it's great to have you as a guest. If you need anything, my name's Cheryl. You just ask for me."

I explained that I was picking up the tab for some relatives who were staying at the hotel. They were registered under my name, and I'd forgotten their room number. One fumbling description of terminal absent-mindedness later, I had a key. Obviously, Cheryl hadn't run into my brother during the two weeks he had been registered. I began to wonder if he was really staying at the Cal-Neva, or if he had indeed stayed at my cabin as he had claimed.

I detoured past the bar, a round room paneled with rich wood. Mirrors above reflected the room's harsh artificial glow, and a stained glass dome high in the ceiling filtered the early afternoon sunshine, so that the bar was a strange mixture of hard and soft light. I heard a high-pitched Richard Widmark laugh rise over a chorus of clinking glasses. Saw the blushing cocktail waitress a second before I spotted the man in the hammerhead-colored suit circling her, his hard little eyes trained on her ample breasts, a long-neck beer bottle with a well-peeled label clutched in his right hand.

I turned on my heel and didn't stop moving until I hit the elevator button.

I was about to slip the key into the lock when the door to room 602 swung open.

She was wearing a white robe and holding an ice

bucket. A smile almost crossed her face, but she spotted my nose before it could take.

"How did you figure it?" she asked.

"It wasn't hard. The Cal-Neva seems a bit tony for our friend. And the bills he rang up at Soule Domaine and Bobby's Uptown were pretty extravagant for a guy who seems to subsist on hamburgers and cheap beer when he's practicing his home invasion skills. It looked to me like he'd had some serious help with the wine list. Just domestic, or did someone named Gabrielle lend her expertise?"

My sister took a step backward. "You're still a smart-ass." She turned away. "Gabrielle didn't work out, if you want to know. Just like the smart little Frenchman didn't work out with Mom. I mean, after a while all that quick-wit shit just wears one down, y'know?" She shook her head, and a strand of dusky blond hair fell over her eyes, confident eyes that betrayed not one ounce of surprise. "I guess that was one thing you got right about me in your weighty tome. No one ever quite lives up to my expectations. I outgrow people. I outgrow habits. I move on to other things." She slipped a slim tie from a lamp shade and curled it between her fingers as if it were an exotic snake. "I like to push the envelope."

I followed her into the room and slammed the door. "I think you've got some explaining to do."

Jo laughed. "Me?" She pointed at a copy of *Killer Cassady* lying open on the nightstand. "*I've* got some explaining to do?"

I wasn't going to let her pull me off course. "I want my movie contract. And the script. I want my credit card." I sucked a deep breath. "I've made some money lately. Sure. I'm not ashamed of it. I'll pick up the credit card tab. We'll call it square. You and Mr. *Wrong Turn* won't have to worry about wasting any time in court."

Jo looked at me, Dad's lips twisting on her pretty face, Dad's eyes hard and unamused beneath her carefully plucked brows. "Did you really think you could get away with it, Tommy? Did you really just think I'd let it be?"

"You'd better," I said.

She laughed at that. Her laughter was just like Dad's, a hissing bray that branded me the most pathetically stupid thing on two legs. "I'll tell you how it's going to be," Jo said. "Because *we* had it all set up—Tom and me. That's his name, too, you know."

I let it go. Best to let her get everything out of her system.

"I was the one who hooked the producer," Jo said. "I met the guy at a party in San Francisco—he's gay, but discreetly so. Anyway, I convinced him to remake *Wrong Turn* with my half brother in the lead. I'd play the hitchhiker because that would *really* push the envelope. A little taste of incest couldn't hurt the box office. He thought that was real sweet."

"And then my book was published."

She nodded. "Right. And suddenly my little incest angle was very *five-minutes-ago*." She ran a rough finger along my nose. "Maybe the producer thinks your nose is cuter than my Tom's." She reached for the phone. "But you're going to change his mind, aren't you, Tommy?"

I stared at the phone, at my sister. Jo's pouting lips twisted into that signature grin that always spelled trouble in Dad's films, the same expression my half brother had worn when he rose from my living room couch with a copy of *Killer Cassady* in his hands.

I hated that look, even when I saw it in a mirror.

"Do you know the number, Tommy?" My name hung there in the quiet room, dripping with sarcasm. "Or do you need me to dial it for you?" I didn't move, and Jo lifted the handset. "And you thought you were so smart. Thought you'd come up here and set what's left of your family straight, buy them off for the price of a couple dinners." It was dark in the room, but her eyes were shining laser-bright.

"Hey now ... let's think about this," she said suddenly, replacing the handset. "Did you ever think of becoming a producer, Tommy? Just how much money did you make from that book, anyway?"

Jo's eyes burned with confidence. She was trying to cut me down to nothing. My hands were shaking. I smelled my own sweat.

And then my world went black and white. I entered the world of *Wrong Turn.* I entered Dad's world. I was in some cheap whore's apartment, and I was beginning to understand that a complete idiot had outsmarted me once again. Jo's eyes were slicing me to ribbons while her laughter marked me a sucker.

And then Jo wasn't laughing anymore. My fingers locked around the phone. The cord bit into her neck, and I tugged on the phone like a fisherman playing a big one on a whispering reel. A tight smile bloomed on my lips as I tried to cut off my father's hissing laughter. The phone was hard and reassuring in my hands, and I couldn't wait for the cord to do its work because then I was going to smash the whole thing against my sister's face, my father's smile.

Her eyes weren't shining now. They were almost empty, nearly colorless. And she wasn't laughing anymore. She couldn't laugh; she couldn't even scream.

And then the door to room 602 swung open. There—live, in living color—stood my father.

Even in that moment I knew the man was my half brother. The hammerhead-colored suit told me that. But it was startling to see his face twisted just as Dad's had been during the climax of *Wrong Turn,* a mask of violent desperation. And I froze up seeing him so close. He wasn't a man in black and white on a television screen, but a man with a face red from alcohol and hurt and hate and pride, a man with knuckles the color of spoiled meat.

He was the same man who stepped into his kitchen one night and found a charming Frenchman fawning over his wife.

He wasn't thinking straight, that man. He wasn't thinking smart.

And I realized with complete clarity that I hadn't been smart in coming here.

I had barely dropped the phone when he laid into me. I should have known it would be a left hook. I should have seen it coming, because I'd seen it coming in all those movies. But I didn't see it, and it dropped me.

He wasn't finished, of course. He took me into the bathroom, where it seemed there was an acre of gleaming tile.

I remember the sound of a human skull used as a hammer.

I remember my sister's screams as she pulled Mr. *Wrong Turn* off me. I remember her yelling something about a goose and a golden egg. And then I remember the hatred in her eyes. "You take this as a warning," she said. "You stay out of our way. Maybe, if you do that, we'll stay out of yours."

The man with my father's face nodded solemnly, cracking his knuckles and grinning the way a man grins after a satisfying meal. "Well," he said by way of conclusion, "it looks like Dad finally gave you a beating, after all."

I passed out for a while. Then I stumbled to the bed and curled up in the bedspread. Somewhere in the middle of the night I made it into the bathtub and cleaned up. I soaked in the steaming water for a long time, eyes closed—the right one swollen shut—and when I opened my eye, the bath water was pink with blood.

At the end of *Wrong Turn*, Tom Cassady is driving. But he's got no place to go. All his life Tom Cassady had nowhere to go. His road was one straight line. He killed a man with his fists and did time for it, but that didn't change him. He lost his wife and family, but that didn't change him. He got another wife, and he was the same way with her that he was with my mother, but wife number two was afraid to do anything about it. And he went back to work in the movies, where he pretended to lose his grip, pretended to hit people, shoot them, hurt them in a dozen inventive ways.

It wasn't much of a stretch.

One day Tom Cassady didn't wake up, and the thing that had burned so hot inside him was dead. But it wasn't gone, nor was it forgotten. I remembered it. So did Jo. We remembered it every time someone discovered who our father was. We remembered how that simple knowledge could make a person's eyes shine, the way the desk clerk's eyes had shined in the lobby of the Cal-Neva when she recognized me.

We all want to do that—put the shine in someone's eyes, I mean. Sometimes, what we'll do for that particular thrill amazes me.

I guess that's why I wrote the book.

I was five when Dad went to San Quentin. Jo was seven. As far as I know, he never laid a hand on me. Never touched Jo, either. I don't remember the man, to tell the truth. He never visited us after his release, never even sent a birthday card. Most of the time I spent with him, he was on a television or movie screen and I was eating popcorn.

The book was a lie. That's what Jo and my half brother had been able to hold over my head. I didn't know my father. But the book was something else, too. It was the little piece of Dad that I had carried inside me for thirty-five years. It was the shadow of anger that always churned in my gut when I tried to assure myself that I was a thinker. Every key I pushed on that computer keyboard was a little jab. Every word I spoke on that book tour was a little knife. And when I cold-cocked that talk show host, I was thinking that I was going to make a million eyes shine all at once, all across America.

The talk show guy had pushed my button. He'd asked about Dad exploiting his crime in order to boost his career. And then he'd held up a copy of *Killer Cassady*, and he'd said, "Like father, like son?"

I couldn't answer, because the thing that had burned

so hot in Dad took hold of me then. I could only react, and for a short instant everything felt so very right. It was the way I felt when I wrapped the telephone cord around Jo's neck; the way Jo felt when she saw our half brother standing there in the doorway; the way he felt when he tore into me.

I don't know why I thought I could steer clear of Jo and get away with the whole thing. But I took the chance. I dug Dad up. I brought him back.

But I knew, soaking in the bathtub in room 602, that it was time to bury him. After thirty-five years, it was time to get off Dad's road.

I had to make sure that I was off it for good. I got out of the tub. My wallet was on the floor, and I picked it up. A few other credit cards were now missing, but they hadn't touched my cash. I took the money and dropped the wallet on the floor.

I managed to get dressed. My face didn't look too bad if you could ignore the shut eye and the gash above it. My lips were puffy and kind of purple, but my nose looked in pretty good shape. Overall, the swelling almost had an odd symmetry. I didn't feel very hot, but seeing that my half brother hadn't managed to crack any tile with my head made me feel a little better.

I didn't drain the pink water from the tub. I didn't wipe the blood off the tile. I didn't hide the bloodstained bedspread. My wallet lay on the floor, stuffed with ID that bore my father's name, and I didn't pick it up. Maybe somebody would make something of it. Maybe they but I had a hard time believing that. The California-Nevada state line bisected the Cal-Neva. Maybe it bisected room 602. If that were the case, the FBI might enter the picture.

It was late. I didn't want to think about it.

I passed the desk, showing my left profile. My right hand covered my swollen eye while I pretended to take care of an itch on my forehead. It didn't matter. No one noticed me. I got to my car without attracting any attention.

I pictured my half brother and my sister driving down Dad's road, running south toward Hollywood, wearing Dad's signature grin on their faces.

I knew they were heading for a wrong turn.

I drove north.

The Zephyr Flash

by James M. Reasoner

In the summer of '52, the club sent me to a wide place in the road called Zephyr, Texas, to see if a kid who played semi-pro in that part of the country could throw smoke as the reports said he could. I'd been over in East Texas looking at a slick-fielding high school shortstop, so it only took me the better part of a day to drive over to Zephyr. Texas and the whole Southwest was my territory in those days, probably because I'd played for the Fort Worth Cats for a couple of years before being called up to the bigs. A collision between me and an outfield wall—said collision having the inevitable winner—put an end to my playing career a few years later, but the club wanted me to hang around as a scout, and what the hell, it was a way of staying in the game.

Anyway, I headed over to Zephyr to take a gander at some farm boy by the name of Ben McKavett, of whom it was said he could throw a baseball over a hundred miles an hour. We didn't have any of those fancy radar guns in those days, but we had *eyes,* and I'd seen enough horsehide coming my way to have a pretty good idea of how fast it was going.

I was driving a '49 Ford, and as I pulled into Zephyr, I saw that it looked just like a hundred other sleepy little Texas towns I'd seen—the state highway was the main street, with about a dozen cross streets and another road paralleling the highway a block to the north. That was where the school was located; I could see the big stone building from the highway. The baseball coach there was the guy who'd gotten in touch with the club, so I wheeled the Ford off the highway toward the school. Classes were over until fall, this being late June, but I wasn't surprised to see a game going on at the baseball diamond behind the school. A couple dozen pickups were parked along the fence around the field. The small towns scattered across the countryside had an informal league that went on all summer, and plenty of folks turned out to see the deadly serious showdowns between Zephyr and places like Blanket, May, Gustine, and Mullin. As I got out of the car, the smell of dust and cow manure on the early evening breeze brought back memories.

The town sold tickets for two bits, although nobody would have stopped me if I'd climbed up into the bleachers without paying. I gave my quarter to a lady in horn-rimmed glasses who sat at a little folding table with a cigar box on it for the money, then strolled over to the home bench. The other team was in the field at the moment, so the bench was crowded with big ol' boys who wore uniform shirts, blue jeans, and feed store caps. They were all young, ranging from high school kids to men in their early twenties, except for a guy who stood at the end of the bench, nervously shifting his grip on a bat he held clutched in his hands.

"You Harry Evans?" I asked him as I leaned on the chain link behind the bench.

He was watching his team's batter; there were men on second and third, and a glance at the numbers chalked on the scoreboard told me there was only one out. The husky kid at the plate looked capable of delivering at least a sacrifice fly. The guy I'd spoken to glanced over his shoulder and said, "Yeah?" Then he did a double take that would have done justice to Sid Caesar and said, "You're Jack Mannion!"

"Guilty as charged," I said. "You Evans?"

The ball cracked off the bat, and I knew from the sound of it that one of the outfielders better get on his horse. I picked up the flight of the ball and saw that it was going to drop into the alley and clear the bases. A minute later, the runner slid into third with a triple and two runs were in. That put the score at Zephyr 5, Goldthwaite 4.

"I'm Harry Evans," the coach said as he turned to me. He reached over the chain link and pumped my hand. "It's an honor to meet you, Mr. Mannion. I saw you play at LaGrave Field when I was just a kid."

I grunted and let that pass, took a cigar from my shirt pocket, and chomped the end without lighting it. The air was hot and wouldn't cool off until a couple of hours after dark, and my short-sleeved white shirt was damp. I waved away a mosquito and said, "Heard you got a pitching phee-nom down here, Coach, so I came to take a look."

About that time the next batter fouled out. Evans clapped his hands, yelled at the kid not to worry about it, and told the guy on-deck to bring home the runner. Then he turned back to me and said, "That's him down there at the other end of the bench. I'll tell him you're here—"

"Rather you didn't," I said. "Don't want him pressing because he knows there's a scout watching."

Evans shrugged. He was a chunky, dark-haired guy in his early thirties, a few years older than the next-oldest man on the team. During the school year he coached football and basketball and baseball and probably taught history or math or something, and during the summer he picked up a few extra bucks, coaching and playing with the town's semi-pro team. He wouldn't get rich, but he looked like he was having fun.

A grounder to second base was the last out and stranded the runner at third. But the team had done well, coming up with a couple of runs to take the lead, and now all they had to do was get through the top of the seventh, which was coming up. I knew without asking that the game would last only seven innings. After that it would start getting dark. There wasn't time after a day's work for a full nine innings before the sun set.

The crowd in the bleachers, most of them farmers and

their families, gave the home team an appreciative hand as the players took the field. Evans went out to play second, a good position for a player-coach since he could direct traffic all over the field from there. Ben McKavett, who was as tall and rangy as his name sounded, took the mound and started warming up. Even throwing half-speed, I liked the sound of the pop his ball made when it hit the catcher's mitt. I studied him with my eyes narrowed and liked the looks of his delivery. Watching him walk around the mound, you'd think his motion would be gawky, but instead it was smooth as silk. A natural? Maybe. It was too soon to tell.

I glanced at the bleachers, and something unusual caught my eye. Three guys were sitting by themselves on the top row, and they looked as out of place in a town like Zephyr as hogs in a ballroom. Two of them wore dark suits, unusual by itself in this heat, and the third guy was dressed as though he ought to be out playing polo or something. A little farming community like this definitely wasn't rich enough for his blood.

Maybe they'd been passing through and decided to stop for a little diversion. I shrugged and turned my attention back to the field.

The PA system was scratchy and had an echo to it, but I could understand the announcer when he said, "Top of the seventh, ladies and gentlemen, and the Zephyr Flash, Ben McKavett, is still pitching!"

The Zephyr Flash, I thought. What would baseball be without nicknames?

The first batter for Goldthwaite came to the plate, and McKavett wound up. His motion was as smooth as ever, but the pitch had a little something extra on it as it zipped by the batter. This time the sound of the ball in the mitt brought an outright grin to my face.

Well, McKavett was as good as I'd heard. He got the first two batters swinging wildly at fastballs that were past them almost before the bats left their shoulders. The third guy managed to get wood on the ball, but it was just a little dribbler that the first sacker gobbled up and scooped to McKavett covering. And that was the game—Zephyr, 5–4. From what I had seen, I guessed that McKavett had given up the runs early and then gotten stronger as the game went on. I liked that, too. I wasn't ready to offer him a tryout yet—I wanted to see him pitch again before I did that—but so far what I had seen was good.

Evans trotted over to me as the fans came out of the bleachers to congratulate the players. He asked, "Can I introduce you to Ben now?"

I nodded. "That'd be all right."

He hesitated. "What'd you think?"

"Kid's got good hard stuff. He got any other pitches?"

Evans grinned at me. "He doesn't *need* any other pitches."

I wasn't going to waste time arguing the point with him, although I knew he was wrong. Nobody can get by in the bigs with only one pitch, no matter how good it is. But McKavett might be able to come closer than most.

Evans led me over to McKavett, who was grinning and talking to a couple of rosy-cheeked farm girls, the kind who looked like they had more than a passing familiarity with what went on behind the barn. Evans got his attention and said, "Ben, this is Jack Mannion. He's a big-league scout."

McKavett looked impressed and stuck out his paw for me to shake. "I've heard of you, Mr. Mannion," he said. "You led the league in hitting in '38, didn't you?"

"Missed by four points," I told him. "You didn't miss much when you were pitching out there, though."

"Thanks." He grinned shyly. I waited for him to scuff his foot in the dirt like Gary Cooper, but he didn't.

"When are you pitching again, son? I'd like to see a whole game."

Evans answered for him. "We're playing DeLeon on Sunday afternoon. That's Father's Day, you know."

I didn't say anything about that. Not having any kids, or even a wife, I sort of lost track of things like Father's Day. I started to say that I would be there for the game, but before I could a voice behind me piped up, "Great game, Benjy. I knew those boys from Goldthwaite wouldn't have a chance against you."

"They had a chance, all right, Mr. Coryell," McKavett said. "They durn near knocked me out."

I turned to see the guy I'd noticed earlier in the bleachers. He wore an expensive sports shirt and precisely creased tan trousers. Shoes were expensive, too, and so was his haircut and his manicure and the capped teeth that were grinning at McKavett. The two undertaker-look-alikes were with him, but up close they didn't look so much like undertakers after all. They looked more like guys who would be responsible for sending business to a funeral home, rather than running it themselves. Tough ginks, in other words. And that fact, plus the name McKavett had used, told me who Joe Polo was.

"Mitch Coryell," I said.

He looked at me in surprise, and the two goons with him paid a little more attention to me. "Do I know you, pal?" Coryell asked.

"Jack Mannion," I introduced myself. "We've never been formally introduced, since associating with guys like you would probably get me kicked out of the game. The commissioner ain't overly fond of gamblers."

If Coryell took offense, he didn't show it. He kept smiling and said, "Mannion, Mannion ... I remember you now, Jack. I saw you track down a drive in deep center one day that I didn't think anybody could get." He lifted an eyebrow. "You cost me some money that day. No wonder I remember you."

It was none of my business, but I asked the question anyway. "What're you doing down here? Last I heard, you'd moved out to Reno."

"Are you kidding? This is home to me, Jack. I was born and raised right here in Zephyr. I've got a club up in Dallas now, strictly legit. The commissioner doesn't have any gripe with me."

That was news to me, all right, but it didn't have anything to do with why I was here. I turned back to McKavett and said, "I'll be back Sunday to see you pitch."

"Thanks," Mr. Mannion."

I stuck the unlit cigar back in my mouth, shook hands with the kid again, and turned to leave. Mitch Coryell and his boys stuck around, talking to McKavett and Evans, and that gave me a bad feeling. Maybe Coryell had gone straight, as he said, but that was hard to believe. He had a reputation for betting on anything from poker to which way an egg would roll when the hen laid it, and rumor had it that he wasn't above trying to influence the outcome of some of the things he bet on. In words even a sportswriter could understand, he was a crook.

I hadn't gotten back to my car yet when I heard loud, angry voices, and I looked over my shoulder to see a big, rawboned old man yelling at Coryell. Ben McKavett was tugging on the geezer's arm, and Coryell had a cool smile on his face. The two bruisers on either side of him kind of trembled like dogs that wanted to be let off their leashes. Evans stood in the middle, looking like he wished he was just about anywhere else as he joined McKavett in trying to calm down the old man.

If McKavett hadn't held on tight to him, the old guy would have taken a swipe at Coryell, which would have landed him in a lot of trouble with the gambler's bodyguards. But finally McKavett and Evans got the old man away from Coryell and led him away, muttering so loud I could hear him even from a distance. The words started with "no-good four-flusher" and got worse from there.

I went to my car, leaned on the front fender, and watched Coryell and his flunkies amble off and get into a sleek little roadster I hadn't noticed earlier among the slew of pickups. I wasn't sure how the big guys fit into it, but they did. They drove off, kicking up quite a bit of dust from the unpaved parking lot, and I heard tires squeal as the roadster turned onto the highway a block away. McKavett and the old man were walking off, so I went after Evans.

"What was that about?" I asked him when I caught up.

"Oh, Mr. Mannion," he said. "That was Anse McKavett, Ben's daddy. He and Mr. Coryell don't get along very well."

That was putting it mildly, I thought. I asked, "What's his beef?"

"He thinks Mr. Coryell is a bad influence on Ben. Ben works for him, you know."

"For Coryell?"

Evans nodded. "That's right. Mr. Coryell owns a beer distributorship that covers the wet counties around here, and Ben drives a truck for him."

I chewed on the stogie. It sounded like Coryell was really going legit, all right, but I still didn't believe it. "And the old guy doesn't like that?"

"Anse would like for Ben to start working on the family farm again. He's afraid that Mr. Coryell is going to lure him away with the bright lights of the big city."

There was a faint touch of mockery in Evans's voice that told me he was a pretty sharp guy for a small-town baseball coach. I said, "If Ben gets a major-league try-out, he'll be leaving the farm for sure."

"I know," Evans nodded. "Anse won't like that, either."

"Then it's a good thing the kid's over twenty-one. He *is* that old, isn't he?"

"Be twenty-two in the fall. I coached him a few years ago when he was still in school here. He was special even then, but his talent's really developed in the last year or so since we started this semi-pro team." Evans looked at me intently. "You think he's got a chance to make it?"

"From what I saw today he does," I answered honestly. "But I've got to see more before I make a recommendation to the club. That game Sunday ought to do it."

"I'm sure he'll pitch his best."

I thanked Evans for his help, said good night, and went back to my car. Dusk was falling now, and I had to turn the headlights on as I drove toward Brownwood, some twelve miles to the northwest. I'd been through there before and knew there were motels where I could find a room. The prospect of spending three days in Brownwood, Texas, wasn't that appealing to me, but I had a stack of paperbacks in the backseat, along with a good radio I carried with me so that I could plug it into the motel room socket and tune in the stations in St. Louis and Chicago that carried ball games at night. I could sit and read and listen to the radio, and that'd keep me from going nuts, I thought.

Life on the road. Glamorous as all hell, ain't it?

The time passed, as it always did, and come Sunday I was in Zephyr again. I got to town just as the Baptist and Methodist churches were letting out, and the thought crossed my mind that it was a little unusual for a ball game to be scheduled on a Sunday this deep in the Bible Belt. I guess that it was a special occasion like Father's Day had something to do with it.

I wondered if McKavett's father would be at the game.

During the time I'd spent in Brownwood, I'd picked up several copies of the local paper and learned that this game against DeLeon had some special meaning, too. Both teams were undefeated, and bragging rights for this whole part of the country were at stake. The DeLeon pitcher was almost as highly regarded as McKavett, at least around here. It was going to be quite a matchup.

I ate lunch at a café on the highway and as I left saw that the benches on the sidewalk in front of the hardware store and the drugstore were deserted. The loafers who usually sat there were probably over at the ball field, along with everybody else for quite a few miles around. I left my Ford where it was and walked over, noticing as I got there that Mitch Coryell's roadster was once again parked among the pickups. I glanced up at the bleachers and saw Coryell sitting in what must have been his usual spot on the two row, flanked by the two bruisers. I wondered if he had driven down from Dallas just for the game.

Coryell spotted me and waved, and I waved back. Legit or not, he wasn't a man I wanted too mad at me. I didn't like him, but dislike doesn't make me stupid. I went over to the Zephyr bench and said howdy to Evans, who looked like he had a lot on his mind. He apologized for his distraction and said, "Big game, you know."

"I know. I've been reading the papers." Around here a showdown baseball game between a couple of small towns was more important than politics or wars or anything else, at least on the day of the game itself.

The bleachers were full, and people lined the fences all around the field, even standing in the pasture beyond the outfield fence. It was hot as hell, but nobody seemed to mind. The men mopped their faces with white handkerchiefs, and the women fanned themselves with bulletins they'd brought from church. Little kids ran around in the shade under the bleachers, more concerned with their own games than the one that would soon get underway on the field. I leaned on the chain link and watched the warm-ups.

McKavett had his stuff; I could tell that already. The catcher, a big, blond, crew-cut kid called Dutch, slipped his hand out of his mitt and blew on it between pitches. I grinned as I watched him.

The team came in for a last few words with Evans, then took the field again as the first batter for DeLeon strolled up to the plate. The batter was trying to look nonchalant as he took a few practice swings before stepping into the box, but I could see the tension in him. He was nervous about facing McKavett.

I would have been, too, and I had hit for the cycle against ol' Diz one day.

McKavett cruised through the first without giving up a hit, then walked a couple of men in the second before striking out the side. That was one thing about throwing as hard as McKavett did: It was easy to throw balls. DeLeon touched him for a run in the third on a single, another walk, and a double, but the relay gunned down the would-be second run at the plate. McKavett got through the fourth, fifth, sixth, and seventh untouched, getting stronger just as I had thought he would. Today's game was a full nine-inning job on account of the afternoon start, and in the eighth DeLeon got lucky. Their right fielder was mud-footed in the field, but he was a hefty fella who got every bit of the bat on a McKavett fastball and sent it a good fifty feet into the pasture. A man was aboard, so that made the score 3–zip, DeLeon, as a groan went up from the bleachers. Zephyr hadn't managed a run all day, which on the surface would make you think DeLeon's pitcher was winning the duel with McKavett. No so; the guy had average stuff at best, but Zephyr kept hitting in bad luck, spanking the ball, but always right at somebody. They hadn't had a man past second so far.

That changed in the bottom of the eighth. Zephyr got a rally going, and McKavett helped himself with his bat by chipping in a timely double that plated a couple of runs. The next batter hit a shot that rivaled the one by the DeLeon right fielder, and just like that it was 4–3, Zephyr, with only the ninth to go.

Nobody could have hit McKavett in the top of the ninth, and I mean *nobody*. The '27 Yankees would have gone down just as meekly as those boys from DeLeon did. And that was the game.

McKavett was mobbed, of course, by all the locals congratulating him. I waited until the crush subsided, then went over and shook his hand. "Good game," I told him.

"I was lucky," he said. "They could've beat me."

I shrugged. "They hit good stuff. That happens."

Mitch Coryell spoke up behind me. "Great job, Ben!" he said excitedly. "You really showed those losers from DeLeon!" Evidently there was enough of the small-town boy still in him to get him worked up over a game like this.

"Thanks, Mr. Coryell," McKavett said, looking and sounding bashful again.

Coryell looped an arm around his shoulders. "You come on out to my place, and we'll have us a little victory party. What do you say?"

"Well ..." Ben hesitated, gazing around, and I had a hunch I knew who he was looking for. Sure enough, I spotted old Anse McKavett standing beside the bleachers, his hands in the hip pockets of his overalls as he glared at the little group of us by the first base line. The old man leaned over, spat on the ground, turned, and stalked off. The message couldn't have been much clearer.

"All right," Ben said with a nod. "I'll come. But only if Coach Evans and Mr. Mannion are invited, too."

"Sure, sure," Coryell said, slapping the kid on the back. "The more the merrier, right?"

I didn't know why Ben wanted me to come along, and I wasn't sure it would look good for me to get pally with a guy like Coryell, but for some reason I felt as though I ought to keep an eye on the kid. Evans, who had been standing by quietly and basking in the reflected glory of the victory, just nodded at the same time I did and said, "Sure, Ben, we'll come with you."

Coryell turned to one of the muscle boys. "Albert, you ride with Mr. Mannion and Coach Evans and show them the way." He glanced at me. "You mind taking your car, Jack?"

I shook my head, even though I wasn't overly fond of the idea of the gorilla riding in my Ford.

Coryell led Ben off to the roadster, taking the other goon with them, while Evans, the guy called Albert, and I walked back to the Ford and climbed in. "Coryell's got a place around here, does he?" I asked Albert.

"Up the Blanket road," he grunted. "I'll tell you where to turn."

I had planned to follow the roadster, but it zipped

along too fast, and I lost sight of it as we drove north on the gravel road that led to Blanket, another little town on the highway between Fort Worth and Brownwood. Albert kept his promise and told me where to turn onto another road, and it led us to a big old stone house that looked like it might have been a ranch headquarters at one time. Somebody had gussied it up a little, adding some hedges and flower beds. This was probably the old Coryell home place, I thought, and Mitch had made a part-time residence out of it when he came back to Texas and opened the club in Dallas.

It was late afternoon when we got there, but the back-yard was shaded by huge pecan trees and was fairly cool as we joined Coryell, Ben McKavett, and a woman I hadn't seen before. Coryell introduced her as his wife, Linda. She was a looker, a blonde with showgirl written all over her, and I knew Coryell must have found her in Reno. She was cool to Evans and me, but considerably warmer to Ben, buddying up to him with an arm around his waist. Coryell didn't seem to mind, but Ben looked a little uncomfortable. He was still wearing his uniform, as was Evans.

Albert's partner went into the house and wheeled a portable bar out the back door. Coryell had every kind of hooch in the world, which came as no surprise, considering he owned both a nightclub and a beer distributorship. He had more in mind than just a booze party, though. A couple of Mexican women brought out platters full of barbecue, potato salad, beans, coleslaw, and rolls. Coryell had been counting on a victory celebration, and he put on quite a spread. He was the lord of the manor, sitting in a big redwood chair and eating barbecue and drinking beer.

Then, as he lifted the mug of suds, somebody shot it right out of his hand.

Shattered glass and beer went everywhere, and Coryell let out a yelp of fear and pain and went rolling out of the chair. Albert and his friend jerked pistols from shoulder holsters and looked around for the source of the shot. Being from Nevada, Linda Coryell knew what to do: She hit the dirt, scrambling under the heavy picnic table. Evans and Ben stood there gawping, so I dropped my plate and took off in a dive that swept both of them off their feet. We hugged the ground, waiting for the next shot to come.

My bad knee had kept me out of the war, but my old man had been a bootlegger for a while, and I'd been shot at a time or two. It was a feeling you don't forget. Now, as I kept my face pressed into the grass of Coryell's backyard and tried to make myself as small a target as possible, my heart was pounding and there was a freight train in my head. I heard Albert and the other goon gallop out of the yard, and I heard Linda Coryell scream at her husband, "I thought this wasn't supposed to happen anymore, Mitch!"

Coryell was crouched behind the chair he had been sitting in before the shot. He said, "Shut up!", then called, "Do you see him, Albert?"

Albert didn't say anything. He was too busy looking for the gunner.

Ben McKavett had something to say, though. He looked over at me and whispered, "Mr. Mannion, that was my father's deer rifle!"

I lifted my head, since there hadn't been any more shots, and hissed at the kid, "Are you sure?"

"I'd know the sound of that old thirty-thirty anywhere," he said grimly.

That put a new light on things. A gent like Coryell might have a lot of enemies, but Ben had narrowed down the source of this particular attack. I'd seen for myself how much Anse McKavett hated his son's employer. Looked like he had taken the direct route to deal with what he regarded as Coryell's "bad influence" on Ben.

There was something else to consider. With Albert and the other goon out there looking for the rifleman, if they found Anse, they'd probably shoot first just out of habit. I didn't want the old guy killed, even if he had been foolish enough to take a shot at Coryell. So far there hadn't been any real harm done.

"Come on," I said to Ben as I pushed myself to my feet. "Let's go find him before he gets hurt."

Evans had heard the exchange, and he said, "I'll go with you," as he scrambled up along with me and Ben.

"Stay down, blast it!" Coryell snapped at us. He was on the other side of the yard, too far away to have heard our whispered conversation, and I wanted to keep it that way. I tugged on Ben's arm, and we lit out with Coryell still bleating behind us.

The big pasture behind the house rolled away in a series of gentle hills. I spotted either Albert or the other guy—the distance was too great to tell which—trotting along a ridge line, skylighting himself. It was a good thing these guys hadn't been in this part of the country when the Comanches still ruled the roost, or their hair would have been lifted in a hurry.

"We'd better split up," Evans suggested. "We can cover more ground and find your dad quicker that way."

Ben hesitated and so did I, not liking the idea much. But Evans had a point, and if we didn't find Anse first, he might not live long. I said to Ben, "Your old man won't take a shot at me if he sees me, will he?"

Ben shook his head. "I told him all about you, Mr. Mannion, and he knows who you are. And in that sports coat he's not going to mistake you for one of Mr. Coryell's men."

I let that indirect comment on my sartorial splendor pass unchallenged and grunted, "Let's go, then."

We headed three ways, and it wasn't long before I was out of sight of all the rest of them, Ben and Evans as well as Coryell's two boys. The country was more rugged than it looked on first glance, with plenty of gullies and draws for hiding places. More memories came back to me as I trotted over the hills. Years of riding subways and fighting crosstown traffic can't completely wipe out the legacy of growing up in the country. I remembered hunting and fishing with my dad in places not much different from this. The old guy was gone now, and I suddenly realized I'd spent too damn many Father's Days on the road somewhere, thousands of miles away from home.

But there was no way to change that now, and I sure as hell didn't want Ben's dad to be gunned down. That would have been one lousy Father's Day present, that was for sure. I kept my eyes open for Anse, but after thirty minutes without any more shots being fired, I realized that this incident was over. We weren't going to find the old man, who had probably run like a rabbit after missing his first shot. Or maybe it hadn't been a miss. Maybe he had just been trying to scare Coryell.

I turned around and headed back to the house, altering my course a time or two when I realized I was going the wrong way. Fifteen minutes later I trotted into the backyard.

And found Mitch Coryell stretched out on his back next to the picnic table, a knife in his belly with the handle sticking straight out, dead as a mackerel. A few feet away, his wife lay sprawled on the ground, an ugly gash and bruise just above her right ear, unconscious but alive.

I had time to drag in a couple of deep, shocked breaths before Albert yelled behind me, "Don't move, you son of a bitch! I oughtta kill you!"

I kept my hands out to my sides in plain sight and turned my head enough to see him pointing his pistol at me, his beefy face set in lines of rage. "Take it easy, Albert," I said urgently. "I just got here. I didn't do this."

"Then who did?" he demanded.

I didn't have an answer for that. I stood there trying to puzzle it out while the other goon came loping up to gawp at Coryell and Linda. He wanted to shoot me, too, but Albert told him to wait. Then Ben and Evans trotted in from different directions and stood around looking shocked and scared. Albert was clearly at a loss as to what to do next. His job for Coryell hadn't required a lot of brain work.

"Did you find him?" I asked Ben and Evans, not putting a name with the question.

Each of them shook his head. I was glad of that. Anse McKavett could get clear of this mess now, and no one would have to know he had taken a shot at Coryell. If the ambush attempt came to light, the old man would have been a natural suspect in Coryell's murder.

Except that he wouldn't have used a knife. I'd never met the man, never even spoken to him, but I was sure of that. If he had walked into this backyard, carrying the thirty-thirty, he would have used *it* on Coryell.

Besides, looking at the corpse with the knife stuck just above Coryell's belt, I knew who had stabbed him. I wasn't sure *how* I knew, or why it had happened, but I could at least guess on the last question.

I looked at Harry Evans and asked him, "How much money did you owe Coryell, Coach?"

He blinked at me and said, "What?"

"I know Coryell's type. They don't change, no matter how much they say they've gone legit." Albert looked like he was going to object to that, but I held out a hand toward him to tell him to wait. I was being either brave or stupid, but I was going to finish the inning anyway. I went on, "It must've looked like a great set-up to Coryell, having his own pet big-league pitcher. Handled right, he could clean up, and Ben wouldn't even have to throw very many games, just one every now and then."

"Throw a game?" Ben McKavett echoed. "I'd never do that, Mr. Mannion!"

"Not even if your old buddy and coach Harry Evans asked you to do it?"

Evans was starting to look sick, and I knew I was on the right track with my guesses.

"What'd you do, Coach?" I asked. "Go up to Dallas and lose a bundle at Coryell's club? Or did you lay the bets here on the ponies or college football or some such? Not that it matters, really."

"I don't know what you're talking about," he said. But he did; I could see it in his eyes.

"I don't believe this, Mr. Mannion," Ben said stubbornly. "One man can't throw a baseball game, not even a pitcher."

"Not very often," I agreed. "By and large, fixing any kind of professional sporting event is a lot harder than the public seems to think it is. But every now and then, a pitcher's in a perfect spot to do it. All he has to do is groove a pitch that ought to be low and on the outside corner, or let one get away from him just enough so that it's a wild pitch. Happens to the best of 'em, and nine times out of ten it's a genuine accident. But it doesn't always have to be." I hammered home the point. "And Coryell could always use his hold over Evans against you. You wouldn't want to see anything happen to the guy who helped you so much in your career, now would you?"

"This is a load of crap," Evans said, trying the angry approach now. "You can't prove any of this."

"What about those gambling debts? Coryell was probably holding some IOUs from you, Coach, and Albert here probably knows where to find them."

I could tell by the look on Albert's face that his brain was finally catching up with everything I'd been saying. And his expression confirmed the theory I'd hatched. The gun in his hand swung from me toward Evans.

"Wait a minute, Albert!" I said quickly. "You can do this the right way for a change. Coryell's gone, so it won't hurt him if the business about the gambling comes out. You can call the Brown Country sheriff out here and spill the whole thing to him about how you *accidentally* found the IOUs from Evans after Coryell was killed and figured out then that your boss wasn't walking the straight and narrow after all, the way you thought. That way you and your friend and Mrs. Coryell are in the clear."

"Yeah, yeah, maybe," Albert grunted, still struggling to keep up.

"And anybody can see that Evans killed Coryell to get out from under the debt and to keep from having to use his influence on Ben to throw some games once he made it to the big leagues. Makes sense, doesn't it?"

Albert nodded slowly, and I began to breathe a little easier. Doing things that way would let Albert and his buddy and the blonde off the hook when maybe they didn't deserve to be, but it also kept Ben and his old man from having to take any heat over something that hadn't been their fault. A good trade helps both teams, they always say.

Evans saw that the trap had closed neatly around him, and he licked his lips and said, "I didn't hurt Mrs. Coryell. I just came up behind her and knocked her out so that she wouldn't see me. All I planned to do was scare Coryell, but he came at me ... Oh, God, I just grabbed up one of the knives off the table and used it on him. I didn't even think about what I was doing. It was all instinct ..."

And that gave me the last answer I needed, which was how in the hell I'd known it was Evans, almost from the first. It was pretty simple, really. I figured neither of the mousy little maids in the house would be the type to stick a knife in a guy's gut, and Linda Coryell was knocked out, so the killer had to be one of us who had gone out to search for Anse McKavett. Neither Albert nor his buddy would kill their meal ticket, and *I* sure as hell hadn't done it, which left Evans and Ben McKavett.

I'd seen Evans play second base that afternoon, seen him scoop up hot grounders and peg them hard to first with that sweet side-arm motion that all of the good second sackers have. Some pitchers throw sidearm or even submarine, but Ben McKavett was strictly on over-the-top guy. Whoever had driven that knife into Coryell's belly had used a second baseman's natural motion, not a pitcher's.

I guess there was some other stuff percolating around the back of my brain, too. It had been Evans who had suggested we split up while we were searching. And if

Ben got that big-league tryout and went on to the majors, Coryell would lose any influence he had over him as his employer—but Evans had been his mentor for years and Coryell could still control the kid through Evans.

A lot of hunches, yeah ... but I was always a hunch hitter and carried a lifetime average of .307, not bad if I say so myself.

Albert still wanted to shoot Evans, but I think the idea of calling the cops must have seemed perversely funny to him, because that's what he did. Evans copped a manslaughter plea and did eight years in Huntsville, where he coached the prison's semi-pro team and had a hell of a record until he pulled a pitcher who didn't want to come out of the game and the guy stuck a shiv in him the next day. I was really sorry to hear about it.

Ben McKavett? I set up a tryout for him, the club signed him to a contract, and he set the minors on fire for a year before being called up to the big league. He threw four shutouts and would've won the Cy Young if he hadn't taken a hot line drive on the pitching elbow and gotten it busted all to hell. He came back enough to work as a reliever for a couple of seasons, then gave it up, and went back to the farm. I saw him a few years ago and think he was just as glad he hadn't had to keep on being the Zephyr Flash. He married a local girl, worked the farm with his dad, and didn't miss any more Father's Days. Better than being on the road all the time, he told me, and he meant it.

Me, I moved on. Always a hot prospect somewhere else that needs a look. That's baseball.

Blest Be the Ties

by Bill Crider

I haven't slept for quite a long time now, almost forty-eight hours. There are several reasons why.

For one thing, I am making a catalog of Harold's ties. Harold was my husband, and for twenty-five years he received a tie from me on Father's Day. And he also received ties from our son and daughter. I bought the ties when the children were young, but they always helped me to pick them out. Later, they bought the ties themselves.

I do not believe that we were unusual in giving ties for Father's Day. I read somewhere just the other day that every year there are 12,000 miles of ties given as Father's Day gifts. Or perhaps it was 120,000 miles. I am not sure, not being very good at recalling figures, but it was one of those numbers. It definitely had something to do with *twelve*; at any rate, it represented a lot of ties.

Harold used to say that the giving of ties represented a lack of imagination. "And the kids are no better than you are. They don't have an original bone in their bodies."

That was perhaps true, but the ties represented to me—and to the children, I am sure—much more than just a gift. They were symbolic; they were the ties that bound us together in love, for all of us loved one another very much. Does such a thought show a lack of imagination? I do not think so, but I never mentioned that to Harold.

"Maybe they aren't original in their giving," I would always answer, "but they're fine children all the same."

He had to agree with that, and he did save all the ties. They hang on special racks that he built in the walk-in closet in our bedroom.

I am cataloging those on the rack that date back to the middle 1970s now. The tie I am looking at is really quite nice. I gave it to Harold myself. It is three and three-quarters of an inch wide at its widest point and has a dark brown background with large white and blue flowers printed on it. It is a Wemlon tie, by Wembley. Here is what the label says:

CRUSH IT . . . KNOT IT . . . EVEN WASH IT . . .
FOR BROWN, GREEN OR BLACK SUIT
100% POLYESTER

Some might think that the murders are the reason I have not slept. You have probably read about the murders. Four young women have been killed within the last two months, all of them within a few miles of where I sit, but I am not worried that I will become another victim.

For one thing, I am no longer what most people think of as young. I am fifty-five years old, which, while it might not be called young by some people, is not exactly old, either—not these days. People are living longer all the time. I read an article not so very long ago that said the fastest growing population group in this country is composed of people from eighty to eighty-five years of age. So fifty-five isn't so old as it used to be.

Of course Harold could not see it that way, not recently at any rate. He had become fascinated with women who were twenty years younger than I—even thirty years younger. I watched him poring over his *Playboy* every month, as if trying to discover a blemish on the perfectly smooth peach-colored skin of the Playmate of the Month.

"Harold," I always said, "those girls are young enough to be your daughters."

He would look up guiltily. "I'm just reading the interview."

I never believed him, however. It wasn't so long ago

that he began asking me to call him Harry. He seemed to think it sounded younger than Harold, perhaps more sporty, but I refused to change. He had been Harold to me ever since we met, more than thirty years ago. Fifty-five might not be old, but it is too old to begin changing the habits of more than half a lifetime. So I did not call him Harry, and now he will always be Harold. That is the name engraved on his stone.

In addition to being fifty-five years of age, I am not of the correct physical dimensions to attract the killer, whose victims are all short and slim, as well as young, much like the Playmates of the Month. I am admittedly somewhat larger than they. I am six feet tall and weigh one hundred and seventy-six pounds. I am not fat, however. Statuesque is the term I prefer. I am quite strong and believe that I could give quite a good account of myself if I were attacked.

"Have you ever thought of joining a health club?" Harold asked me one day as he was looking through the sports section of the paper.

He had never cared for sports, and I knew perfectly well what he was looking at. He was certainly not reading the box scores from the previous night's baseball games, or even the advertisements for health clubs. He was looking at the advertisements for the "gentlemen's clubs" that feature prime-rib specials for under four dollars and entertainers with names like "Brenda Boobs," who are fresh from their careers in "XXX Rated Hits." I have seen the advertisements.

I asked what he meant about my joining a health club, though I thought I knew.

"Get a little exercise," he said. "Do you good. Tighten you up a little."

He himself had recently begun exercising every morning with a "Tummycizer," which purported to be a device that would reduce his waistline by several inches within a month. So far as I could tell, it had not yet had any effect.

The tie I am looking at now came, according to the

label, from Sears—The Men's Store. It is four and one-quarter inches wide and is one hundred percent polyester. It is dark green, and the scene repeatedly depicted on it is that of a decaying forest, with falling brown and yellow leaves, gray stumps of trees, and four mushrooms with brown tops. The label does not instruct the wearer as to the color of suit that would be appropriate.

Harold and I were married for twenty-seven years. In all that time I do not believe he was unfaithful to me even once; that is, not until near the end. Then it was a different story, though not a very original one.

He was two years older than I, and I believed that he had successfully avoided the midlife crisis I had read about so often in *Reader's Digest* and other publications. He had not, however. He had only delayed it a bit longer than most, and it struck him hard when it finally arrived.

He was, naturally enough, humiliated when I caught him out in one of his clumsy lies and told him that I knew about what was going on.

It is possible that his humiliation only increased when he later told his intentions to the young woman—I believe that she could have been no older than thirty—with whom he was currently involved. Now that I knew all, he explained to her, he would divorce me and marry her. Though it would be a struggle, since it was possible that he would soon be out of work and since no doubt the divorce would strip him of a considerable portion of his assets, he was certain that they would be happy because of the love they had for one another.

She laughed at him, of course.

She did not love Harold and was not interested in marriage with a fifty-six-year-old man, grown slightly bald, sporting a paunch that the Tummycizer had not reduced, and having no prospects for a decent income. She had gone out with him, let him pay for her meals, and accepted his gifts of money and clothing. She had probably even given him sex as a reward—though he never admitted that to me—but she was not in the least interested in marrying him. So her reaction to his declaration was predictable. Had Harold asked me—as of course he did not—I could have told him what she would do. I might have done the same thing myself at her age and in similar circumstances had I ever been involved in anything so sordid as an extramarital affair, which of course I never was.

I could never have told Harold, however, how he himself would react. I would never have expected it, and I am sure that he did not expect it, either.

At home Harold had always been mild. Not meek, exactly, but certainly mild. He never raised his voice to the children when they were growing up, not even on the day that Dwayne put the cat into his wagon and rolled it into the street in front of the oncoming traffic.

This time was quite different, I suppose because Harold had been under a great deal of pressure at home— from me—and at work. The job that he had held for nearly thirty years was being eliminated, and while the company had a private pension plan, it was not a very good one. Too, it did not go into effect until the worker reached the age of sixty-two. Add to all that the crisis of masculinity, or whatever it was Harold was experiencing, and the stress must have been considerable.

Not that I am trying to excuse him. He should never have done what he did, and I can never hope really to understand why it happened. There are no doubt circumstances, besides those I have cited, that I do not know about. I can never know them now.

What Harold did was to kill the young woman and dump her in a ditch on a deserted section of a county road that branched off Highway 288. She was found shortly therafter, becoming the first in the series of victims I referred to above.

I am looking now at an Arrow tie, four and one-quarter inches wide. It is brown, with three narrow diagonal white stripes crossing it near the bottom. It is, like the others from this rack, made of one hundred percent polyester. It is not, of course, the tie that Harold used to strangle the young woman. Ties these days are much narrower, though perhaps they are still made of polyester. I have not come to the newer ties as yet. They are on another rack.

"Why, Harold?" I asked him when he came home and confessed everything to me.

He had his own little apartment by that time, but I am sure he felt a need to talk to someone, and he knew that I could never turn him away. I had not even wanted him to go in the first place. I had never been comfortable without him in the house, and I would have tied him to me if I could have. Leaving was his idea, not mine.

At any rate, that night he came home. He tried to explain himself, I suppose, but he was unable to do so.

"Because," he said. "Because . . ."

But that was all he could say. He was sobbing and incoherent, and I told him to get undressed and go to bed. I told him that everything would be all right, though of course it would not. How could it be?

I was hoping, however, that what had happened might bring him back to me. As far as I was concerned, the woman who had almost succeeded—though perhaps that had never been her intention—in breaking up my home was dead. She had received no more than she deserved. Justice was served, Harold's fling was over, and he was at home where he belonged. I gave him a pill to help him sleep, but I am not sure that he took it. Most likely he did not.

I went to the closet at that time and looked at all the ties. He had taken only a few of them with him to the apartment, but I was glad that he had taken them. I had felt that somehow they would bring him back to me, and I suppose they did, if hardly in the way I had expected.

I am sure I know which one he used. It was one of his favorites, the one that Dwayne gave him last year. It had a gaudy floral pattern, but I did not recall the name of the manufacturer.

Harold died sometime very early the next morning, somewhere between four and five o'clock. I was sleeping in another room, and while I cannot be sure that he was sleeping as well, I hoped that he was. That would make his death at least a little easier to bear. I would hate to think that he lay awake torturing himself by agonizing over that woman, who so richly deserved her end.

But because I was not with him, I cannot really be sure of the time of death, only that it must have been between four and five o'clock. That is what the doctor estimated.

His heart had not been strong for several years. The doctors repeatedly had warned him about his blood pressure and his cholesterol count, both of which were elevated. They had even told him to stop smoking, and he had done so for a while. Recently, however, probably because of the stress, he had started again. I had spoken to him about it, but to no avail.

So the young woman—the young *women,* as I am sure there had been more than one even though he never admitted as much—took Harold away from me a second time. Permanently. The ties did not bind, not forever.

The funeral was distressing, to both me and the children, who loved their father almost as much as I. I did not tell them of their father's infidelities. It would have done no good at all and might have done much harm. Nor did I mention the death of the young woman. I did not want to upset them needlessly. It was right for them to remember their father as he had every right to be remembered.

I have passed the time since Harold's death in various ways. I read the newspapers thoroughly every day. I watch television. Recently, I have begun to catalog the ties, and each one reminds me of what a good husband and father Harold was until very near the end of his too-short life.

The tie I have here now, for example, is particularly nice. It has a geometrical pattern of browns, blues, and blacks. It was designed by Oleg Cassini, whose name, I believe, is highly respected in the world of fashion, though oddly enough the tie was made in Burma. That seems a strange place for a tie to have been made, and surely Oleg Cassini is not a Burmese name.

The young women continue to die, all of them strangled with ties, which also seems strange. They are very careless it appears, leaving their "gentlemen's clubs" unescorted at all hours of the night, prey for anyone clever enough to await them at the right place or stupid enough to allow themselves to be lulled by someone they do not expect to kill them.

Harold is not the killer. He did kill the first one, as I have explained, but he can kill no more. I am not sure that I know who killed the others.

I do know, however, that I have dreams, strange dreams. In some of them I am waiting in lighted parking lots, looking lost and distracted, as if I need assistance. Young women ask if they can help, and I ask them for a ride. I do not remember what happens after that, though I have tried.

There are no female serial killers, or very few. I read that in an article not so long ago. The article mentioned that there was one woman who, I believe, posed as a hitchhiker and killed a number of men, but there have been no other women I am aware of who have done so.

The dreams trouble me, however, and that is why I prefer to remain awake. If I do not sleep, then I cannot dream. And if the dreams are more than dreams, then what have I become?

That is why I am cataloging the ties. There seem to be fewer of them now than there were when Harold died. But there are so many. It is hard to be sure.

Next time, I will know. I will have the list I am working on, and I can check to be certain. If one is missing, then I will know. I do not know what I will do then.

But that is then, and this is now. Now I believe I will have a cup of coffee, very strong coffee. And then I will work on my catalog of ties again, beginning with that bright orange one there—not quite as wide as the others, but certainly from the same time period.

The 1970s were a very colorful era, and Harold was a

man who liked color. He particularly liked that orange tie, which Dwayne gave him for Father's Day. He swung Dwayne into the air and said, "Blessed be the ties that bind, right, Dwayne?"

Dwayne laughed and laughed, and Harold put him down, winking at me. I wonder if he somehow knew what I secretly thought about the ties. I wonder if the ties bind us even now, but if they do, it is in a way that I do not care to think about any longer.

I will make the coffee especially strong.

And then I will look at the ties.

Father's Day

by Ruth Rendell

Teddy had once read in a story written by a Victorian that a certain character liked "to have things pleasant about him." The phrase had stuck in his mind. He too liked to have things pleasant about him.

It was to be hoped that pleasantness would prevail while they were all away on holiday together. Teddy was beginning to be afraid they might get on each other's nerves. Anyway, it would be the last time for years the four of them would be able to go away in October for both Emma and Andrew started school in the spring.

"A pity," Anne said, "because May and October are absolutely the best times in the Greek Islands."

She and Teddy had bought the house with the money Teddy's mother had left him. The previous year they had been there twice and again last May. They hadn't been able to go out in the evenings because they had no babysitter. Having Michael and Linda there would make it possible for each couple to go out every other night.

"If Michael will trust us with his children," said Teddy.

"He isn't as bad as that."

"I didn't say he was bad. He's my brother-in-law and I've got to put up with him. He's all right. It's just that he's so nuts about his kids I sometimes wonder how he dares leave them with their own mother when he goes to work."

He was recalling the time they had all spent at Chichester in July and how the evening had been spoilt by

Michael's insisting on phoning the baby-sitter before the play began, during the interval and before they began the drive home. And when he wasn't on the phone or obliged to be silent in the theater he had talked continually about Andrew and Alison in a fretful way.

"He's under a lot of stress," Linda had whispered to her sister. "He's going through a bad patch at work."

Teddy didn't think it natural for a man to be so involved with his children. He was fond of his own children, of course he was, and anxious enough about them when he had cause, but they were little still and, let's face it, sometimes tiresome and boring. He looked forward to the time when they were older and there could be real companionship. Michael was more like a mother than a father, a mother hen. Teddy, for his sins, had occasionally changed napkins and made up feeds but Michael actually seemed to enjoy doing these things and talking about them afterwards. Teddy hoped he wouldn't be treated to too much Dr. Jolly philosophy while on Stamnos.

Just before they went, about a week before, Valerie Wilton's marriage broke up. Valerie had been at school with Anne, though just as much Linda's friend, and had written long letters to both of them, explaining everything and asking for their understanding. She had gone off with a man she met at her Commercial French evening class. Apparently the affair had been going on for a long time but Valerie's husband had known nothing about it and her departure had come to him as a total shock. He came round and poured out his troubles to Anne and drank a lot of Scotch and broke down and cried. For all Teddy knew, he did the same at Linda's. Teddy stayed out of it, he didn't want to get involved. Liking to have things pleasant about him, he declined gently but firmly even to discuss it with Anne.

"Linda says it's really upset Michael," said Anne. "He identifies with George, you see. He's so emotional."

"I said I wasn't going to talk about it, darling, and by golly I'm not!"

During the flight Michael had Alison on his lap and Andrew in the seat beside him. Anne remarked in a plaintive way that it was all right for Linda. Teddy saw that Linda slept most of the way. She was a beautiful girl—better-looking than Anne, most people thought, though Teddy didn't—and now that Michael was making more money had bought a lot of new clothes and was having her hair cut in a very stylish way. Teddy, who was quite observant, especially of attractive things, noted that recently she had stopped wearing trousers. He looked appreciately across the aisle at her long slim legs.

They changed planes at Athens. It was a fine clear day and as the aircraft came in to land you could see the wine jar shape of the island from which it took its name. Stamnos was no more than twenty miles long but the road was poor and rutted, winding up and down over low olive-clad mountains, and it took over an hour for the car to get to Votani at the wine jar's mouth. The driver, a Stamniot, was one of those Greeks who spend their youth in Australia before returning home to start a business on the money they have made. He talked all the way in a harsh clattering Greek-Strine while his radio played bouzouki music and Alison whimpered in Michael's arms. It was hot for the time of year.

Tim, who was a bad traveler, had been carsick twice by the time they reached Votani. The car couldn't go up the narrow flagged street, so they had to get out and carry the baggage, the driver helping with a case in each hand and one on his head. Michael didn't carry a case because he had Andrew on his shoulders and Alison in his arms.

The houses of Votani covered a shallow conical hill so that it looked from a distance like a heap of pastel-colored pebbles. Close to, the buildings were neat, crowded, interlocking, hung with jasmine and bougainvillea, and the hill itself was surmounted by the ruins, extravagantly picturesque, of a Crusaders' fortress. Teddy and Anne's house was three fishermen's cottages that its previous owner had converted into one. It had a lot of little staircases on account of being built on the steep hillside. From the bedroom where the four children would sleep you could see the eastern walls of the fortress, a dark blue expanse of sea, and smudgy on the horizon, the Turkish coast. The dark came quickly after the sun had gone. Teddy, when abroad, always found that disconcerting after England with its long protracted dusks.

Within an hour of reaching Votani he found himself walking down the main street—a stone-walled defile smelling of jasmine and lit by lamps on iron brackets—toward Agamemnon's Bar. He felt guilty about going out and leaving Anne to put the children to bed. But it had been Anne's suggestion, indeed Anne's insistence, that he should take Michael out for a drink before supper. A whispered colloquy had established they both thought Michael looked "washed out" (Anne's expression) and "fed up" (Teddy's) and no wonder, the way he had been attending to Andrew's and Alison's wants all day.

Michael had needed a lot of persuading, had at first been determined to stay and help Linda, and it therefore rather surprised Teddy when he began on a grumbling tirade against women's liberation.

"I sometimes wonder what they mean, they're not 'equal'," he said. "They have the children, don't they? We can't do that. I consider that makes them *superior* rather than inferior."

"I know I shouldn't like to have a baby," said Teddy irrelevantly.

"It's because of that," said Michael as if Teddy hadn't spoken, "that we need to master them. We have to for our own sakes. Where should we be if they had the babies and the whip hand too?"

Teddy said vaguely that he didn't know about whip hand but someone had said that the hand which rocks the cradle rules the world. By this time they were in Agamemnon's, sitting at a table on the vine-covered terrace. The other customers were all Stamniots, some of whom recognized Teddy and nodded at him and smiled. Most of the tourists had gone by now and all but one of the hotels were closed for the winter. Hedonistic Teddy, wanting to have things pleasant about him, hadn't cared for the turn the conversation was taking. He began telling Michael how amused he and Anne had been when they found that the proprietor of the bar was called after the great hero of classical antiquity and how ironical it had seemed, for this Agamemnon was small and fat. Here he was forced to break off as stout smiling Agamemnon came to take their order.

Michael had no intention of letting him begin once more on the subject of Stamniot names. He spoke in a rapid violent tone, his thin dark face pinched with intensity.

"A man can lose his children any time and through no fault of his own. Have you ever thought of that?"

Teddy looked at him. Notions of kidnapping, of mortal illness, came into his head. "What do you mean?"

"It could happen to you or me, to any of us. A man can lose his children overnight and he can't do a thing about it. He may be a good faithful husband, a good provider, a devoted father—that won't make a scrap of difference. Look at George Wilton. What did George do wrong? Nothing. But he lost his children just the same. One day they were living with him in his house and the next they were in Gerrards Cross with Valerie and that Commercial French chap and he'll be lucky if he sees them once a fortnight."

"I see what you're getting at," said Teddy. "He couldn't look after them though, could he? He's got to go to work. I mean, I see it's unfair, but you can't take kids away from their mother, can you?"

"Apparently not. But you can take them from their father."

"I shouldn't worry about one isolated case if I were you," said Teddy, feeling very uncomfortable. "You want to forget that sort of thing while you're here. Unwind a bit."

"An isolated case is just what it isn't. There's someone at work, John Frost, you don't know him. He and his wife split up—at her wish, naturally—and she took their baby with her as a matter of course. And George told me the same thing happened in his brother's marriage a couple of years back. Three children he had, he lived for his children, and now he gets to take them to the zoo every other Saturday."

"Maybe," said Teddy who had his moments of shrewdness, "if he'd lived for his wife a bit more it wouldn't have happened."

He was glad to be back in the house. In bed that night he told Anne about it. Anne said Michael was an obsessional person. When he'd first met Linda he'd been obsessed by her and now it was Andrew and Alison. He wasn't very nice to Linda these days, she'd noticed, he was always watching her in an unpleasant way. And when Linda had suggested she take the children up to the fortress in the morning if he wanted to go down to the harbor and see the fishing boats come in, he had said:

"No way am I going to allow you up there on your own with my children."

Later in the week they all went. You had to keep your eye on the children every minute of the time, there were so many places to fall over, fissures in the walls, crumbling corners, holes that opened on the empty blue air. But the view from the eastern walls, breached in a dozen places, where the crag fell away in an almost vertical sweep to a beach of creamy silver sand and brown rocks, was the best on Stamnos. You could see the full extent of the bay that was the lip of the wine jar and the sea with its scattering of islands and the low mountains of Turkey behind which, Teddy thought romantically, perhaps lay the Plain of Troy. The turf up here was slippery, dry as clean combed hair. No rain had fallen on Stamnos for five months. The sky was a smooth mauvish blue, cloudless and clear. Emma and Andrew, the bigger ones, ran about on the slippery turf, enjoying it because it was slippery, falling over and slithering down the slopes.

Teddy had successfully avoided being alone with Michael since their conversation in the bar but later that day Michael caught him. He put it that way to himself but in fact it was more as if, unwittingly, he had caught Michael. He had gone down to the grocery store, had bought the red apples, the feta cheese, and the olive oil Anne wanted, and had passed into the inner room which was a secondhand bookstore and stuffed full with paperbacks in a variety of European languages discarded by the thousand tourists who had come to Votani that summer. The room was empty but for Michael who was standing in a far corner, having taken down from a shelf a novel whose title was its heroine's name.

"That's a Swedish translation," said Teddy gently.

"Oh, is it? Yes, I see."

"The English books are all over here."

Michael's face looked haggard in the gloom of the shop. He didn't tan easily in spite of being so dark. They came out into the sunlight, Teddy carrying his purchases in the string bag, pausing now and then to look down over a wall or through a gateway. Down there the meadows spread out to the sea, olives with the black nets laid under them to catch the harvest, cypresses thin as thorns. The shepherd's dog was bringing the flock in and the sheep bells made a distant tinkling music. Michael's shadow fell across the sunlit wall.

"I was off in a dream," said Teddy. "Beautiful, isn't it? I love it. It makes me quite sad to think we shan't come here in October again for maybe—what? Twelve or fourteen years?"

"I can't say it bothers me to have to make sacrifices for the sake of my children."

Teddy thought this reproof uncalled for and he would have liked to rejoin with something sharp. But he wasn't very good at innuendo. And in any case before he could come up with anything Michael had begun on quite a different subject.

"The law in Greece has relaxed a lot in the past few years in favor of women—property rights and divorce and so on."

Teddy said, not without a spark of malice, "Jolly good, isn't it?"

"Those things are the first cracks in the fabric of a society that lead to its ultimate breakdown."

"*Our* society hasn't broken down."

Michael gave a scathing laugh as if at the naivety of this comment. "Throughout the nineteenth century," he said in severe lecturing tones, "and a good deal of this one, if a woman left her husband the children stayed with him as a matter of course. The children were never permitted to be with the guilty party. And there was a time, not so long ago, when a man could use the law to compel his wife to return to him."

"You wouldn't want that back, would you?"

"I'll tell you something, Teddy. There's a time coming when children won't have fathers—that is, it won't matter who your father is any more. You'll know your mother and that'll be enough. That's the way things are moving, no doubt about it. Now in the Middle Ages men believed that in matters of reproduction the woman was merely the vessel, the man's seed was what made the child. From that we've come full circle, we've come to the nearly total supremacy of women and men like you and me are reduced to—mere temporary agents."

Teddy said to Anne that night, "You don't think he's maybe a bit mad, do you? I mean broken down under the strain?"

"He hasn't got any strain here."

"I'll tell you the other thing I was wondering. Linda's not up to anything, is she? I mean giving some other chap a whirl? Only she's all dressed up these days and she's lost weight. She looks years younger. If she's got someone that would account for poor old Michael, wouldn't it?"

It was their turn to go out in the evening and they were on their way back from the Krini Restaurant, the last one on the island to remain open after the middle of October. The night was starry, the moon three-quarters of a glowing white orb.

"There has to be a reason for him being like that. It's not normal. I don't spend my time worrying you're going to leave me and take the kids."

"Is that what it is? He's afraid Linda's going to leave him?"

"It must be. He can't be getting in a tizzy over George Wilton's and Somebody Frost's problems." Sage Teddy nodded his head. "Human nature isn't like that," he said. "Let's go up to the fort, darling. We've never been up there by moonlight."

They climbed to the top of the hill, Teddy puffing a bit on account of having had rather too much ouzo at the Krini. In summer the summit was floodlit but when the hotels closed the lights also went out. The moonlight was nearly as bright and the turf shone silver between the black shadows made by the broken walls. The Stamniots were desperate for rain now the tourist season was over, for the final boost to swell the olive crop. Teddy went up the one surviving flight of steps into the remains of the one surviving tower. He paused, waiting for Anne. He looked down but he couldn't see her.

"The Aegean's not always calm," came her voice. "Down here there's a current tears in and out like a mill race."

He still couldn't see her, peering out from his lookout post. Then he did—just. She was silhouetted against the purplish starriness.

"Come back!" he shouted. "You're too near the edge."

He had made her jump. She turned quickly and at once slipped on the turf, going into a long slide on her back, legs in the air. Teddy ran down the steps. He ran across the turf, nearly falling himself, picked her up and hugged her.

"Suppose you'd fallen the other way?"

The palms of her hands were pitted with grit, in places

the skin broken, where she had ineffectually made a grab at the sides of the fissure in the wall. "I wouldn't have fallen at all if you hadn't shouted at me."

At home the children were all asleep, Linda in bed but Michael still up. There were two empty wine bottles on the table and three glasses. A man they had met the night before in Agamemnon's had come in to have a drink with them, Michael said. He was German, from Heidelberg, here on his own for a late holiday.

"He was telling us about his divorce. His wife found a younger man with better job prospects who was able to offer Werner's children a swimming pool and riding lessons. Werner tried to kill himself but someone found him in time."

What a gloomy way to spend an evening, thought Teddy, and was trying to find something cheerful to say when a shrill yell came from the children's room. Teddy couldn't for the life of him have said which one it was but Michael could. He knew his Alison's voice and in he went to comfort her. Teddy made a face at Anne and Anne cast up her eyes. Linda came out of her bedroom in her dressing gown.

"That awful man!" she said. "Has he gone? He looks like a toad. Why don't we seem to know anyone any more who hasn't got a broken marriage?"

"You know us," said Teddy.

"Yes, thank God."

Michael took his children down to the beach most mornings. Teddy took his children to the beach too and would have gone to the bay on the other side of the headland except that Emma and Tim wanted to be with their cousins and Tim started bawling when Teddy demurred. So Teddy had to put up a show of being very pleased and delighted at the sight of Michael. The children were in and out of the pale clear green water. It was still very hot at noon.

"Like August," said Teddy. "By golly, it's a scorcher here in August."

"Heat and cold don't mean all that much to me," said Michael.

Resisting the temptation to say bully for you or I should be so lucky or something to those lines, Teddy began to talk of plans for the following day, the hire car to Likythos, the visit to the monastery with the Byzantine relics and to the temple of Apollo. Michael turned on him a face so wretched, so hag-ridden, the eyes positively screwed up with pain, that Teddy who had been disliking and resenting him with schoolboy indignation was moved by pity to the depths of himself. The poor old boy, he thought, the poor devil. What's wrong with him?

"When Andrew and Alison are with me like they are now," Michael began in a low rapid voice, "it's not so bad. I always have that feeling you see, that I could pick them up and run away with them and hide them." He looked earnestly at Teddy. "I'm strong, I'm young still. I could easily carry them both long distances. I could hide them. But there isn't anywhere in the civilized world you can hide for long, is there? Still, as I say, it's not so bad when they're with me, when there are just the three of us on our own. It's when I have to go out and leave them with *her.* I can't tell you how I feel going home. All the way in the train and walking up from the station I'm imagining going into that house and not hearing them, just silence and a note on the mantelpiece. I dread going home, I don't mind telling you, Teddy, and yet I long for it. Of course I do. I long to see them and know they're there and still mine. I say to myself, that's another day's reprieve. Sometimes I phone home half a dozen times in the day just to know she hasn't taken them away."

Teddy was aghast. He didn't know what to say. It was as if the sun had gone in and all was cold and comfortless and hateful. The sea glittered, it looked hard and huge, an enemy.

"It hasn't been so bad while we've been here," said Michael. "Oh, I expect I've been a bore for you. I'm sorry about that, Teddy, I know what a misery I am. I keep thinking that when we get home it will all start again."

"Has Linda then ... ?" Teddy stammered. "I mean, Linda isn't ... ?"

Michael shook his head. "Not yet, not yet. But she's young too, isn't she? She's attractive. She's got years yet ahead of her—years of torture for me, Teddy, before my kids grow up."

Anne told Teddy she had spoken to Linda about it. "She never looks at another man, she wouldn't. She's breaking her heart over Michael. She lost weight and bought those clothes because she felt she'd let herself go after Alison was born and she ought to try and be more attractive for him. This obsession of his is wearing her out. She wants him to see a psychiatrist but he won't."

"The trouble is," said Teddy, "there's a certain amount of truth behind it. There's method in his madness. If Linda met a man she liked and went off with him—I mean, Michael could drive her to it if he went on like this—she *would* take the children and Michael *would* lose them."

"Not you too!"

"Well, no, because I'm not potty like poor old Michael. I hope I'm a reasonable man. But it does make you think. A woman decides her marriage doesn't work anymore and the husband can lose his kids, his home, and maybe half his income. I mean if I were twenty-five again and hadn't ever met you I might think twice about getting married, by golly, I might."

Their last evening it was Anne and Teddy's turn to baby-sit for Michael and Linda. They were dining with Werner at the Hotel Daphne. Linda wore a green silk dress, the color of shallow sea water.

"More cozy chat about adultery and suicide, I expect," said Teddy. Liking to have things pleasant about him, he settled himself with a large ouzo on the terrace under the vine. "I shan't be altogether sorry to get home. And I'll tell you what. We could come at Easter next year, in Emma's school hols."

"On our own," said Anne.

Michael came in about ten. He was alone. Teddy saw that the palms of his hands were pitted as if he had held on to the rough surface of something stony. Anne got up.

"Where's Linda?"

He hesitated before replying. A look of cunning of the kind sane people's expressions never show spread over his face. His eyes shifted along the terrace, to the right, to the left. Then he looked at the palm of his right hand and began rubbing it with his thumb.

"At the hotel," he said. "With Werner."

Anne cottoned on before he did, Teddy could see. She took a step toward Michael.

"What on earth do you mean, with Werner?"

"She's left me. She's going home to Germany with him tomorrow."

"Michael, that just isn't true. She can't stand him, she told me so. She said he was like a toad."

"Yes, she did," said Teddy. "I heard her say that."

"All right, so she isn't with Werner. Have it your own way. Did the children wake up?"

"Never mind the children, Michael, they're okay. Tell us where Linda is, please. Don't play games."

He didn't answer. He went back into the house, the bead curtain making a rattling swish as he passed through it. Anne and Teddy looked at each other.

"I'm frightened," Anne said.

"Yes, so am I, frankly," said Teddy.

The curtain rattled as Michael came through, carrying his children, Andrew over his shoulder, Alison in the crook of his arm, both of them more or less asleep.

"I scraped my hands on the stones up there," he said. "The turf's as slippery as glass." He gave Anne and Teddy a great wide empty smile. "Just wanted to make sure the children were all right, I'll put them back to bed again." He began to giggle with a kind of triumphant relief. "I shan't lose them now. She won't take them from me now."